EU

Will this be
how it ends?

Terry Palmer

EUROSLAVIA

TERRY PALMER voted to stay in the Common Market in Britain's referendum in the 1970s. He watched European affairs grow, knowing nothing of what was going on. Gradually he began to be uneasy about the European Economic Community, with talk of a single currency and a federal Europe.

He regretted losing his dark blue passport for the maroon version, and slowly he became aware that he had absolutely no say in what was happening in Brussels.

He listened to Margaret Thatcher's outbursts at Brugge, wondering why she was saying "No!" — and he decided to find out.

He was horrified by what he found. He was staring into the face of a political monster whose sole purpose in life was to grab every nation which wandered too close to its fangs, and swallow it.

This book is Palmer's only way of trying to fight the Euromonster, and it is partly autobiographical. Palmer was born in Wisbech, he later lived in Montmédy in France, and in Spain. He wrote guide books to numerous places, and ultimately lived in Clacton with his wife, whom he met in Spain.

Also by Terry Palmer:
The Ghost At My Shoulder, Discover Guernsey, Discover Jersey, Discover Florida, Discover The Gambia, Discover Tunisia, Discover Morocco, Discover Gibraltar, Discover the Isle of Man, Discover Malta, Discover Cyprus, Discover Turkey, The Cairo Alternative, Discover the Suffolk Coast, Discover North Norfolk, The Lower Stour, A Day Out In Aldeburgh, A Day Out In Southwold.

Euroslavia

...can you escape it?

Terry Palmer

PALLAS PUBLISHING

Euroslavia.
First published: 3 September 1997
First printing July 1997

Typeset by Paragraph Typesetting, Witham
Printed and bound by Cox & Wyman, Reading
Published by Pallas Publishing,
47 York Rd, Brentford, London, TW8 0QP

© Terry Palmer, 1997

Dedicated to the ancient Greeks for inventing democracy, to the early Norse peoples of Iceland and the Isle of Man for inventing the parliamentary system of Government, and to the millions of people who died in the twentieth century defending the free world against dictatorships, autocracy and tyranny.

EUROSLAVIA

FAREWELL NOTE

My dearest Lisa.

This is goodbye. I've been thrown into a dungeon in some medieval castle in Region FR41 and abandoned. Nobody will ever come for me, or for the other people with me. One of them died last night, & I think his wife is dead as well; haven't heard a thing from her for ages. No food, no water, no heat, no light. I'm writing this in almost total darkness — can't even see the paper.

It's bitterly cold in here. I have to keep walking up and down my cell all night to keep alive. Three paces each way. I fell asleep several times but couldn't sleep for long.

It was the Security Service who picked me up. No charge. The boss just wants me dead. Before tomorrow is out he'll get his wish. They'll find our bodies sometime — next week, next year, next cent? Hope this note will still mean something to you, my darling.

I'm not even sure we managed to do our job. Is Euroslavia dead, or has it come back to life?

If I'd had a trial, I suppose they might have said high treason, but I was only telling the truth. You know that all I ever did was straight reporting, telling things as they happened & as I saw them. And that, in these enlightened days, is a major crime. But then, Euroslavia has been rewriting European history for several years, telling it like they wish it had been. And it has been silencing its critics with threats of heavy fines.

I haven't seen you since that last meeting in Castletown, but you have been always in my thoughts, partic during the motorcade advance on Brussels. You're certainly in my thoughts now, when all I have to do is wait for death in whatever form it will take.

You know I'm not a politician — I deal in the truth. And I certainly couldn't live a lie like some of them. They spent 30 yrs telling us black was black, then they admitted they knew it was white all the time. And we all believed them.

Which is why I'm here. I tried to tell the truth that nobody else dare tell. I tried to warn people what was in store. I tried to tell them of the civil liberties they had already lost, and didn't yet realise. When things got very difficult & we moved over to Brussels, I began to guess I was putting my life in jeopardy.

My uncle George was gassed in the 1st War — the war to end all wars, they called it. I saw some of the 2nd War for myself. A dog-fight over the Fens. A Spitfire come down under full power & bury itself 30 ft deep in a field. Bombs raining down over Wisbech — why Wisbech? — & next morning seeing wallpaper waving from a second-storey room: the rest of the house had gone. After the 2nd War nobody would dare try again, they said: the threat of nuclear annihilation was too great.

I saw the Cold War at 1st hand when I was in the RAF. I was there at RAF Benson when George Blake came home in triumph — but they didn't then know he was a spy. The Cold War was the war that didn't happen.

& now we've lived through the 3rd War these past few days — most of us. The war that never fired a shot. Maybe it didn't, but it certainly killed thousands by other means. & now I'm going to be one of the victims — one of the last, I hope.

We all know who laid the groundwork for the 3rd War. The lying politicians, then the faceless few, the bureaucrats whom nobody knew about. But who were the victims? The common people, as ever. The people who were lied to for decades, until they woke up one morning & realised it was too late. Their country had been stolen from beneath their feet.

It's never the ordinary people who want a war, but this time they had to start it. & now, if Euroslavia is dead, the ord p'ple must see that their sovereignty is never again stolen. I wish I could be there to help in the cause, but it isn't to be.

I shall watch down on you from wherever I go, & wish you all the best for the future. Even though you are out of Euroslavia's clutches, it's not going to be an easy time. See you in the next life, my darling.

Terry.

ONE

ON THAT DAY in May, six months before I wrote my farewell letter from an icy dungeon, I was struggling to save my chat show on television. The ratings were stagnant and the adverts were only just breaking even, but what more could you expect with fifty other channels to watch, plus the cinema, bingo, books, radio, and shady spots down country lanes?

Tell Tel had a catchy title, but neither I nor the producer had yet found a formula that would click. That evening we were going to try something controversial, in a controversially new way, aware that it would almost certainly make or break the programme.

On that same day, Archie McGovan was skippering his sixty-foot (twenty-metre if you must go metric) fishing boat *Good Hope* in the northern North Sea, sticking strictly to the zone he had been allocated by the Common Fisheries Policy and enforced by fishery protection officials in all English and Scottish ports, particularly Aberdeen, in Region UKA4. In the old days, he had gone where he thought the cod would be, but now some civil servant told him exactly where to drop his nets, and could check on him at any time of day or night with EGNOS, the European Global Navigation Overlay System.

EGNOS was brilliant. It was a satellite navigation system, and every subscriber merely had to press the 'home' button to get his position shown on his computer screen, correct to within two hundred yards — alright, metres. It was much more accurate than the American Global Positioning System, and the Russian Glonass system, but it had its drawbacks.

It told the skipper exactly where he was. It also told anybody else exactly where the skipper was. If the fish — what remained of them — were half a mile beyond his sector boundary, he couldn't go for them or EGNOS would know all about it.

McGovan cursed perpetually about Scotland and England's failure to grab a two-hundred-mile (*mile* — not kilometer) exclusive fishing zone for themselves, after the Cod War. The European Economic Community knew this was on the way, but it managed to impose a policy whereby all EEC states shared their fishing stocks. And that policy came in *less than one day* before Scotland would have got its exclusive zone.

I say Scotland and England because the United Kingdom is no more. Tony Blair's Labour Government saw to that by offering devolution, and by offering regional assemblies to various bits of England.

EUROSLAVIA

It was all part of the European policy to smash the governments of the member states and put Brussels in their place. A Europe of regions, they said. Much more manageable than a Europe of nations.

In any event, now that we have a European Union stitched up as tight as the old Soviet Union was, how can one of its provinces be called the *United Kingdom*? Monarchies have gone. Monarchs were heads of state, and how can a mere province claim such an honour? The abolition of the British Monarchy spelt the end of the British aristocracy, the Trooping the Colour and millions of euros of tourist earnings, the Lord Mayor's Parade, and the House of Lords. Of course, there never had been any plan to print the Queen's head on euro banknotes.

Oh, yes, I should have had Archie McGovan on the show. He would have stirred things up.

ON THAT DAY in May, Father Erich Zimmerman was conducting his morning offices as he had done for many more years than he cared to count. He lived in Liechtenstein, an independent principality of sixty-one square miles stuck between Switzerland and the Austrian Province of the Europäische Vereinigung, the European Union. Zimmerman had been born in October 1918, shortly before the end of the First World War, which made him 86 on that day. By the time he was 87 he would become one of the victims of the Third War, the war that lasted for just one day.

Also on that day, Xavier Yzurdiaga, the Basque with the ridiculous name, was living in Andorra as a refugee from his native Euzkadi, the Spanish Basque homeland. For years the Basques had fought for independence from Madrid, then in 1986 they had seen independence and freedom fade into nothing when Madrid started giving its powers to Brussels.

Yzurdiaga believed in shock therapy. He had planted bombs in several provincial capitals, such as Paris, Copenhagen and Madrid, and his ambition was to plant a super bomb in the heart of the European Government. One day.

Meanwhile he managed to run his coach company in Euzkadi from his hideout in the picture-postcard village of Sant Julià de Loria, safe in the knowledge that Andorra, that tax-free haven in the Pyrenees, was not entangled in Europe's far-reaching tentacles.

ON THAT DAY in May 2005, Annette Dugard was, as usual, totally disillusioned with life in the Province of France and had found a new life in an island community which knew the meaning of independence. Alderney had been self-governing — except for defence and foreign relations — ever since the Middle Ages, but the German occupation of 1940 brought an end to that. Now, however, Alderney and Guernsey, with Sark, had formed an independent nation which was one of the outposts of the beleaguered Sterling Zone.

Miss Dugard was born in the French town of Montmédy in what is now Region FR41, and made a modest living as an artist and photographer, but she was continually aware of the menace lying on the eastern skyline: Region FR25, Basse-Normandie, part of the Province of France, had laid claim to the entire Channel Islands.

ON THE MORNING of that day in May 2005, the post had just been delivered to the House of Keys, the parliament of the Isle of Man, the independent island state lying in the Irish Sea between the Province of Ireland and the Province of Ulster, on the west, the Scottish Province to the north, and the English Province to the east. Wales, to the south, was merely Region UK91 of the English Province.

When the mailroom clerk saw the big envelope printed overall in mid blue with twelve gold stars on it, he sensed trouble. Nothing that came from the European Union was good news.

He studied the envelope. It had a hard red plastic seal on the back, indicating that the Brussels bureaucrats who had sent it deemed it to be important. He looked at the automatic franking of the Europost service, which had recently replaced the individual post offices of the member provinces of the Union Européen: the monster's name was used in any of eleven languages. He put the envelope with the others in the receptionist's 'in' tray.

The receptionist glanced at the envelope but knew better than to open it. Instead, she put it in the tray with other mail for the attention of the Chief Minister, Sir John Faulds. When the remaining stack of envelopes was sorted, the receptionist took the tray through to Sir John's office.

Twenty minutes later the Chief Minister arrived at the classical-style building on the corner of Bucks Road and Finch Road, containing the administrative offices of the world's oldest Parliament, established on a field a few miles away around the year 979.

Sir John was proud, and suitably humbled, to be shouldering the weight of the duties of Chief Minister of such a bastion of people-power, and every Sunday he renewed his personal vow to die in his people's service rather than allow the Parliament to be usurped or overthrown. These days the struggle was particularly keen, at least as keen as it had been, centuries ago, when the Norwegians and later the Scots, held supreme power.

"Morning," he smiled at the receptionist as he swept into the office block.

"Good morning, Sir John," she answered.

The Chief Minister still had his smile as he entered his office. He glanced out of the window as he hung his hat on the rack, paused to absorb the glint of sunshine on the quiet waters of the bay, and noticed that the mountains of England's Lake District — Region UK12 — were clearly visible on the skyline. It was indeed a good morning.

His smile faded as he tipped the contents of his mail tray across his desk and saw the distinctive livery of the European Union on the large envelope. He ripped it open and pulled out the letter.

> Office of the European Commission
> 200 rue de la Loi,
> B-1049, Brussels
> Tuesday, May 3, 2005

Mr John Faulds,
Chief Minister,
Administrative Offices of Tynwald,
Bucks Road,
Douglas, IM1 3PG
Isle of Man.

Dear Mr Faulds...

He felt his heartbeat accelerate slightly as he read the salutation. Since the European Union had abolished the European aristocracies, his own knighthood had been ignored, although the Brussels autocrats had no authority whatever in the Isle of Man. It was a self-governing Crown Dependency, historically independent of the Parliament at Westminster, and every Manxman was eternally grateful that Tynwald had negotiated no more than associate membership with that cuddly puppy, the European Economic Community. Puppies grow up, and the EEC had now become a baying hound, ready to tear the flesh off the Manx bone and swallow it whole if ever Tynwald dropped its guard.

He began reading the letter.

Dear Mr Faulds,

At their recent meeting in Brussels the Commissioners of the European Union decided that it is increasingly difficult and unnecessarily expensive to undertake commercial transactions in the less viable currencies of the world.

To this end the Commission has proposed, and the Council of the European Union has ratified, that under the terms laid down by Article

228 of Chapter 4 of the Maastricht Treaty, from August 3, 2005, three months hence, all transactions between the Isle of Man and the European Union must be made in Euros. This will mean that all invoices from Manx companies to companies within the Union, will be charged in Euros, and all payments made by Union companies will likewise be in Euros.

From the nominated date, invoices made in these less viable currencies will not be considered valid and Union companies will be advised not to make payment thereon. This is enshrined in Directive 1620/05/Z, a copy of which will be sent to you.

We trust you will advise Tynwald of this pragmatic decision and do all in your power to ensure compliance by Manx companies.

Yours most sincerely,

Hengst Berghofen
Financial Commissioner

Sir John realised his hands were trembling with rage as he read the letter again, digesting more of its underlying meaning. Finally he slammed the offensive paper on his desk. "The Brussels bastards on the warpath again! Damn their hides! This is the final straw — we will *not* give in to them!"

He snatched up his phone, dialled, and tried to speak calmly when his call was answered, but it was difficult.

"Good morning, Governor," he said testily. "Yes, it is a wonderful morning. At least it was. I have on my desk a letter which I'm sure will ruin your morning as well. May I read it?"

The Lieutenant-Governor, Air-Marshal Sir Quentin Harvey, was the representative on the Isle of Man of the latest in its line of rulers, the Lord of Mann, spelled with two Ns. And the Lord of Mann was, of course, Her Majesty the Queen, now known in Euro circles as Mrs Elizabeth Windsor, and in New Zealand where she lived, as Queen Elizabeth with no designating number.

Sir Quentin had had a distinguished career in the Royal Air Force from 1973 to 1995, notably in the Falklands Campaign and the shorter Gulf War. He had taken up his post in Douglas in 1997 and had suffered a minor heart attack in 2003 when he learned that the armed forces of all member provinces were to be absorbed into the Euroforce or Euromacht, according to whether one's preferred language was French or German. Worst of all, the RAF was to become a minor part of the Armée de l'Air Européenne, known in German as the Euroluftwaffe. He quailed at the thought of what those gallant fighter pilots who died in the summer skies over Kent — now Region UK57

EUROSLAVIA

— in the Battle of Britain, would have thought had they known the ignominy of such a sell-out.

He was not surprised at the large number of desertions even after the loyalty scrutiny had supposedly removed all those who still considered themselves English, Scottish, Welsh or Ulsterpersons rather than European, and he took great delight in the knowledge that the Royal Falklands Air Force continued the traditions of loyalty to all things British, including the Royal Family. Mrs Windsor? A major insult!

"You may read it, Sir John. What are they trying to steal this time?" His voice was suddenly tired, showing the stress he felt whenever the word Brussels entered the conversation.

"It's yet another attack on the beleaguered pound, sir. All Manx companies have to invoice Europe in their damned euros, or forego payment. Comes into force in three months."

"Or forego payment! That's preposterous as well as illegal. You'd better read it to me now, then copy it to me later." He listened as the Chief Minister read the entire letter aloud, then he snapped: "What is this confounded Article 228 of Chapter Four? You don't happen to have a copy of the damned Treaty in front of you, do you?"

"I've taken it from the shelf, Governor. Maastricht: I keep it between 'Knavery' and 'Malevolence.' It's in the usual obtuse language, so I'll cut it down to the bone. Here goes. Where this treaty provides for the conclusion of agreements between the Community and other States, the Commission shall recommend action to the Council, which shall then go back and tell the Commission to get on with it and open negotiations. There's a bit more, but it doesn't add to the issue." He paused. "It's all bluff, sir. Article 228 merely tells the Commission to get on with negotiations."

"Which can be as one-sided as the Commission, in its infinite wisdom, decides, eh, John? What sort of negotiations can one make, with a loaded shotgun held to one's temple? Ah! I'm sick of them! I wish we could tow this island into the South Pacific!

"You want us to pursue it through the European Court of Justice, sir?"

"You know as well as I do, John, it's a court of injustice. It's nothing but a puppet to manipulate European laws and plug any loopholes. We haven't a hope in hell of getting a fair hearing."

The Chief Minister nodded to his phone. "I agree wholeheartedly, sir. We're in a cleft stick, and they can roast us over the fire any time they want."

"What do you propose we do? Surrender yet another slice of our precious independence? I'd pay them in Yankee dollars or pieces of eight before I'd touch their damned euros."

Sir John glanced out of the window once more at the view of the rooftops of the lower part of Douglas town, at the Irish Sea an unusually dark blue, at the distant Cumbrian Mountains and, to the left, the mountains of Galloway in Scotland, Region UKA2, now emerging from the morning mist. It was a view he could sit and watch for an hour or more.

"No, sir," he said firmly, aware that the words may yet have far-reaching implications. "I propose we resist. I feel this infernal diktat is merely the beginning. If we have to deal with them exclusively in their damned currency, they'll soon come back with another diktat and before we know what's happened they'll find some fine-print clause that says we'll have to abandon the pound altogether, even within our own island, if we want to trade with them. And then they've got us. Remember how they cheated Britain?"

"I do indeed, John. A really shabby piece of work. The infamous Article 104c. My God — we certainly don't want to go the same way."

Sir John thumped his desk in his suppressed anger but managed to keep his words under control. "You won't remember it, Governor, but at the end of the Second War sterling was a major currency. There was such a thing as the Sterling Zone, with the British Isles, the entire Commonwealth except for India and Canada, and quite a few other places as well, such as Palestine that was, and Egypt. The Sterling Zone! Now it's a few islands scattered from here and down the Mid-Atlantic Ridge. If it weren't for the billions of barrels of oil in the Kingdom of the Falklands the currency would have collapsed when Westminster capitulated to Frankfurt. No, Governor, I'm damned if I'm going to give those Brussels bastards another inch — or should I say centimetre?"

There was a pause on the line before the Lieutenant-Governor replied. "You know, John, I agree with you wholeheartedly. You'll forgive my reminding you that Pitcairn opted to become a New Zealand colony when Britain met her nemesis." He paused again. "So we resist. You realise what it will do to our economy?"

"Of course I do, sir. The United Kingdom — I'm not going to concede that it's split into bits — is our major trading partner by far. We'd lose all that. We'd have to import our oil direct from Libya or The Gambia — or even the Falklands — and our grain direct from North America. No trans-shipment anywhere in Britain. Damn it, Governor — we'd even have to forego our Scotch whisky!"

"But we'd retain our financial services — and I thank God they're doing very well. But if we show any weakness at all, we shall undermine the stability of the pound. There'll be a run on the currency, and we'll be finished."

"Perhaps that's what they're hoping for, sir."

"My God! You're probably right! We operate a much more liberal financial market than Frankfurt does. Lower taxation. Far less bureaucracy. And we're still picking up business whereas I do hear tell that Frankfurt can't hold on to what it's got."

"Once we let it be seen worldwide we're refusing to give another inch — inch, mind you — to the Union, we may even claw some business direct from the lion's mouth." Sir John crumpled his fist. "I almost relish the idea of a fight, Governor. David against Goliath. David won, didn't he?"

"I'm just a biased English comeover," the Lieutenant-Governor said from his home in Governor's House, Onchan, "and I'd give everything I have to see the United Kingdom regain its freedom. But you're a Manxman born and bred, John — do you think Tynwald will go for it?"

The Chief Minister sighed. "What choice do we have, Sir Quentin? We've been giving way to the European monster ever since we signed the Treaty of Association, and I'm damned glad we never signed the full Treaty of Accession. If we give way on this one, sir, we upset confidence in sterling, and then it's only a matter of time before the whole financial pack of cards crumbles. Inside a year we'd be destitute, and then the Euro monster just picks us up, squeezes us dry, and drops us in the frying-pan. Frankfurt would be delighted to have our business."

"And what about the other bastions of the Sterling Zone, John? Guernsey, Jersey, Gibraltar? They've all been tax havens for years. And what about the Falklands? D'you think this Berghofer crook has tried the same trick on them?"

"I'd better contact them right away, Governor. Tell them we propose resisting." He studied the distant view of the mountains, trying to picture them as being in enemy territory. It was difficult, but necessary. "I'm sure I can tell you Tynwald will go for it, Governor. *Quoconque jeceris stabit,* Sir Quentin."

"*Quoconque jeceris stabit,*" the Lieutenant-Governor repeated, studying a wall-mounted plaque of the ancient symbol of the island, the Three Legs of Man. *Quoconque jeceris stabit;* whichever way the legs are thrown, they stand up. Manxmen had learned to survive many adversities and they would withstand this latest threat with equal determination. It was just a pity they didn't have the oil revenue of the Falklands. "Then you must put it to the House as soon as possible, Chief Minister. *Aigh vie* — good luck!"

EUROSLAVIA

THAT EVENING, 3 MAY 2005, we broadcast the controversial issue that we guessed would be the turning-point for *Tell Tel* — either way. The theme was the Union Europeo which had been something of a dead duck lately. After all, the United Kingdom had gone and we were all citizens of the União Europeu (that would pacify the Portuguese), like it or not — and the vast majority of Brits did not. Why show people how green the grass was on the other side of the street if they couldn't get over for the traffic?

The actual subject matter was the vandalism of statues of the Founding Fathers right across the provinces of England and Scotland, and the interviewee was Mr X, a well-spoken man in his middle years whose voice we distorted slightly and who sat in silhouette, for reasons that would soon be obvious.

"You admit, do you, Mr X, that you destroyed the statue of the former President of the European Union, Neil Kinnock, that stood at the entrance to the Channel Tunnel in Region UK57?"

"No. I can't admit to that, Mr Mason, because I don't recognise Region UK57 or anything else belonging to that so-called Euronation. Ask me if I blew up the statue of Kinnock in Kent and I'll agree I did."

"And do you admit to tearing down the statue of Leon Brittain outside the new Welsh Provincial Assembly building in Cardiff, Region UK92?"

"You're at it again. Cardiff is the capital of the Principality of Wales, and it's in South Glamorgan. And I pulled down the statue."

"Why, Mr X?"

"Why? It's obvious, surely. Everybody hates these monstrosities. I'm doing the people a favour. I tore down Jacques Santer at the new terminal at Manchester Airport, and I tried to pull down Ted Heath in Parliament Square, but he must have been standing in Superglue."

"You don't accept that these eminent people deserve statues?"

"I certainly don't! Take Neil Kinnock, for example. For years he'd been criticising Europe. He lost two general elections, and John Major offered him the consolation prize of being a commissioner in Brussels at a salary far greater than he'd have got in Downing Street. So he jumped at the chance. Then he became President of the Commission — President of Europe, in effect. Way above the Prime Minister. Way above the Queen. He became the most powerful man in the world, outstripping the President of the United States who had a mere two hundred and fifty million people. Kinnock had three hundred and seventy million, not counting the Poles. *And the ordinary person didn't have a say in the matter!* How can you possibly call that being eminent?"

Now, here was where we were going to be different. It's common practise for the interviewer to take the opposite viewpoint from his victim, but nobody in the British regions supported these monstrosities, so why lose more viewers? We had decided that I should agree with our guest, and see where it took us.

And it worked. Mr X told me of his background: born in a council-owned tower block in Newcastle-upon-Tyne, sent to a comprehensive school, started work in the water supply industry. From there he dragged himself up by taking a degree at the Open University, started a part-time business in making fancy bricks, and earned himself a million by the end of the century. Pounds, that was, not euros.

Not that there's anything wrong with tower blocks, but a detached house in Derbyshire is undeniably better, and Mr X had an obvious appeal across the social spectrum: he had worked hard, taken risks, and succeeded. "And you can't say the same for many of those commissioners. Yet they're the ones who make the rules and bugger up the lives of the rest of us who pay their inflated salaries."

It was a live broadcast, and by midway through the calls were coming in fast, an overwhelming support for Mr X's one-man campaign to rid the provinces of provocative statues, and a good endorsement for the programme itself. *Tell Tel* looked as if it was going to survive.

SIR JOHN FAULDS e-mailed a copy of the threatening letter to the Chief Executive of the Government of the Kingdom of the Falkland Islands, marking it *Personal. For information only.* It arrived on his desk in the sparsely-appointed head office of Falkland Fisheries Ltd around midday, local time. This was five hours later than Europamittelzeit, European Mean Time, with which the European Union, the Europäische Vereinigung, had replaced Greenwich Mean Time at the start of 2005 although the rest of the world (except Saudi Arabia, which wouldn't adopt any time imposed by a Christian country) had been content to stay with GMT. EMZ was one hour in advance of the outdated system.

The six-foot-two-inch-tall chief executive, Sir Tom Smith, read the letter three times. After the first reading he snorted in disgust that the European Union could be so petty and vindictive to a small nation state struggling to retain its independence.

After the second reading he felt his anger rising. For more than a decade the world's second-largest autocracy — China was still in top position — had been negotiating to mould the member states of the old European Economic Community into a European superstate, regardless of what the common people had wanted. "Sodding Euroslavia! I'll see them bastards in hell before they pinch one more acre of free territory."

After the third reading he crashed his ham-sized fist onto his desk with much more force than Sir John Faulds had managed. "Right, Brussels! You want war — you can have it!" He snatched up his phone, then dropped it and bawled across the office: "Fred! When you've got a minute!"

Fred Barnes was a craggy third-generation Falklander who had spent most of his working life rearing sheep on the windswept, treeless Campo. He was smaller in stature and personality than the founder-owner of Falkland Fisheries who had won a landslide victory when he stood for election in 2003 as a member of Desire The Right, the islands' only political party. He had won a landslide — if you can have a landslide with a total population, including juniors, of little more than two thousand. Subsequently, he had been elected Chief Executive.

Fred had been returned as another of the eight Elected Councillors of the Lower House of the new Parliament, replacing LegCo, the Legislative Council of colonial times, and also carrying the banner for Desire The Right. In retirement he had come in from the Campo, married his childhood sweetheart Beryl, and taken a job with Falkland Fisheries, which kept him under the eye of Sir Tom Smith.

He came from the stockroom to the main office in response to the Chief Executive's bellow. "Aye, Tom?"

"Just look at this bilge," Sir Tom grunted, thrusting the e- mail across his large desk. He waited until the older man had read it, then snapped: "You can see what they're up to?"

"Clear as crystal. Germany started two world wars in the Twentieth Century, and lost 'em both, thanks to British intervention. Ever since they picked themselves out of the rubble of the Third Reich they've been planning how to try it again. And the bastards did it, without a shot being fired. They *talked* their way to victory. Norway was the only one with any sense: it quit while the going was good."

"And Greenland."

"Oh, ah — Greenland. But just look at the way them bureaucrats talked everybody stupid. Must join the Iron and Steel Community. Must join the Common Market or you won't sell your goods. Must stay in when it starts calling itself the European Community, but I bet you nine tenths of the average people had no idea what was going on behind their backs."

"Or even under their noses."

"Sure. If you've got troops fighting out in the Campo, like we had when the Argies landed, you know you've got an enemy and you can see where the buggers are. But when they come dressed in business suits and offering handouts, you never know where you are. Then the European Union. That's when they started showing their true colours, I hear. Pettifogging rules. Masses of paperwork that changes its meaning as it goes through a dozen translations. An' now it's the United States of Europe: I like your name for it, Tom — Euroslavia. More'n three hundred and fifty million people in Europe deprived of democratic government. Boy! I thought when the Berlin Wall came down we'd seen the end of fascism and communism."

The chief executive poured two tots of whisky from a bottle of Johnny Walker Black Label. "You've been doing your homework, by the sounds of it."

"Homework! I'm British, aren't I? I want to know what's going on in the old country, even though I've never been there."

"You ain't seen the half of it yet, Fred. They're just waiting to pick up the bits from the Isle of Man and the Channel Islands. Then it'll be Gibraltar. Then they'll try to pinch *us*."

"Like bloody hell!" The old sheep-farmer's weatherbeaten face puckered into a deep frown. "We're strong, Tom. We're bloody strong. Seven thousand top-flight servicemen, an' half the civil population's ready to take up arms at a minute's notice. We're sitting on as much oil as Iraq or Iran. We ration ourselves to a million barrels a year but even so it brings in fifty-five million dollars gross. And the Falklands Pound is one of the strongest currencies in the world — beats the bloody euro into a cocked hat, with all their unemployment and social chapters and pension frauds and employment tax and God knows what else. We pay every kelpie a hundred quid a week just for waking up in the morning, and your average sheep farmer could run around the Campo in a Rolls-Royce if only they'd fit the bloody things with four-wheel drive. What could Europe do to us?" He swallowed his whisky at a gulp, staggered for a moment, then breathed out. "Thanks, Tom."

Sir Tom Smith sipped his whisky. "You forget one point, Fred. Our defences are aimed at Argentina. But our planes couldn't even make it to Buenos Aires and back without refuelling."

"You're surely not suggesting we're just going to sit back an' watch these little places have a hernia and die? They're British as well, for God's sake!"

"I didn't say that, Fred. We all remember second April, 1982 when the Argies came. What had we got? Thirty Marines and a dozen sailors, guarding eighteen hundred sheep farmers on some godforsaken islands in the South Atlantic. We all remember what Britain did for us, don't we? Maggie Thatcher, the Iron Lady, the one who was forever shouting 'No!' at Europe."

"I know, Tom. I was here, don't forget."

The Argentines, he recalled, had landed in a creek south of Port Stanley a little before midnight on April 1-2. Twenty Amtrack armoured personnel carriers came ashore north of Stanley at six in the morning and seized the airport and lighthouse without seeing any British resistance. They moved on and had captured Stanley by eight o'clock, although there was some little fighting before Government House — the building now used for the Royal Falklands Parliament — surrendered at nine-thirty, acknowledging defeat.

In the invasion, one Argentine soldier had been killed and two wounded, with no casualties to the British or the islanders. And the Falkland Islands, the Malvinas, were back in Argentine hands for the first time since 1832. It was a phenomenal success for an army in which every private soldier was a nineteen-year-old conscript called up for his year's service in January and not properly trained until April — autumn in the Southern Hemisphere.

The Argies had assumed that was it. World opinion would be on their side and Britain would not bother to rescue a mere eighteen hundred sheep farmers almost seven thousand miles away. They were wrong. By mid-April the first British ships were sailing south from Ascension, and on 26 April they recaptured South Georgia after just twenty-three days under Argentine rule.

Fred Barnes remembered the first of May, when the British struck back. A Vulcan bomber made a large crater in the runway. The next day the Sea Harriers took off from their carriers *Hermes* and *Invincible*, destroying several enemy Pucará planes on the ground at Goose Green's tiny airfield. Fred Barnes remembered that day with bitterness after the Argies' decision to move the entire population of the remote village of Goose Green, the second largest community in the islands, into the village hall and lock them in, while the invading soldiers commandeered the private homes. Fred was among the hundred incarcerated, but for him there was one good thing to come out of the incident: he was thrust into close contact with his childhood sweetheart Beryl, by then widowed, and they married in Stanley Cathedral after the conflict.

Fred's war was effectively over with the Goose Green imprisonment. He never heard about the sinking of the *General Belgrano*, but he heard the later controversy about the death of 321 of its crew of 1,093. He deplored the loss of life, particularly of young conscripts but, after all, they had come to steal his homeland.

He and Beryl, and the other Goose Green inhabitants, were released in time to follow the events of the Argentine defeat on 14 June, when five thousand British troops, thousands of miles from home, forced the surrender of ten thousand Argentines, fighting on their back doorstep. Fred was astounded to learn the size of the British task force, and the effort that the home country, under Mrs Thatcher, had put into liberating the sheep farmers.

He was shocked to hear of the loss of the *Sir Galahad*, dismayed to learn of the *Atlantic Conveyor*'s sinking, and utterly amazed to hear that the luxury liner *Canberra* and thirty Royal Naval vessels had sailed south. He learned of the loss of the *Coventry* and the damage to the *Sheffield* and *Glamorgan*, adding to his sense of profound gratitude to Britain. He decided at that time that his debt, indeed the Falkland Islands' debt, to the mother country, was so great that it could never be repaid.

Fred Barnes poured himself another whisky, uninvited, and toasted the map of the islands, hanging on the wall behind Tom's desk. "Sure, Tom. I remember. And I know that if the Argies had invaded us today — we still being what we were back then — Britain *couldn't* have come to help. She hasn't got a defence policy any more. She hasn't got any armed forces of her own — hell! *We've* got what's left of the RAF, down here! She'd have to go cap-in-hand to Frankfurt to beg for some of her own money back, to fight the war, and the answer would be 'get lost.' Europe wouldn't have cared a damn about us, and Spain would have vetoed any move Britain tried to make." He put down his glass, reluctantly. "We owe everything we've got to Britain. *Everything*. An' now she's gone. Sunk, like the bloody *Belgrano*. You know, Tom, there are times when I'm ashamed of myself, that I didn't do more when Britain needed us, when Europe pulled that fast one about Article 104c and told Westminster she'd been voted into the single currency, like it or not."

"The Brits should have pulled the plug and got out fast."

"Trouble with this world, Tom, is that we're plagued by governments who think they know best and never listen to the people."

The Chief Executive of Her Majesty's Royal Falklands Government laughed. "That's rich, Fred! You're in the Lower House — do you listen to your constituents?"

"Sure I do. Every one of the hundred and eighty-seven who had the good sense to vote for me. I even listen to the seventeen who didn't — and I think I know which are which."

"And what do you think your hundred and eighty-seven supporters would do about this?" He slapped the e-mail.

"I know damned well they'd say Europe has gone too far. We *couldn't* have helped Britain — two thousand of us and fifty million of them. But we *can* help these other places, Isle of Man, Channel Islands, maybe Gibraltar. And we've got to do it, boss. We can't stand by and see 'em picked off one by one."

Sir Tom Smith studied the map of the Falklands on his wall — 4,700 square miles of treeless, windswept bog and moorland with a mean annual temperature of 6°C, 42°F. The civil population was a little more than two thousand, vastly outnumbered by its sheep. The military population after Britain's collapse had increased from two to seven thousand men, including a few women, whose task was to prevent a repetition of the invasion of April 1982, particularly now that the Falklands were on their own and they had infinitely more to lose.

They had, at the last estimate, a hundred billion barrels of crude oil to lose — a 1 and eleven noughts — possibly much more. The government and the oil companies had a policy of extracting no more than a million barrels a year but, at the present price of $55 a barrel, that gave the Kingdom of the Falklands a gross income far in excess of its needs.

But it didn't end there. One of Westminster's last acts before it surrendered control over its own finances was to grant the Falkland Islands complete independence, and control over South Georgia, the six hundred and sixty thousand square miles of the British Antarctic Territory — population sixty — and the islands of the South Atlantic: Saint Helena, Ascension, Tristan da Cunha and Gough, and the South Orkney and South Shetlands. Including territorial waters, the oil-rich Falklands controlled a huge chunk of the world's surface from the South Pole almost to the Equator, with the United States of America acting as guarantor.

Sir Tom Smith nodded and turned away from the map. "When I saw this damned bit of paper my first reaction was predictable. I wanted to make war on Europe. Totally impractical, of course, if we're talking about guns and bombs. But we could fight them with their own weapons — words. Words, Fred. By hell, we could fight them with money. We could wage an undeclared economic war on the European Union. How does that grab you?"

Fred's wizened face crumpled as he contemplated the prospect. "Economic war? Are you serious, Mister Chief Executive? We may have the highest income per capita for anywhere in the world, including Brunei, but we're still leagues behind Europe. So how the hell?"

Tom Smith smiled. "Leagues. I like that, old friend. Has a nice imperial tone to it. Goes well with ounces and inches."

"That's all very well, Tom, but I haven't a clue what economic war is. All the same, we've got to do something, so you may as well count me in. But could we win?"

"Could we win? How would you define victory?"

"Buggered if I know, boss. Get Britain out of the mess? Give her back the pound?"

"By all that I hear, it's too late. Those prats in Westminster gave the Bundesbank a good ninety percent of Britain's reserves. If she leaves the party now, she's got nothing but the clothes she stands up in. An' not even the Kingdom of the Falklands could pay for a new wardrobe. Our income for a year would give a quid to each Briton — not enough to do any good."

Fred sank down into one of the Falklands Fisheries' sheepskin-lined chairs and sighed. "I want you to remember I'm only a simple kelper, Tom Smith, a retired sheep farmer. I know about scab and scrapie and foot rot. I wouldn't know a balance sheet from a statement of insolvency. But I'm still with you all the way. So what's the first move — put it to the House?"

"Aye. On Thursday. Leave it to me, Fred. I'll introduce a Green Paper about offering economic aid to Jersey, Guernsey, Gibraltar and the Isle of Man. That's for starters." He leaned over Fred, putting his massive hands on the chair arms. "I know you can keep a secret, old friend."

"Keep a secret? I've been married twenty years; I've had to learn the hard way! Why?"

"Our goal, Fred. Our ultimate victory. Our mark of success."

"Aye?"

"We've got to get Britain out, and get her money back. The way I see it, getting her out isn't impossible, but getting those bloody muggers to give her back what they stole, is another job altogether. For that, we've got to destroy Euroslavia. Wreck it. Smash it to bits. It may take years, but if we start this thing, we've got to be ready to take it all the way."

Fred Barnes smiled, and the smile broke into a laugh. "Destroy Euroslavia? Destroy bloody Euroslavia?" He struggled to his feet and smashed his fist gently into the Chief Executive's forearm. "My God, boss — it's the best idea I've heard in years, but I wish you were serious. Two thousand kelpers down here, freeing three hundred and fifty million slaves in Europe? Don't forget they don't all want to be freed — there must be millions with their noses in the trough."

"It's the principle of the thing, Fred. Think what the Brits did for us."

"I know, boss, I know, and I tell you, I'm with you all the way, and then some. But you're not talking about setting an ant against an elephant — this is one tiddly ant on it's own against a whole herd of elephants. With the best will in the world, it's just not possible. You must've left your brains in the Campo."

The Chief Executive stomped over to the window and looked out on the colourful corrugated-iron roofs of Royal Port Stanley, and at the bleak Murrell Peninsula to the north of the harbour. "You read anything about the Second World War, old friend?"

"Of course I have. Don't forget, I was born before it started. Again — why?"

"So you know about nineteen-forty-one. Britain stands alone. Germany controls all of Europe from the Pyrenees to the gates of Moscow, and even the Spaniards are agin her. The Japs are spewing all over south-east Asia. But did the Brits give in? Did they say there wasn't a hope in hell of winning, so let's hang out the white flag and chant 'Heil Hitler'? Did they hell!"

"There were fifty *million* of them, for God's sake. Be reasonable, Tom. There's no way you can stretch two thousand to fifty million."

The Chief Executive ignored the objection. "There's another thing, Fred. I've been to Britain several times. I know the place. Damn it, I'm a kelper through and through, but I'm also British to the core. I take all this European nonsense personally. It's like Brussels was kicking *me* up the arse."

"Me too, Tom. Me too. Every one of us."

Sir Tom Smith looked at the low clouds of early winter sweeping over the rugged crest of the Murrell and recalled the scene twenty-three years earlier when Argentinian troops held the islands. His was an insular personality and he did not like being subjugated by another race, either now or then. He reasoned that the average Briton had the same insular mentality and, for good or bad, would agree with him. "But there is a way, Fred. There is a way."

"How?" The old sheep-farmer joined his employer, friend and political leader at the window. "Just tell me how?"

"We give the little places — Man, Gib, and the others — all the help they need to cock a snoot at Euroslavia. That's well within our power. Then we all pull together to get Britain out of the mire, even if she's got nothing but the clothes she stands up in. God knows how we'll do it, but we'll do our damnedest. We can pay her wages for a few days even if we can't give her a new wardrobe."

"And then?"

"And then we're back to nineteen-forty-one. Britain has freed Europe twice in the past hundred years, and by God, Fred, she can do it again!"

XAVIER YZURDIAGA HAD chosen to live in Andorra because it offered him sanctuary from the Eurosicherheitsdienst, the European Security Service which, he was convinced, had good reason to be searching for him.

He had liked Andorra since his first visit thirty-five years earlier. He admired it for its independence, despite being squeezed between two much greater powers. When he had seen it in 1970 it had no police force, no army, no air force, no customs officers, no taxes, no immigration officers, no post office, nobody to stamp your passport. It had been ruled for centuries by the Compte de Foix and the Bishop of Urgell, but the compte had been superceded since the French Revolution by the President of the French Republic, nowadays by the President of the Province of France. The bishop's successors held the other half of the reins.

Until the end of the Second War Andorra had no tarmac road either, and traces of the ancient mule path were still visible. The road had crossed the Pyrenees into France some years after the war — and had opened the way to tourism.

On Yzurdiaga's first visit — though he was not to know it — the vote was given only to third generation Andorran-born males who had passed their twenty-fifth birthday.

By 1981 the country was swelling with immigrants who had come for the tax-free existence, despite the heavy snows of winter. Two years later the people voted to introduce Income Tax, but the Cap de Govern, the Head of State, didn't approve.

In September 1986 the co-principality was host to a memorable visit by President Mitterand, acting as the Compte de Foix, and Dr Joan Martí Alanis, the current Bishop of Urgell. The two gentlemen, in consultation with the Govern, decided that Andorra should not apply for membership of the European Community although in 1994 it was to become the 184th member of the United Nations.

And so it was that a tiny tax-free, bureaucracy-free bolt-hole was preserved high in the Pyrenees. The Govern decided to impose a quota on immigrants, who must be either French or Spanish nationals and who would work in the tiny country. Yzurdiaga's activities with Herri Batasuna, the political side of Basque demands for independence, and later with Euzkadi ta Askatasuna, the terrorist side, convinced him that he should get in on the Andorran quota.

Now that he was a refugee in Andorra, he was glad of his foresight. On that day in May he was thinking — as always — of his humble but renowned beginnings. His grandfather, the fanatical Padre Fermín Yzurdiaga, had joined the Falange in 1934 and served for a while as head of propaganda at Generalísimo Franco's headquarters. The padre had swallowed the Nationalists' own religious propaganda although Franco hadn't bothered to mention God until he saw that his revolution had a chance of success. In the turmoil of the Civil War, Yzurdiaga had to flee his native Santander to join the Nationalists in

EUROSLAVIA

Logroño, where he settled long enough to form a friendship with another Basque family who had left Sandander in a hurry. Despite his vows of chastity Yzurdiaga married the family's elder girl and made her pregnant, but the call of a much greater loyalty, to the Falange, took him from Logroño never to return.

Francisco Yzurdiaga, named from the Generalísimo, was born in August 1936 and went with his mother and her family to San Sebastian the following spring in the wake of the Nationalist advance, which still left Santander in Republican hands. San Sebastian was so much closer to France, to where the family would flee if the murderous Republicans threatened to recapture the territory. Apart from that, the town was the summer capital of Spain and so much cleaner, away from the heavy industry of Bilbao which, on bad days, poured so much filth into the atmosphere that day turned into night and old people were known to choke to death in the streets.

Shortly after their arrival the little Basque market town of Guernica, held by the anti-Franco Republicans, was targeted by German aircraft and was to experience the world's first attempt at blitzkrieg. At half past four on 26 April, 1937, a flight of Heinkel 111s dropped bombs then came back and strafed the streets with machine-gun fire. It was a market day and the town centre was packed. Then came the Junkers 52s, dropping incendiary and high explosive bombs before taking their turn at strafing. By the time the raids had finished at quarter to eight, the centre of the little town was a mass of rubble and bodies: nobody counted the dead when the clearing-up began.

Some Basques considered it a sign from God that the Basque Parliament building and the sacred Guernica oak tree nearby, were untouched. For many centuries the oak had been the spot where Basques had met the Spanish kings every two years to hear the sovereign swear to uphold Basque rights. The more cynical of the survivors realised the ferocity of the German war machine and vowed that neither they nor their descendants would ever submit to German rule.

Francisco Yzurdiaga, proudly bearing his father's family name, grew up in poverty, like so many of his compatriots. He saw that Franco had not kept his promise to give the Basques the autonomy they demanded; like the Catalans, they were even forbidden to speak their native language in school and on the streets. The Guernica bombing had in reality been a bad omen for the nationalists. By the time Franco's ally, Adolf Hitler, had taken his own life in his Berlin bunker, young Francisco was beginning to question the Falange cause.

His mother's family managed to scrape together enough money to give Francisco a decent education and so get a job in the back rooms of the Banco de Bilbao in San Sebastian, where the lad met fellow-thinkers and soon found himself campaigning for Basque independence.

Franco's dictatorship had lost much of its brutality from the days of the Civil War but even in the early 1960s it was still a repressive regime. Everybody in public service, from a government minister to the meanest roadsweeper, had to be seen to go to church every Sunday or lose his job. To criticise the *Caudillo* in public was such a serious offence that it wasn't even safe to mention Franco's name to your best friend. Poverty was rampant, with thousands of people living in caves, entire villages sharing a single well, virtually all the land being worked by man and beast, with quite a number of women slaving from dawn to dusk. There was no social security whatever. In a Western European country, in the second half of the Twentieth Century, one could still starve to death.

When the young man went across the border on a brief honeymoon and saw the relatively affluent life in Bayonne, in the French Basque lands, he knew he wanted it — but he wanted it in Euzkadi, not in France.

In 1959 the message was passing through the Spanish Basque lands that the revolution was coming. The Basques were a separate race and had nothing in common with the Spanish — nor the French, for that matter. Their language, broken into distinct dialects, was unique as well as near-impossible for foreigners to learn. The Euzkadi were the only people in Iberia to withstand the advance of the Moors in the eighth century: and the world should remember it was the Euzkadi who had begun the reconquest and so saved Spain from Islam.

Euzkadi ta Askatasuna!

But the young bank clerk's bride's belly was swelling and his loyalty was divided. He listened when he first heard the words *Euzkadi ta Askatasuna* mentioned — Euzkadi and Liberty — but he also heard the crying of his firstborn son, Xavier Yzurdiaga. He decided to keep his head down and his family safe, but his sympathies laid with the new cause, ETA.

When mass tourism hit the Spanish costas in the 1960s, the country rapidly began to catch up on the rest of Europe, despite Franco's demands for loyalty to the Falange. The first tourists found it strange that the police, identified by those funny hats, would not allow women to wear the new two-piece bathing costume, the bikini, as the Catholic Church had decreed it was an abomination. Visitors found life in Spain rather restricted yet remarkably cheap, but the people who had to live there still found it abysmally poor as well as restrictive. The bank clerk hid his allegiance to Euzkadi ta Askatasuna but passed on any useful information that came his way, and as he gained promotion he suspected that some of ETA's coups were the result of his groundwork.

Young Xavier Yzurdiaga was raised on the doctrine of Basque independence: why should one of the wealthiest regions of a poor country be penalised to help support the run-down economy of the rural areas? Damn it — in the mid-sixties the country didn't have more than a dozen farm tractors, and the new Pegaso lorry factory practically made its vehicles by hand.

From then on, tourism made a vast impact on the Spanish people. The Industrial Revolution and the Cultural Revolution arrived side by side, financed by the franc, the Deutschemark and the pound sterling. Spaniards saw their strict social customs relax and then collapse; they saw wealth flooding into places such as Benidorm and Palma de Mallorca, and penetrating deep into the interior. There were good roads, new cars, big tractors. Factories sprang up in the cities, drawing peasants by the million — and villages crumbled into dust. Spain had found prosperity, but Madrid's grip on Euzkadi and Cataluña tightened.

Xavier Yzurdiaga formally became a member of ETA in 1977, two years after Franco died in his eighty-third year. The new recruit took part in a few terrorist attacks, but when he saw the results of the car bomb assault on the police station at Vitoria, he began to have second thoughts. It wasn't right that they should blast a hole seven metres deep and smear the guts of three innocent men across buildings on both sides of the street.

Yet it still wasn't right that the enterprising Basques should be penalised for being an unwilling part of a foreign country.

As tourism brought affluence and liberalism, ETA's campaign seemed to be of less significance, but the movement refused to be granted autonomy on Madrid's terms in the 1978 constitution, although Cataluña accepted. Both regions were allowed to put road signs up in their own languages, so San Sebastian became Donostia and Vitoria was Gasteiz. Over in restyled Catalunya, Gerona became Girona and Lérida renamed itself Lleida. But they were all governed from Madrid. The Basques repeated their longstanding demand for total independence, to which the government of King Juan Carlos replied by establishing the *Grupos Antiterroristas de Liberación,* aimed at smashing Basque nationalism. It worked. By the mid-nineties, although ETA had been responsible for some eight hundred deaths, around six hundred of its leaders were long-term guests of His Majesty.

Except for Xavier Yzurdiaga.

After seeing blood and guts used for external decoration, he had eased out of Euzkadi ta Askatasuna, although he never gave up on its ideals. His father had lent him two hundred thousand pesetas in 1980 — it was worth only a thousand pounds — and Xavier had bought his first coach. When he rented a small garage in the coastal town of Zarautz, a few miles west of San Sebastian, he couldn't resist the temptation of calling his company XYZ — Xavier Yzurdiaga de Zarautz.

Carrozas XYZ made its fortune on its name — but Yzurdiaga's timing, location, and marketing were also crucial. In the early eighties, tourism was in its infancy on Spain's rugged and rainy northern coast, and XYZ offered attractive young women as couriers speaking French, German, English and Spanish, to guided tours for specialist or all-purpose groups. Whatever Yzurdiaga learned that his customers needed, he provided.

By the end of the first season he had three coaches and a sizeable overdraft from his father's old bank. Gradually he whittled the loan down as he increased the fleet of coaches and their destinations. When he began offering coach tours to Germany and Britain for Spanish customers, he thought that not only had Spain arrived, but so had XYZ. It was truly a case of *Arriba España,* even though Euzkadi was no nearer independence.

And then in 1986 Madrid cheated on the Basque nation. It took the country — the entire country — into the European Community.

Yzurdiaga marked the event by draping his fleet of fifteen luxury coaches in black ribbon and getting blind drunk. "They've taken us to market," he told anybody who would listen. "We want to get rid of the Spanish handcuffs, but they've shackled another set on us." For the first time his vehicles started carrying stickers in the back window, proclaiming *Euzkadi ta Askatasuna,* but Yzurdiaga was meticulously careful to keep his nose clean. The police could never pin anything shady on him, or his company, although they tried numerous times.

From the day that Spain became a member of the great European adventure, Yzurdiaga felt the enthusiasm start to drain from him. The excitement of planning fresh excursions, getting new vehicles, improving XYZ's service, gradually began to fade as the paperwork started to increase.

There was, for a start, the dreaded *impuesto de valor adicionál*, Value Added Tax, the brainchild of the Brussels bureaucrats. It certainly wasn't a good time to take a wife, but he had been courting Victoria Monzón for several years and the upper class of Zarautz expected him to make an honest woman of her. After all, he was twenty-seven and she was twenty-five; if he abandoned her now, she would be on the shelf, and shopsoiled.

"Damn Europe!" he swore almost daily, turning his anger towards Brussels rather than Madrid, yet he realised his impotence. ETA had failed to make much of an impact on the Spanish Government and the chances of hitting the European Commission were much more difficult. Besides, ETA wasn't thinking on that scale.

Yzurdiaga slowly realised that he must act alone; not even Victoria could be in on the scheme. She wasn't thinking on that scale either for by 1990 she was nursing José Antonio named — but not too obviously — from an early Basque Nationalist leader.

As the directives issuing from Brussels became more restrictive and occasionally downright stupid, Yzurdiaga suddenly realised the balance of power was held by Germany, made even more powerful by its reunification after the collapse of the Berlin Wall.

"Guernica!" he swore. *"And we haven't yet had our revenge!"*

TWO

THE HOUSE OF KEYS had been in session for less than half an hour before Sir John Faulds raised the matter of the letter from the Financial Commissioner of the European Union. All but one of the twenty-four members of the House had read copies in advance — the missing member was on business in the Province of Italy.

Sir John rose to his feet. "Madam Speaker," he began, with a nod towards Lady Olga Maughold, "I'm sure we all realise the underlying message of this most intrusive of letters and see the danger in which it puts the Kingdom of Mann? If we accept the euro as the only currency for negotiations with the European Union, we can, in effect, forget sterling. And forget our financial services sector, as well. Frankfurt would grab the lot — indeed, Sir John and I believe that's what's behind it all. Greed. Apart from the money markets, nine tenths of our general trade is with Europe, and the other tenth is a mixture of dollars, yen, and Norwegian kronor. We do virtually no external trade in pounds — even our Guernsey tomatoes come via England."

"The Province of England," Keysman Bridget Norris groaned in an undertone.

"Indeed the Province of England. And may I remind you that Europe has issued a map claiming that Guernsey, and Jersey and Alderney, belong in Region FR25, part of the so-called Province of France? How could the politicians have been so *bloody stupid* to give away what wasn't theirs in the first place, and reduce themselves to fifth-rate characters in what's no better than a county council?" Sir John shook his head woefully sadly. "But I prefer not to use offensive language while the House is in session." Mrs Norris led the applause.

Barry Kelly raised his arm and the Speaker recognised him. He rose. "If my Honourable Friend the Chief Minister is working up to a proposal that we tell Europe to go to hell, then may I make the proposal for him — with no apologies for offensive language, which is the only way to talk about Europe." He sat down angrily.

Mrs Norris rose. "If you want to show off and talk regions, I can join the club. As you all know, I run that souvenir shop on Victoria Street. I'm so disgusted with all this region and province nonsense that I get my customers to write their region number in the most suitable place I can find — on a lavatory seat. Half of them don't know their number, and don't damn'well care, but they scribble something. They love it. Those that do know their number; I've had them from Penzance in UK62 to Wick in UKA3. I've had plenty from what they now call the Irish Province, but they don't like the bog seat idea so much because Brussels has bribed them for years."

She smiled, bestowing most of it on Sir John. "When I get a new one I put its real name beside it, so I can tell you I've had them from SE08, Lappland; DE3, Berlin; ITA, Sicily; GR42, Rhodes; and PT15 — the Algarve."

"You know them by heart, Bridget?"

She nodded. "Most of the capitals, any way. *Provincial* capitals, I mean. It's a kind of morbid fascination. Madrid, ES63; Lisbon, PT14; Paris, FR1; London, UK55; Stockholm, SE01; Copenhagen, DK with no figures; Rome, IT6; Helsinki, FI11; Brussels, BE1."

"They're not based on postcodes, are they?"

"Postcodes? They're a damned sight more ominous than that. You know Britain gave its last colonies independence? France didn't go all the way. Guyane in South America is in the European Union, and it's FR93. I don't know the numbers for Réunion and Martinique and Guadeloupe, but they've got 'em."

"Bloody hell! Is Tahiti in the European Union?"

"No. Nor is Bora-Bora, nor Fatu-Hiva where Thor Heyerdahl lived, and New Caledonia is free. I guess it's got independence. The Canaries are ES7, and Portugal's got special numbers for the Azores and Madeira." She paused. "I'll tell you what. France owned a couple of windswept islands off the coast of Newfoundland — St Pierre and Miquelon; most stamp collectors know of them. They're about a hundredth the size of the Isle of Man and they've only got a few fishermen on them — but they're in the European Union as well, and they've even got their own regional number! It's the height of lunacy!"

There was some scattered laughter, and Stuart Kelly the coach operator said: "Do I take it that this Euro Union has territory in every continent except Australia and Antarctica?"

"So if it grabbed us," Sir John concluded, "we'd have absolutely no chance of escape. That was very revealing, but may we now get back to the agenda?"

The Finance Minister, Sir Arthur Stanley, rose. "I say to this House that the pound sterling is the cornerstone of all that Britain has stood for, for centuries. We, plus a few other islanders scattered the length of the Atlantic Ocean, have been honoured to preserve the legacy." He smashed his fist into the palm of his other hand. "We are, if you like, the keepers of the Holy Grail. *We must never let the pound die.* No matter what it may cost us in time, in effort — even in pounds sterling — we must preserve the currency at all cost."

He sat down to a storm of applause, with all twenty-three keysmen, and the Chief Minister, rising to their feet, but a keen observer would have noted that Keysman Anthony Callan was the last to rise.

"So — how?" Sir John asked when the noise abated and the members sat down.

Keysman Barry Kelly didn't wait to catch the Speaker's eye. "Pull out of all dealings with Europe. Don't trade with them at all. Forget they're even there!" He held up his hand for silence. "Alright. I know I'm going to be one of the first to suffer. I shan't offload any more herrings at Fleetwood. Not that I've been catching all that many since those bloody..." He glanced at Lady Olga. "I beg your pardon, Madam Speaker. Since those *naughty* Spanish fishermen registered in English ports to cash in on England's quota. Fact is, I'm surprised they haven't abolished national fleets and gone for one big European fleet — they've been heading that way for years. I always thought that was why they clobbered the British fishermen so much."

"It'll be the end of my shop, Madam Speaker." Mrs Norris was on her feet. "But for the sake of a greater cause, I'll offer myself for sacrifice."

"Not so, Madam Keysman," Anthony Callan protested. "Provided we still keep the ferry links with the United Kingdom, I feel we'll be even more attractive to the tourists. There'll be the hint of notoriety..." Keysman Callan, whose name signified his long family links with the island — the Callans were descendants of the Scottish McAllans — had lived for years in Britain, the United States and The Netherlands before coming home.

He tended to keep his affairs to himself so that most people knew him only as a banker who went to Europe quite often. Rumours told that he was wealthy, having made some big financial killing when Britain was wheedled into the single currency, but other rumours said that he was always hungry for money.

"Only to *some* tourists," commented Margaret Knight. "A few will think we're stupid and obstinate, and should throw our lot in with Britain. They won't want to know us."

A voice murmured in the background: "We can do without them any day."

"And we can forget the Irish," Keysman Miss Knight continued. "The Euromonster has pumped billions of pounds into their economy. They're head over heels in love with Europe."

"We can do without them, too," the voice murmured and the Speaker recognised Keysman Stuart Kelly. "Never had a colony, Madam Speaker. Never had much of a Stock Market. Never had much of an export trade, except of people. Never had an allegiance to London — for understandable reasons, I don't deny. In fact, they sided with the Kaiser in the First War and they didn't do much to help Britain in the Second War..."

"Thousands of Irishmen joined the British armed services, Madam Speaker."

"Aye." This Kelly was a coach operator and no relation to the fisherman Kelly; the family name is more common in the Isle of Man than Smith is in Britain. "I'm talking about the government, not the people. It was always a bit Germanophile, or whatever the word is. No wonder the Euromonster pumped money into the country until it nearly burst at the seams. Encircling tactics, that's what it was. Ever since Maggie Thatcher said 'No' at the Bruges Summit, the European Commission or Union or whatever, had its beady eyes on poor old England. Single currency? The Dutch were keen to jump in at the deep end; the Belgians lapped it up. And the Luxemburgers? Well, the European Union was tailor-made for them. They were glad to join the euro; they'd been juggling with four currencies for years."

The Chief Minister rose. "Madam Speaker, it appears we have strong sentiment in favour of refusing the Brussels invitation to trade in the euro. This will inevitably mean we cease trading with the European Union. Before we vote on the proposal, may I suggest my Honourable Friend the Minister of Finance tells us exactly what that entails?"

Sir Arthur Stanley, Minister of Finance and Home Secretary to the Manx Government, rose again. As every Manx schoolchild and every Keysman knew, Sir Arthur could trace his ancestry at least six centuries to an unscrupulous family whose head was also the King of Mann. During the Wars of the Roses the reigning Stanley changed loyalty to make certain he always supported the winning side, thus Thomas Stanley II feigned illness to avoid fighting for Richard III at Bosworth in 1485, and turned out for the rival to the English throne, Stanley's stepson Henry. When Henry won the battle, Stanley rescued the dead Richard III's crown from a thornbush and personally put it on the head of the man who became Henry VII, the first of the Tudors.

Thomas Stanley, thereafter created the First Earl of Derby — named from the family estate in Lancashire — became an obvious royal favourite. Henry VII offered him the Kingdom of Mann on the death of the Stanley who had enjoyed the title for some years, but this Stanley said he would prefer to be a powerful lord rather than a puppet monarch: from that time on, the Crown's representative on the island was to be the Lord of Mann although the territory remained a kingdom.

The ancestors of the present Finance Minister continued to live by treachery, as shown by the Fourth Earl, Henry Stanley, when he helped condemn Mary Queen of Scots to her execution at Fotheringhay Castle. Some 32 years later the Seventh Earl of Derby, James, Lord Strange, took up residence in his island. Known as *Stanlagh Mooar,* the Great Stanley, he strengthened Derby Fort in the south, built barracks at Peel Castle on the west, and a vast defensive earthwork on the flat lands of the north. Then he began racing horses by Derby Fort and so started what was to become one of the world's most prestigious events, the Derby. It moved to Epsom in England much later.

But the Great Stanley was as perfidious as his forebears. He wanted to introduce the feudal system to the Kingdom of Mann, but met stiff opposition from Edward Christian, a shipowner who had made his fortune in the East India Company and was to become Captain of the Troops, an archaic Manx title even in the seventeenth century.

Meanwhile, Stanlagh Mooar was defending his little empire against the English Parliamentarians. He took some troops to fight at the Battle of Marston Moor — the first time the Stanleys had backed a loser. Stanley escaped back to Mann and Charles I escaped south.

Victorious Parliament demanded that Stanlagh Mooar surrender the Kingdom of Mann, but he refused, threatening to hang the bearer of the next such request. In 1651 he was back in Lancashire fighting for the man who would one day be Charles II, leaving his wife, the Countess de la Tremoille, alone in Castle Rushen in Castletown, in Mann. Stanley was captured at Wigan, put on trial at Chester and executed at Bolton.

The Countess offered the Isle of Man in exchange for Great Stanley's life, but too late. William Christian, a relation of shipowner Edward and a forebear of Fletcher Christian who led the mutiny on H.M.S. *Bounty,* seized the island and negotiated a surrender to England. William — *Illiam Dhône* or Brown- Haired Bill — was to be rewarded with the title of Governor of the Kingdom of Mann, but the Manx people refused to accept him. Charles Stanley, the Eighth Earl of Derby and the new Lord of Mann, brought William to trial in an English-speaking court before a jury of six illiterate Manx-speaking labourers who nevertheless brought in a verdict of not guilty — twice. When forcefully told of the verdict that was required, they convened once more and agreed that Christian was guilty. He was shot near Castletown beside the Derby racecourse.

The Tenth Earl of Stanley was the last of the aristocratic line, but the Stanley family continued to support the Royal cause from the Kingdom of Mann, even though the new Lord of Mann was the Third Duke of Atholl.

Atholl turned a blind eye to the growing business of smuggling

Jamaican rum, oriental silks, and anything else that had high value for little bulk. Dozens of Manxmen in the villages of Castletown, Peel, and Dughglais — soon to be the capital town, Douglas — dug cellars to store the contraband knowing they were safe as long as they paid a small bribe to Atholl.

But Parliament at Westminster, now much stronger than the Crown itself, decided that the smuggling was hitting its own revenues and so it passed the Revestment Act in 1765, a typical example of dictatorial democracy which the European Union was to emulate some 240 years later. The Act gave the British Government the right to buy up the title of Lord of Mann and to control Manx excises. By the middle of the nineteenth century the Lordship of Mann had passed by default to the British Crown, but it was in the second half of the twentieth century that Westminster revived memories of the Revestment Act.

And Westminster did it by adopting the European invention, Value Added Tax. As this was levied by customs officers — excise men — instead of revenue men, it was applied to the Isle of Man despite protests that the isle had never come under Westminster rule.

What about the principle of no taxation without representation, the Manxmen cried, reminding Westminster that that was the issue which had lost them the United States of America.

Now, as Sir Arthur Stanley — the first Minister of Finance of the twenty-first century, and also Home Secretary to the House of Keys — rose to address his fellow members, he began: "Chief Minister, Madam Speaker, ladies and gentlemen, I expect you all know sufficient of our history for me not to bore you with a repetition. You will know that my ancestors were kings of our island home, and later Lords of Mann, until the Duke of Atholl ruined the status quo by his negligence."

"Hear, hear," echoed in the chamber.

"I continue to support that tradition. Although a Stanley is no longer a ruler here, this Stanley and all my family loyally support the present Lord of Mann, Her Majesty Queen Elizabeth the Second..."

"Mrs Elizabeth Windsor, in Eurospeak," Keysman Barry Kelly commented with scorn.

"We also support the British Government — the English Government, I should say, in deference to the Scottish Assembly — even though it's now a rump with much less power than we have. However, the question of whether we could cut ourselves off completely, in an economic sense, needs very serious thought. Last financial year this kingdom spent sixty-five million pounds in Europe, almost all of it with England and Scotland. Ireland took the great majority of the remainder, with tiny amounts spent in Germany,

France, Sweden and the United States of America."

"BMWs, Peugeots, Volvos, and Disneyland," a voice murmured, drawing a few laughs.

"We earned sixty million, so we have a deficit which needs urgent attention." Sir Arthur paused, and Barry Kelly's voice obliged.

"Tourism, finance, a bit of industry, and the fish I sold in Fleetwood."

"My honourable friend has it in one," the Minister smiled. "That's around a thousand pounds per head of the population. If we cease trading with Europe, we save around fifty-five million, and we cut our income back by only twenty million. Our industry would suffer, but we could expect to increase our business in the financial services sector. So on those figures, with tourism untouched, we have a surplus of thirty million pounds a year."

"So what are we waiting for?"

The Minister of Finance raised a finger. "Unless, of course, Europe retaliates by denying us ferry access..."

"Which it will, Madam Speaker," Barry Kelly snapped. "It wants to conquer us, not give us handouts."

The Minister nodded. "I'm inclined to agree with my honourable friend. If so, it leaves us much worse off than we are now. We'll need to find alternative sources for the goods we shall no longer buy from Europe. Oil, grain, cars and lorries, almost all our manufactured goods. Even such luxuries as bananas and whisky." He paused. "Are you still in favour?"

"We can buy those goods from America, or the oil from The Gambia or the Falklands, Madam Speaker," Keysman Margaret Knight protested. "And what we can't, we can do without. My parents managed in the war."

"But it will all cost more," Sir Arthur cautioned. "We would need to ration our imports quite considerably. And if Europe in its wisdom decided to close its ports to the Isle of Man Steam Packet Company, and its airports to Manx Airlines, then we lose our tourist trade at a stroke, and both those admirable companies will go to the wall. Can we risk that? Would those companies try sueing us for mismanagement of the economy?"

Keysman Bridget Norris rose. "And I go out of business, too; who'd want a tourist shop, with no tourists? And my husband would almost certainly lose his job in the docks." She shrugged. "But I think we'd be prepared to make the sacrifice if it were in a good cause, and..." She flashed a lightning-quick glance at the Finance Minister. "...I'm sure we'd manage to survive, somehow."

"Admirable sentiment," the Finance Minister acknowledged, with a smile at Mrs Norris.

Stuart Kelly the coach operator, was recognised. "In that event we could take our case to the European Court, Madam Speaker."

The Finance Minister sighed and transferred his gaze to Kelly, inspecting him as if he were a troublesome schoolboy. "Do me a favour, Stuart," he said in a voice just loud enough to be heard.

"Sorry, all. I forgot." He sat down, shamed.

Keysman Callan had been listening intently. It was part of his overall plan to use his position in the House of Keys, along with his contacts in the merchant banking world, to bring the island economy almost to its knees, then throw it a lifeline. Maybe he could hint at that lifeline right now?

He caught the Speaker's eye. "There is another aspect to the entire debate, Madam Speaker. Let us suppose we go along with the EU's suggestion..."

There were roars of protest, but Lady Olga Maughold waved them down from her seat of authority. "Let the Keysman continue, please."

"If we accepted the euro, we'd be part of the vast market. We'd be inside it, not trading on the outside. At the moment we are merely *associate* members of the Union. If we join the single currency but keep associate status, we keep control of our taxation system. We could be in an insurmountable position — a tax haven within the Union. We could invite foreign investment — we could have a motor manufacturer here, turning out ten thousand cars a year for Europe..."

"Ha! An' they'd drive to Liverpool across the Irish Sea? Rubbish! What about freight costs?"

"Negligible," Callan replied. "The cars are shipped from the Far East at the moment. The Irish Sea is nothing."

"Labour costs are a lot higher here. And if we wanted heavy industry we could have got it years ago — we've been a tax haven, as you call it, for ages."

"Order! Order!"

Callan sat down. *I tried,* he thought. *If they don't want it the easy way, then they can have it the hard way.*

The Finance Minister continued. "We have three months to make a decision. I suggest we close the debate without a vote, and examine the prospect from our own personal points of view. Could each one of us survive? If so, could the Manx economy survive? We must also take the pulse of Manx businesses likely to feel the pinch." He paused, studying a somewhat bemused gathering.

"There are two final points I'd like to make, Madam Speaker. Poor old England, as a province, doesn't have the authority to represent us or the Channel Islands — or even Rockall — to foreign governments.

Personally I find it like a bad dream whenever I think about it, but our House of Keys is infinitely more powerful than Westminster is. So, since England gave up the ghost, we've been in charge of our own defence and foreign relations — in charge of everything, except that anomalous Value Added Tax."

He paused. "I feel that, at the moment, our arrangements for defence and diplomacy are sadly lacking and, in view of recent developments, I propose we approach the Kingdom of the Falkland Islands to see if we, them, and the Channel Islands, can arrange joint diplomatic representation. As for defence, we must look very carefully on how we can keep the Euromonster at bay."

Margaret Knight, a poultry farmer from the flat lands of Andreas in the north, said: "It's absolutely impossible to defend ourselves against military attack. What we have to protect against is the economic attack, like this crazy letter. And like Keysman Callan's suggestion, which would merely allow Europe to get its foot in the Manx door."

Sir Arthur Stanley nodded. "Isn't it a pity? If the Tenth Earl of Stanley had been better in bed, then maybe I would have been Lord of Mann today. No disrespect to Her Majesty, but if I *were* the lord, the Revestment Act would never have been passed and we would not be liable to pay that damnable tax."

"How much do we owe at the moment?"

"A little over a million pounds."

"Don't pay it!" Bridget Norris called. "Let them sweat!"

"On the contrary, Madam Speaker," Sir Arthur Stanley said with a twinkle in his eye. "I propose we wait until after August the third, by which time all transactions must be made in euros." He waved a copy of the letter from the European Financial Commissioner. "'Invoices in sterling will not be valid,'" he quoted. "So I propose we pay our tax debt in sterling."

The chamber echoed with laughter and applause, until Keysman Callan called: "They'll take it. They'll take it even if we pay in cowrie shells."

"Then we shall know exactly what kind of Euromonster we're dealing with, won't we?"

Keysman Stuart Kelly, the coach operator, rose to his feet with difficulty due to his troublesome left leg, shattered in a motorcycle crash during the 1975 Tourist Trophy race. "Just one point, Madam Speaker. If we want to break our Treaty of Association with Europe — will they agree to it?"

"Of course not, Madam Speaker," Chief Minister Sir John Faulds replied. "Europe is a land-grabbing autocracy on a par with all empires, including the late and lamented British Empire and the USSR until it collapsed in its own excrement. We shall give notice that we're breaking the treaty unilaterally. And we shall revoke the Revestment Act: we'll no longer pay VAT in any currency. No taxation without representation, and we certainly don't want the latter."

"Can we get away with it?"

"Legally, I'm sure we can't. A contract is binding on all parties unless there's a get-out clause, and I very much doubt there is such a clause in our treaty — or in the Revestment Act. Escape clauses are noted by their absence in treaties with Europe. Maybe we should ask the Attorney-General Sir Marcus Wimbury to start reading the small print."

"Tell him to put his bifocals on, Minister," Keysman Miss Knight interrupted. "Some of those clauses read differently five minutes later."

"So what do we do, sir?" Keysman Kelly insisted.

"The Balkan States and the Warsaw Pact countries broke away from the Soviet Union, although I must agree the Soviets didn't have the heart, or the power, to prevent it. Europe is different. We shall need to prepare our diplomatic and defence strategies very carefully before we show our hand, Madam Speaker. And then we should hang our garlic over the door." Several eyebrows puckered, and Keysmen looked at each other in bewilderment. "Keeps the witches and warlocks and evil spirits at bay," the Chief Minister explained with a wry smile. "We shall need all the help we can get."

Ten minutes later, after the closing formalities, the Keysmen began drifting out of the chamber. Mrs Bridget Norris, the woman who ran the tourist shop on Victoria Street, worked her way closer to the Finance Minister. "That was a wonderful speech, Sir Arthur," she said loudly.

"Thank you, Mrs Norris," he replied with a smile, then stopped. The remaining Keysmen passed and within seconds they were alone. In a much more seductive voice Sir Arthur said: "Going my way, Bridget? Care for a lift?"

She smiled and murmured in a voice meant for his ears only: "I thought you'd never ask, my dear."

KEYSMAN ANTHONY CALLAN, the banker who had worked in The Netherlands before it became the Dutch Province, collected his Jaguar from a backstreet and drove north-east to the suburb of Onchan, although his home was in his constituency of Ballasalla to the south-west. He stopped at a call box owned by Manx Telecom, part of the Concert conglomerate, looked up a number in his diary then pulled on a pair of thin rubber gloves. He ripped open a bag of fifty-pence pieces fresh from the bank and fed them into the slot. He dialled. Before his call could be answered he pushed a large piece of rubber in each cheek.

"May I speak to Commissioner Boeke?" he asked in English-accented Dutch, his voice sufficiently disguised.

"Who shall I say is calling?"

"A friend. A friend from Amsterdam, three years ago." He waited for a few moments, feeding the kiosk with coins, until a familiar voice came on the line.

"Who is that?" it asked in Dutch.

Callan said: "Remember 104c, Commissioner? Look, sir, I need to see you. Can we meet on Sunday around 1600 hours?"

"Sunday? You choose a very inconvenient day, my friend."

"I regret, Commissioner, I cannot make it any other time in the near future. May I suggest the same place as last time?"

"And is it that urgent?"

"I believe so, sir. This is about Commissioner Berghofen's ultimatum to the Sterling Zone. Another 104c."

The Dutchman paused only briefly. "Sunday. Same time, same place."

Keysman Callan put down the receiver, confident that there was no way his call could be identified with him. He didn't want anybody in the Isle of Man to know that he had been talking to a European Commissioner, although when he brought a multi-million-euro motor-manufacturing industry to the island from Korea after the Manx community finally had to abandon sterling, he knew who would be the hero.

SIR CLAUDE WARNER, Her Majesty's Vicereine in the Kingdom of the Falkland Islands, sat in at the reconvened meeting of the Royal Falklands Parliament on Monday 16 May, 2005, an observer who could speak only when invited, but everybody knew the invitation was permanent. The Chief Executive, Sir Tom Smith, opened the proceedings in his bucolic fashion.

"Right. I hereby declare the Lower Chamber to be in session. Everybody here?" He noted the ten members seated at the single circular table, and nodded. "We open, as usual, with the singing of the National Anthem, *God Save The Queen*." When all twelve members of the government, plus the journalist in the Press box and a few people in the public gallery, had offered an off-key and out-of-tempo version of one of the easiest tunes ever composed — nobody counted those who merely mouthed the words — Sir Tom said again: "Right. Item one. You've all had a chance to read it. If not, where have you been the last week? Now we've had time to sleep on it, we've got to vote on it. The proposal before us is that we offer any help we can to the Isle of Man, the Channel Islands and Gibraltar. Who's going to open the debate?"

Mrs Sheila Coward raised her hand and simultaneously spoke. She was in her early seventies but still carrying the freckles of her youth. "There's nothing to debate on, Mr Chairman. We had a chat a while ago among ourselves, and we agree. We offer any help we can to the places you named. You can take it as a unanimous vote — assuming you're in favour?"

Sir Tom was slightly deflated. "Huh! Good! Right, then. Item two. What do we offer them? You want to start, Sheila?"

"We can offer them wool, fish, mutton, oil or money. It's pretty obvious it's got to be money, but I don't see why they shouldn't have some oil as well, if they want. Where else are they going to get it? Libya? The Gambia? The Gulf?"

"Objection, Mr Chairman," Verdun Reeve called. "Not in principle but in substance." Reeve was fifty-three and often joked that he was underheight for his weight. "I agree we should let them have oil. Free, if everybody agrees. But what are they going to do with it? These little islands don't have any refineries."

There were murmurs of surprise from the Elected Councillors.

"It'll be a year or so before our own refinery is in production. It seems to me we'll have to send them a tankerload of crude and barter it for a lesser amount of refined products — petrol, diesel, avgas, whatever."

"Where can we do that, Verd? Not in Europe."

"Certainly not in Europe. It's too far to ship the stuff to the United States. Ideally we need some staging-post on the direct route from here to destination." He paused to offer a smile. "That's why I did some research on Morocco. There's the capacity to refine four million tons of crude at Mohammedia or Sidi Kacem, so I propose we give the Moroccans a supertanker of our light crude and send on the equivalent value in refined petroleum products. What do you all say?"

Sir Tom nodded in mild admiration. "Sounds good to me. How much do we send 'em?"

"As you know, it makes economic sense to send a supertanker, especially as we're seven thousand miles away. The refined oils can go in much smaller tankers that these little islands can manage; we don't want a repeat of the *Torrey Canyon*."

"What's that, Verd? Some theme park?"

"It's only the biggest oil disaster in the English Channel. Supertanker went onto the rocks near Guernsey in 1967 and plastered thick oil on hundreds of miles of beach."

"How small do you call a small tanker, Verd?"

"Ten thousand tons, top size. We could store all the refined stuff from Morocco in Gibraltar. There's a second city carved out inside that lump of limestone. I saw it once — hospitals, military places, rocket launchers, fuel and food stores, water. You could probably put every kelper in those caves and still have room for the Pitcairners. Gib could certainly take seventy thousand tons and let the other places share ten thousand among them.

"Right," the Chief Executive said again. "We're getting through the agenda pretty quickly. Anybody else like to add something about material help?" Heads shook. "Then what about money? If them islands break off all trading links with Euroslavia, they're pretty soon going to feel the pinch. Are we going to offer them financial help?"

Mrs Mary-Ann Chesters snapped: "Of course we are. We cannot stand by and do nothing, after what they did for us in 1982. The question is... no, the questions are — must get my grammar right: who wants what and for how long? Are we looking only at the Isle of Man or are we looking at Jersey and Guernsey as well? And what about Gibraltar? Surely we must ask them for a reasonable estimate of what their needs may be, and for what length of time."

Several heads nodded, and Peter Hepplethwaite, an ex-officio member who came out to the Falklands after the war with Argentina, to run a fish-and-chip shop, commented: "Trust a teacher to come up with the most sensible answer. Good thinking, Mary-Ann."

Mrs Chesters, whose enormous bosom ideally matched her name, smiled.

Sir Tom looked around him. "So. The first proposal is that we offer these other sterling places a tanker full of crude, swapped in Morocco for refined oils. All in favour?"

Eight hands went up; Stewart Christian and Peter Hepplethwaite were non-voting officers appointed by the Lower House.

"Second proposal: do we charge an economic rate for it?"

Verdun Reeve raised his hand. "Two points, Mr Chairman. First — it's not our oil. It belongs to the exploration companies. We can ask them to donate it, or we can buy it ourselves as a gift. Second — if we're going to vote on giving these places financial aid, there's no point in charging them for the oil. Give with one hand and take back with the other. May I suggest we vote on the question of economic aid before we vote on charging for the oil?"

Sir Tom gave a wry smile. "Well spoken, Verd. If ever you want to take over the chair... Right. Proposal three: economic aid. In favour?"

Once again all eight hands rose.

"Proposal two: we give them the oil. In favour?"

Eight hands.

"We'll sort out the details of that one later, and who exactly makes the offer to Morocco. Right. I'll ask the Civil Service to get the letters drafted to Mann, Channel Isles and Gib. Next issue..."

Reeve put up his hand once again. "Mr Chairman, may I introduce an item that's not on the agenda?"

"Can't it wait until any other business?"

"Not really, Tom. It's about oil."

Governor Sir Claude Warner settled back in his chair. He knew, more than anybody else, that Verdun Reeve was one of the most meticulous of men. An oil broker, he researched his subject like a cricket fan would study *Wisden* — if only there were a copy in the Falklands.

Verdun Reeve, who had stood five-foot-three at the age of ten and had not grown another inch in forty-three years, stood up and spoke without the aid of notes or script. "We're talking about giving oil and money to a few small outposts of the former British Empire. Why? To help poor old Britain that's now trapped in the web of this enormous and voracious arachnid called Euroslavia..."

Fred Barnes coughed. "For God's sake, Verd, use words we can all understand. Some of us are only kelpers off the Campo."

Reeve smiled. "Fine. Monosyllables."

"Aye — an' that's a good one for a start!"

"It seems to me, governor, ladies and gentlemen, honourable members, that our efforts will be futile on their own. What does it matter to Brussels if a hundred thousand pound-proffering people on their periphery starve to death?"

Barnes groaned, but with humour: "You'll be one of 'em if you're not careful, Verd. Get to the point, man."

Reeve smiled back. "The point is, while we're supplying oil to these little states, we should try to cut off the oil to Euroslavia. Now, don't you think that's a good idea?"

Everybody sat up, suddenly alert. "Brilliant," Sir Claude Warner commented. "How can we do it, Verd?"

"Turn the screw, Sir Claude. Simply turn the screw. Euroslavia is totally dependent upon imported oil. Western Europe has about twenty-five billion barrels of accessible reserves — and half of those are in the British sector of the North Sea. Or what was the British sector," he corrected himself wryly. "Most of the rest is in the Norwegian sector — eleven billion barrels. Sadly, because of the geography of the sea bed, all of that is pumped ashore in Britain."

"Can we get the Norwegians to turn off their taps?"

"I'm sure we can, especially if we give them enough oil for their own domestic use. But we've got to stop anybody else in the world supplying Euroslavia, and that's not so easy."

He glanced around the chamber and realised he had total attention. "Saudi is the first place we target. It's got two hundred and fifty billion barrels in its reserves, two and a half times what we have. It also has the world's greatest production. So, can we induce Saudia Arabia to stop supplying oil to Euroslavia?"

There was a pause. "Well?" Sir Tom Smith asked anxiously. "Can we?"

"Saudi is still grateful to Britain and France for what they did in the Second Gulf War, when Iraq invaded Kuwait. It has no allegiance to the rest of Euroslavia. By the way, that's a very descriptive name, isn't it? And Saudi is still worried about the heavyhanded way in which the European Union dismissed the European monarchies. King Fahd is trembling in his shoes — and he's got a growing anti-monarchist, pro-democracy rebellion in his own country to consider." He paused. "Yes, I think we can ask our Ambassador in Riyadh to..."

Mrs Chesters interrupted. "Ambassador in Riyadh? We don't have any ambassador in Riyadh, or anywhere else for that matter! We use the American diplomatic service, or had you forgotten?"

"We shall be having our own diplomatic service, Mrs Chesters. That's an item further down the agenda. We're going to share ambassadors with the rest of the Sterling Zone. In fact, I have a good idea some ambassadors are being head-hunted about now."

BRIAN HUTCHINSON ENJOYED his retirement in Jersey. He had qualified for residence on several grounds, none of which was sufficiently strong in its own right. His paternal grandfather had been born in St Helier, but had left the island during the 1930s Depression and gone to find work in England; the young man had become a farm labourer in the Cambridgeshire Fenlands.

The grandson was wealthy: he could afford to live comfortably on his pension from the diplomatic service although he was well short of the £1,000,000 in assets which was the unofficial minimum level for acceptance — and for buying into the 'open' property market, in which all permit-granted immigrants had to trade. Prices there were at least four times higher than in the 'local' market which was exclusively for people born in the island.

But Brian Hutchinson's greatest asset was his services to the States of Jersey performed some years back while he was on a posting in the Far East. There was absolutely nothing shady about the deal, but the negotiations were so confidential that Hutchinson had to refer to them in a closed committee room when he made his application for residence.

Putting all three qualifications together, he soon found himself enjoying the very great privilege of joining immigrants such as John Nettles of the 80s TV series *Bergerac,* cricketer John Edrich, and pop singer Gilbert O'Sullivan. His particular permit was granted under Section 1 (1) K, for social or economic reasons, labelling him a K-man.

He and his wife Rebecca had settled comfortably in to the cheapest open-market property they could find, a stone cottage in the Parish of St Peter, within comfortable walking distance of the Jersey Motor Museum and St Peter's Bunker, and the parish church with the tallest spire in the Channel Islands. The bunker was built by the occupying Germans in 1942 and now, sixty years later, holds the largest collection of Occupation relics in the island, including an Enigma decoding machine which helped prevent World War Two lasting even longer.

Hutchinson's main interest in retirement was his garden, some of it created in the Japanese style to remind him and his wife of their years of service in Tokyo. He was working in it one morning in May, 2005, when Rebecca called him from the kitchen. "Telephone, darling. Somebody from the States."

He hurried into the cottage, mentally calculating the time lapse between Jersey and New York, but his caller introduced himself as a member of the States of Jersey, the island government.

"Mr Hutchinson? I wonder if you would consider suspending your retirement for a short while? We have a delicate situation confronting us and we believe you may be the ideal person for the job."

"Depends what it is."

"Would you like to come into St Helier and discuss your possible appointment as Ambassador to the Sterling Zone?"

"RIGHT," VERDUN REEVE commented. "When we get our Ambassador, I reckon he can put in a very strong case for a major reduction in supply, if not a complete stoppage, subject to the agreement of the producing companies. It would have to be for a very limited time, of course, but the President of Europe needn't know that."

"But there are other suppliers," Sir Claude suggested.

"Indeed there are. We can forget the United States; it's a net importer even with Alaskan oil. Kuwait will follow Saudi in support of its great friend the United Kingdom. That's another major supplier out of the picture — again, subject to the companies agreeing. Russia has a hundred and fifty billion barrels but they're in Siberia or under the Arctic Ocean, and they can only come out on the Trans-Siberian

Railway. Forget 'em. Iraq is anybody's guess; the workings of Saddam Hussein's mind are beyond the understanding of mortal man, but he'd have to send all his production to Europe if the superstate is to survive. Oman would back Kuwait and Saudi, so would Bahrain. Iran is another enigma."

"So in the Gulf area, it's Iraq and Iran we'd have to convince?" Mrs Coward asked.

"That's it. In the rest of the world, Mexico is happy to sell to the USA, Venezuela's got its local markets, so has Indonesia. Nigeria and Algeria are getting worked out — and I can't see Algeria coming to France's help."

"It wouldn't be France," the governor said. "It would be Europe."

"Of which France is a major part," Reeve pointed out. "The Gambia's only just started production, and it's reserves are pretty small. China's got fifteen billion barrels on tap, but most of its spare capacity goes to Japan." He paused. "So there you have it, ladies and gentlemen. We can call in on favours due to Britain, remind people who their real friends are, and perhaps apply a little pressure where needed. But that still leaves Libya, Iraq and Iran. If we can persuade any one of them to stop selling to Euroslavia, then the country is in trouble. If we can persuade any two, and nobody else steps in to take up the slack, then Euroslavia has six months to live." He sat down.

Sir Claude shook his head. "A wonderful idea, Verd, but the major oil companies would never agree to cut supplies for six months, or even three months. It's just not politically possible. Besides, they have no incentive to do so — they're interested in money, not democracy."

"We'll have to offer them a quid pro quo — something in return."

"Such as?"

"A major concession on oil extraction? If supplies to Europe are reduced by half for — say — three months, could we make up the companies' lost revenue by granting them the right to extract extra oil from our fields, spread over two or three years? After all, we've got plenty of the stuff."

"Provided they don't sell it to Europe, you mean?," Sir Tom asked.

"Doesn't matter who they sell it to. Europe wouldn't survive even a three month ban."

"I just can't see it happening, Verd," Sir Claude sighed. "It's morally indefensible to cut off oil supplies because you don't like a customer nation's politics."

"We did it to Iraq. The world stopped buying Iraqi oil for years. Had the same effect as cutting sales."

The debate gradually floundered until Sir Tom tried to bring it to a conclusion. "Right. We can't vote on this but the way I see it the suggestion is that we do all in our power to find ways to persuade the oil producing companies and countries to impose an embargo on the European Union." He paused. "Next item..." He saw the Governor trying to catch his attention. "Sir Claude?"

"Thank you, Mr Chief Executive." The Governor grasped the lapels of his jacket and peered at the assembly over the top of his spectacles, rather like a Victorian Prime Minister in London. When all eyes were on him, he spoke gravely.

"Sir Tom, friends. Do you realise the proposition we have been debating is nothing short of high treason? It could also be construed as an act of war although we're not advocating military action. More importantly, it could be considered an act of downright stupidity, and of a blatant disregard of the chances of success and the penalties of failure. We, the two thousand civil inhabitants of these remote islands, have decided to do all in our power to bring down the non-elected autocratic government of the European Union so the three hundred and seventy million or so population can deliver themselves from tyranny."

Fred Barnes murmured audibly: "My God. So we have!"

"My duty as Vicereine should be to do all in my power to persuade you this action is totally wrong from start to finish. Tactically, it's impossible. Morally, its indefensible. But my duty as a citizen of this world tells me beyond the slightest doubt, that we cannot stand by and do nothing. We owe Britain our liberty and independence, a debt we can never hope to repay. Ethically, you've made the right decision, an honourable choice. I am absolutely convinced that the majority of the European peoples long for freedom, particularly those in Poland who're just about to join despite having suffered years of horror under Nazism and then under Communism. I know there are large minorities in the other Union provinces who bitterly resent having been taken blindly down this road to federalism. England isn't the only country to lose her sovereignty, although it probably hurts her the most."

He paused. "For the record, immediately after the signing of Maastricht, only Denmark and France had a referendum. The governments of Spain, Portugal, Greece, Germany, Italy and the Benelux countries, refused to listen to their own peoples' wishes. Whatever tragedies befall those governments — provincial councils, I suppose I should say — they've brought it on themselves."

"Hear, hear!"

"So, my friends, if we in the Sterling Zone can liberate England, with or without Scotland, I feel that together — England and the Kingdom of the Falkland Islands — we can topple the Union bit by bit. Tactically it's impossible. But who cares for tactics?" He paused again, looking every person eye to eye.

"I also know, with total certainty, that our sovereign, Her Majesty Queen Elizabeth, Queen of the Falklands, Duke of Normandy, Lord of Mann and Queen of Gibraltar, will support you once she knows of your decision. Here's to the day when she returns to Buckingham Palace and becomes Queen Elizabeth the Second once more! I shall inform Her Majesty of your decision by e-mail today."

"Aren't you with us yourself, Cloudy?" Fred Barnes called, invoking the Argentine pronunciation of Sir Claude's name.

Suddenly Sir Claude put aside his formality. He waved his right fist in the air and called: "Of course I am, Fred. Here's to the liberation of Britain and the downfall of Euroslavia!"

EUROSLAVIA

THREE

LONG BEFORE BRITAIN had been compelled to join the single currency, the Royal Families of Europe had seen their nemesis. There was no room for provinces which pretended to be separate kingdoms within the boundaries of a superstate. There was no room for monarchy any more, nor for aristocracy.

When the European Union's anthem, *Ode to Joy,* from Beethoven's Ninth Symphony (they had to choose a *German* composer, of course: what was wrong with Benjamin *Britten*?) was played in preference to *Rule, Britannia* — and, for that matter, ousting *La Marseillaise* as well — then the message was plain to see. Whatever the tune, the policy was still *Deutschland Über Alles.* For years, there had been predictions that Prince Charles would never become King Charles III, but most people thought it would be because of his amorous affairs, not that the British Monarchy would be dismissed.

Now, in 2005, the seventy-nine-year-old Queen lived quietly at Eden Palace on the northern edge of Auckland, New Zealand, with her mother, who would be 106 on the day after the European Commissioners imposed the ban on handling sterling from the lesser isles around the Scottish and English provinces.

Queen Elizabeth was no longer designated the Second as the Antipodes had never known the First Elizabeth, Good Queen Bess, but she was still head of state of New Zealand and Australia, despite an active republican movement in the latter. She had been a widow for a few months, the erstwhile Duke of Edinburgh not having been able to adapt to the severe change in the Family's circumstance and surroundings. Queen Elizabeth the Queen Mother, although permanently in a wheelchair or a bed, kept up to date with world affairs.

Prince Charles, once the heir to the throne of what had been a vast empire in his grandfather's day, had no British throne to claim, so he renounced his right of accession and married Camilla Parker-Bowles, a commoner, and his admitted mistress during his marriage to the Princess of Wales. He lived in California and managed to make a decent living as an architect. His estranged and divorced wife, Diana, was still at the centre of American high society, usually on the Atlantic seaboard, but her sister-in-law, known worldwide as Fergie, had slipped from centre stage after making a few blunders as a chat-show hostess on American television.

The Queen's secretary brought her morning mail on this day, Friday, 17 May, 2005, as on all other days except Sundays. Among today's was an e-mail from the Governor of the Kingdom of the Falkland Islands.

Almost half an hour passed before the Queen reached it. She skimmed it, as was her custom, then read it again, thoroughly. Governor Sir Claude Warner — Cloudy Barn-air she thought irreverently with a faint smile; no wonder he didn't like the Spanish-speaking world — had sent her the full text of a Bill which the Lower Chamber of the Royal Falklands Parliament had debated and passed in one session without any committee stages, and the Executive Council had approved without amendment. Sir Claude now humbly sought the Royal Assent that would turn the Bill into the Act of Restitution: its full title was An Act To Allow The Royal Falklands Government to Subsidise The Economies of Beleaguered Members Of Her Majesty's Crown Dependencies.

She hu-hummed her approval and read the Bill in its entirety. It was short, merely touching on the proposal to divert funds from the exchequer to settle any shortfall in the economy of Britain's offshore islands should they decide to ignore the European Union's directive on the refusal to handle sterling. The Islands Government may also supply the other islands with their oil requirements, at no cost to the recipients. There was no mention of any proposal to try to start an oil embargo on Euroslavia.

The Queen eased back in her chair and thought nostalgically of Buckingham Palace, of Ascot, of the rhododendron woods around Sandringham House, and the splendour of Deeside. Wouldn't it be wonderful to be able to go back home again as Monarch, and not as a dispossessed Mrs E. Windsor? Since Britain was forced to adopt the Euro on 1 July 2003, Westminster had lost its right to make its own economic policy. No more Budget Days. Chancellor Brown had been usurped; Commissioner Hengst Berghofen in Brussels was now the *de facto* Chancellor for what had been fifteen European nations from Lisbon to Frankfurt-an-der-Oder, with stupid Poland still waiting outside the door.

And Commissioner Kinnock had been nominated — purely within the Union hierarchy — to be president for a five-year term. President Kinnock, in 2003, had been the most powerful man in the world.

"How in heaven's name could he have done it?" Her Majesty wondered for at least the thousandth time. The abolition of the Civil List, the Royal Family's income, had come only a few weeks later, followed by the imposition on the British provinces of the new European Union Income Tax, the top band of which demanded 70% of all income above E50,000 — around £37,500.

And there was *nothing* anybody could do about it, except get out of the Union's territories before the trickle of economic refugees became a flood, and the recipient countries closed their borders. In view of the punitive restrictions that the old Westminster Government had imposed on economic refugees, the prospect of closed borders was very real.

Queen Elizabeth closed her eyes and realised how lucky she had been, despite the loss of most of her income. She could have gone to almost anywhere in the world, excluding only a few of the Arab states and China. Her dear friend King Juan Carlos de Bourbon y Bourbon, King of Spain, had gone to Argentina in self- imposed exile. Albert II, King of the Belgians, now seventy-six, had retired to the United States with his family, while Queen Margrethe II of Denmark had soldiered on as a commoner in Copenhagen but at 65 she was still seven years away from collecting her EU pension.

Of all the monarchs in Europe in 2005 Margrethe was the most popular in her own country. For years she had been approachable, and had many genuine friends among the community. She knew what life was like for the average Dane; bills, family, jobs. It was this bond between sovereign and citizen that had virtually compelled her to stay when crowns had collapsed, but she bitterly regretted her government's decision to hold that second referendum on the Maastricht Treaty, when the Danish people had voted against it on the first time around. But then, the Queen recalled, the Folketing, the Danish Parliament, had told the citizens how they should have voted; in the second referendum they approved Maastricht by a tiny majority and now, Queen and country alike, all were paying the penalty.

King Carl XVI Gustaf of Sweden had moved across the unmarked border into Norway where he told anybody who would listen that the Norwegians were damned lucky to have got out of Europe when they did. If only they could split the Scandinavian Peninsula up the watershed, Norway could actually separate itself physically from the rest of the continent.

But the Strait of Dover hadn't done the poor British sods much good, thanks to Article 104c of Title VI.

Grand Duc Jean of Luxembourg considered himself, at eighty-four, too old to start a new life even though he had been manifestly overshadowed by his fellow countryman, President Jacques Santer, acting as if he were King of Europe. When the Grand Duke realised that Santer's successor Neil Kinnock really was, in effect, king of the continent, he took a one-way ticket to Australia, his entry Down Under guaranteed by the family fortunes — or what remained of them. Queen Beatrix of the Netherlands negotiated her way into the United States and at the age of sixty-seven was doing well as an after-dinner speaker, often earning $5,000 a time. Not bad. Bloody good, in fact, since she didn't pay tax at 70% on the top band.

Neither, of course, did the European Commissioners, that band of twenty non-elected men and women who now ruled the continent. And neither did the elected Members of the European Parliament, who had next to no legislative powers. They were puppets but, like their political masters, their tax bills were very low.

Queen Elizabeth of New Zealand realised more than most people what a clever ruse it had been. When commissioners had first been appointed by their parent states, they had been excused paying their native Income Tax as they were working most of the time in another country — Belgium. When the Union had taken control of national budgets from the start of the common currency, the Commissioners had forgotten to include themselves in the Union tax laws. There was, of course, nobody who could jog their memories as they were answerable to absolutely nobody. Their power was supreme — just as Hitler's, Josef Stalin's and Atilla the Hun's had been. Pretty soon, the Queen thought as she gave the Falklands Bill its Royal Assent, the Commissioners would ask God to move over and make way for them.

YOUNG XAVIA YZURDIAGA had realised that God could not help Euzkadi get its revenge on the country that had tried to annihilate Guernica and its famous oak, the symbol of Basque nationalism. He did his homework and when he realised that that country had been the leading force in the creation of the European Iron and Steel Community, followed by the European Economic Community and now the European Union, he had determined to stop it, either with a small group of trustworthy friends, or single-handed if need be. Any help from God would be a bonus.

When he saw that political union was looming, he did more homework. He studied the Constitution of the United States of America and found that each of the fifty states, from tiny Rhode Island to mighty Texas, had more control over its own destiny than Spain would ever hope to have within Europe. And Euzkadi, Region ES21, would have far less voice.

He learned that the states of America set their own income taxes and sales taxes. They decided whether to adopt the national minimum wage, to allow abortions, gambling, and shooting the traffic lights at red. They also decided what to do with their convicted murderers — shoot, gas, or inject them, or lock them up for life. They decided whether to make it compulsory to wear seat belts; they agreed their own time zones — none of this obligatory *tiempo mediano europeo*, Europamittelzeit — they even had border controls between themselves: no Schengen-style nonsense over there. And Arizona retained the right to give much of its territory back to its original inhabitants, the so-called Indians. The Navajo people, he learned, had their own nation with its own police force, its own government, its own taxes — and its own time zones.

All that the federal government in Washington controlled was foreign policy, diplomatic relations, the armed forces, federal taxes and the Post Office. It never dabbled in fishing quotas, farm quotas, straight bananas or crooked commissioners.

"The damned Navajo are better off than the Basques!" he cried.

Shortly after Spain signed up to the Maastricht Treaty in 1992, Yzurdiaga bought a copy and studied it meticulously. He soon realised the wording was so loose that any lawyer could drive a coach and horses through it.

One section in particular gripped his attention: it was Article J.2, clauses 1 and 2 of Title V, 'Provisions on a common foreign policy.' After a few days he knew it by heart:

1. Member States shall inform and consult one another within the Council on any matter of foreign and security policy of general interest in order to ensure that their combined influence is exerted as effectively as possible by means of concerted and convergent action.
2. Whenever it deems it necessary, the Council shall define a common policy.

He showed it to Eustaquio Arrieta, a fellow sympathiser and a member of the political front, Herri Batasuna. The two met outside the church of Zarautz one cold Sunday in January 1993. Arrieta whistled between his teeth in amazement as he read it. "What nincompoop dreamed up this nonsense? Just look at it! Paragraph one — member states shall try to agree a policy on some issue or other. Paragraph two — if it wants to, the Council will override them and make its own policy. *Cojones!* No messing about: *whenever it deems it necessary,* the Council will step in."

Yzurdiaga nodded vigorously. "So if member states dream up something that's workable between them, the Council can come along and say it deems it necessary to define its own policy. Not that you've got it wrong, lads — just that the Council doesn't like it. *Jesús Cristo!* I'd rather live under the Madrid Government than under this lot!" Yzurdiaga snapped. "What happened to democracy?"

"There is one strange little anomaly, Xav. I wonder if anybody in Madrid has spotted it," Arrieta added. "El Peñon. The dear little Rock of Gibraltar. Madrid has wanted it for centuries but London says it's hanging onto it." Arrieta stopped in the street, allowing the churchgoers to pass around him. "Take this simple little case. Let's say Spain and England make an agreement that El Peñon comes back to us in a hundred years, like Hong Kong has got to go back to China. Got it?"

"I think I'm already in front of you, but go on, friend."

"Right. Is the Council going to agree to a deal like that? Is my sister a Moslem! The Council is going to rule that El Peñon is given back to Spain in just one year."

Yzurdiaga nodded. "At the moment The Rock is not in the European Union. As soon as it's handed back to Spain — it is. But it wouldn't do Spain any good. Under European rules it wouldn't be Spanish any more than the Eiffel Tower would — the land- grabbing European Union would have it."

Arrieta rolled his eyes to the heavens. "I prefer to say the East Wind would blow it away." 'East Wind' translates literally into Spanish as *el viento oriental,* but Arrieta used the poetic term *euro*.

"So, if Spain and England make any agreement *at all* over Gibraltar, the East Wind could come in and grab The Rock? And they must make an agreement at some time, because if England becomes part of a federal Europe it loses its sovereignty — just like Spain does. And a country without sovereignty isn't a country at all, so it can't have colonies. Clever. Damned clever. I must admit, friend, I hadn't spotted that one." Yzurdiaga whistled. "I wonder if London and Madrid know about it and are keeping quiet? By the way, I like your name East Wind. Reminds me of ice cold weather coming out of Russia and freezing everybody rigid."

"And that's exactly what Brussels is trying to do. Communism is dead in Russia, so now they want to introduce it to western Europe."

Yzurdiaga stared at his friend, pleased that they had come to the same conclusion independently, but he feigned surprise. "Communism? You don't mean it?"

"I don't know what it is, Xav, but I do know it isn't democracy. It's some new form of autocracy that's deadly dangerous. It's going to make slaves of every one of us, if we let it."

"I know. I can see that much, friend. Take these Members of the European Parliament we vote in. I don't think many Spanish people realise they haven't the power to pass the slightest bit of legislation. They couldn't even lick a postage stamp unless the Commission says so. It's as if we're voting for the Cortes and we know every one of them will spend the next five years sitting on his arse. Why in God's name do they do it?"

"Money, Xav. One of the most powerful forces in the world, if there's enough of it. It even beats sex. They'd slit their mother's throat if the pay was good enough, that lot."

The boss of XYZ Coaches recalled that he had known Eustaquio Arrieta for a number of years. They had attended several Herri Batasuna rallies held in secret locations; they had once worked together on a mission to spy out the possibility of bombing an army barracks in Burgos for ETA. Yzurdiaga thought he knew his friend well enough to test the waters a little further. "I'd love to drop a bomb on Brussels," he said casually.

Arrieta stared at him. "I do believe you're serious."

"It's enough to make anybody serious." He began counting on his fingers. "As if business isn't difficult enough, we've had the tachograph, the limit on driving time, the tyre regulations, the value-added tax, the new driving licence, the Euro passport, the controls on who you can employ and who you can't. We've got to provide restrooms and toilets for the staff, fill in the forms for this, the forms for that..." Having run out of digits, he paused to spit forcefully in the street. "Well, friend — are *you* serious?"

"Shall we put it to the committee?"

Yzurdiaga spat again. "Let's string ourselves up under the nearest bridge, and save them the time."

"What do you mean?"

The coach proprietor looked around him. "How many ETA leaders are rotting in Spanish jails? Enough to fill half my fleet of coaches. And why do you think that is, friend Staqui?"

"The *Grupos*, of course. They must have fifth columnists in *Euzkadi ta Askatasuna.*"

"Fifth columnists!" Yzurdiaga snapped as he led his friend out of the main street into a small alley which ended in open fields. "Don't you dare spout Francoist policies at me," but he spoke with a smile on his lips. Generalísimo Franco had used the expression when his troops besieged Madrid in November 1937: 'I have four columns outside the city, but I have a fifth column inside.'

When there was grass under foot, Yzurdiaga said quietly: "Are you truly serious, friend Staqui? Would you like to bomb Brussels?"

Arrieta met Yzurdiaga's eyes with his own. "Xav, I will do anything in this world to liberate Euzkadi from oppression. Madrid had no right to negotiate our entry into the European madhouse. I will bomb the Palace of Europe. I will blast the European Commission sky high. Then, for good measure, I will blast the German Government to pieces. Like it did to Guernica." He dropped his glance and shrugged helplessly. "But seriously, Xav. Guernica was sixty years ago. We can't do anything, can we? Two stupid men against the might of the East Wind?"

Yzurdiaga kept his eyes on the grass, frozen in places from the cold spell. "If the will is there, we can move mountains. But we must go about it the right way. Just two of us. No more. We mustn't even talk about it to our wives."

Arrieta stopped. "You *are* serious, Xav."

Xavier Yzurdiaga slowly raised his eyes. "I am deadly serious, Staqui. Are you?"

Arrieta paused only briefly before thrusting his hand out to shake Yzurdiaga's. "I will bomb the Palace of Europe."

The coach proprietor turned away. "No handshakes in public, friend Staqui. Who knows who may be watching? No more talk now. Come round to the garage tomorrow evening and we can talk there in safety. *Euzkadi ta Askatasuna.*"

"*Euzkadi ta Askatasuna,*" Arrieta replied, then turned and walked back into Zarautz. Yzurdiaga followed a few moments after.

SIX MONTHS LATER, at the height of the summer of 1993, Yzurdiaga and Arrieta exploded their first bomb. It was a small device, planted in an unused French customs post on a minor road near the Col du Somport in the Béarn. It exploded at night, killing nobody — as planned. The only possible link with the conspirators was that an XYZ coach had parked on a nearby layby thirty-seven hours earlier so the passengers could appreciate the view, but at the height of the tourist season, dozens of other coaches and hundreds of private cars had done the same. The blast was not reported in the Basque daily paper *Euskaldunon Egonkaria* — which was to be expected — and the driver of another XYZ coach passing along the same road a week later, quietly noted the damage. That second driver was Xavier Yzurdiaga.

After that, there were several unexplained, unclaimed bombs left in strategic places over the next year. None was big, none caused any injury to people or animals, and certainly there were no deaths. Yzurdiaga and Arrieta were perfecting their technique in locating suitable places and placing the explosives.

"I'm not going to have an XYZ coach travelling within five kilometres of any road we bomb, and certainly never on the road itself," Yzurdiaga stated as they refined their strategy. "Two casual sightings reported to the police, are two too much."

"And we ought to use different kinds of explosive," Staqui said. "Fertilizer and diesel oil will soon be a giveaway."

Eustaquio Arrieta took a longish holiday from his ironmonger's shops in Donostia, the old San Sebastian, in Tolosa and Durango, and took his wife and family on a tour of northern England and the

Scottish Highlands. He stopped shaving as soon as he had driven across what was once the Franco-Spanish border and near the end of the holiday once his family had departed on a five-day package trip to the Shetland Islands, Arrieta bought an airline ticket from Aberdeen to Belfast, paying cash. At Belfast he chartered a taxi with the request to find him a contact in the Irish Republican Army. He was careful to cover his tracks all the way, and spoke an absolute minimum to the driver, in carefully rehearsed but broken English.

His faulty English was good enough to make contact with a lieutenant on the fringe of the IRA, who fed him up the line until he had an arranged meeting in a pub car park at night on the Springfield Road in West Belfast; he used a different taxi for every journey.

This latest contact blindfolded him, bundled him not too comfortably into another car, and took him into the open countryside; he had no idea where.

Another passenger joined him on the back seat of the car and began the negotiations without removing Arrieta's blindfold. His hands were sticky with the effects of fear, he could feel his heart pounding, and his throat was desert-dry, but he tried to present a businesslike composure.

"ETA?" the Irishman snapped. "Prove it."

"I cannot prove it," Arrieta croaked. "I do not carry proof. It not *seguro*."

Instead, he listed some of ETA's publicised attacks and stated his determination to carry on the independence campaign single-handed: he guessed the IRA would go for that in preference to an attack against the European Union.

"On your own?" the Irishman asked, but Arrieta could not understand the brogue no matter how often it was repeated. He nodded when the question became: "You. One man. No more?" Then: "Why?"

"Leaders in prison. Six hundred. I work solo."

A nervewracking hour of negotiations followed with no indication of the outcome, until the Irishman suddenly said: "Okay, ETA. You get Semtex. Ten kilos for start, in half-kilo packs. You collect in Munich. Savvy?"

"Savvy? What is that?"

The Irishman laughed. "For God's sake, ETA. Can't you speak English?" He talked on, giving an address in Munich, a password, and a price to be paid in American dollars, which made Arrieta wince. He was forced to repeat the instructions ten times in differing sequences, then his passenger slipped out into the short summer night and the Basque found himself lying on the floor as the car sped back into

Belfast.

He was in Aberdeen, clean shaven, in time to meet his family off the P&O ferry from Shetland, unaware that his voice, bearded face, and physical features were being analysed minutely from a videotape shot by a tiny security camera concealed in the taxi he had hired to make the initial IRA contact.

THE ROYAL ULSTER CONSTABULARY could make little of the video beyond that a thin man in his forties, wearing a black goatee beard that was probably false, asked the undercover taxi driver to introduce him to the IRA. The man was under great stress and spoke little, but a phonologist placed him as coming from the northern part of Spain. An anthropologist working independently thought the visitor had some of the Basque characteristics. Identification was even more difficult as the man hung his head all the time, and the security camera was hidden near the roof of the cab.

All the same, a Basque trying to make contact with the Irish Republicans could only spell trouble, and several stills from the tape, plus a voice recording, were sent to interested parties in London and Madrid, but nobody recognised the mystery man. Gradually all interest was lost, but the information remained on computer.

IT TOOK A YEAR for word to come through to Arrieta — as arranged, on a postcard written in Castillian Spanish and posted in Prague. The simple message stated that Maria had bought some eggs and hoped to take them to a friend in Munich, to make a big cake.

In that year, neither Yzurdiaga nor Arrieta had planted a bomb, but they had continued their research. They knew the location, the full postal address, and the role, of every European Union building in the central area:

The Council of the European Union at 175, rue de la Loi in Brussels, where ministers of the member states (as they then still were) interpreted the diktats passed down from the Commission and converted them into any of three forms: regulations, applied directly to member states without the need to consult national parliaments; directives, equally binding but which gave the national parliaments a choice in how to apply the laws; and decisions, which were binding on those to whom they were addressed — such as health shops, specified trades unions, companies, dentists, fishing fleets, farmers, or unemployed candlestick makers. The two Basques learned that the members of the Council were nominally responsible to their home governments, but they were all so pro-European that the average johnny in the street had no say whatever, and didn't know what diktats had been made law until he was told to start obeying them.

"Bloody marvellous!" Yzurdiaga commented scathingly. It was rare for a minister to try to block any new law, and the most publicised bloody-mindedness to be seen in the Council was back in 1996 when Britain was protesting against the ban on the sale of its beef around the world. But Britain had had to back down on every issue.

Then there was the European Commission itself, a little way along the same Brussels road, where ex-politicians who had never had to face election to this particular job enjoyed enormous salaries for the responsibility of creating those regulations, directives and decisions which would rule the lives of millions of people from the Mountains of Kerry in Ireland to the Oder River in central Europe.

There was, of course, no doubt that the directives were essential to the smooth running of half a continent, as they had covered and would continue to cover such important issues as standardising the size of fruit, renaming Vitamin E tablets as lecithin-retinyl acetate, and ordering that 'set aside' farmland be ploughed in high summer, when the soil was often as hard as concrete and when, in northern latitudes, many ground-nesting birds were rearing their young.

It fell to the commissioners, too, to protect the health of European citizens by banning in 1995 the sale of all beef and beef derivatives produced in Britain after the stupid incidence of bovine spongiform encephalopathy. What could one expect after feeding meat to animals who didn't have the means to digest it? The commissioners also safeguarded the health of tribesmen in Papua New Guinea and Kurdistan, among other places, by banning the sale of British tallow for candles, but they forgot to impose a similar ban on other member states which had reported mad cow disease. But then, nobody is perfect. Perhaps the commission would be remembered for its greatest achievement, the standardisation of dress sizes across the continent.

Xavier Yzurdiaga and Eustaquio Arrieta made careful notes of all they found, avoided keying one byte on their computers in favour of old-fashioned pencil and paper, and hid their notes in the cylinder of an early diesel engine concreted into the floor of the reception office at XYZ Coaches; either man could get access outside working hours.

They had a ground plan of the European Parliament buildings, the formidable Palais de l'Europe at Strasbourg, the optional building on rue Belliard in Brussels, and the new multi-billion-peseta monstrosity going up in the Leopold complex in the centre of Brussels. It was being built without a car park to encourage members to use public transport. They knew that 622 members had — or would have — seats in these three buildings, of whom 64 were Spanish and 87 represented France, with an identical number from the United Kingdom. They also knew that, now the Berlin Wall had collapsed, a unified Germany had 99 seats. Just one seat was reserved for the spokesperson whose territory included Guernica.

And they knew what these honourable members did. On taking office, each had to swear loyalty to the European Parliament and to its aims and ideals, including monetary union and federalism, with all that that entailed. There was no need to swear loyalty to the country — ultimately, the province — from which each member had come.

It was, of course, financially well worth one's while to be elected to the European Parliament. The pay at the end of the twentieth century had been the same as their domestic MPs back home — £43,000 for the British, which was almost E54,000; rising to L160,000,000 for the Italians, which was around £75,000 or E94,000. In addition they collected around £20,000 or E26,500 housing allowance, plus a similar amount for living outside their own country — the Belgian and Luxembourger commissioners lost out there — plus around £5,500 for personal entertaining. And there was no real obligation to do any work. Scores of members drifted in during the working day, clocked in — a bizarre ceremony reminiscent of unskilled labourers in factories of half a century earlier — took their seats in the great semicircular assembly, read a few papers and drifted out again, having earned E230 — £175 in proper money — for the effort of attending the sitting.

Those that put in a full day could do little more useful work, although they had the power to approve or reject individual commissioners, or to reject the Union's budget in its entirety — but not bit by bit. As so many of them lived far from home it was to be expected that they received suitable travelling expenses, based on the use of club class flight and Mercedes cars.

Yzurdiaga and Arrieta researched the European Court of Justice in Luxembourg, which had pronounced some strange verdicts over the years, such as compensating women who were sacked from the armed forces for becoming pregnant. Yet the same court would have been outraged had a pregnant private been forced to give birth in a Bosnian bunker. But it would be churlish of critics to suggest that reinforcing the commissioners' directives was its most important role.

The European Investment Bank was also in Luxembourg, on boulevard Konrad Adenauer, named from the man who began Germany's long journey down this road to a unified Europe of free and independent nations removed from the fear of another war.

The European Monetary Institute was, of course, in Frankfurt-am-Main, on the Kaiserstrasse and not so terribly far from the Bundesbank. The Basque plotters were less concerned with the

Economic and Social Committee buildings on Brussels's rue Ravenstein, or the Court of Auditors in Luxembourg, and they totally dismissed the European Office for Veterinary and Plant Health, in Dublin. Arrieta, for one, had no desire to set foot again anywhere in the island of Ireland.

AND SO THEY made careful arrangements for the next XYZ coach tour to stay at the Meisterhof an der Isar hotel in Munich to collect a very important package.

Yzurdiaga's timetable called for him to spend half his time in Zarautz, and the remainder travelling with his coaches, trying to visit every destination once a year, so there was nothing whatever unusual about this trip.

Nothing unusual — until the pick-up truck arrived at the hotel in the early evening. The driver, a rough-speaking Bavarian in a filthy boiler-suit, lounged by his truck until Yzurdiaga came out to meet him.

"*Ihr Reifen'st hier. Sie hab' das Gelt?* — here's your tyre: got the money?"

"*Natürlich.*" In his travels, the coach operator had picked up a working knowledge of German, French, Portuguese, English and even Dutch. "You will help me fix it?"

There was nothing clever about hiding ten kilogrammes of Semtex and ten detonators inside a spare wheel; it was one of the most obvious places. But lorry and coach wheels had one big advantage over car wheels: the hub was in two parts. The tyre could be packed with whatever contraband was being carried, and the hub assembled around it, then lifted into place under the vehicle. There were two hazards: police at roadside checks could ask for the wheel to be removed for weighing, or they could put sniffer dogs under the suspect vehicle.

But why should a coach belonging to a reputable firm, whose name was emblazoned in three letters each a metre high, be suspected of smuggling? In any event, the IRA had promised the explosive would be in a lead foil bag, soldered airtight, and wrapped in three old inner tubes to give the authentic smell.

It still took around half an hour to manoeuvre the wheel under the coach and crank it up, which Yzurdiaga thought was too long and might attract the attention of some schoolkid with time to watch and wonder. The ten thousand US dollars changed hands while both men were busy underneath — and Yzurdiaga knew that no accountant studying the firm's books would query the expenditure. It had been accumulated from tips and other takings while the Basques were waiting for the merchandise from the Czech Republic. And there were another seven thousand when needed.

There were no problems. The party continued its tour of Augsburg, the Black Forest and Strasbourg, before heading home. As the coach paused to let the Spanish passengers view the wonderful Palacio de Europa, one of the homes of the Parliamento Europeo, Yzurdiaga wished he could stick a fuse on the spare wheel and trundle it in through the front door. It would save so much time and effort. There were no police checks, no excise officers, and certainly no border controls at Hendaye or Irún. They arrived back at Donostia with the passengers sitting on enough explosive to remove the Council of the European Union. Yzurdiaga wondered why he hadn't done it.

THE FIRST SEMTEX bomb went off in the autumn of 1997 in the Grote Markt in the heart of Brussels. The police and army estimated it had around half a kilo of explosive with three kilos of 15-cm nails wrapped around it. It detonated around one in the morning, shattering windows and pitting the stonework of buildings. It reduced a telephone kiosk to particles of glass and shards of twisted metal, killing the courting couple who were making a call.

Hours later a communication, made of words and letters cut from British, French and Belgian newspapers published in the previous week, was delivered to *Le Soir,* which forwarded it to the police. There were no fingerprints on the envelope or the paper, which read in English and French: *No to Europe. Non á l'Europe.*

That night an old van had been stolen from a backstreet in the Sint Jans Molenbeek area and was found days later in the Canal de Charleroi: Police suspected it could have been used as the drop-off vehicle for the bomb, but it was as clean as a nun's nightdress. That same night an XYZ coach was on a scheduled stopover at a hotel in the suburb of Anderlecht, two miles away. The next day as the coach headed for Brugge, Yzurdiaga complimented himself on a job well done. It was the first real protest against the European Union, but he was determined it would not be the last. The next one would hit the proper target.

EUROSLAVIA

FOUR

THE MANX AIRLINES flight from Ronaldsway Airport had terminated at Birmingham's Elmdon Airport, where Anthony Callan had transferred to a British Midlands flight to Schipol, Amsterdam. On that day in the summer of 2005, with the British provinces now committed to the Schengen Agreement on the abolition of all border controls within the European Union, passports were used only when visiting real countries outside the Union, so Callan showed an identity card, the precursor of the long-threatened Eurocard, issued to one Anton Cavan. The document was two years old and Callan had acquired it by the simple forgery of writing his name in untidy capital letters. Callan had been in Maastricht at the time and so the card bore the code for the region of Limburg, NL42.

Callan paid for the airline ticket in euro notes, four twenties and a ten, thereby closing any trail. But who would be hunting him?

Now, if he'd come in his own Piper Cherokee he would have left a trail as recognisable as a motorway. Log book, air traffic clearances, fuel purchase, landing fees, flight clearances, plus the odd awkward schoolboy collecting aircraft registration numbers. In any event, it would be quicker by commercial airlines. He wasn't worried about the cost, in view of what he hoped to gain when he pulled off the big one and brought a new motor industry to the Isle of Man.

Cavan — Callan — was smartly dressed for a Sunday, his tall frame carrying his business suit well. At Schipol he walked straight into the airport terminal, took the moving walkway to the vast check-in hall, and found his way by memory to the restaurant, taking his seat at 1435hrs. He had plenty of time to kill.

His contact strolled in almost an hour later, dressed as immaculately as befits a man on a salary of E180,000 a year, plus extremely generous expenses for which he need never give account. Callan rose and with the slightly deferential manner that he knew was expected of him, extended his hand.

Commissioner Gisbert Boeke took Callan's fingers, gave a slight squeeze and released them; commissioners were the salt of the earth and never failed to impress the fact upon their minions. Boeke's eyes never made contact with Callan's.

"Callan," he said. "Let's go through to the VIP lounge. So much more comfortable, don't you think?" His English was excellent but with the near-unavoidable shift of his esses to a shushing sound.

Callan followed the commissioner who walked through the crowd like an ocean liner heading for harbour and expecting all the little craft to make way. As Boeke weighed 110kg, what Callan still thought of as seventeen-stone-five-lbs, and was 188cm tall (Callan didn't need to calculate it was six-foot-two) almost everybody did give way to him. He looked nobody in the eye; after all, he was the most important person in the restaurant by far. Within Europe, only the President and the two Vice-presidents of the European Commission ranked higher, with mere ex-monarchs some considerable way below him.

Callan had been in the VIP lounge before as Boeke's guest, but the outrageous opulence never failed to impress him. The first occasion had been when Article 104c had come up for discussion; much more recently it had been when Callan had met the Commissioner with another brilliant interpretation of the Maastricht Treaty that could prove detrimental to the islands around the European coast, still using the outdated sterling currency.

Now, back in the lounge again, Callan wondered how mere chromium, stainless steel, cut glass, flocked wallpaper, deep-pile blood-red carpeting and exotic wood panels, could be fashioned to exude such luxury? He wasn't so much concerned at the cost, or who paid, as long as it wasn't him.

Boeke snapped his fingers to bring a waiter at a run, and ordered for them both, a quick glance seeking Callan's assumed approval. "The sturgeon was out of this world last week." He inclined his head a little towards the waiter. "How is it today?"

"Excellent, Commissioner."

"Then we'll have some." He ran through the menu until Callan wondered how his own stomach was to hold it all: the Commissioner obviously could manage. Once the waiter had gone, Boeke eased back in his chair and steepled his fingers. "So, Callan. What have to to tell me that I should come out to Schipol on a Sunday afternoon?"

"You are no doubt aware that Commissioner Berghofer has sent the suggested letter to the House of Keys..."

"Indeed, indeed. And to the States of Jersey, the States of Guernsey and to the Government of Gibraltar. We are once again grateful of your interpretation of Maastricht, Callan, for to be quite frank it is not worth the bother collecting sterling payments from these trifling little island states." A flicker of a smile played briefly on his jowls. "I know you're an ardent Keysman, but I also remember the excellent role you played in persuading the United Kingdom to abandon its opt-out and take its role as a full member of the European Monetary Union. The famous Article 104c. I know I don't offend you."

Callan smiled. "Not in the least, Commissioner."

"So what results has this letter produced?"

"Perhaps you would care to report back to Commissioner Berghofer..."

"I shall let him know what I feel he needs to know, have no fear, Callan. Continue."

Callan cleared his throat. "It is very much as I predicted. The House of Keys is extremely offended and at the moment is considering cutting all economic ties with the Union. Buy nothing, sell nothing."

The Commissioner picked at a bread roll in a side basket. "As you said, exactly as one would expect. But Mann has no bargaining power. What is sterling these days, Callan? The outdated currency of a few islands scattered down the Mid-Atlantic Ridge. It is time they all saw sense; at the rate they are going, one would expect them to do business with tally-sticks next. I hope you brought them to their senses? We're relying on you to smooth the waters and get them to come where the real money is. But of course, you know that. Eh?"

"Indeed, Commissioner Boeke." Callan knew exactly what depended upon his persuading the Isle of Man to surrender the pound: his own seat in the European Commission. He had so nearly been marked down for filling the next vacancy after, from the safety of his bank in Amsterdam, he had seen an interpretation of Article 104c of the treaty that ideally fitted the mood of the moment. It was worded in such a way that, given the circumstances, the United Kingdom could be persuaded to go all the way in to a federal Europe and rule out the other option, of pulling out of Europe altogether and facing the cold world alone. He knew what Maggie Thatcher would have done in the old days: she would have told Europe to get lost. He doubted whether John Major would have found the courage to go it alone, at the cost of losing half his Cabinet, but neither Thatcher nor Major was actually faced with the reality of the conquering euro.

Tony Blair was at 10, Downing Street when the eurobombshell came, with its ultimatum: *all the way in, or all the way out.* Within days of winning his landslide victory in May 1997 his government had signalled its friendliness to Europe by freeing the Bank of England of political control, a prerequisite of joining the single currency, and by establishing a Department of the Regions.

A Department of the Regions! That was ominous — but nobody in the great wide world outside of politics was aware of the menace. Europe was about to promote itself as a republic 'of the regions' — and there was the British Government waiting at the starting post.

The European Commissioners knew that Prime Minister Blair would be a pushover for the single currency and when they tempted him with an oath of secrecy, which was normal policy for Europe, Blair had given in to the relentless pressure and surrendered more than nine hundred years of independence.

He did it with the extreme reluctance of a skilled showman, but he did it nonetheless.

Without a referendum.

Callan had used his contacts in the banking world to pull every string possible to establish contact with a commissioner — *any* commissioner. Gisbert Boeke had been the one who listened, and who had led the campaign that cost Britain its economic and political liberty.

Callan smiled. "I'm working on it, Commissioner. I'm confident that when the Manx people see the stark options facing them — nothing short of ruin — they'll come running."

"They had better, Callan. They had better, if you still have thoughts of claiming your reward."

"Reward, Commissioner? I'm doing it for the good of the Union, and for the Isle of Man."

The Commissioner raised an eyebrow. "No quid pro quo anywhere? Then you're a very odd man, Callan."

Callan ignored the probe: no point in giving away his plans to make himself a million or more in consultation fees for introducing the motor manufacturer to Douglas. The other prize was equally tempting: a seat in Brussels at the pudding bowl of the gods. There was no harm in carefully suggesting that his motives were purely altruistic — but nobody would be stupid enough to believe him. "You'll recall, Commissioner, that this was precisely the initial reaction which I predicted when I made you the proposal?"

"Indeed, Callan." The meal arrived and the conversation came to an abrupt halt. When they were alone again, Boeke continued. "They didn't consult Maastricht to see the justification of our proposal?"

"No, Commissioner," Callan said as he tried the sturgeon. It was delicious, but he knew he would find the caviar utterly tasteless. "They accepted it at face value. Europe is so big, the treaty so damnably difficult to read — at least, in the English version — and the Isle of Man is so small. They realise they cannot fight Europe so, for the moment, they're going to try the total trade embargo."

"These stupid island nations," the Commissioner commented. "They become so insular they lose touch with the real world. In France the Maastricht Treaty was a bestseller. How many people in Britain have ever seen a copy, far less read it? Even your Chancellor Clarke claimed he hadn't read it." Gisbert Boeke ate his caviar as if he had been fed on it from birth, instead of being brought up in an orphanage.

"Indeed. But they'll change their minds when they realise the total absurdity of going it alone." And that's when I throw them the lifebelt, Callan reminded himself. He would negotiate for the Isle of Man *in absentia*, seeing that the island kept its associate status, and therefore could set its own tax levels — twenty cents in the euro — which would more than offset the extra freight cost to get the Manx-built cars across the water to the British provinces.

Callan added: "By the way, Commissioner, the House of Keys proposes waiting until after the deadline before paying its Value Added Tax — in sterling, of course."

Boeke's face crumpled into a smile. "The fox when cornered by the hounds will try anything to escape. But we will accept it, have no fear. We would accept Vietnamese dong, so we will certainly accept Manx dung."

THE COMMISSIONER, WHOSE specific role was the protection of the environment, including river fish, became so engrossed in his sturgeon that conversation lapsed. While Callan enjoyed the best meal he'd had since his last visit to this lounge, his mind went back to the exact details of one tiny section of the Maastricht Treaty, which had allowed him to meet Commissioner Gisbert Boeke two or three years ago. It was the now infamous Article 104c of Title VI, Economic and Monetary Policy, and the crucial bit began at Paragraph 2:

The Commission shall monitor the development of the budgetary situation and of the stock of government debt in the Member States with a view to identifying gross errors....

And then to Paragraph 3 (1), which began:

If a Member State does not fulfil the requirements ... the Commission shall prepare a report....

The Commission may also prepare a report if, notwithstanding the fulfilment of the requirement under the criteria, it is of the opinion that there is a risk of an excessive deficit in a Member State.

Callan liked the careful wording of that part of the Article.

The Commission may also prepare a report if it is of the opinion that there is a risk of an excessive deficit in a Member State.

In other words, if the Commission *thought* there was a *risk* of a *deficit*, it could act. Every time an airliner took off, a passenger could *think* there was the *risk* of a crash. Clever! But it got better!

Paragraph 5 was pungent:

If the Commission considers that an excessive deficit in a Member State exists or may occur, the Commission shall address an opinion to the Council.

Paragraph 6 was even better:

The Council shall, acting by a qualified majority on a recommendation from the Commission, and having considered any observations which the Member State concerned may wish to make,...decide whether an excessive deficit exists.

But Paragraph 7 was the gem, particularly its last sentence:

Where the existence of an excessive deficit is decided,...the Council shall make recommendations to the Member State concerned with a view to bringing that situation to an end within a given period. Subject to the provisions of paragraph 8, these recommendations shall not be made public.

That was it! *These recommendations shall not be made public!* To hell with democracy and open government! Keep the people in ignorance — deprive them of their most basic rights!

Oh, it was so clever! Callan admired the brilliant mind of the lawyer who had built that trap! If the European Commission considered that a deficit *may* occur, it would go and tell the European Council of Ministers. And the Council, acting on a majority vote — no veto, certainly not from the Member State under investigation — and having considered any observations — *that* could take all of five minutes — would decide whether an excessive deficit exists.

The Treaty of Maastricht never faced the difficulty of defining 'excessive' yet the British delegation of 1992 signed the document. Lambs to the slaughter! And, in 2003, the Council having decided there was, or *may be,* such a deficit, made recommendations to the Member State in question — Britain.

Callan recalled Boeke telling him what those recommendations had been: that Her Majesty's Government should sign up to the European Monetary Union forthwith.

The final sentence was a wonderful face-saver for the Labour Government. *These recommendations shall not be made public.* In other words, Mr Tony Blair, you can tell the nation whatever you like and your new master, the Euromonster, will back you. Tell your nation, while you still have one, that you've decided that EMU is the best policy after all. There's no need for the referendum you promised while the Tories were still in office: you know what's good for the country, and you're going to take it there! And with the biggest Parliamentary majority of the Twentieth Century behind you, the Opposition was utterly impotent.

The lamb had gone to the slaughter with considerable reluctance, Boeke had told Callan afterwards; in fact, there had been quite a strong influence of the old British Lion. The Westminster Government's response — within the committee rooms of the European Commission and far from the ears of any journalist — had been to invoke the Protocol under Article 23 of Chapter IX, 'Transitional and Other Provisions.' The Labour Government had protested that this gave them the much-publicised opt-out:

> *Unless the United Kingdom notifies the Council that it intends to move to the third stage [of economic union], it shall be under no obligation to do so.*

Unofficially the European Council had let it be known that it would not tolerate a piddling few words like that to stand in the way of German domination of Europe. Officially the Council agreed to refer to Article 23, and found it read: *In accordance with Article 109/1 of this Treaty, the EMI shall go into liquidation...*

Incredibly, but nonetheless true, Chapter IX had *two* Articles 23. Having located the article it favoured, the Council bluntly refused to accept the existence of the unfavourable one.

When Callan learned the truth of the backstabbing agreements which had cost Britain her independence and would bring him his own reward, he realised with a sense of smugness that he was in possession of information held by nobody else in the former United Kingdom except members of the Labour Cabinet of 2003, just two years ago. The information was not only the way in which the opt-out had been nullified, but also the precise nature of the 'excessive deficit' of which the Council was of the opinion that there may be a risk. It was that the Labour Government *may* increase taxes and public borrowing to increase spending on the National Health Service, and *may* consider increasing war pensions to the few remaining claimants.

The glorious part of the whole affair was that the British government didn't *need* to increase taxes; it wasn't even considering it but, being Labour, it was *suspected* of *thinking* of doing it — and that was excuse enough. Brilliant political lateral thinking on the part of Keysman Callan. If only he could cash in on it!

But, of course, that was precisely what he was negotiating to do. A seat in the European Commission. The only problem was: who would nominate him? Certainly not the demoted MPs at Westminster, and most other provinces had their own sycophants awaiting a place at the Great Pudding Bowl. Failing which, Callan had decided he may just be persuaded to tell the British press. He calculated he had around two years to take that option, for after that time the news media throughout the European Union would be censored. Nothing detrimental to the Union would be allowed to be broadcast or published. He knew from Boeke's remarks at their last meeting that the Commission was already planning how to do it.

He also recalled another snippet that the Commissioner had let slip. From the 1990s every car built in the Union or imported into it, had a mini-computer aboard. A software manufacturer, eager for increased sales in any field, had approached the Commission with a dynamic proposal. The company could insert a tiny *personalised* chip which could use a pulse of energy from the battery to do a range of things: if the vehicle had a suitable video screen it could receive its exact location from the EGNOS satellite-tracking system. More to the point, EGNOS could report the *individual* car's position to any authority which might be curious.

But the computer could be programmed to do other things as well: on instructions from a radio message transmitted from any mobile telephone mast — or any combination of masts — an individual car, or every vehicle within range, could be ordered to blow selected fuses, burn selected cables, even weld the bonnet lock. Just think of it: at the press of a button there could be gridlock in any selected city within the Union, if ever the common people thought of protesting. That was more than Hitler or Stalin could have managed!

Commissioner Boeke had told Callan that the Eurosicherheitsdienst was looking into the possibilities of remote control, but he had refused to elaborate on what the Eurosicherheitsdienst may have been.

Callan's knife and fork could not keep pace with Commissioner Gisbert Boeke, who had had several years of practise at the dinner table. The Manxman cleared his thoughts of all extraneous matter and concentrated on one thing: being able to put the hallowed words *European Commissioner* after his name.

"So, Callan," the Commissioner asked as he put down his cutlery, "did these merry little Manxmen query the legality of Commissioner Berghofen's letter? Article 228 of Chapter 5?"

"Not a bit, sir. I suspect some of them read the article, but they accepted that if the Union says it's going to do something, it's going to do it, regardless of what the Manx people say."

"They have learned some common sense, then. And how long do you give these tiddly little outposts of the Sterling Zone? Three months? Six months?"

"They'll fall within a year, Commissioner. One hard winter and they'll be ready to negotiate."

Boeke sat up as the waiter approached to take his order for dessert. "Negotiate? Whatever gave you the idea we would negotiate? They come in on our terms or they stay out there and starve. Finish your plate, man — we're having black forest gâteau followed by a compôt of tropical fruits."

THE MEMBERS OF THE Emergency Committee for Oil Embargo — ECOE — met over lunch in a small room in the new social centre in Royal Port Stanley, capital of the Kingdom of the Falklands Islands.

The committee had already elected Verdun Reeve as its chairman on the strength of his knowledge of the oil industry, not only in the Falklands but also in the North Sea, Alaska, Saudi Arabia and Kuwait. He had started in the industry on the rigs of the Viking Bank, his oilskins covered in sludge as he helped drill the wells that brought the first oil ashore in Sullom Voe in the Shetland Islands. Later, he took time off to study geology and, equipped with his BSc degree and practical experience, he had seen some of the world while being paid handsomely. He had retired from the graft in 2002 and moved to the Falklands in time to start up as an oil broker when the first black gold came ashore.

He smiled at the four other members of ECOE and said: "Do we agree that we can cut out formality, as long as we keep things legal?" Four heads nodded, so he continued. "Press is welcome, but I don't see anybody here. Right, I can report that the *Goose Green* is currently off the coast of west Africa, due in Mohammedia in Morocco in two days with a hundred thousand tons of light crude. She'll offload the lot and come back under ballast, then smaller tankers will carry the same cash value in refined oils to Gib, the Channel Islands, Mann — and to Norway."

"Norway?"

"Norway. It's agreed to turn its taps off — or rather, to tell the oil companies to do it — so we're making a gesture by giving it some petrol. And the stuff's free, courtesy of all the oil companies down here — which are the same companies operating in Norway."

The door opened to admit a breathless young woman who was wiping mud off her tweed skirt. "Sorry I'm late. Sheep was defending its lamb, chased a dog; dog got head caught in a fence."

Amid a ripple of laughter the chairman said: "Here we are, discussing items of world importance, and the *Penguin News* decides animal antics are more urgent." He smiled. "Sit down, Peggy, girl. Right.

And we're going all the way through, are we: chartering the smaller tankers to go right to Bergen?"

"We are, Mr Chairman. It makes a finished job."

"Good. Thanks, Verd. Now to the nitty-gritty. The oil embargo. One e-mail to the Norwegian Government brought an almost instant response — and we didn't even have to write it in Norwegian."

He waved a paper. "And here it is. Norway is very sympathetic towards the shabby way Britain was treated, and it's still grateful it didn't surrender to Brussels, so it agrees to shut down its oil production in the Viking field where I started in the business years ago, in return for oil from us. The shut-down is for maintenance, mind you, which explains why we're sending the tanker on to Bergen."

"Why can't it use its own oil, Verd?" asked Sheila Coward, the 70-year-old widow.

"Because there's a trench in the sea bed off the Norwegian coast. You have to pump Norwegian oil to Scotland and nobody can trust Euroslavia not to pinch it, when the going gets rough. As it will." He glanced at the *Penguin News* reporter, scribbling her shorthand in an attempt to keep up.

"The next bit's confidential, Peggy. You can stay if you like, but not a word of what we say can go into print just yet. Okay?" He laughed. "I bet that's not how they conduct press business in Europe. Any rate — on to the major oil producers. If we're going to succeed in rescuing Britain, we have to make the oil embargo almost totally effective. Short and sharp. A month total cut-off, minimum; three months on reduced deliveries, maximum. Now, the producing companies are the people who actually ship the crude or the refined stuff to their customers around the world. They buy the stuff from the producing countries, like it may be us, on contract. If we're going to make this work, we've got to get them all on our side — companies and countries."

"That's a tall order, Verd."

"You're dead right. Take the countries first. We've got to get the Saudis on our side. I can now inform ECOE that the Falklands, the Channel Islands, Gibraltar and the Isle of Man have formally agreed to share their diplomatic representation under the title of Her Majesty's Sterling Zone. We are now appointing ambassadors and consuls — not many, I grant you — and we have just appointed one to cover the Gulf States and the Middle East. He hasn't been down here yet but I met him, you may recall, a month ago in Ascencion. Excellent fellow. Been a career diplomat for Britain and now lives in retirement in Jersey."

"I suppose that's how you found him? Jersey nominated him?"

"Jersey's interests are our interests, so what's good enough there is good enough here."

"Good, Verd. What's this fellow's name?"

"Brian Hutchinson." He smiled. "And the next bit of good news is that he presents his credentials to King Fahd of Saudi Arabia tomorrow, and meets the Minister for Petroleum and Mineral Resources on Saturday. If he gets over that hurdle he'll have to try begging the likes of Shell and Esso and Texaco and Q8 and all the others, to see things our way, just a little bit."

"If he can pull that one off, I'll personally pin a medal on him," Fred Barnes added.

THE AMBASSADOR IN the Middle East to Her Majesty's Sterling Zone was very much aware of the compromise title he carried. He represented the last territories in the world which had sterling as their currency: the Isle of Man, the Channel Islands, Gibraltar, and the islands that came under Falklands administration. The name had been chosen deliberately, and the ambassador suspected he had been selected as much for his opposition to Euroslavia as for his diplomatic triumphs. He had studied Japanese at university and spent the largest part of his service in Toyko, where he carved out an exemplary career. His final posting was as British High Commissioner in Malta before he used family ties and influence to retire to Jersey.

Just a few days in office, Brian Hutchinson, OBE, was feeling his way around Jeddah. He had always been a keen linguist but he had got no further with Arabic than being able to read *There is no God but Allah, and Muhammed is the prophet of Allah.* It wasn't too difficult: it was the Arabic script on the Saudi national flag.

At five minutes to ten on the first Saturday in July, 2005, (according to the Christian calendar), Ambassador Hutchinson was driven to the palatial offices of the Minister of Petroleum and Mineral Resources. It was a sweltering day, but four labourers were watering the grounds where bougainvillea, daturas, petunias and poinsettias grew among other flowers he couldn't yet identify. It was a sign of affluence, for in this holy city, water was much more expensive than petroleum.

Servants ushered him in from the sunshine to a waiting-room that out-splendoured the best manor house in Jersey, but only a moment passed before the door at the far end opened and another servant ushered in Sheikh Ibn al-Houri. "The Minister of Petroleum; Her Majesty's Ambassador to the Sterling Zone," the servant mumbled in perfect English, then withdrew backwards, bowing all the way to the door.

"Ambassador!" Sheikh Ibn al-Houri smiled, extended his hand, and took two significant paces forward. Brian Hutchinson was instantly relieved: if these signs of friendship persisted, there should be no problem. But the Minister had only a vague idea of what was to come. "How are things in the Channel Islands?"

"You know them, Minister?"

"Indeed. I have a house in St Peter's Valley. A little retreat, you understand. I manage to take the family there once or twice a year."

"I'm impressed, Minister." Not only impressed, Ambassador Hutchinson thought, but thrilled. This gives us common ground. "My home is only a mile or two away, near the airport. I understand it's because of my Jersey connections that I was invited to represent the Sterling Zone. But sadly, access to Jersey will soon become very difficult; one will be obliged to fly in from Switzerland or Norway."

Sheikh Ibn al-Houri frowned. "Why is this? I usually fly in from Heathrow."

"Not so for much longer, Minister. From early August the European Union is closing all sea and air links with the Sterling Zone islands I represent."

"This is preposterous! You mean I shall have to fly to Zürich and take a flight from there? Who dreamed up this nonsense?" The Ambassador noticed that the Petroleum Minister was mainly concerned about how the problem influenced him; it was an angle to pursue.

"It's one of those directives that comes from Brussels, Minister. It is retribution for the Sterling Zone islands' refusal to invoice for goods and services in the euro currency."

"Why should you have to? Sterling is still an important world currency, now that the Falkland Islands have joined the oil club."

"Indeed, Minister." It was the ideal opening for him to introduce the idea of an oil embargo, but business wasn't conducted like that in the Arab world. He veered away from the subject, accepted a tiny cup of hot and strong Arab coffee, and watched the minutes tick by on a case clock that could have come from the Fabergé workshops.

Twenty minutes passed before Ambassador Hutchinson began steering the conversation towards the origins of the state of Saudi Arabia. Before the discovery of oil, the Ottoman Empire controlled the Red Sea and the Gulf coasts, while nobody wanted the dead heart where a few nomads lived. The Ambassador touched on the British treaty of friendship with Ibn Sa'ud, the leader of the tribes on the Gulf coast, but didn't mention the later arrangements with the tribes on the Red Sea coast. If he could gently stress the longstanding friendship between Britain and the Sa'ud family of Arabia, he was half way there.

The Six-Day War between Israel and her Arab neighbours was an obvious problem, but both men glossed over it while the servant brought sugary-sweet cakes and more coffee.

They recalled the troubles of 1988 when Saudi Arabia, for half a century one of the world's wealthiest oil-exporting countries, cut diplomatic relations with Iran over that country's war with Saddam Hussein's Iraq. Within weeks the Americans had doubts about selling arms to Saudi but in July Britain stepped in.

"Twenty thousand million American dollars, I think it was," the Minister said, rubbing his hands as if his country had received the money, not paid it. "Your country helped us a great deal."

"Your country helped us, too, Minister." The Ambassador had done his homework: military aircraft, minesweepers, and the construction of two air bases. It was as good as striking oil in Piccadilly Circus.

"And then came Operation Desert Shield, and the attack on Saddam, Operation Desert Storm. Without the help of Britain we should not have managed to defend our frontier with Iraq."

The Ambassador smiled. "Of course, the United States also helped. And the Pakistanis and the Egyptians." He couldn't think at the moment of any other Islamic countries that had joined in.

Sheikh Ibn al-Houri was the most senior cabinet minister who was not a prince of the Royal Family, and he had been appointed on his wit as well as his wisdom. By now he knew what was coming. "But Britain cannot help us ever again," he began. "It is a terrible thing to see a nation vanish from the face of the earth and become little more than occupied territory."

"Indeed, Minister. Even though Britain still has an effective arms industry, it cannot sell a single rifle outside the European Union, without permission from Brussels."

The Sheikh sighed. "And that permission, of course, is given according to political decisions made in Brussels."

"And economic decisions, Minister."

"Of course. I seem to remember that France helped us during Operation Desert Shield, but the other member states weren't interested." He paused, waiting for the Ambassador to pick up the cue.

"Although those other member states receive much of their oil from Saudi Arabia and the Gulf. It is indeed strange, Minister. It lets one know where one's friends are."

"Indeed. More coffee, Ambassador?"

"If you would be so kind."

The Minister's eye twinkled. "I am so sorry it is nothing stronger.

You would be taking stronger drink if you were back in Jersey?"

Brian Hutchinson decided it would be stupid to deny a liking for alcohol. "Of course, Minister. But in moderation."

The conversation drifted, with frustrating waste of time, onto subjects that the Ambassador found difficult to follow. Cricket! He didn't know a leg stump from a maiden over, but Sheikh Ibn al-Houri went to several matches in Jersey. Damn!

After the third round of coffee the Ambassador steered the conversation onto the German occupation of Jersey, and the gaunt and terrifying Underground Hospital. Again, Brian Hutchinson knew his facts. "The Germans employed slave labour to dig out fourteen thousand tons of rock, Minister. It was the most impregnable hospital the world has ever seen."

Sheikh Ibn al-Houri's eyebrows rose. "Really? I didn't know that. But it's quite a revelation to see the massive gun emplacements the Nazis built, isn't it? Tell me, why do you not destroy them?"

"They're a part of our history, Minister."

The Minister paused. "Tell me something else, Ambassador. The implementation of Clause 104c of the Maastricht Treaty. Would you say that had gone down in British history as one of the nation's greatest achievements?" He looked firmly into the Ambassador's eyes, defying him not to speak his mind.

Ambassador Hutchinson knew this was the moment he had been waiting for since he entered this palatial building. "It was an act of betrayal, Minister. It was a day of infamy. It was Britain's equivalent of Saddam Hussein's invasion of Kuwait." He drew a deep breath. "I represent a few small islands, Minister, so I cannot speak for the British provinces of the European Union, but I was born a Briton, I have served Britain much of my life, and I would desperately love to die a Briton, not some citizen of some obscure region in a..."

He stopped abruptly. He was about to comment that Euroslavia was the antithesis of democracy, but he remembered that Saudi Arabia was an absolute monarchy with no legislature and no political parties. He remembered that the king ruled by Shari'a, the holy law of Islam, that petty thieves had a hand chopped off in public, adulterers were stoned to death, and murderers were likely to be beheaded in public. In those circumstances, could he really hope that a sheikh, who was appointed through family ties, would help restore democracy in a country whose religion was anathema to him? Even if he did have a holiday home in Jersey?

Sheikh Ibn al-Houri seemed to sense the dilemma. "Ambassador, you have a problem. You are representing one sovereign country but I feel your interests are for another. Am I right?"

"Indeed you are, Minister. My heart bleeds for Britain, as your heart would have bled for Saudi, had Iraq managed to invade. Through the stupidity of elected politicians, my country has lost its identity. It has lost its sovereign, its currency, its armed forces, its common law: even its culture is under threat. There are times when I feel it has lost its will to survive. In the late 1990s it was having an economic boom, but now it is struggling, like all of Europe. It is being bled to death so that central Europe may be the first to recover from the economic downturn, and yet the rulers do not address the basic reasons for the depression." He sighed deeply, aware that he was acting, but also aware that he was telling the absolute truth.

"You wish for Britain to escape from the European Union?"

"It is my dearest wish, Minister."

"And how can we help bring that about?"

Ambassador Hutchinson added the dramatic pause. This was the opening he wanted. Would he fill it diplomatically?

"Europe has very little oil, and most of that is British." He let the statement hang.

"So you are looking for a diplomatic way in which to ask the Kingdom of Saudi Arabia to cut off all oil supplies to the European Union. Is that not so?"

Brian Hutchinson swallowed. There was no more fudging; his answer would probably have major political and economic repercussions around the world, and could bring down the latest empire.

"That is so, Minister. For a very limited time, of course."

"And what excuse do we give to Europe? The average European has a distorted opinion of Arabs as it is. He sees us as men dressed in nightshirts who bow to Mecca five times each day and stone our adulterers to death. Whereas in the West few of your people ever go to pray and you glorify your adulterers in your popular press. Why should we alienate ourselves even more?"

"Let us not accentuate the differences, Minister, but concentrate on the similarities." God, he thought: what similarities are there? "We are united in our love of sport. Football, horse racing..."

"Cricket," the Minister added with a smile.

"And any reduction in supplies of oil to Europe would, of course, be bitterly regretted."

"Bitterly," the Minister agreed, his tone suggesting that he had not closed the door to any such idea.

The Ambassador thought of Sheikh Ibn-al-Houri's problems when next he flew to Jersey. "You could try the same approach that Europe tried on Jersey, Minister. You could state that payment for Arabian oil must be made only in — for example — Saudi riyals. Euros are no longer acceptable. American dollars are not acceptable. It is, perhaps, possible?"

"It is possible, Ambassador. It is quite possible. But you are certainly aware that Saudi Arabia does not sell its oil to countries. It sells it to the oil producing companies."

"Indeed, Minister. And if I were to have persuaded those companies to stop selling to the European Union, you would rightly be greatly offended that I had cut into your income without having the courtesy to ask if you had objections."

The Minister smiled. "You should be an Arab, my friend. Your process of thought is so logical. Your major problem, I fear, is that those companies have no political vision. They will sell to whoever has the most money. You must give them a very good reason in the medium to short term, why they should help."

Ambassador Hutchinson had seen this problem. "I am empowered to enter into negotiations with them, whereby the Kingdom of the Falklands will be prepared to offer them extra oil at very favourable terms. If, for example, there were reasons why oil supplies to Europe should be disrupted for, let us say, one month, then after resumption of supplies, the Falklands could release sufficient oil at — for argument's sake — half price until the financial shortfall be recovered. Producing countries, such as your own, would welcome an explanation of such a policy long before my government put it into effect." He smiled. "Is that not so, Minister?"

The Minister nodded. "Within the terms of our contracts with the extraction companies we too are permitted certain freedoms. We can demand that any specific field be shut down. We can insist that pipelines be closed for inspection. We can, for example, dictate the exact currency in which we wish to be paid. This inevitably means the producing companies demand payment from their clients in the same currency. It saves on the overheads."

"Indeed."

"You say, Ambassador, that Europe refuses to accept sterling from the Sterling Zone? In essence, that is the problem?"

"Quite so, Minister."

"Then suppose the Kingdom of Saudi Arabia demands of its producing companies that all payments for petroleum products must be made in sterling? Specifically, Falkland Islands pounds? In actual banknotes bearing the name? Would that not be poetic justice?"

The Ambassador was delighted. "It would be the most poignant message the European Union could ever receive. There are, of course, nowhere near enough Falkland bank notes in circulation to pay for even one tanker."

"That would cause an interruption to supplies, would it not, Ambassador? That would create the very situation you desire?"

Ambassador Hutchinson was surprised things were going so easily. Was the sticking point yet to come?

"It most certainly would, Minister."

The Minister crossed the room and studied the gardens beneath his window, where colourful butterflies danced from one exotic flower to the next across lush green lawns. He turned and smiled at Ambassador Hutchinson. "But why should Saudi Arabia oblige? Why should we cut our income even for as little as a month, so that the oil-rich Falkland Islands should increase their already phenomenal income?"

"The Falklands would not increase their income, Minister. Any shortfall we make up would not benefit us by one penny."

"So it would benefit the oil companies instead? And surely they have enough money already?"

"It would recompense them for their losses during the month — or whatever period — of shutdown."

"So we would be the ultimate losers, Mr Hutchinson? Why should we agree to that?"

Hutchinson swallowed. "What is it that we have, Minister, which we could give you in return for your co-operation? More arms, perhaps?"

"But the islands of the Sterling Zone do not produce weapons. Your main business, apart from oil, fish and meat, is money. Money, Mr Ambassador."

"We would, of course, offer you adequate financial compensation, Minister," the Ambassador said as calmly as he could, aware that that hadn't been suggested in his briefing. "I assumed that that went without saying."

"On the other hand," the Minister said slowly, "there is something my country would welcome more than money."

"My governments will do whatever they can. What is this thing that you would like which is greater than money, Minister?"

"For a start, more coffee, Ambassador?" He snapped his fingers and the waiter at the door hurried away. "You know our economy is almost totally dependent on oil?"

"Indeed."

"And you know world supplies of oil will be running down by 2040?"

"I wasn't aware of the date, Minister."

"Take it as the truth. When there is no oil, how will aeroplanes fly? On stretched rubber bands?"

"We will find a substitute."

"Indeed *you* will. But how will Saudi Arabia survive?"

"I confess I hadn't thought of that, Minister."

The Minister leaned forward, slightly but ominously. "We have. I can tell you that the technology already exists, but the industrialised nations want to drain the Arab world dry of its oil before launching the hydrogen motor or the water motor, or whatever it will be. That way the Arab world would lose its power, and the Western world would be happy."

The Ambassador was lost for a reply.

"You cannot deny the Western world would be happier to see the Arabs as nomads in the desert?"

Brian Hutchinson took a deep breath: was he going to lose it all, so quickly? "Indeed, Minister, with respect I can deny it. It would be virtually impossible for the Arab tribesmen to revert to their old ways, any more than Europeans could go back to the days of the horse and cart."

"Which you certainly will not do when you harness your new technology."

The Ambassador was struggling, but never showed it. "Let me say, Minister, that I cannot deny it would be easier for the West if it had control of its own fuel." That was it: goodbye to any hopes of the oil embargo.

Sheikh Ibn al-Houri smiled. "Thank you for your honesty, Mr Hutchinson. I think we can do business."

The Ambassador gently raised his eyebrows.

"First, Mr Hutchinson, we realise you cannot speak for Britain; you can speak only for the Sterling Zone. We shall require a treaty stating that the members of the Sterling Zone — specified — undertake now and in the future to do all that they can to give to Saudi Arabia all the technology that is needed to make an alternative to petrol, kerosene, diesel and aviation spirit. There are vast reserves of hydrogen and oxygen in sea water and we have adequate sunshine, even if we were to cover half the desert with solar panels. As soon as Britain is liberated, the Sterling Zone will do all in its power to persuade London to agree to the same treaty." The coffee arrived. "Now — is that fair, Mister Ambassador?"

Hutchinson smiled. "I think it is certainly fair, Mister Minister. Shall we get the lawyers working on it?"

The Minister shook his head. "First, we must agree, you and I, that this contract is negotiated and conducted in the terms of maximum secrecy. The oil companies must never get to hear of it, for understandable reasons."

The Ambassador nodded.

"Fine. The Kingdom of Saudi Arabia will honour this agreement,

Ambassador, but before it can be put into effect you will need similar deals with the other oil producing nations, but you will not offer them the means to produce alternative hydrocarbon fuels. Even more importantly, you must persuade the oil producing companies to impose a trade ban. I feel the most you can hope for is one month and I also feel the only carrot you can dangle before their noses is the offer of discounted oil from the Falklands." The Minister held out his hand. "I see two possible reasons why a short-term interruption to supplies — which sounds better than a ban — could be engineered. One: payment should be made in Falkland currency. Two: a major potential defect has been discovered in the world's tanker fleet. All ships are to undergo detailed structural survey before they carry any further cargos."

"Excellent, Minister," Ambassador Hutchinson said, shaking the offered hand and reflecting dismally on the task before him. "I particularly like the tanker maintenance suggestion." The other motive, demanding payment in Falkland notes, could easily backfire and force Europe to accept sterling again — and he knew that his masters, from the Irish Sea to the South Atlantic, had gone beyond that ambition. They wanted nothing less than Britain's emergence from Europe, unscathed.

The Minister casually added: "By the way. I may be able to persuade other members of OPEC to support your governments' aims. We have our own private accounts to settle: debts of gratitude for favours done, you might say. In the long term, it would be so useful to know that Saudi Arabia, which has nothing except its oil, would be able to look forward to a future on the world stage. After all, you will need Iran, Iraq, Kuwait, the Emirates, possibly Libya, to support an embargo, won't you? I feel you may have to work on Venezuela on your own."

"Indeed, that is most generous," the Ambassador agreed, scarcely able to believe his good fortune, despite the strings — or hawser-sized ropes — attached. "The Sterling Zone acknowledges the enormous debt of gratitude that it owes to the Saudi Kingdom and will not rest until it is repaid in the manner indicated."

But more was to come. "This interruption to supplies will, of course, have a detrimental effect on the economy of the European Union?"

"Indeed it will, Minister. A grave effect."

"And will adversely affect the value of the euro?"

"One assumes this is inevitable, and to be bitterly regretted."

"Bitterly regretted, indeed. However, I feel I should advise my companion, the Minister for Finance and National Economy, to move the Royal investments from Frankfurt." He smiled. "Where would you

EUROSLAVIA

suggest we transfer them, Ambassador?"

"I hear that Jersey is still a wonderful financial centre, Minister. And Guernsey, and the Isle of Man..."

"And Gibraltar, too, I believe? Consider it done, Ambassador."

FIVE

IT WAS AROUND that time that I found myself caught in the great European net. *Tell Tel*'s controversial new format — to examine European issues and avoid being controversial — was a winner, and several more imposing effigies of the Brussels hierarchy were defaced around the province, notably the bas-relief of Edward Heath on the new town hall at Broadstairs in Region UK57.

We followed it with a quickly-researched programme on the Eurocard which was being introduced throughout the Union in stages, replacing all the national ID cards — after all, the only nation was the Euronation — and imposing one on the English and Scots for the first time since World War Two.

Our interviewee was another Mr X, a high-ranking civil servant in what remained of the Whitehall machinery, and he was, of course, shown in silhouette with his voice slightly garbled. But the liturgy of disasters which he told was shocking in the extreme. The card was purely voluntary, but the only people who didn't need one were tramps and those with severe mental handicap. It had to be shown to employers, who were not allowed to pay salaries without sliding the card through an information-grabbing slot. "This information is used, of course, to check your tax returns from your main employment."

"What about jobs on the side? Moonlighting?"

"You'll need the Eurocard if you want to open a bank account, and you have to present it every time you use any savings account," the anonymous civil servant said. "So any money you earn from moonlighting should be taken in cash and stored under the mattress."

"That's been going on for generations."

Our Mr X nodded. "So what's gained by introducing the card? Only more jobs for more civil servants in Brussels — not here in London. Moonlighting still goes on. But you need the card to buy or sell property, buy or rent a car, buy an airline ticket, or stocks and shares. So any ill-gotten gains had better stay under the mattress. And, as we all know, you'll need the card to get a passport, a driving licence, and to get married. Your criminal record will be kept on the card, and your medical record — so if you're an epileptic and apply for a job as a lorry driver, you won't get very far."

"Isn't that a good thing?"

"Why should your employer know you have hay-fever? Or that you broke the speed limit ten years ago? This is just Big Brother looking down on us, twenty-one years after Orwell's nightmare."

Mr X then told of some harrowing incidents of people who had been tripped up by the information on their Eurocard within days of its issue. A county court judgement on a disputed debt prevented a man getting a mortgage. A woman who couldn't get her headaches cured, tried to change doctors and was refused: she died of a brain tumour.

Oh, yes, it made compulsive viewing — and it was going out on satellite as well, with pan-European coverage.

The next programme would be about the regions, and that promised to be a troublemaker. Why was the European Union divided into regions? The English Province, for example, had Somerset and Dorset as Region UK63; Norfolk, Suffolk and Cambridgeshire were UK4; and all of Wales except the Glamorgans and Gwent were UK91. Northern Ireland was UKB, and the Scottish Highlands and Western Isles from Fort William to Stornoway were UKA3.

Our researchers were already working on it, and concluding that it was a ploy to deflect people's interest in their now-defunct national government: a Geordie's interest would centre on Newcastle or Brussels, never on London.

The Irish Republic wasn't regionalised — but the Irish were wholehearted supporters of Europe, anyway.

But, I would ask: why did Region FR25, Basse-Normandie, claim the Channel Islands, which had never been consulted? Why was all of Spain divided into seventeen regions — with Gibraltar as the eighteenth, Region ES63?

Even the Isle of Man was included in the English regions: *did Europe have long-term plans that we didn't know about?*

CHRISTINE BOUDERON HAD managed to snatch a few days' leave. One of the three deputy presidents of the Service de Sécurité Européenne, known in German as the Eurosicherheitsdienst, she had snatched a long weekend at very short notice and had flown from Berlin's Tempelhof to Luxembourg, and continued by train to her home town of Montmédy in the French Ardennes.

The beautiful woman with the shoulder-length honey-blonde hair wanted to relax and sort out her feelings for her boss. She was twenty-seven, had never married, and was aware that time was beginning to pass her by.

"Any nice young men working in your office?" her mother asked.

"Stop trying to marry me off, mother." Bouderon relaxed, then added: "There is, actually. But he's my boss."

"That could be difficult, my dear. Is he a good Catholic?"

She shrugged. "I haven't asked him." Catholic, Protestant, Hindu or agnostic — what did it matter these days? Her grandparents had been so rigidly Catholic that they wouldn't have tolerated any of their offspring marrying out of the faith; her parents were only a little more tolerant. "He's German," she added. She decided not to add that he was also married.

"German? Oh, well, we're all in Europe together these days, aren't we? But there are some good German Catholic families, I hear."

When Bouderon was a child, exploring the tiny historic town and the rolling wooded hills with her brother, she had often walked up the steep hill on which old Montmédy sat. Montmédy Haut in those days was a run-down collection of ancient stone houses gathered around a large market square on the top of the pimple-shaped hill.

Now, to escape her mother's gentle inquisition she borrowed the family Renault and drove to these grim haunts of her childhood, and wandered from the square into the abandoned castle. The Romans had come here, seen the military advantages of this steep-sided hump, and called it Mons Medius, the mountain in the middle, because it was surrounded on three of its four sides by a river. Centuries later the thousand-foot-high peak found itself in the Spanish Netherlands, later to become Belgium.

Bouderon found the only entry to the castle, a timber door that was never locked because nobody ever bothered to come here. She pushed it open and walked carefully down a flight of steps which were dank, dark and chilly even in midsummer. She turned, found another stairway which led up to the crumbling battlements, and stood there for a while, admiring the undulating wooded countryside of what is now the Province of France. This was the terrain which had once held Belgium's enemies, and so they, the Belgians, had built the fortress to repel attack from the south-west. Therefore after Louis XIV's troops captured it in 1657 the new French occupants found it facing the wrong direction: *their* enemies were in the north-east.

Despite this problem, the French fortified Montmédy castle, but lost it to the Prussians in 1870 after a two-day bombardment which left the place in considerable ruin.

Eighteen-seventy, Bouderon thought. The Franco-Prussian war ended and France regained Montmédy. Her ancestors once again became French citizens.

But the following year saw momentous events to the east. Prussia and the minor German states to its south began fusing into one powerful nation, the German Reich. That fusion inevitably led to the First World War, and the Germans seized Montmédy and its castle within weeks of its outbreak, holding it right to the end.

War, Bouderon thought. Her home town had changed hands three times — then it was seized again by Hitler's hordes during the Second

World War. That's why she had accepted her job in the European Union: to make a fifth war in Montmédy, a Third World War, impossible. She had been very idealistic when she was appointed to her post in the fledgeling security service seven years ago.

She left the south-west battlements and looked southwards, over the modern town lying at the foot of the hill. In seven years she had seen unbelievable changes in her career. The tiny security service, which had no true role at the start, was now a monster controlling the lives of every one of the three hundred and seventy million citizens of the Union. It could reach into any of the provinces and pick up people for questioning. It had implanted cars with bugging devices. It was now beginning to put microchip implants into new-born babies. It was almost out of control.

And she was in love with its boss — or was she?

THE MODERN TOWN of Montmédy was still quite small. A century ago it had made hats and vinegar, it had tanned leather and sold livestock. Now it was involved in high-tech livestock breeding and a bit of forestry, and had scarcely grown since she had known it. Far in the distance, on the main road to Luxembourg, she could see her parents' house, a Swiss-style chalet behind an ancient stone building on the edge of the road; her grandparents had scraped a living from a small farm and lived in one end of the old stone place while her mother, their daughter, had run the other end as a roadside bar and bistro. The bistro was now a smart restaurant: how things had changed!

She saw the flash of sunlight on a windscreen and knew that a car had just pulled away from the restaurant. She followed the car as it came closer, then turned from the main road that went around the hill, and entered the town. She lost it behind trees, then caught it again as it began climbing the steep slope that would bring it, within the minute, to this ancient village on the top of Mons Medius.

She walked around the parapet until the crumbling masonry blocked her path, but she could just see the car when it pulled up beside her own.

A man stepped out, inspected her car — damned cheek! — then looked up at the old castle walls. And then she recognised him.

Her boss!

She hurried down the gloomy stairs and met him on the edge of the market square. No kiss. No handshake: she hadn't revealed her feelings for him, although she knew that he would have her in bed at the first opportunity.

"Christine! Your mother said I'd find you here."

"Mother? You've been talking to her?" But she'd seen the car leave the restaurant. "You wanted me?"

"Of course, it's nice to see you at any time, my dear." He was still talking in German and she lapsed easily into it: absolute fluency in German and two other Union languages was a requisite of the job. "I'm on the way to a meeting in Paris and I have a day to spare, so I thought I'd call in and give you a surprise."

"You certainly did that," she murmured, feeling a blush tingling her cheeks. "When are you due in Paris?"

"Oh, not until tomorrow." He looked again at the castle. "I remember you telling me about this place. Is this where you used to play as a child?"

"Not too often. It can be dangerous." She stared at him, then glanced at his Mercedes. He had come without his chauffeur and his wife, and she read faint danger signs into the omissions. "Would you like to see the old castle?"

"Would you like to show me around?"

She paused. "Of course, sir."

Sir: that should indicate she saw this as official business. Axel Teutoburger, her boss, was handsome, tall, and carried himself as if he were still a brigadegeneral in the Wehrmacht: he had resigned his commission before the German army had been integrated into the Euroarmy although he had become, for lack of anyone better, the political head of Europe's armed forces. She knew from a surreptitious glance at his personal file on CD-ROM that he was thirty, just three years older than she; that his father had been something influential in the Wehrmacht and later in the Bundesrat, and had probably pulled a few strings to get his son into the position of President of the European Security Service at a time when no more than a hundred people knew of its existence. But Axel Teutoburger had ideal credentials: apart from his father's influence he had a degree in criminology and brief experience as a military attaché in Moscow.

"Did you have a pleasant journey, sir?" she asked over her shoulder as she led him up those same crumbly steps she had just descended.

"Not bad at all. But why the sir? We're six hundred kilometers from the office. Why not call me Axel — Christine?"

Six hundred kilometers? Her mind did some quick calculations: her boss must have been at the wheel for a good six hours.

"You must have left Berlin very early this morning...Axel?"

"I did." He blinked as they came out into strong sunshine.

"Go carefully, or you'll get down a lot quicker than you came up." Then why, she wondered, didn't he mention the trip to her when she left Berlin? It could only mean that he wanted to catch her on her home territory. And was that for sinister reasons — or was he going to try to seduce her?

"It's a wonderful view," he breathed, taking her elbow.

Acutely aware of his touch, she nodded. "Due south, out of sight behind the hills, is Verdun. North-west is Sedan."

"Where thousands of men died ninety years ago. It is our job, Christine, to make certain that your land and mine never go to war again."

"I prefer to think of it as the place where they invented the Sedan chair," she smiled.

She showed him everything there was to see of the castle's upper structure, but couldn't keep him from wanting to clamber down into the interior. "Those dungeons you talked about. I'd love to have a look at them."

She went again to the stairway which descended into the gloom and chill, even on a day such as this. Their voices echoed in the eerie darkness, and she shivered.

"Feel the grilles," she whispered. "Great iron gates that close off the cells."

"Horrible." He reached a hand forward until it touched rusting metal, then he fumbled around, tracing the size of the ironwork which formed the doorway to each dungeon.

"How many are there?"

"Six. All the doors open except one."

He felt for a hinge or a lock. "How?"

"Slide up and down." She shivered again. "This is a terrible place. I've only been down here two or three times. I think it's time we went up again."

She felt his hand take her elbow, then his other hand found her other arm, and she realised he was facing her. She guessed what was coming and braced herself for the kiss.

It was gentle. For a tall, muscular man who always got his own way, it was a featherlight kiss on her lips, and it made her spine tingle. She began to respond, then realised what it may lead to: he was still her boss, and he was still married. Luckily, this was no place to make love.

When they reached daylight again she had made up her mind. Axel Teutoburger was not for her.

BACK IN 1998 the terrorist bombing campaign had started again in May with a small explosion outside the Palais de l'Elysée, a phenomenal achievement or a great humiliation, depending upon one's viewpoint. The Palace, on the southern side of rue du Faubourg St Honoré, lies between the sidestreets known as the avenue Marigny and the rue des Elysées, and was subject to some of the highest security in Paris. It was built as a private mansion in 1718 and among its visitors were Queen Victoria, Madame de Pompadour and Napoleon. In 1998, as for many years past, it was the official residence of the head of state.

When Yzurdiaga strolled down St Honoré two months earlier, in March, he was surprised to see a high wooden fence along the front boundary, and the pavement closed to pedestrians. Cars were not allowed to stop on the road, and — by day, at least — there were enough police on patrol to form a football team.

Back in Zarautz he planned his move meticulously so that by May, nicely into the tourist season, he was ready. While the XYZ coach he travelled on, was overnighting in the 18th arrondissement, he went out on foot and stole a tatty old black-painted Renault from the 17th. Wearing thin gloves from that point on, he drove out of the city and into the Bois de Boulogne where he hid the car among the trees. He walked fifty yards to retrieve a small suitcase that he'd hidden the previous week on a separate coach tour, and worked steadily for half an hour, rigging the bomb in the boot, with a two-minute delay on the detonator. He pulled a boiler-suit over his clothes and had one leg of a pair of dark tights on his head, ready to pull down over his face.

He drove carefully but not too slowly to the end of the rue du Faubourg St Honoré, aimed it down the almost-empty street, then reached down to drop onto the throttle pedal a brick which he had collected at a roadside stop in the Loire Valley. Then, as the car surged forward, he jumped out and ran northwards until he reached the boulevard Haussman. Before he was half way there an explosion rent the night air, its echoes rumbling through the cavernous streets and waking half the city's dogs.

He dropped to a purposeful walk, glancing around as if wondering where the noise came from. Nobody was following him. He crossed Haussman at the dead of night and paused in the shadow of the St Augustin church, watching. Ten minutes passed without seeing any sign of pursuit. It had been remarkably easy!

As emergency vehicles screamed their way towards the Elysée Palace, Yzurdiaga stripped off his unused mask and thrust it in a boiler-suit pocket. He strolled leisurely along rue de la Pepinière to the great Gare St Lazare, the railway station serving the north-west of the Province of France. He dumped his boiler-suit in a street waste-bin beyond the reach of the first CCTV camera.

Dressed now in light but casual clothes, Yzurdiaga walked into the station holding his head downcast but acting as if he knew where he was going: the toilets.

He allowed himself a sleep while he sat on the rim of the lavatory pan, but his mind woke him with a distorted image of the night's events. Yzurdiaga smiled, confident that he had shaken French security, even though his car bomb never did a scrap of damage to the palace where the Council of Ministers, the rump of the French Government, met every Wednesday. It had done absolutely nothing to shatter the bastions of the European Union.

At half past four, with the sky outside registering the coming of the dawn, Yzurdiaga walked out of the station and headed north-east, to the 18th arrondissement and his coach. He could catch up on his sleep on the long haul back to Euzkadi.

IN JULY, a slightly smaller explosion scarred the stonework on the front of the Palazzo Chigi on the street called Corso, the seat of what remained of the Italian Government, after the European Union had taken its pick. There was far less security and Yzurdiaga suspected he could have hurled a larger delayed-action bomb as he drove past at night in a stolen car which later splashed into the Tiber. But he felt he was making his point: targeting the seats of government of the members of the European Union. One day he would strike where it really mattered: at the East Wind itself.

This time he was starting to get his message across. He had included a hundred sheets of paper each laboriously photocopied from an original made in Letraset — transfer letters. That original proclaimed *A bas l'Union. Down with the Union. Abajo el Union. Nieder mit Europa! Abasse Europa.* Somebody should get the message.

The polizia collaborated with the French police and came up with the conclusion that both bombs were prepared by the same person or organization; the parts of the detonator found in Paris matched the almost-complete device from Rome, and both had used Semtex.

Both police forces submitted their findings to their domestic governments, which forwarded them to the European Union.

Chancellor Kohl had been furious at this unnecessary intermediate step, particularly as the Union itself was seen as the ultimate target. He had hinted in 1996 that the Union needed its own police force on the lines of the United States's FBI, but initially the suggestion had met considerable opposition, particularly from Britain. The Euro-FBI was therefore once again on the agenda of the 1997 Amsterdam Conference: it just would not go away.

Britain's Home Secretary had told Westminster, and the Council of Ministers in Brussels: "Police forces historically have been organised on a county basis. This was done deliberately to prevent the creation of a nationwide police force which would have the latent ability to overthrow a government of which it didn't approve. Consider the

American case where each *city* has its own police force, and its authority doesn't go one inch beyond the sign saying 'city limits.' This government firmly opposes giving control of the law to any force which may abuse the privilege, and creating a pan-European police force is a prime example of building a cannon then standing in front of the muzzle."

His advice was ignored.

As a direct result of Yzurdiaga's bombing, the German Government therefore did what it and its predecessors had done too often. Within a month of the Rome attack it began secret trials. In high summer of 1998 a skeleton security service was born, working totally independently from Europol and Interpol, but collating information from the many police forces of the first member states — Germany itself, France, Italy, and the Benelux countries. Europol, of course, was similar to UCLAF, *Unité de Coordinations pour la Lutte Anti-Fraud*, the pan-European fraud squad, in that neither had teeth. The first couldn't make its own investigations, and the second couldn't prosecute.

The Eurosicherheitsdienst, the ESD, to become known to a few English-speaking people as the European Security Service, would rectify all that and have teeth to spare. It was at the start a semi-autonomous body of men and women whose main qualification was that they all had an excellent command of German, the established common language of the service, since it was to be based in Berlin, far from Brussels, Strasbourg and Luxembourg. Brigadier-General Axel Teutoburger was appointed officer in charge of the new force, with an absolute mandate to retain security: neither he, nor any of his staff, was to breathe one word of the existence of the ESD; the penalty was never spelled out, but Teutoburger was under no doubt that he wouldn't see his next birthday.

The ESD was indeed so secret that no members of the European Parliament knew of it, and only a very select few of the commissioners were aware of developments.

Back in 1998, in order to save time in setting up the infrastructure of ESD, the responsible Bundesrat officials had engaged the services of two elderly men who had worked in the old Geheime Staats Polizei of the Third Reich; they remembered the essential skills of a proper security service — infiltration and investigation. There was, originally, no intention of introducing torture, either mental or physical, into the regime; tactics such as those of the old Gestapo belonged with the Nazi era. There were to be significant other differences between the Gestapo and the ESD, notably that the new force was to be multi-provincial from the outset.

Recruiting was handled extremely delicately as the service could not advertise itself, and failed candidates must have no idea about the organisation that had rejected them. Above all, not a word — not a *letter* — must be allowed to leak out to the German citizens who would be appalled to learn their country was taking such a step.

The French girl Christine Bouderon, freshly graduated from Heidelberg University with a first class degree in German and English, was the first recruit, sworn to secrecy and hired to handle criminal records. The second recruit came from Spain: Sergio Gonzáles, to run political surveillance. The third was Belgian — Frans Casbergen, fluent in French, Dutch, German, English, and with a good knowledge of Spanish and Italian. He was in charge of electronic surveillance and as soon as he had passed his probation he was gradually introduced to the workings of the EGNOS satellite system, and the early experiments on the bugging of cars — but Teutoburger maintained a strict oversight of this highly controversial system.

Naturally, the first cases that the infant ESD was given were the Paris and Rome explosions. They had next to nothing to go on: no terrorist organisation had claimed responsibility for either blast and no demands were made. The only clues were the few leaflets that survived the Rome explosion — but the choice of targets indicated distinct disillusion with the aims of the European Union.

AND THEN THINGS changed. In September of 1998 a bomb was detonated by the front wall of the Cortes, the Parliament building in Madrid. It exploded near a window at around seven in the morning and severely injured a cleaner in the room behind that window; she died two days later of her wounds.

Now it was triple murder.

The *Guardia Nacional* began the investigations, shortly to have the *Grupos Antiterroristas* take over, as the incident appeared to be a revival of the ETA campaign. But when it became obvious that the bomb had been lobbed into the Cortes precinct over a sturdy brick wall, and it had a timing device identical to those used in Paris and Rome, the ESD moved in, displacing the Antiterrorist Group. The head of the group, Coronel Juan Martín, protested loudly to the Jefe de las Fuerzas Armadas, but a day later the Chief of the Armed Forces summoned the colonel to his office to give a strict warning to keep his mouth shut or risk a sudden transfer to the Canaries.

Teutoburger saw the significance of this bomb and brought his entire team down from Berlin in a private jet to conduct investigations on site. The team was still very small: the three deputy presidents whom he was retitling as heads of section, and ten clerks, mostly women. Teutoburger was still shocked that he had been appointed; he still wondered how he had achieved the rank of brigadier-general in the Wehrmacht, but his selectors knew of his excellent degree in criminology — and of old man Teutoburger's ability to pull strings where they mattered. Axel Teutoburger, like the rest of his small team, wore civilian clothes, never showed any interest in their own or other people's rank, and followed orders to the letter by absolutely refusing to say one word about their job even to their families.

The Madrid Government had given them a small office at the rear of the Cortes building, and Teutoburger's first move had been to order Frans Casbergen, head of the electronic surveillance section, to check the place thoroughly and set up their own telephone line with the latest scrambler device.

Two days into their investigations Christine Bouderon, head of criminal records, laid a computer print-out on his desk. "It's a long shot, sir, but it's the most positive lead we have so far."

Teutoburger looked from the metre-long strip of perforated paper into the bright eyes of the French girl, who must have sent a thousand Gallic hearts into overdrive; Teutoburger knew even then that at some time he would have to try seducing this beauty. "Tell me all."

"We can confirm beyond doubt that all three explosions have the markings of the same operator. So how does he travel?"

"Or she. Mustn't be sexist, Christine." My God, he thought, I'd love to be sexist with you any day of the week.

"So I've compiled a list of coach operators known to have had vehicles in the appropriate cities on the nights of the explosions. Two hundred and forty-three in Paris, in May; three hundred and two in Rome, in July, the height of the tourist season; and forty-four in Madrid in late September. Here they are, sir."

She continued talking as she unfolded the print-out. "There are a hundred and two operators in both of the first two lists, sir. I've highlighted them in yellow. But of those hundred and two, only seventeen also had coaches at Madrid — also marked in yellow."

Teutoburger smiled. "So you're suggesting our man travelled on one of these coaches?"

"Not suggesting, sir. Just hypothesising." She smiled back. "Unless he was a woman, of course." She laid an A4 sheet of paper on top of the print-out. "And here are the seventeen. Four are Spanish, so we would expect them to be in Madrid. Coches Aranjuez, with a fleet of ten. Lineas Madrileños, with sixty-four — but they're based in Madrid so we can assume they're always here; Carrozas del Sol from Seville, with thirty-four; and Carrozas XYZ from Zarautz in the Basque lands."

"Do you mean Lineas Madrileños is the only coach operator based in Madrid?"

"Not a bit of it, sir. The list is only of those that travel to other countries, and I'm sure there must be a number of small companies we don't know about."

"So your research is defective from the start?" His left eyebrow rose questioningly.

"Yes, sir, but due to a lack of information, not to a lack of interpretation."

"Anything on any of them?" He let his eyes linger for a second on the fascinating curves of her eyelashes, then remembered he was faithful to his wife Louise, and dropped his left brow suddenly.

"Carrozas del Sol had a coach whose driver was blown to bits while he was doing a hundred km on the road up to Poitiers. Forty people died when the coach crashed into a house; forensics concluded the driver was carrying a World War Two hand-grenade in his pocket and the pin must have shaken out."

"Christ," Teutoburger grimaced. "Any more?"

"There are still thirteen non-Spanish coach lines to check." She paused. "Then I checked with the list of suspicious contacts of whom nothing more has been heard. There were thousands, sir, right across the Union. I put them through the computer to sort out links with explosives or coach operators; that's brought both lists down into the hundreds, but they're still too big to be meaningful."

"So?"

She smiled, sending Teutoburger's heartbeat a little higher. "So I put both lists through the computer again, looking for specific Spanish connections. And I came up with these, sir." She dropped another print-out onto his desk. It was half as long as the first, and it specialised on individual people, giving every scrap of information available. "There are five I think you'll be interested in, Axel."

He glanced up at her at the surprising use of his first name. Then she leaned over his desk and her long honey-blonde hair framed her delicate face to perfection. He swallowed hard and concentrated on the five suspects.

"No name, Spanish-speaking, probably from Cádiz. Graffitus artist... Specialises in anti-European sentiment. H'm. Nice photo of the back of his head. Next — no name, female," He fed his desire with another glance at the French girl's features. "So we do have women?" The third on the list had a poor photo from a high angle, showing a man with a black beard sitting in a taxi. "No name, noted in Belfast trying to make contact with the IRA. Spoke broken English with a strong Spanish accent; voice taped; phonetic expert hints at Basque origins." He studied the remaining two before folding the paper. "Any preferences, Christine?"

"None, sir. But what I've done for Spanish suspects I now have to do for French and Italian and..." She let her voice trail off, then added: "They're probably all holding down proper jobs and supporting a family, but I think we should keep the list under review when the next bomb's dropped. It's all we have to work on."

"And you think there will be another?" he mused.

"I certainly do, sir. Don't you?"

"You can bet on it, my dear."

THE NEXT BOMB went off outside the Folketing in Copenhagen during the Christmas shopping spree, and scared a man walking his dog in the snow at twenty to seven in the morning. An absence of prints in the thin dusting of snow indicated the device had been thrown over the boundary fence at least four hours earlier, and therefore had a timer attached — fragments found showed that it was exactly the same as in all the other bombings. There was considerable damage to the exterior of the building but the series of blasts was still only an irritant: the big one had yet to be planted.

The ESD was in place before nightfall, and before midnight Christine Bouderon had a list of all known coach tour operators in the city the previous night.

"Ten," she moaned to Teutoburger. "And only one of them is on any previous lists — Paris. It's a Dutch company."

"You'll check it, Christine?" God, Teutoburger thought: she gets more beautiful every day. Either I'll have to get her transferred or seduce her.

"Of course, sir." She gave him another of those smiles, and he wondered if she was aware what they did to his self-control. "So we have a quandary, sir. Either our man couldn't travel by coach this time, or he realised it would be too dangerous with so few coaches around."

Axel Teutoburger brought his thoughts under control. "Either way, his coach company didn't run. That's assuming he came by coach before." He tapped his teeth with a pencil. "So how did he travel this time? Car? Rail? Air?"

"Or sea, sir?"

"He didn't take a ship to any of the other places, Christine."

"He didn't come to Copenhagen by coach, either, sir." She shrugged. "Back to the metaphoric drawing-board."

XAVIER YZURDIAGA WAS pleased with his handiwork. He had deliberately been creating a signature to his campaign: delayed-action

Semtex, half a kilo a time, thrown at night at parliament buildings in EU countries. Sometime soon, somebody would get the message. The trouble was, if he was caught at any time he would be charged with the complete series of bombings, including the three deaths to date.

He had come by train from Donostia via Paris and had arrived at Copenhagen Central Station in mid-morning on the sleeper from Bonn. Using a forged Euro-French passport that had cost him a quarter of a million pesetas a year ago, he verified there was a leather case in that name at the station's left luggage office: it had been there since the last XYZ coach had visited Denmark in September.

With the day to spare he had bought a Copenhagen Card, used it to wander around the Tivoli Gardens on Vester Brogade just outside the station, then he caught a tourist bus for an acclimatisation glimpse of the main attractions. He wanted to remain unnoticed but a woman sitting beside him realised he was a foreigner and insisted on pointing out some of the features to him, talking in English. "The Round Tower," she pointed. "Good views from the top. And look at the Toy Museum." The coach crossed a bridge and the woman said "Christiansborg Castle Square. This is our Parliament, our Folketing. A terrible pity the power has gone to the Europæisk Forening in Brussels. All the Danish people are angry about it. And over there is the Stock Exchange with its funny steeple."

He knew it all, but he paid attention.

"Bishop Absalom built a castle here in twelfth century, but the modern place was built in nineteen-sixteen. You want to look inside?"

"Can I?" he asked, not explaining that he had been inside three times.

"Sure. Royal sitting rooms. Royal stables. Cellars." Then she began telling him about the Carlsberg Brewery and he lost interest.

He got off the bus at the Central Station, smiled at the woman then walked back to Castle Square and verified that Christiansborg Castle had only a simple iron railing fence around it, and still no CCTV security. When he had a thorough knowledge of the layout of the streets around the Castle Square, and with the biting easterly wind off the Baltic bringing a snow flurry, he sought shelter, choosing the Gran Hotel Herlev because it was hosting the European Scrabble Contest and he could lose himself in comfort.

He went back to the station to collect his leather case then as darkness fell he walked to the northern suburbs, stole an old van, and drove it to within a thousand metres of the Parliament building. He sat in the cab, shivering, until sometime after midnight, when he drove at a moderate speed through Castle Square, stopping briefly to hurl a package from the case over the railings. He saw it land near the wall of the building as he drove away. He parked the van in a backstreet near Kastrup Airport, ten kilometers away, and tried sleeping again until he was defeated by the intense cold.

He took his second delayed-action device from the case; this was an incendiary based on phosphorus. He rigged it under the driver's seat so it would destroy any clothing fibres or flakes of skin, which could prove damning in a forensic examination, then he set the timepiece, put the case on his seat, and began walking to the airport.

He was on the first flight out of Copenhagen that morning, the 0650 to Århus delayed half an hour by snow on the runway. From Århus he caught a train to Hamburg, then a reserved seat to Nice on the last flight before Christmas. A taxi to Cannes put him in contact with one of his coaches which took him back to Zarautz early in the new year.

CHRISTINE BOUDERON WAS also pleased with her handiwork but, despite the extensive computer system at Eurosicherheitsdienst's disposal, crime detection still depended on the human brain and its intuition. She received lists of all the passengers who flew from Copenhagen's Kastrup Airport throughout the day but by 0915 she had developed an interest in a Xavier Yzurdiaga who had taken the first flight of the day.

She called in her companion, Sergio Gonzáles, the third of Brigadier-General Teutoburger's heads of section and threw the name at him.

"Yzurdiaga? Basque, without a shadow of a doubt. That language throws up the most unpronounceable words in western Europe. Even worse than Finnish."

"So what would a Basque be doing here at this time of year?"

Gonzáles shrugged. "Was he at the European Scrabble contest?"

She stared at him. "You've got to be joking?"

"No way. I've just found out about it; I'll check it out for you."

But Christine Bouderon had her own hunches. She went back to her lists of coach operators and ran her finger down those who had vehicles in the member states' capitals — as they then were — coincident with explosions. The very last entry was *XYZ, Carrozas*.

"Gotcha!" she cried, and slapped her delicate hand on the desk. "Brussels, Rome, Madrid — XYZ!" She called in one of the ESD mobile clerks and told him to get the names of everybody who flew out of Århus that day, until he came on the name of Xavier Yzurdiaga. Unless he spotted the name on a car hire rental agreement first.

She smiled. She wouldn't tell her boss yet; she'd wait until she'd got the case neatly tied up and the Basque with the ridiculous name safely in the pen.

But she couldn't tie it up. The name Yzurdiaga didn't come up in any other checks: it was next to impossible to check through all the passenger lists of every flight taking off in the Union in the next two days, at the height of the pre-Christmas exodus the sun. Carrozas XYZ was very busy, but its coaches were going to Mediterranean coastal resorts, ski resorts in the Alps — and one lone vehicle to Prague. Of course: Christmas, Wenceslas Square and the castle built by the good king. When she learned that the castle site is now occupied by the Cathedral of St Vitus she gave a wry smile. Yzurdiaga was leading her a fair dance; she didn't want to involve St Vitus as well.

She reluctantly reported to Axel Teutoburger. "If we're still allowed feminine hunches, sir, I'll say I'm damned sure this Yzurdiaga is in it somewhere. I'll ask Sergio to go and have a quiet chat with him — my Spanish isn't that good — but even if he can talk his way out of it, which I'm sure he can, I feel we should flag this inquiry and keep it under review."

XAVIER YZURDIAGA WAS horrified when a man in smart civilian clothes came into XYZ's office with an air of total authority and quietly suggested a private meeting. In the board room the visitor introduced himself as Sergio Gonzáles from the Transport Commission of the European Union. Yzurdiaga knew he was in trouble but he kept the smile fixed on his face as he offered his guest a glass of sherry.

"You were in Copenhagen recently?" the ESD man suggested without preamble.

"Yeeees," the coach operator hesitated. "Why?"

"I wonder if you would tell me what your business was?"

Yzurdiaga swallowed. This was no gentle chat; this was an investigation, but he hoped it was not going to be on the lines of the Republicans' torture squad in the Civil War, or Hitler's Gestapo. Yzurdiaga thought quickly: this thug obviously knew his basic facts so a denial was useless. Think! "Yes," he said as calmly as he could. "I went to the Scrabble contest."

Gonzáles's eyes narrowed in anger and frustration. "You did *what?*"

"Scrabble," the coach operator smiled. "There was a contest. I went to it."

"But your name was not on the list of competitors, Señor Yzurdiaga."

"Oh, you checked, did you?" Yzurdiaga asked calmly, yet he was aware of his heart pounding with fear. "I was just a spectator. Who were you looking for?"

"That is none of your affair. I assume you can prove what you say?"

"Why not? It was at the Gran Hotel Herlev. Hold on a minute — I may have a ticket." He went to his coat hanging on the door and took out several crumpled pieces of paper. One was the relevant ticket and he offered it with a smile and a very dry throat. The visitor scowled at the slip of paper as if willing it to change into a signed confession of treason.

"You mean to tell me you went to Denmark just to watch a Scrabble contest? Then I suppose you know who won? What was the score? What clubs do you belong to down here? And why did you fly to Århus instead of coming straight home?"

Yzurdiaga shrugged. "I'm not interested in the players, only the game. I don't care who won."

Gonzáles thought of a clever question. "What language were they playing in?"

The Basque managed to smile; he had been intrigued by the same thought. "English," he answered. "Or German, if English was your mother tongue."

"And why Århus?"

"Why not? It's a charming town. A little bit like Donostia, don't you think? Besides, I had a business meeting there — and another in Copenhagen before I went to the Scrabble."

Gonzáles closed his eyes. "What business?"

Yzurdiaga emptied his sherry glass and offered a refill. He relaxed as he thought of the perfect alibi. "Why, coach tours, of course. I'm thinking of running them to Scrabble conventions."

He kept the smile until the visitor had gone, then Yzurdiaga locked himself in the lavatory and was gut-wrenchingly sick. What had gone wrong? Had he used his real passport as identity for the flight out of Copenhagen? As a cold sweat broke out on his forehead he decided he'd keep his nose absolutely clean for the next two or three years — to the dawn of the new millennium, at least: 2001. And probably a bit longer.

When he planted the next bomb, it would be a monster, and all of the East Wind would know. He had made five half-kilo bombs from the ten kilos of Semtex collected in Munich. Seven and a half kilos, and five detonators, remained.

SIX

THE HEAVENLY TWINS researched into the events of 1st July, 2003, the day on which Britain had bowed her head in shame and surrendered her currency and ultimately her sovereignty, to the unelected bureaucrats of rue de la Loi, Brussels. Law Street! What irony there could be in names!

It was also the day on which Scottish Devolution came into effect, thus revoking the Act of Union which had brought the two countries together in 1707. It solved other problems, since a mere province could not go under the name of the United *Kingdom*.

Following the new interpretation the European Commission had put upon Article 104c of Chapter 1 of Title VI of the Maastricht Treaty, back in the spring of 2003, on the suggestion emanating from Commissioner Gisbert Boeke of the Dutch Province — although it wasn't until much later that we learned this person's identity — the European Union had given the United Kingdom, still opting out of the single currency despite Tony Blair's occupation of Downing Street, three months to put its financial house in order. This had meant the Labour Government promising to drop the tax rises which it had not in truth considered implementing, and preparing itself for entry into the single currency with the only option being to leave the European Union — the British Union was already in its dying days. President Kinnock of the Commission — in effect, President Kinnock of the European Union — had explained all the implications in a man-to-man talk with Prime Minister Blair. As England and Scotland were the last of the member states to hand over their worldly goods, they would have financial assistance, if required, to meet the convergence criteria.

The Westminster government had found little time to consider its dependent territories and it rushed legislation through Parliament giving independence to Anguilla, the Bahamas (which took the Turks and Caicos Islands), Montserrat, and the Cayman Islands. Bermuda accepted independence but began negotiations to become part of the American state of Florida: they had a similar climate and were equally dependent on tourism. The British Virgin Islands joined the American part of the group, while Cyprus willingly accepted the gift of the British Sovereign Bases on the island — Episkopi, Akrotiri, Dhekelia, the observatory atop the Troodos Mountains, and the fifteen patches of land around the island.

Fanning Island, and the Christmas Island that was in the Pacific, had been easy: the USA had gladly accepted them.

Gibraltar had been a tricky one. In the Treaty of Utrecht, signed in 1713, Spain had ceded The Rock to Great Britain (according to the official English translation) on condition that if *it shall hereafter seem meet to the Crown of Great Britain to grant, sell, or by any means alienate therefrom the propriety of the said town of Gibraltar, it is hereby agreed and concluded, that preference of having the same shall always be given to the Crown of Spain, before any others*.

But who paid attention to treaties? The previous paragraph had stated that *no leave shall be given under any pretence whatsoever, either to Jews or Moors, to reside...in the said town of Gibraltar*. Yet Jews had lived there for at least two centuries, and dozens of Moroccans had held work permits in the closing years of the twentieth century.

When Britain had given The Rock self-government and created the LegCo, Spain had responded by closing the border. But when England gave Gibraltar total independence in 2003, Spain made no protest at all. Had it done so, and begun negotiations with England, then, regardless of the outcome, the European Union could have invoked Article J3 of Title V of the Treaty of Maastricht — Maastricht town was only ninety miles from Utrecht — and forced England to cede The Rock, just as Eustaquio Arriaba had foreseen some years earlier.

So Gibraltar had escaped the noose and responded by proclaiming its Britishness, although most of its inhabitants were of Spanish origin. It flew the British Union flag, the last place in Europe to do so, as well as its own flag, the royal coat of arms presented by Queen Isabella of Spain in 1502. And, responding to public demand, the Gibraltar Parliament issued a law stating that only sterling, the US dollar or the Moroccan dinar were to be accepted as legal tender. Euros were to be exchanged at the banks or the border.

In its dying days, Britain offered independence to Pitcairn, but it opted to become a dependency of New Zealand where its governor lived. With a population of only eighty, a drastic drop from the two hundred who lived there in 1936, there was no way the islanders could run their own affairs.

The British Indian Ocean territory was abolished, the Chagos Archipelago going to its northern neighbour, the beautiful Maldive Islands, while Diego Garcia went to the United States which had built the massive runway there years before.

And that left only the Falkland Islands. A liability until the turn of the century, the isles of sheep and penguins and damn-all else, had joined the world's wealthiest nations on gaining independence. Oil was the salvation. A hundred billion barrels of the stuff at conservative estimates. Eternally grateful beyond human understanding for their deliverance in the Falklands War, the two thousand islanders had determined to show their patriotism and had petitioned Her Majesty Queen Elizabeth II to grant them the right and honour to call themselves the Kingdom of the Falkland Islands. Almost the last Act of the Westminster Parliament before it went into a rest-home for the aged and infirm was to grant their wish, and to permit the creation of the Royal Falklands Parliament. The new kingdom offered its monarch a royal residence anywhere she chose, from the tropical isle of Ascension to a palace to be built at Royal Port Stanley, to royal design. Nobody was dismayed when the Queen declined; Ascension was understandably remote and insecure, and the Falklands too bleak and cold.

But Her Majesty and Prince Philip called in for a day on their way to their new home at Mount Eden in New Zealand's North Island. They knew that once England and Scotland were swallowed in Europe, with no chance of escape, the provinces of Germany and France planned to sweep away all the monarchies and aristocracies of Europe. There must be nobody with higher status than the President of the European Commission, currently Mr Neil Kinnock, elected to office only by the other commissioners who, in turn, were nominated by their home provinces and approved by the European Parliament. The royal families of Britain, Spain, Denmark, Belgium, Luxembourg, the Netherlands and Sweden had seen it coming: the President was the new king, and the king was Neil I.

TELL TEL WENT from strength to strength. We put on a programme about European Union extravagances, some of them dating back a few years but exposing facts that never had a proper airing at the time. We did a complete programme on libraries, starting with the one that was built in Luxembourg in the 1970s when the European Economic Community held regular sessions in the Duchy. It was now reserved for the sole use of the 626 members of the European Parliament, who seldom went inside its doors — because they were now based in Brussels and Strasbourg. Its costs of providing books, translating them into the other Eurolanguages, salaries of the forty staff, and other overheads, worked out that in the late 1990s it cost £48,000 — around E60,000 in today's currency — for each of the 125 or so books loaned each year.

We did a snippet, for insertion wherever there was a gap, on the sheer effrontery of Brussels's whizz-kids changing the twelve Euronation languages *by diktat*. In English, an enema was to be called a 'rectal solution' and a mouthwash an 'oromuscular solution.' I hope nobody confused the purposes of the two solutions. Probably the greatest lunacy we had yet come across was that scallops from St Pierre and Miquelon, the French possession off Newfoundland, were to be called by their Latin names.

When we researched the amount that Europe had spent on propaganda across the continent — £20,000,000 a year in the last years of the old century — we learned that the Union had set up libraries right across Britain, as she was then, to publicise its cause. They were not necessarily large, but each university had one, and collectively they must have brainwashed a small percentage of the electorate.

We also unearthed some apt quotations from politicians and academics, which the Referendum Party had used in its 1997 campaign and seemed worth reviving, for old times' sake. *Monetary union is the motor of European integration,* said by Jean-Luc Dehaene, former Belgian Prime Minister. *There are some in this country [Britain] who fear that, in going into Europe, we shall in some way sacrifice independence and sovereignty: these fears, I need hardly say, are completely unjustified.* What a blatant misrepresentation of facts from former Prime Minister Edward Heath!

A spokesman for Chancellor Helmut Kohl, former German leader and a staunch Europhile, said for his master: *The only way to deal with Britain is to present it with faits accomplis.* And: *Monetary union is the highest and purest form of integration. Through it, national sovereignty would be transferred to a European body.* And, again: *Currency union is part of political union — a central part of political union. Once that Rubicon is crossed, no country will be able to resist closer integration.*

We flew up to Manchester and filmed in the university library there and in Liverpool; it was on the Mersey that we came across Euronation maps of all the member provinces, showing how they were divided into regions. Quite truthfully, the system was called NUTS, but we couldn't find out what the suitably-apt acronym meant.

While in the educational field we went to a primary school in Liverpool to sit in on a history lesson, and we were appalled.

Afterwards we had a private interview with the teacher on the understanding that we masked her identity.

"I'm near retirement," she began, "but that doesn't mean I don't have a conscience about what I teach. You saw it, didn't you? I'm obliged to use the school books the Government provides — the Brussels Government, I mean. The history books have been rewritten. I mean — Napoleon was a tyrant! He tried to conquer Europe! But I have to stand there and teach these children that he was a hero. He was an early exponent of the European ideal, wanting to create one superstate."

"And was Adolf another hero?"

"He certainly wasn't all that bad, according to the books. He tried to unite the continent but his methods were too strict and half a century before their time."

"And do you believe it?" I asked her, knowing her response.

"Believe it! It's educational pigswill! It's brainwashing! And the other humanities subjects are no better. Earth studies — what you would probably have called geography. We ignore Norway and Iceland. We have to ram home everything about the provinces and the regions, so Newcastle and Edinburgh are just as important as London. To talk about the United Kingdom is taboo."

"More to the point — do the children believe it?"

The teacher stared at me. "I ignored the syllabus for a lesson a few weeks ago and talked a bit about World War Two. It was as if I was teaching them ancient history. They'd all heard of Neil Kinnock, of course, but most of the ten-year-olds had never heard of Winston Churchill. What is this country coming to?"

The quotations proved so popular, even to a nation — sorry, province — sunk into the mire of monetary union, that we threw in some more. *The single currency is a political objective,* from Raymond Barre, former French President and former member of the Pig Trough Club. Otmar Issing, chief economist of the Deutsche Zentral Bank had stated: *There is no example in history of a lasting monetary union that was not linked to one state.*

We touched again on the subject of finance. Before Armageddon and the single currency, Britain contributed *ten thousand million pounds a year* to the bottomless European coffers, and got back around £6,300,000,000 in grants, leaving Britain £3,700,000,000 out of pocket, almost £10,000,000 *a day*. I stressed that any normal person would have no objection to giving to the poor, but our extra cash was being hauled away to pay super-expenses to the filthy rich autocrats and to finance schemes which we could have financed ourselves for far less extravagance. What many people didn't know, even now, was that since the mid-nineties, every project financed by a 'grant' from Europe had to carry a permanent sign saying so.

And what about the show when we called in an economist who argued that, again before Armageddon, we'd have been financially much better off outside the Slave Market, because in the nineties the General Agreement on Tariffs and Trade — GATT — made membership of the Suicide Club economically pointless?

We were overwhelmed by the response we were now generating, with many people asking us why we hadn't done this long ago, when the peoples of the continent still had a chance — remote in some areas, I know — to oppose the final union. Only a few letters were protesting, and there were just three in the first month which contained threats of physical injury to me or to the production crew. After we analysed them, we stopped publicising the production company's name and address.

Philip Andrews, our producer, came in with a newspaper cutting. "Look at this nonsense," he said. "It's an old story now, but a Londoner developed a glasshouse which used solar energy to convert sea water into fresh water so it could grow fruit and salads in the desert."

"Brilliant," I answered. "And?"

"The European Commission gave him a million-pound grant — pounds, so that dates it — and he built the thing in Tenerife. It worked, but he needed more cash to bring it to a marketable stage. Europe promised it, then changed its mind. The Directorate-General VI — I've never heard of that — gave him some waffling excuse in French, and left him to his own devices."

"And one more brilliant British invention bites the dust? Are we going to have him on the show?"

"We're going to try. Then he can tell us what he found out — that fruit and salad growers in southern Europe didn't like the idea of competition and put pressure on Directorate-General VI to kill off the scheme."

"Typical!"

Europe itself objected to that programme a week or two later, saying it was dragged up from the mid-nineties, and bombarded us with a strongly-worded letter from the legal department warning us to be ready to substantiate any claims we made which were critical of the Union.

"Big Brother is coming," Philip said calmly; he's a nice guy, but at times I wish he would show more emotion.

We were picking up story leads all over the place, and we threw in more quotations. *The European Court of Justice is a court with a mission* — said Judge Mancini, a former judge of the same court. Sir Patrick Neill, QC, formerly of All Souls College at Oxford, explained, although not in the same context: *A court with a mission is not an orthodox court. It is potentially a dangerous court, the danger being that [which is] inherent in uncontrolled judicial power.* Professor T C Hartley, formerly of the London School of Economics, had said: *The policy of the European Court of Justice may be summed up in one phrase: the promotion of European integration.*

The viewers loved it. But then, the British always have had a bizarre pleasure in having their noses rubbed in cowshit.

EUROSLAVIA

We dug into the archives of a decade earlier and found evidence that the Εοροπαικ Συντεχνια, otherwise known as the Eurooppalainen Yhtymä (that was to placate any Greeks and Finns who may be watching; we put the words on screen as subtitles) had paid the Mafia a subsidy on non-existent olive groves, and that back in 1994, the total of exposed and admitted fraud of European funds had been £4,000,000,000 in that year alone.

We rehashed another scandal from the nineties, of Spanish fishing boats registering in Britain and putting into British ports for a minimum of eight hours, six times a year: they were then entitled to catch fish on the British quota, which had been sorely depleted but was still more productive than their own quotas.

As a nasty tail-stinger to that story I asked viewers what I should call England, Wales and Scotland collectively if our dearly beloved lords and masters in Brussels were to ban the use of the word *Britain*, on the excuse that Britain no longer existed. After all, the United Kingdom was no more — but did Britain still survive? Obviously it was no longer Great.

The loss of Britain's greatness led us to look at the City of London, which was almost a ghost town. After we had given our £46,000,000,000 of gold and foreign reserves to Frankfurt, the City had nothing left in the bank with which to trade. Thousands of jobs had gone, some of them extremely well-paid. And the Stock Exchange, along with the Bourse in Paris, had faded into insignificance, as we all knew. Yet a decade ago the City of London had handled more financial business than the rest of Europe put together — including Zürich.

"Where," I asked viewers, "was the sense in committing political, economic and even cultural suicide? Experts had been pontificating that the City couldn't survive outside the Union. We now know it couldn't survive within it. Frankfurt saw to that."

We came up with yet more quotes used by the so-called 'Barmy Army' of General Sir James Goldsmith: *The purpose of information services [for which read 'propaganda'] by the European Union, is to disarm opponents of integration.* Said by Max Kohnstamm, a eurocrat of the day. *The Europe of Maastricht could only have been created in the absence of democracy,* quoted from Claude Cheysson, former French Foreign Secretary and member of the commission.

In view of what was soon to happen, this statement by the CDU, the ruling Christian Democrat Party of Germany, was particularly apt: *Deployment of troops or weapons should be decided by the majority.*

On a lighter note we covered the EU directive compelling council gardeners to wear green uniforms to create a common European identity, and we contrasted that stupidity with the Chinese blue boiler-suit worn in the days of Chairman Mao. Did we want than kind of compulsory common identity?

Brussels didn't like that one, either. To hell with Brussels — the British viewers loved it, and so did the hundreds across Europe who managed to let us know, despite our lack of on-screen identity.

We followed up the common identity theme with several spoof items. Shouldn't Santa Claus or Sint Niklaas be made to conform? He covered much of northern Europe on Christmas Eve, yet he didn't touch Spain until the *Fiesta de los Reyes* on 6 January. Didn't that contravene some European diktat?

And why was it that France and Belgium should have their *Fête des Morts* — the Festival of the Dead — on All Saints' Day, 1 November, when the English and Scottish provinces didn't even have it as a public holiday?

From that point we carried the spoof theme a bit further, and I think that's where we began going wrong. We made it plain we were merely suggesting nonsense items for the European Union to adopt, and challenging the viewers to separate them from the genuine laws. As an example we gave the Royal British Legion six months' notice to change its name: 'British' was offensive now that Britain no longer existed, and 'Royal' was meaningless when Mrs Elizabeth Windsor had fled to New Zealand.

Then I suggested a Euro directive to order British wineries to close because they were too far north. Philip brought in an actor to play the role of Minister of Agriculture of the Greenland Government, inviting the vintners to move to latitude sixty, since Greenland had been a major vine-grower in Viking times. By now, everybody in Europe knew I was poking fun at Brussels.

I suggested that all bicycles must have lights fitted at all times, but there should be no law making it compulsory to switch them on at night. I hinted that people moving animals in horseboxes had to tell the police the postcode of where they were going — but nobody in Brussels had realised that fields don't have postcodes.

It was all good clean fun.

Until Brussels struck back and turned my stupid suggestions into real directives. You know that the Royal British Legion must change its name by 2006, that British vineyards are really under threat, and that Europost is working on a method of postcoding the open countryside.

By that time, it wasn't funny, and the broadcasting company ordered us not to make fun of Brussels ever again. It didn't matter much: you may remember that in July Brussels ordered *Tell Tel* off the air. The only thing that pleased me was that I hated the name Tel.

AND THEN CAME the first death threat.

It was a phone call to my home in Clacton in Region UK54 from some man who told me in a muffled voice that I had a week to live. I dialled 1471 but, of course, the call had come from a public box. Lisa and I took the threat seriously from the start, as we'd realised that a few people were such fanatic supporters of autocracy that they'd kill to prevent democracy coming back.

I decided not to go out of the house for at least a week: I didn't have a job any more. On the fourth day as I was admiring the back garden from behind the net curtains in the bedroom, I heard the angry buzz of a radio-controlled model aircraft. It was travelling in a straight line, as if programmed, and I never saw it until it was maybe twenty yards away, and coming straight at me.

I threw myself onto the floor and rolled under the bed just as the aircraft struck the window (we don't have divan beds, if you're wondering). Double glazing didn't matter; the missile came through both panes and crashed on the mattress. If the bomber had used high explosive he would have killed me, but he chose incendiary material.

The room was ablaze by the time I rolled out on the other side. I screamed for Lisa and we rushed from the house without even finding time to dial for the fire operatives ('brigade,' it appears, is considered too military these days). As soon as we reached the pavement I realised I was a prime target and that *this* could be the true assassination plot. I thrust Lisa into our car, which she'd left at the kerb, and drove off — but not soon enough. Several bullets ripped through the Rover, without hitting us or any vital part of the vehicle.

"What about the house?" Lisa screamed.

"Sod the house — do you want to be a widow?"

"I've got to go back — what about Cat?" It was the animal's name as well as its species.

"I'm going to miss Cat every bit as much as you are, but we can't look after her if we're on the run."

Lisa choked. "On the run? Why? What have you done?"

"I suppose I'm a threat. Free speech isn't welcome."

She stiffened. "Free speech? You can't be serious, Terry!"

"Did you know that fishermen who speak up against the Common Fisheries Policy risk a fine of fifty thousand pounds — or whatever it is in funny money?"

"Now you've got to be joking."

"No way. It's been so since the nineteen-nineties. And with the closed shop coming into effect across Europe, how long before the law applies to journalists? How long before journalists are banned from criticising their own union? Or the Euro unions? Or Europe itself? Europe took my stupid programme off the air, didn't it?" I saw traffic lights ahead at red, and cut down a side street. "It's all very insidious, like everything to do with Europe. But it looks as if free speech is the latest victim."

"You scare me."

"I scare myself. Who'd have thought this could happen in Britain — sorry, the bloody Province of England, the so-called land of the free?" My diversion threw me towards the same set of lights but from a different angle: I'd lived in the town for twenty years and thought I knew my way around. But the lights were green and I shot over.

"So who are we running away from?"

"Europe, in its broadest sense."

"But who in Europe, Terry?"

"I wish I knew. More to the point right now — where are we going?"

She mentioned three of our closest friends, but I shouted back: "No! No way! We'd still be targets. We've got to lose ourselves completely. Go to earth."

"They don't want *me*, Terry. I could go back."

"Rubbish. They'd get at me through you. Sorry. You're in it as much as I am. And that's up to here." I snatched a second to draw the edge of my hand across my throat.

"Shall we go abroad?"

"You mean Europe? If it's the Eurosicherheitsdienst after us, they may be watching the tunnel, the ports and the airports. Depends how much of a menace they think I am. Y' know, this bloody island used to keep the enemy away. Now it's keeping us prisoners. But you've got an idea, Lisa: we'll borrow a boat." I negotiated the last roundabout from town, tyres squealing, and took the dual carriageway which headed west from our home in Clacton-on-Sea. Our former home. Once on the straight I glanced in the mirrors, but couldn't see any sign of pursuit.

"Eurosick-of-something? What were you talking about?" Lisa asked me, her voice registering a mixture of shock and horror.

"Eurosicherheitsdienst. European Security Service. The old Gestapo come back to haunt us. You're not supposed to know about it so forget the word."

"I can't even remember it, so I can't forget it. But why you, Terry?"

"I made a number of enemies over *Tell Tel*, but I made a hell of a lot of friends as well. You saw the fanmail."

EUROSLAVIA

"You're joking about the Gestapo, aren't you?"

"No more than I'm joking about freedom of speech." I overtook a lorry at seventy; no point in going faster and attracting police attention from one of those roadside spy cameras. "Somebody rang me just before Brussels ordered the programme off the air and said the old Gestapo was back again under another name. Apparently it was started in 1998 or so."

"Good God, Terry! I hope not."

"Of course, there'd been talk of a European-style CID for several years. I think Chancellor Kohl of Germany suggested it, and it came up again at the Amsterdam Conference in 1997."

"He didn't suggest the Gestapo, surely?"

"No, but back in 1972 Ted Heath didn't talk about the federal European Union, although he knew that was what they all wanted."

"And you've known for some while about the Security Service?"

"Nothing concrete — I suppose it's too secure for that. The programme researchers were trying to find out how true it was. Maybe one of them wasn't discreet enough, and this is the result." Then I realised. If it was this so-called Eurosicherheitsdienst trying to bump me off, it would be watching my escape route on these bloody cameras. Then I realised further that it would have planned everything better: I wouldn't escape two attempts on my life within five minutes. And it wouldn't have sent me a death threat on the phone. No. It had to be some fanatic after me, but a fanatic clever enough to find out where I lived and to target the house with a flying bomb. The first point wasn't so difficult — at the start of *Tell Tel* we'd put the production company's name on the closing credits and a discreet inquiry could have revealed that I lived in Clacton. The rest was easy.

From now on, was the difficult part. Provided I covered our tracks I felt we'd be reasonably safe, but Lisa was in it as much as I was. I noticed she was crying softly and I touched her gently on the hand. "Cat. I'm sorry, too. She'll find a good home."

It was the worst thing I could have said to a cat-lover, but she cried her sorrow out of her system.

There was nobody behind us close enough to read our numberplate as I approached the second roundabout. I took an exit that quickly led to rural lanes and for the next fifty miles we travelled across country, with Lisa doing her best at navigating us towards Birmingham. We lost our way only twice, so some things were improving.

"Remember the Isle of Man?" I asked after an hour without casual conversation.

Lisa nodded. "We had some happy times in Castletown."

EUROSLAVIA

"I'd feel happier if you went back there."

"You're coming too?"

"I'll come and see you settled in, but I shall be back in England pretty soon. I want to find out who's got it in for me."

"She gently took my left forearm. "Don't get yourself killed, Terry. It's not worth it."

I smiled. "I want to draw the retirement pension for another twenty years — unless Europe pinches all Britain's funds, and I wouldn't put it past it." Minutes later I added: "We won't be short of money. I took thirty thousand euros in cash to the Isle of Man Bank in Douglas and changed them into sterling."

Lisa stared at me. "But you can't send money out of the Union. How did you manage?"

"Remember that trip to Manchester and Liverpool a few weeks ago for *Tell Tel*? I flew out to Ronaldsway with pockets full of banknotes."

"And you didn't tell me?"

"I didn't want to get you worried, but I'm damned glad I took the precaution." Ten minutes later we saw the first motorway sign promising that Liverpool and Manchester lay ahead. "Why don't you get some sleep, Lisa?"

"Sleep? I'll never sleep again. Why couldn't we have brought Cat with us?"

WE REACHED LIVERPOOL late in the day and I drove straight to the docks, following those funny signs that look as if a ship has done a Jonah and swallowed a car. But at the gate to the docks I saw a sign: *Isle of Man ferry service closed for the season. Sailings from Heysham only.*

"Stone the perishing crows. That's another sixty or seventy miles." Even at that moment of stress, my mind latched onto the question of how long the European Union would tolerate four of its provinces — England, Scotland, Ireland, Ulster — clinging on to miles.

I drove on, reached Heysham after dark and checked on the next sailing to Douglas. Ten o'clock in the morning. We were there waiting, the first in the queue.

As we were driving aboard the ferry I saw crew members putting up signs: *This service will be suspended after the 1000 sailing on Thursday 4 August 2005 due to circumstances beyond our control.*

"Hey," I called. "How do we get back?"

"Swim, or fly to Switzerland, mate."

"Why're you packing it in?"

"Eurobloodyunion. Won't accept sterling no more. So Manxmen

won't accept Mickey Mouse money."

Lisa and I stared at each other. "I'd heard it might come," I said, "but I never thought it'd be this quick."

"We'd better turn back, Terry."

"No. I want you safely out of Europe."

"But the Isle of Man..."

"I mean out of the European *Union*. If you're safe, I can look after myself so much better." The driver behind pipped, and I moved forward, into the hull of the last Isle of Man Steam Packet Company's ship to sail from England for the forseeable future. The rump of the Sterling Zone had been forced to sever the last contact with mother England.

I could see that the showdown was not far off. I desperately hoped that 2005 would be the year when Britain regained her freedom, but the omens were definitely against it.

I BELIEVED WE HAD shaken off our own particular devil when we drove ashore at Douglas in the Rover saloon with three entry bullet holes on the driver's side and three exit holes on the other. Several people stared at them, but nobody asked anything. As we drove into town we noticed the absence of tourists although this was the height of the season. Of course — the ferry had made its last crossing. There were no more tourists because the Euronation and the Manx nation were warring over money. And I hoped the little island would win.

Our first task was to rent a room in a guest house; the second was to add Lisa's name to the account in the Isle of Man Bank in its Castletown branch. We got a bodywork shop to patch over the bullet holes in the car, but there was nothing we could do about the damage to the interior trim.

Then we spent a couple of days touring the beautiful island by car. I knew the place well from my researches for the guide book I had written on the place almost twenty years earlier. We took a nostalgic ride from Douglas to Port Erin in the south-west aboard the oldest working train in the British Isles — I hadn't found a Euro alternative to *that* name, either. Had the Euromonster (I soon picked up the Manx name) controlled Mann, of course, the entire railway would have been condemned. As it was, ten of the little 2-4-0 steam locos were from the early twentieth century, and much of the track was laid in the *nineteenth* century. But it worked, and it was wonderful.

And then we, too, went to work. We found a small, stone-built terrace house in Castletown and signed a year's rental with the option to buy, subject to my being granted a work permit. The house was within walking distance of Ronaldsway Airport, now closed to all flights except to Jersey, Switzerland, and Bergen in Norway, but the address would be useful when — or if — flights resumed to England.

We looked around the airport, which was certainly not among the world's largest. I found one of the senior admin staff, mainly because my face was familiar to anybody who had been watching *Tell Tel*, and asked her what the problem was, exactly.

"Mann was given an ultimatum three months ago," she told me. "We had to invoice all our accounts in Britain in euros, and pay all bills in the same currency. The Manx Government saw it as a way of taking control of the island, so we had a series of public meetings and the people overwhelmingly decided we didn't want to dirty our hands with euromoney. So the Euromonster told us that as there was no way of paying landing fees and other expenses, Manx Airways was denied landing rights in Europe." She shrugged. "It'll kill us in the long run. We just can't survive without trading with Europe — but we're all agreed we'll go down fighting."

"You can't pay in dollars?"

"Euros or nothing. I know it's just a symbol on paper, an 'E' instead of a pound sign, but they're adamant — and so are we."

I looked through her office window at the airfield where a miscellany of commercial and private planes was parked. "So there's no way I can get a flight back to Wonderland?"

She smiled. "There's a very remote chance. We have one man in the island with business ties in Holland. He says he's also going over to England now and again on business, and will pay his fees in euros. He owns a plane — that one over there." She pointed to a Piper Cherokee standing some way off. "He's a merchant banker."

"He must be highly unpopular," I ventured. "As well as filthy rich."

"His name's mud, but he calls himself Callan. Keysman Anthony Callan."

"Keysman! He's in the Manx Parliament? And he's breaking the voluntary ban?"

"He says we must keep a minimal contact, and I suppose he's right, but not many island folk see it that way." She turned from the window and the view of a lot of aircraft sitting on the tarmac and losing a small fortune. "He lives in Ballasalla. He might give you a lift."

Ballasalla village was less than two miles from our house in Castletown, with Ronaldsway Airport separating us. Lisa and I remembered it as a quaint little village famous for its ancient packhorse bridge and the ruins of its abbey. We asked around until somebody pointed out Callan's house, a stone-built mansion hiding behind mature trees in its own grounds. It looked the sort of place for a merchant banker with his own private plane, and I wondered if we would need an appointment merely to ring the front door bell.

After waiting half a lifetime, a woman answered the door; obviously not Mrs Callan, more like the housekeeper. She suggested we ring that evening and fix a time to see the keysman.

"Why don't we live in a place like this, and you insist on people making appointments?" Lisa asked as we drove away.

"I'm no merchant banker. I'm just an out-of-work chat show host."

The sight of Callan's mansion reminded us of our home — fourteen rooms on three floors and far too big for the two of us, but now probably burned to the ground. I daren't think what had happened to Cat.

I rang Callan that evening and spoke to him directly. "You have a nice-looking aircraft at the airport," I began. "I'm staying on the island for a while, a sort of political refugee from the English Province, if you know what I mean. But I need to go back now and again. I'm wondering if you take paying passengers?"

Callan paused. "It can be done, but with some discretion. Perhaps we ought to meet? Are you on the island at the moment?"

"We've just rented a house in Castletown."

Callan sounded quite cautious, and since he was going against public opinion I could see why. "Can you make it tomorrow afternoon? Let's meet in the bar at Rushen Abbey. What did you say your name was?"

"I didn't, but it's Mason."

I distinctly heard an intake of breath before Callan replied in a falsely-relaxed voice: "Fine. Three o'clock tomorrow, Mr Mason? Look forward to seeing you."

THE NEXT MORNING we walked around Castletown, renewing our acquaintance with the ancient Castle Rushen and its one-handed clock, supposedly given by Good Queen Bess. The castle, rebuilt over the ages, had been the island parliament, the House of Keys, for close on nine centuries, and stood at one corner of Parliament Square.

Looking at the place again after an absence of too many years, I thought of my first meeting with a keysman, due that afternoon. I wasn't comfortable about it.

"What about seeing if you can go by boat?" Lisa asked. There were plenty of private yachts tied up, resting on their twin keels on the gravelly harbour floor. Although it was the height of the tourist season, few people were about, and I didn't think it was due to the tide being out. Lisa pointed to a fishing-boat and as we strolled towards it we saw there was a man aboard.

EUROSLAVIA

An hour later we had arranged tentative bookings on the *Viking Maiden* from Castletown to some secluded spot on the north coast of Wales — Region UK91. Fifty pounds each way, payable in cash. If five people travel together, ten quid a time. And the man wanted sterling, not Mickey Mouse money.

I kept my appointment with Keysman Callan more out of politeness than necessity. I was dead on time, which gave me ample opportunity to study the inside of this peculiar place which had been a magistrate's court, lunatic asylum, prison, and barracks, as well as the island's parliament. And now it was privately owned, run as a museum, a bar-restaurant, and a disco in the evenings.

I was nursing my drink when Callan arrived. He was tall, suave, well-dressed, and around fifty. His smile was built-in as he advanced on me, hand extended in greeting.

"Mr Mason! How nice to meet you. I've seen you on the television many times, of course. What's happened to *Tell Tel*? Off the air for the summer?"

"Off the air," I said. "Permanently. Brussels didn't like some of the things we were saying, and it started turning the screws. But I didn't come here to talk about that — out here, you're free of the influence of the Euromonster."

He smiled. "I see you've caught the local jargon remarkably quickly. But how did you get to the island? Did the little folk bring you over?"

"Pardon?"

"The fairies. Surely you've heard of Manx fairies? The original garden gnomes. They're the only people here not under the influence of Europe, and they're the only ones likely to fly you back to England, no questions asked. Incidentally, the European Union has *not* closed the sea and air links. The Manx people decided they weren't going to use the euro currency, so they effectively closed the ferries themselves."

"But *you'll* be flying to Britain some time?"

He nodded, and I decided then I didn't like him. He was just too smooth, too self-assured.

"And you don't carry passengers." I made it a statement.

"It can be arranged, Mr Mason. I often go at very short notice, but... When do you want to go back?"

"Sometime next week."

"Possible. Possible. Do you want to return to Mann?"

"I shall do, but I can't say when. How's that arranged?"

He gave me his card. "Call me. We'll see what can be done."

I suddenly wanted to get this meeting finished. "And the fare?"

He shrugged. "I've never carried anybody before. Fifty pounds each way sound alright? Sixty euros?" When I nodded, he said: "There's just one thing, Mr Mason. You can appreciate the anti-European feeling on the island? I wouldn't want anybody to know I'm carrying you."

"What about the people at the airport?"

"Particularly not them. You can get through the perimeter fence on the east, quite easily. That's the far end of the runway. We arrange a time and I pick you up there. Straight into the aircraft — alright?"

I nodded again, and we parted. When I got home I said: "I don't like it, Lisa. Someone tried to kill us with a bomb strapped onto a model plane, and now this guy doesn't want anybody to know I'll be on his plane. What's to stop him dropping me off half way across the Irish Sea?"

She stared at me. "So what are you going to do?"

"Take the next crossing with the *Viking Maiden*."

IN MID-AUGUST I sailed from Castletown aboard the *Viking Maiden* with four other passengers. We landed at a quiet spot on Holy Island, off Anglesey, only twenty minutes' walk from the railhead. There were no hold-ups on the journey to London, from where I phoned the police at Clacton. I gave them my name and address and asked about the damage to the house.

"Mr Mason! We're glad you called. No, the damage was confined to that one room, because the fire operatives attended within two minutes."

"And what about the guy who shot at me?"

"That's what we'd like to see you about, sir. We've found the bullets and we'd like to do some ballistic tests on your car. I understood several shots went through it?"

I never told him where the car was. "Any leads yet?"

"Not yet, sir. We've found the remains of the model plane he used. Standard production radio-controlled toy with quite a price tag. Incendiary device set to detonate on impact. Built by somebody who knows something about aerodynamics and explosives, who's got a bit of cash to spare. Does that bring anybody to mind, sir?"

It did, but I dismissed Callan straight away, although he still gave me the jitters. In all honesty, what motive could he have? "The world is full of nutters. Say something controversial on the box and they'll all beat a path to your door."

"True, sir. By the way, I enjoyed your comments on Europe. I just wish you had the strength to get us out of this mess."

"Thank you, officer," I said, genuinely pleased. "By the way — any news of our cat?"

"Cat? Oh, the neighbours have it, sir."

"I'm glad, and my wife will be thrilled. I'll see you soon."

I decided I still couldn't trust anybody. *Somebody* wanted me dead and while it wasn't likely to be any Euromonster official, I couldn't take risks.

I caught a train to Clacton and booked in at a guest-house on Marine Parade, pleased that my old clothes and two-day stubble were sufficient disguise.

The next morning I walked to within sight of the old home and satisfied myself there was no major damage. Was it coincidence, I wondered, that the flying bomb struck the very room I was in? I walked towards the house and turned quickly into the neighbour's drive. And there was Cat, sitting on the doorstep. She greeted me with such enthusiasm that I thought I might cry, but our neighbour saved the embarrassment by coming to the door.

"Terry! We didn't know what had happened to you! Are you OK?"

"As well as a badly-aimed handgun will let me be." I was very much on edge and confined the conversation to the damage, the cat, and my reluctance to give a forwarding address. "Make it *poste restante*, Douglas, Isle of Man," I said at last. "But for God's sake don't tell anybody." I looked him in the eye. "Mind if I slip over the fence and go in the back way?"

I gave the family home a quick security check. Lawn was getting long and the lettuces were bolting, but inside, the room where the flying bomb had landed was a total mess. There was no damage elsewhere, beyond chips to the paintwork and water soaking through the kitchen ceiling. I checked all the services were off, collected all our documents — passports, insurances, and the deeds — then picked up the post from inside the front door and left by the way I'd come in. The cat tore at my heart, but what could I do?

Feeling more confident, I walked to the smart new police station whose front looked like the bridge of a cruise ship, and answered most of their questions, passing only on our present address. They had nothing on my would-be assassin so by mid-morning I was on the train back to London.

That was when I opened the mail. There was another death threat, presumably from the same nutter. I stiffened in shock as I read the words cut out from what appeared to be *The Times*:

Mason, you are in the way. You talk nonsense about Europe. You are indescribable menace so shut your mouth or WE SHUT it 4 you.

God! Whoever was behind this must be raving mad! What the hell damage did he think *I* could do? Britain was in, the door was locked behind her, and Germany had thrown away the key. Besides, *Tell Tel* was off the air and I had no more voice than the poor old cat. The postmark told me nothing so I put the entire missive into my inside pocket and resolved to post it back to the Clacton police as soon as I could.

Ignoring bills and circulars, the next real letter gave me even more of a shock. It was from CCC, Central Cable Channel, one of the fifty-odd television franchises trying to make a living after the free-for-all when digital television came in. It offered to put *Tell Tel* on nationwide cable and Europe-wide satellite, provided I could get the same production team together and we were as scathing and as controversially anti-Europe as we had been. The letter explained:

> The majority of stakeholders in CCC see the Union as the greatest retrograde step that Britain has ever been forced to take in its thousand-year history since the Norman Conquest. We firmly believe that individual free will and free speech in the Union must increasingly be repressed if the conglomerate is to survive.
>
> We are totally committed to being the voice of the opposition for as long as we can maintain that voice, and we are prepared, ultimately, to risk the station's licence in the cause of democracy.
>
> We are able to offer you several extra researchers, and, using our contacts in Brussels and elsewhere, we shall be able to provide a limited amount of fly-on-the-wall television from within the seat of power.
>
> Despite our name, we have access to satellite coverage across the European Union.

I sat back and thought about it. One letter threatened my life if I said another bad thing about Europe; another offered me an excellent fee to say as many bad things as I could.

At least, I could look forward to dying a rich man.

I called at CCC's offices in a smart building in Soho Square, in mid-afternoon without an appointment and came out three hours later with the best contract I could ever have hoped for. *Tell Tel* would go on air from early September, an unprecedentedly speedy scheduling for a current affairs series that didn't have a production team — apart from Philip, whom I'd persuaded over the phone to join us.

The next morning I took the train back to Clacton, carrying a cat box. I collected the family puss, who purred in ecstasy as I eased her into the box. I phoned Lisa in Castletown and told her all the good news then asked her to arrange for the *Viking Maiden* to meet me at the same spot around about midnight.

EUROSLAVIA

Thirty hours later, Cat and I were back in our new home in the Isle of Man.

ANOTHER THIRTY HOURS later, Conseiller John Doyle, the aged descendant of the man who drained the marshes of Guernsey, was lamenting the decision of the States of Guernsey. "We've really done it now. We've got to pay mooring fees and landing fees in euros. If we don't, we're cut off from the Eurinal, effectively as isolated as we were in the war. If we do pay fees in euros, we've agreed to their proposals and we've done the biggest U-turn in our history. So which is it to be?"

"Point of order, Mister President." John le Mesurier, the poet-painter and one of two representatives from Alderney, said. "While I fully endorse the name of Eurinal — indeed, I can think of even more descriptive names — may I suggest we don't use it in this house? Let us not desecrate the States of Deliberation, although my throat suffers from blocked drains every time I have to say European Union." He smiled and sat down.

The humour passed over Conseiller Doyle's head. He continued. "As I've consistently said, heads we lose and tails we don't win. If we give in and accept that we have to use the euro, they'll find something else to grumble about, until we find we've signed up for the slaughter. As it is, our ships and planes aren't welcome anywhere in Europe, except Switzerland and Norway, so we're cut off, just like we were in the war. And if we give in, we're going to lose our independence and we'll be ruled by Germany — again."

He studied his audience. "Those old enough to remember, will still have nightmares of the thirtieth of June 1940 when the Luftwaffe landed on the old aerodrome. Does anybody here — apart from me — remember the next four years and 326 days under German occupation?" The old conseiller looked around the members of the States of Deliberation gathered in the Royal Court in St Peter Port, the pretty capital of the Channel Island of Guernsey.

"Mister President," interrupted Conseiller Mark Hatton, the only pro-Europe member of the island government. "I commend Conseiller Doyle for his memory, but the German people have changed since Hitler's day. They're some of the most polite and educated tourists I've ever seen. Ask yourself — who gives us the most trouble? Answer: the British lager louts. The Germans are impeccable — and they invented lager!"

Conseiller Doyle groaned in despair. "For the umpteenth time, I'm not talking about the common people. I'm talking about governments. Governments that are *not elected* by the common people.

Governments that are autocratic, dictatorial, meet in secret session, and don't care one damn about the people. And that's what we've got in Brussels — and Strasbourg, and Luxembourg, and Frankfurt-on-the-bloody-Main. I'm seventy-three, man. I saw it. Guernseymen sent to concentration camps in Germany for listening to the BBC on the radio. Concentration camps in Alderney, our own neighbour, with slave labourers starving to death. But the worst of it was the loss of hope for those of us under the Jerry jackboot. How long was it going to last? Four years? Forty years?"

Two of the young conseillers made winding motions with their right hands, and the old man seized the bait.

"They can make mock of me, Mister President. Ignorance is bliss. But if we knuckle under to the Eurinal one more bit, I warn you, we'll be under German rule once again, and it won't be for four years this time. Or for forty. More like a thousand years as Adolf threatened." The old man clung to his seat and waved a menacing finger at his protagonists. "Don't forget, Britain isn't there to fight for us this time. Poor old Britain has had its chips. We should show solidarity with the Jerseymen and the Manxmen who are all in the same boat as we are..."

"A boat that isn't going to France," Conseiller Saumarez chipped in, provoking laughter.

"...and with those selfless Falklanders seven thousand miles away. Mister President, we have cut ourselves adrift from the Eurinal so I move that we accept the Falklands offer of help with open arms. We've been buggering around far too long as it is."

The old man sat down, exhausted. Did it still matter that he was of British, not French, origin? His ancestor, Lieutenant-General Sir John Doyle, had drained a marsh in the north of Guernsey and so joined Ancresse to the rest of the island. Now another Guernseyman of British descent, that insolent Mark Hatton, wanted the island to accept the Treaty of Rome, the Treaty of Maastricht and the Treaty of Amsterdam, and be swallowed up in an enormous, unwieldy superstate called the European Union. Conseiller Doyle insisted on giving it its accepted name, the Eurinal, and he noticed that the Bailiff, who acted as Speaker but was addressed as Mister President, had given up trying to correct him.

His attention returned to the proceedings as the Bailiff, Rear-Admiral Sir Rodney Bullen, the Crown Representative, was winding up the debate. He touched on the decision the Isle of Man had made, which could have had a serious impact on the Manx economy until the Falklands offer had come two months ago. He nodded to the representative from the States of Jersey, which had also voted to break off all ties with the Eurinal, and he commented that the Gibraltar

Government voted fifteen to nil to hold onto its independence. If these three remaining outposts of the Sterling Zone thought it so vital to keep their currency — and, with it, their sovereignty — then why should Guernsey be any different?

"We Guerns thrive on our independence," he said. "Back in 1830 we had an argument with the Privy Council and dropped the monarch's head from our currency." He smiled. "Well, he *was* the German-born George the Fourth." Then his voice rose. "But do we want to send our ferries back into Normandy and tug our forelocks and pay our fees in funny money? Do we want to risk our unique States of Guernsey pound, our twenty-per-cent tax rate, our financial services interests? Do we want to become a tiny part of Region FR25? Do we want a top rate of income tax at seventy cents in the euro? Do we want VAT on top of that at — what — twenty percent? Do we want to be ruled by another unelected bureaucrat of the likes of President Kinnock? He never had a scrap of government experience in Westminster yet he could be given the job of ruling three hundred and seventy million people! Ladies and gents — I ask you: *do we want that?* If we do, let's send our ferries and our planes back into the Eurinal and dance at our own funeral."

He paused, but there were no interruptions. "If we don't want it, then we go back to our island mentality and we tell them to sod off! We've pulled up the drawbridge: let it stay up until Europe comes to its senses, be it next week, next year or next century!"

There was a pause before Mrs Conseiller Marguerite de la Roche caught the President's eye. "I merely wished to emphasise the point about Guernsey's financial services. When I first became interested in 1993 we had seventy-five financial institutions with deposits of £37,500,000,000, and rising. The deposits continued to rise after the euro was introduced. They took a little dip when Britain lost her way in oh-three but, as you know, they soon picked up, although we get next to no investment from Europe — it's not encouraged. I feel that with the help of Falklands oil, the sterling countries from Mann to Falkland can offer a far greater stability than the European Union with its high unemployment and civil unrest. I predict we shall do very well once we prove to the world that the pound is safe with us. Thank you, Mister President. We have chosen our way, and now may God go with us." She sat amid mild applause, which made her smile in embarrassed pleasure.

John Doyle stood up for a final comment. "And while God's going with us — may He give us a little help us as well."

SEVEN

FATHER ERICH ZIMMERMAN was troubled. He had prayed for days for God's guidance, but so far there had been no sign. Father Erich was old, but he knew that age maketh wisdom, while so many of the younger generations believed that they already knew it all.

He knew things were going badly in the superstate that surrounded him, and he was looking for a sign from Heaven to tell him whether he should intrude. But, so far, there had been no sign.

Father Erich had been born in Liechtenstein in the closing days of the Great War, the war to end all wars. He had grown up in the tiny capital city, Vaduz, and in his teens had seen, from a comfortably safe distance, the resurgence of nationalism in a defeated and shattered Germany.

In his formative years he learned that the Armistice, signed on 11 November 1918 in a railway carriage in the Forest of Compiègne, north of Paris, had humiliated the defeated Germany. As he was of German blood himself, although he lived in the tiny principality squeezed between Switzerland and Austria, he could understand the feeling of resentment that permeated the Reich. Germany had not only lost the war, it had lost prestigious territory. Limburg, with its capital city of Maastricht, had gone to the Netherlands; the Saar was almost independent; Alsace and Lorraine were now French; the Poles had driven a corridor through Prussia, and even the Danes had nibbled at Schleswig-Holstein.

And Germany was forbidden by the Treaty of Versailles to move troops west of the Rhine, or to re-arm. France and Britain had been afraid of the might of Germany since the empire emerged from the mass of squabbling city states in the early nineteenth century; after 1918 they tried to keep the monster under some sort of control.

The young Erich Zimmerman knew, as did millions of Germans, that the controls were too restrictive. As the country faced ruin, it was obvious to all but the politicians that Germany would avenge its humiliation.

Adolf Hitler had looked the least likely candidate to restore the nation's fortunes. At thirty, the man had no friends, no money, no trade, no profession, no job, no education, and he was also a foreigner. Zimmerman learned that when Hitler joined the German Workers' Party it had around a hundred members and a kitty of seven marks fifty pfennig.

Hitler used what he did have — a commanding personality and a driving urge to lead. With those features he created the Nazional Sozial Deutsche Arbeits Partei, soon to be known as the Nazi Party. By 1923 the mark was losing its value faster than an iceberg can melt in midsummer. In January of that year you would need 18,000 to buy a US dollar; by July the price of a dollar was 160,000, and on 1 August 1923 you needed a million marks. In November the mark had sunk so low that four thousand million were needed, and the value was sinking so quickly that you couldn't count the notes fast enough to keep up.

Within days, Hitler stage-managed the Beer Hall Putsch which led him, ten years later, to become Chancellor of the Third Reich, and the most powerful and megalomaniac dictator that Europe had seen since Napoleon — and probably long before that.

The Second World War was inevitable as a Nazi Germany tried to recover the lands and glory that it had lost a generation earlier. And for the second time in the century, Britain went to war against the Germans. For the second time the Americans helped Britain, and for the second time Germany was defeated. On this occasion she lost yet more territory: Pomerania and Silesia, which the victorious Russians seized and gave to Poland, while they took East Prussia for themselves. And almost a third of what remained, including their capital, became a separate state.

Would it happen a third time?, Zimmerman wondered. As he studied for the priesthood in neutral Switzerland, he watched his blood brethren, and continued wondering. The German race, he knew from his place within it, never did things by halves. In defeat, they despised militarism. In striving to rebuild their cities and industries they didn't know when to stop, and so created the Economic Miracle. In their private lives they sought perfection and the absence of complication: if they were to have a social security system it had to be the best; if they wanted to reserve deck chairs by the holiday hotel pool then they would get up before dawn to do it. They wanted the smartest cars, the healthiest food, the most virile sex life. Second best was a failure in the German way of thinking.

But their leaders, notably Helmut Kohl, didn't want to impose their superlatives on other countries. Prussia, later Germany, had tried three times — and had failed every time. Therefore the Germans didn't want to go to war ever again: they didn't want second best.

So they would make war impossible. They would integrate their nation with all the others in Europe...and it was purely by chance that in the resulting cake mixture, Germany would have the most currants. If having the most currants made them the most powerful part of the mixture, then that was fine by Germany. The Germans would willingly oblige by taking the lead in Europe, in deciding how much icing to put on the cake, and because they instinctively knew they were right, it would be tough luck on any dissenters.

After all, the dissenters hadn't been *conquered* this time: they had queued up to pour their individual sovereignties into the pudding bowl. If they didn't like it, and wanted to go back to being the unbroken eggs, or the flour in the packet — tough luck.

And so, once again, Germany had become the dominant force in Europe — and this time there was no going back. They had won not by the bullet, but by the ballot — at the outset, that is. The ballot would be phased out so slowly that nobody would miss it until it was gone. The new Germany, der Bundesrepublik Deutschlands, had capitalised on the continent's natural fear of the Teutonic race by creating a union of nations. The capital city would not be within Germany; that would be too blatantly obvious and menacing. No: it would be in a smaller land that nobody could accuse of wanting to invade its neighbours — how about Belgium, and why not Luxembourg as well? Nobody would notice until too late that the *real* power, however, was German.

At first Zimmerman, like millions of people in Europe, including the average German citizen, thought it was a wonderful idea. The nations would bind together and so truly make another war impossible; nobody would ever imagine that Nordrhein would ever attack Niedersachsen, or that Alsace would declare war on Saarland.

The Bundestag found a likeminded thinker in France: Jean Monnet. Monnet, who had had reason to fear the Germany of the Third Reich, was an ardent supporter of the idea. He, too, wanted the nations of Europe to be be unified, consolidated, federated, fused irrevocably into one block, just as the United States of America or the Union of Soviet Socialist Republics were.

And once in, all the way, there was to be no way out.

Zimmerman, like millions of other citizens, was never aware of the secret agenda. The French and the German top politicians decided that the average factory worker or housewife, fisherman or farmhand, would not appreciate the great future that was to be engineered on their behalf. Lenin had had the same benign sentiments two generations earlier. Zimmerman did not see any danger in the creation of the European Iron and Steel Community in 1951: why should he? Where was the threat to sovereignty and democracy?

He, and millions others, merely shrugged when they heard of the founding of Euratom. It obviously meant less chance of France and Germany dropping a nuclear bomb on each other.

Europe's farmers welcomed the Common Agricultural Policy, for it brought controlled prices and subsidies. The French, still a nation of small farmers scratching a living off a few hectares of marginal land, thought Heaven had come early.

But the CAP didn't stop the bigger farmers gobbling up the smaller ones, who drifted to the towns in search of jobs in the factories. Britain had seen it start a century earlier, in the Industrial Revolution.

The paperwork was increasing, but one must expect that. Commissioners were being appointed, but nobody realised they were under European and not state control. True, the state politicians knew, but it was all part of the master plan to keep the messy details from the people who actually financed it all — the common taxpayers.

And then came the European Common Market, another wonderful idea. Jean-Paul Monnet, the French Premier, said at the time that *"this union would compel nations to fuse their sovereignty into that of a single European state,"* but he never said it loudly enough for the common masses to hear.

Zimmerman, now qualified as a priest and working as a curate in a parish church in Vaduz, was not to know the details of Britain's entry into the European Economic Community: the Prime Minister of the day, Edward Heath, told the nation that membership would pose no threat whatever to the sovereignty of Great Britain. That was the quotation he wanted the people to hear and accept, but he had actually added that Britain would fuse its sovereignty. If anybody heard those other words the explanation was that Britons would give a little sovereignty to the other member countries, and get a little back in return.

Bland, meaningless and harmless words at the time, but years later people began to realise their true meaning: they would have as much sovereignty as part of a federal state as they had as Britons — but *it would be the sovereignty of another nation* — the European Union — and not their own. It would be like swapping a comfortable old typewriter for a brand new computer, then realising you didn't like it or want it. Too late.

It was only twenty years too late that Heath confessed on television that he knew all along that ultimate union and *total* loss of sovereignty were part of the plan from the very outset.

Monnet later said that in May 1970 he explained to Heath: "I told him how we had proceeded from the start, step by step,...and that I was convinced we should proceed in the same manner."

When Zimmerman began to realise the enormous fraud that was being perpetuated on the European peoples, he began researching notes and opinions of the politicians involved in the destruction of the right to vote. He learned that Raymond Barre, French Prime Minister in the late 1970s, said of the European Union: "I never have understood why public opinion about European ideas should be taken into account."

Suddenly the middle-aged priest saw the Union in another light. It became for him, *der Urian,* the Devil, and he began paying much more attention to the evil monster. He noted that all member states had to ratify the Treaty of Maastricht in 1992 and so commit themselves to discard their own currency in favour of a common coin, later to be called the euro. He noticed that the French people, responding to a heavily-financed government campaign urging them to vote yes, did so — by a majority of one percent.

He noticed that the Danes ignored their Folketing's advice and voted *Nej.* But they were sent back to the polls with the instructions to approve Maastricht. Reluctantly, they did so.

Zimmerman also noted with keen interest that the British people were never given a referendum. After inquiries, he learned that the politicians assumed the answer would be a resounding *No!* So British democracy survived unscathed by being stifled.

Bundeskanzler Helmut Kohl, Zimmerman learned, said of the Devil that "The future will belong to the Germans...when we build the house of Europe." He added: "In the next two years, we will make the process of European integration irreversible. This is a really big battle but it is worth the fight." Later, the priest heard Kohl predict in forceful tones that if Europe did *not* unite under a single currency, it would lead to war.

That was when Erich Zimmerman saw the future, and it did not look good. He saw the prospect of a third major war in Europe within a century, not from a Europe that wouldn't unite, but from one which had united — and bitterly regretted it. He saw once more a Germany dominating the nations of Europe — but this time there was no independent Britain standing alone in defiance; this time there would be a subjugated Britain without its government, and with armed forces from other countries occupying its soil, the first time since 1066. Germany would have won the next European war without a shot being fired — but at some time in the future there would be vast bloodshed as the people struggled to free themselves from the Devil.

The world had already seen many such struggles for freedom at the demise of empires; the Roman, the Byzantine, the Ottoman, the Spanish. More recently, the collapse of the attempted Nazi Empire, then the British, French, Dutch and Belgian empires, and lastly in the downfall of the mighty and oppressive Soviet Union as it crumbled from within, freeing first the vassal states in eastern Europe — the tiny Baltic states, occupied since 1941; Poland, whose occupation by Germany had started the Second World War. Romania, Bulgaria,

EUROSLAVIA

Czechoslovakia. And what had happened? Zimmerman wanted to shout it to the world. Romania had spawned Moldova. Czechoslovakia had spilt into halves. And then the Russian Empire had disintegrated into a loose collection of republics.

Finally, the old Yugoslavia, held together by years of Communist suppression, had exploded when the lid had been taken off. Civil war and ethnic cleansing had followed, resulting in the re-emergence of long-buried nations: Croatia, Slovenia, and those others with unpronounceable names.

What chance had der Urian? None, Zimmerman told himself. *Absolutely none. Gar nicht. Rien du tout. Totalmente nada. Inte alls. Wcale nie. Ei lainkaan. Oydamos. De maneira nenhuma.*

And yet the liberated countries of eastern Europe were queueing up to subjugate themselves once again — to a power led by Germany. Poland was almost in the Urian. The Czech Republic wanted to join, with Slovakia — so the two would, in effect, be united again — and Hungary, Slovenia, Bulgaria, Romania, the Baltic States of Lithuania, Latvia and Estonia, and even Cyprus. Malta appeared to have given up on the idea of joining the lemmings' mass suicide. The old priest just could not understand the fatal attraction of the governments' giving up what the people had fought for over half a century.

Unless it was for money. Did these countries, with lower standards of living, expect handouts from the great Pudding Bowl, as Greece and Ireland, Spain and Portugal, had received? If so, they should ask the very pertinent question: *where was the larg*esse *coming from?* There were already too many spoons dipping into the bowl; if another dozen ladles were to plunge in, there would be nothing left for anybody.

Mixing metaphors, Zimmerman thought of the children's fable of the animal who gave up his liberty in return for regular meals. But the free meals stopped once the harness was around his neck, and the animal realised he had been a true donkey.

Turkey had vowed to resist expansion of NATO unless it could thrust its head into the EU noose; Greece had argued that it would not attend any conference to which Turkey was invited, and would also block any expansion of the Urian unless Cyprus was given the key of the door. And by Cyprus, the Greeks meant the entire island, including the third that Turkey had occupied since 1974.

How *could* the European Union succeed?

Father Erich Zimmerman rose stiffly. He had been at prayer in the Church of Heilige Maria for an hour, pleading for God to send him a sign. He, the humble priest, could see that the ground was being prepared to sow the seeds of a third European war within a century. He desperately needed to know what action he should take. Intervene? Or turn the other cheek? Christ had not turned the other cheek and Erich Zimmerman believed that he should follow the Master's example.

He leaned on the back of the pew in front of him until his old knees regained their use. Then, feeling the fingers of arthritis testing his joints, he walked slowly to the door and looked out onto the road.

At that moment a cyclist hurried past. She reached behind her to check the stack of books in her saddlebag, but never noticed that she knocked the top one out. It fell onto the pavement and slid towards Father Zimmerman, coming to rest two paces in front of him. Its front cover was uppermost, and presented itself as if laid out for him.

Trembling, Zimmerman stepped forward and picked up the paperback, before any other pedestrian could reach it. He stared at it, and the words burned themselves into his mind. *Der Urian Liebt.*

It was the sign! He walked slowly back to the church, as if in a dream, marvelling at the coincidences: the book falling from the cycle bag at that precise moment. Its landing in front of him, right way up. And its title: *The Devil Lives.*

Father Zimmerman had his sign from God. He went back to his pew and onto his knees for another half hour; he had to offer his thanks and explain that he understood what he had to do.

Erich Zimmerman was a computer buff who regularly surfed the Internet. He would have to use his knowledge of computers to build up a Resistance Movement. The Devil lives — but the Devil must die!

He sat at his computer keyboard for ten minutes, thinking what he would write. Then he keyed it in, almost without the need for correction.

DID YOU SEE THE TRAP
BEFORE YOU STEPPED INSIDE?
OF COURSE NOT. WHO AMONG US DID?

But now we know the worst. Citizens of the provinces of Austria, Belgium, Denmark, England, Finland, France, Germany, Greece, Ireland, Italy, Luxembourg, Netherlands, Portugal, Scotland, Spain and Sweden. You have been cheated. Citizens of the nations of Bulgaria, Cyprus, Czech Republic, Estonia, Hungary, Latvia, Lithuania, Poland, Romania, Slovakia, Slovenia, and Turkey. You are about to be cheated.

You are now — or soon will be — governed by the unelected bureaucrats of the European Commission and by the members of the Council of Ministers who are deaf to your pleas. Your own government has little more power than a town council. And what can you do about it?

Nothing. Absolutely nothing.

Democracy is dead. You did not vote your commissioners into power — you cannot kick them out. They are all-powerful and now self-perpetuating. These men and women, with more to come from the new member provinces, have the power of life and death over you.

They set your taxes. They spend your money. They govern every move of your daily life. Can you start a company outside of the European Union? Not without permission, which will not be given unless you have a very clever lawyer.

If you employ 20 people and wish to expand, your 21st must be disabled. You have nothing for a disabled person to do? Too bad. You cannot even find a disabled person? Not surprising. They are so much in demand they can name their own salary.

You want to teach your children the words *black, cripple, man, mental*? Be prepared for heavy penalties. Maps will soon be renaming the River Niger and the Black Forest.

You want to sell your business and take the money out of the European Union in dollars, francs (Swiss, of course), yen? Do not even think about it.

You want to take a private pension fund to pay for your retirement? Put the money under the mattress instead — it is safer.

You want to teach your children the unbiased truth about Napoleon, Adolf Hitler, Winston Churchill? Then do not read the newest history books.

Is this the life that you want? If not, contact me on the WWW, for there truly *is* a way out of the mess.

He translated his message into English, added his e-mail address and, through his access company, logged his message on the appropriate bulletin board, which would allow anybody in the world who had compatible computer equipment to access it and copy it into his or her own system where it could be saved on disc or printed on paper. Finally, he keyed in instructions for the message to be screened from midnight, Europamittelzeit, for twenty-four hours, then be erased.

SIR ARTHUR STANLEY couldn't sleep. Damn Rebecca! Lying there beside him and snoring like a stag in the rutting season. He should have taken Bridget's suggestion and spent the night with her, except that he dare never run the risk of being discovered in some other woman's bed. Think of the scandal. The headlines in the *Isle of Man Courier*: "Home, Secretary!" followed by the tag-line "Home Secretary Sir Arthur Stanley found in Keyswoman's bed." Then the damning report: Sir Arthur, distant descendant of the Great Stanley, was found in bed with Mrs Bridget Norris by dockworker Brian Norris coming home early on Sunday morning from night shift. His chances for a bit of canoodling would vanish in the next few days when Norris felt the effects of the trade embargo with the Euromonster, for the Douglas Sea Terminal would be reducing staff to just two.

The mid-August humidity didn't make sleep any easier and finally Sir Arthur slid out of bed, careful not to disturb the rhythmic rumblings issuing from his wife's nasal passages. He had been awake ever since he turned down Bridget's offer, with great reluctance, but his imagination had given him a sharp warning on the perils of being caught.

Needing something to occupy his mind, he went up to his computer room. Rebecca had her fuchsias and her home-made wine: he had his computer. At a little after three on that Sunday morning he decided to see what he could find on the Internet and began skimming through the vast index; he refused to think of it as 'surfing'. *Europe* caught his eye and he opened some of the many files on the subject. History, geography, travel, politics... he sampled a dozen before a headline snatched his attention: DID YOU SEE THE TRAP BEFORE YOU STEPPED INSIDE?

He read on to the end, hesitating over the invitation to contact the unnamed writer on the World Wide Web. He copied the file onto his own hard disc then wrote his reply.

THIS IS NOT THE LIFE WE WANT
We never stepped inside the trap, but Brussels wants to capture us now. We are fighting back. If you can help us please fax details to...

He ended with his private fax number, thought for twenty minutes about the possible repercussions of his actions, then sent his reply.

He went back to bed and was asleep within minutes, regardless of the rutting stag.

XAVIER YZURDIAGA TOOK a phone call. "Can you get the Internet, Xav?"

"Staqui! How goes it these days, old friend?" Yzurdiaga was forcefully reminded that he and Eustaquio Arrieta had decided not to be seen together, after that grilling by the man who knew far too much about Yzurdiaga's movements in Copenhagen at the time of the Folketing bombing. The campaign had lapsed, and the remaining 7.5kg of Semtex was stored in an airtight, damp-proof cool container, where nobody would find it. "Of course I can get the Internet. Why?"

Arrieta identified a bulletin board. "Try it now." He named the appropriate heading. "Let me know what you think, eh?"

"What's it about?"

"The East Wind. Remember?" The line went dead.

SINCE ITS BEGINNING in 1998 with a staff of five, under Brigadier-General Axel Teutoburger, the Eurosicherheitsdienst had grown phenomenally. By 2005 it was sited near the old Checkpoint Charlie in a new office block fronted by smoky-glass walls from roof to ground: everybody could see out, but nobody could see in. The notice on the insignificant door said simply: ESD, Friedrichstrasse 1000. Scarcely anybody used the door; all 357 staff and the very few accredited visitors parked their cars under the new church next door, and entered the ESD building through a tunnel. To complete the camouflage, ESD people were the only ones to use the church, which was open to the public only on Sundays.

Within the ESD complex, known to its staff as Kristallkoffer, the Glass Box, Teutoburger's original three assistants still headed their sections. Christine Bouderon controlled personnel surveillance and, while the first faint lines were appearing beside her eyes, she was still as beautiful, and unknowingly had given Präsident Teutoburger several wet dreams.

Franz Casbergen had deepened his knowledge of electronic surveillance and his computer equipment was the best in Europe, outside the offices of the European Union itself, but it was still not admitted that the ESD was part of the surveillance arm of the Brussels autocratic empire.

Casbergen had, at all times, four of his staff monitoring the Internet for anything which might be the slightest subversive; he had another dozen checking up on the information sifted out.

Early on that Sunday in August one of the monitors picked up the letter with the heading DID YOU SEE THE TRAP? She decided it was worth downloading, and it went into the file for further research. Gradually all four of the staff began noticing a steady trickle of replies, and copied each one of them. For each one publicly displayed on the Web they guessed at least a hundred were being sent direct, in private.

THE NORTHERNMOST TIP of Alderney, in the Channel Islands, carries a fortress built around 1739 and reinforced in 1845. The Château à l'Etoc, 'Stock Castle,' was one of nine fortresses built on prominent headlands to deter the French from landing. Instead, the Germans had come in 1940, built their four death camps and murdered around four thousand slave labourers, mostly Russians. It was a strange irony of World War Two that Alderney was the very last place in Europe to be liberated from Nazi oppression, five days after the German surrender.

After a few years to recover from the bitterness and resentment of occupation, Alderney folk again welcomed German tourists to their island home, but many visitors were humbled to see the vast concrete gun emplacements that Hitler had had built on this tiny outpost. For every twelve tons of concrete the Germans had poured into their Atlantic Wall from Heligoland to the Bay of Biscay, one ton had been poured in the Channel Islands.

Annette Dugard knew all about it. She had become enraptured with windswept Alderney from her first visit in 2001, and had decided to live there. Born in Montmédy, a hilltop town in eastern France, she was a freelance writer and painter and had developed an almost paranoid hatred of every aspect of the European Union. In Alderney, she believed, she could regain some of her lost freedom.

But freedom stopped short of buying her own home as the island authorities pointed out she was not eligible as she was not a subject of the Sovereign. Dugard argued that the Sovereign herself had taken refuge in New Zealand, and that Britain had lost herself irrevocably in the Eurinal.

And so she had rented an apartment in the converted Château à l'Etoc, from where she kept in touch with European affairs and wrote ascerbic features for the large chunk of the French press which was still anti-European.

It was on a Sunday afternoon in August 2005 that her computer threw up a letter keyed by a priest in Liechtenstein — although she didn't know his identity. She downloaded the letter and sent a terse reply offering her services, preferably as a writer and publicist. She printed off a copy, then dialled a local phone number.

"John? Annette here, at Château à l'Etoc. Are you free for a few moments if I drop by?"

John le Mesurier, among the many Alderney men to have carried the name down the generations, was one of the two island representatives in the States of Deliberation, Guernsey's Lower House. "Is it poetry or politics?" he asked. He and the French girl shared a love of poetry, in French and in English, and both had managed to pick up a small income from writing it. Until recently.

"There's no poetry in the Eurinal. There's somebody on the Internet who looks as if he's gathering names of protestors. I've replied."

Le Mesurier sucked in his breath. "Could be risky. We're dealing with unknown forces. Still — why not? Come round as soon as you like."

The French girl cycled the two miles from her apartment in the château to the Crabby part of St Anne, the island's capital village, and leaned her machine against the front wall of Le Mesurier's small house. The tall, bearded conseiller answered her ring within seconds and put his hand on her shoulder to welcome her inside and into the kitchen-diner. Fiona Le Mesurier was preparing the midday meal and added her smile of welcome. "Take a seat, my dear."

The conseiller swung his chair around and sat leaning on its back rail. "Politics, not poetry." He shrugged. "There's no market for poetry anymore, now the economic blockade has begun."

Annette nodded. "I know. All my magazine contacts in England and France have dried up since I refuse to accept payment in euros. Anyway..." She handed him the printout of the message on the Internet, and Le Mesurier read it aloud for his wife's benefit.

"You think he's starting some form of resistance movement?"

The French girl nodded. "Looks that way. It's about time somebody did — there's a vast opposition across France, I know. You remember the referendum after Maastricht? Forty-nine percent of French people were opposed to a single currency."

Mrs Le Mesurier said over her shoulder: "You were lucky to have a referendum. Denmark was the only other country to have one, then the Referendum Party in Britain forced the three big parties to commit themselves to one, but only on the issue of the single currency, not about getting out of Europe altogether. Nobody else in Europe had a chance to vote on it. Democracy? Even the Greeks never had a vote, and they invented democracy."

"So how's the blockade going, John?"

"Depends on your viewpoint. You know Guernsey, Jersey and the Isle of Man have formed a partnership? Gib and the Falklands are in it as well. We're all opposed to handling a single euro note. So the trade war has started in earnest."

"And the televisions' been full of it."

"As long as Channel TV's not buying any programmes from Britain, what else can it screen? You know all the ferry links to England and France have been shut down. You'll certainly know our ferry to Cherbourg has stopped, and it's going to Guernsey instead. All flights to the mainland have been cut, but Guernsey Air and Manx Airlines are going to start up a direct link soon."

"Overflying England?"

Le Mesurier shrugged. "Depends on how snotty the air traffic controllers are. They might just make it damned awkward and route us around Cornwall."

"Takes more fuel."

"Ah! You won't know the latest on the Falklands issue. The first load of free oil is on its way. The tanker discharged Falklands crude in Morocco and two smaller ships are bringing the refined stuff to us poor beleaguered souls up here. And there'll be financial help for people who can prove their income has suffered as a result of the trade embargo."

"So we stand to get some dole money?" Annette smiled.

Fiona Le Mesurier swung around from her cooking preparations, anger in her eyes. "I hope to God we do. John's lost his entire income because of the trade ban — photography, painting, poetry: who wants to know now? Mind you, I'm with him. Somebody has to do something." She pointed a rolling-pin at the French woman. "But is it enough? Are we just tilting at windmills? Who the hell in the Eurinal cares one jot what we do? They'll just laugh at us and wait for our silly little protest to grind to a stop. But this mustn't be the end of it — this has got to be the start of something meaningful."

Le Mesurier nodded. "I agree. But what can a handful of people on a tiny island do?"

"Fight," Annette Dugard said with grit. "Your parents and grandparents did it in the war. So did mine — my grandfather led the Résistance in the département of the Meuse, and that wasn't very far from Luxembourg."

"I don't want to disillusion you," le Mesurier groaned, "but Alderney people didn't fight in the war. The whole island population was evacuated. When the people came back in November 1945 the place was in ruins. Alderney was independent before the war, but after — it was a shambles. It was all gone. The islanders had the option of abandoning the place, joining with Hampshire, or joining Guernsey."

"So they chose Guernsey," Dugard added. "If they'd joined Hampshire, you'd be well and truly in the Eurinal by now. Think yourselves lucky." The Frenchwoman slammed the kitchen table in her anger. "Germany cost you your freedom once. Don't let it happen again. Fight!"

"WE'LL BLOODY FIGHT!" snapped Archie McGovan after he read the text under the headline *DID YOU SEE THE TRAP?* which he picked up on the Internet on Sunday morning. He was playing with his computer in the back room of his granite house in Aberdeen, while his wife and children were at the kirk. "Whoever you are, Mac, if you're goin' to do somethin' aboot the bloody Common Fisheries Policy, I'm wie ye all the way."

McGovan was a weatherbeaten deep-sea fisherman who had been sailing out of Aberdeen since 1970. He learned the industry the hard way, by watching the gulls and gannets as they harvested the shoals of whiting and herring; by listening in to fishermen on other boats and hearing what they *didn't* say. There were no transponders, no factory ships, no EGNOS satellite tracking system in those days. The Cod War with Iceland was in the future, there were no quotas, and the Spanish fishermen were confined to plundering their own seas, scooping up inch-long hake by the million and frying the lot.

He had seen the fishing industry slide into difficulties. Sonar location allowing nothing to escape, and factory ships coming from Russia, both leading to declining catches. Then came quotas, imposed by politicians for political — not conservation — reasons. The Cod War of 1976, when Iceland justifiably tried to preserve its own fishing territories.

Then came the Common Fisheries Policy itself, with Britain applying the directives with a rod of iron while other countries, notably Spain, almost ignored them. What was 'common' about such a policy? Then came quota-hopping, with twenty percent of British fish going to Spanish and Dutch markets — including almost half the hake and plaice caught in what had been British waters.

Then the British Government had been slow to join the decommissioning scheme, so Spain had picked up the modernisation grants while Britain had let them slip. *Politicians!* Then the mountains of paperwork.

Then the Spanish, who were notorious for keeping everything they caught, were allowed to send forty new and efficient ships into the Irish Box for the first time, while Britain's two-hundred-mile territorial waters declaration was waved aside by the Brussels bureaucrats because it came a few hours too late.

Then the Greeks and the Austrians, who knew sod-all about the North Sea, were allowed to vote on every goddam' issue. It was pointless to argue that the Brits could vote on Mediterranean issues — they didn't understand them either. Then the satellite monitoring and the electronic log-book — where was the bloody incentive to go to sea?

But the thing that sickened him most was being told to throw back fish because he'd filled his quota. Did the politicians in Brussels know — did they even *care* — that the throwbacks were already dead, and there was as much conservation in that idea as there was snow in Cuba?

He could see the way the industry was going: he could see the way it had been planned for years. There would be *no* national fishing industry — by which a Europhile would understand no *provincial* industry. It would all be European, the whole damned lot of it.

The Eurobloody Commission would issue licences and control the show. No quotas for England or Scotland or even Spain. Everything ruled from Brussels. It was obvious, when you thought about it: why else had the British fleet been hammered to the verge of extinction? Why else the fifty-thousand-pound fines for speaking out? Why else had the Spanish been given the key to the Irish Box?

No boats registered in Newlyn or Aberdeen, or even Dunkirk or La Coruña. One overall registration system. One commissioner telling every fisherman from Rockall to Rhodes just what he may — and may not — do. What a sodding prospect!

"We'll bloody fight, given half a chance. I want Britain back again. I want my bloody country out o' the bloody European Disunion. I want Spanish fishermen out o' British waters. An' I want politicians out o' the fishin' industry. Contact him on the Web? You bet, Sonny Jim."

McGovan keyed in his adamant agreement that this was not the life he wanted, and he sent it to the Internet address given.

Then he sat back and thought. He would be taking the *Good Hope* out on the ebb tide in an attempt to catch cod in his designated sector east of the Shetlands and, as usual, he would risk being picked up by the EGNOS spy, and offload in Bergen any that were surplus to his quota. It would probably be sold back to the English regions at a higher price. His choice was either that or throw the damned fish back into the water, dead, which would only feed the gulls. Bloody quotas! Luckily Norway wasn't embroiled in the Union.

Then, he had to remind himself, there were plenty of people in the fishing industry, particularly in the Scottish Province, who were in favour of the policy despite having had their country snatched from under their feet. My God! How money talks! There were fishermen in the Shetlands who were millionaires. Yet there were hundreds of fishermen in southern England who had taken the subsidy to get out of the industry, and there were hundreds of others who'd gone broke, with no fish and no subsidy.

He read the letter again. It was sent from somewhere in Switzerland, which was also free from the Union and, judging by the sentiment, it wasn't written by a politician.

Politicians had created the Union and made a soddin' mess of things. Other politicians down in Westminster had blathered about it for years — get in, get out, wait an' see — until that blackest of days when some other politician in Brussels had re-interpreted Article 104c.

"We need a government without bloody politicians," he muttered to himself, aware that that was a contradiction.

But maybe it wasn't.

"People power," he said to his computer. "They used it years ago when I was a kid. The Philippines and Cory Aquino. The collapse of the Berlin Wall. The end of Communism in Europe. Palestine and the Intafada. Collapse of Yugoslavia. India. Albania. Java. Even bloody China. Doesn't always work, but it's damn' well worth a try. Leave it to the polibloodyticians and you'll get nowhere."

People power.

Good idea, but how do you get it off the ground? And what do you do when you get going? Send a hundred thousand people down to Westminster an' block the streets solid for days?

"Westminster has had it," he mused. "May as well go an' campaign outside Aberdeen City Council offices, or the Rangers' ground in Glasgie."

But the idea persisted. People power. Need a hundred thousand people who feel strong enough about the Europe issue to get off their backsides and make a protest. But where the hell d'you get such a list?

He switched off his computer and went out to meet Helen on the way back from the kirk. A hundred thousand people: maybe his mind would come up with something.

It did, the moment he reached the front gate. *The Referendum Party!* Sir Jimmy Goldsmith's lot. The Barmy Army, according to the real politicians who were messing their pants before the general election in May 1997.

"The Referendum Party!" He stopped with his hand on the gatepost. Eight years ago. The database would be hellishly out of date. Maybe it had been wiped clean long ago. And even it were still around, how would he find it? And how would he get hold of it — or a copy? And even if he got it, how could he physically phone or write to two hundred and fifty thousand, or however many?

Then he smiled. "You bloody fool!" Some guy in Switzerland was sending out a letter on the Internet: DID YOU SEE THE TRAP BEFORE YOU STEPPED INSIDE? All Archie McGovan had to do was reply via the Internet: Helen could find her own way home. He hurried back inside and keyed his appeal.

DID YOU VOTE "REFERENDUM" IN 1997?
GRAND REUNION COMING UP 2007
Contact:

He added his e-mail address and posted his appeal on the Internet. The revolution had begun.

EUROSLAVIA

FATHER ZIMMERMAN WAS shocked. The first reply to his letter came onto his screen at twenty-three minutes past midnight on that Sunday morning. Five minutes passed before the second response, then they came in a steady stream with scarcely a pause. He recorded them all straight onto hard disc but diverted a few onto his screen to take a sample.

They came from all over Europe, and most gave some story of loss brought about by directives from the Urian, the European Devil: businesses forced to close because their owners couldn't afford to comply with directives — many of these were from abbatoirs in northern Europe. Directives that contradicted each other, such as confusing soft cheese and yoghurt. Directives that were obviously dreamed up in some office and were totally impossible to put into practice in industry. Directives that were selectively punitive because they ignored a small section of an industry.

He hadn't solicited praise for the Devil, and he didn't think he'd received any, but he was astounded at the strength of the criticism of the Urian that he had received.

He broke off twice to conduct Mass, and begged a curate to take the confessions; the old man was astounded at the stories of betrayal, bitterness, injustice, frustration, anger, and sometimes near-suicidal desperation that were flowing in to his computer.

They never stopped at midnight, although when he checked, his message had been withdrawn, as requested. A few minutes later, when he logged into his directory to check on the number of replies, he learned there were one thousand five hundred and thirty-two, and still counting.

They came in all through that night, but on a reducing rate. He went to bed at one in the morning and was back at his computer desk by seven. There were distinct pauses now between the responses, but another four hundred and two had been logged on. And then at a few minutes past eight, while he was sampling a reply from Greece, written in poor English, the text suddenly turned to gibberish, a confusion of symbols and letters. Seconds later, the screen went blank.

Father Zimmerman booted his system but could not log back into the Net. He tried his computer on normal functions and saw it was working perfectly, but the apparatus would not speak to any other computer. Zimmerman shrugged. "Modem," he diagnosed. "Unusual for that to go wrong."

ARCHIE McGOVAN HAD his first reply within half an hour of posting his letter on the Internet, and by late afternoon there was a steady flow of responses which he was saving on hard disc. When he could delay the sailing of the *Good Hope* no longer, he asked his wife Helen to keep an eye on things.

"Ye ken Ah know nothin' o' your computers?"

"I know, gerrl. It's merely seein' that things keep runnin' as they are. Ye'll see the messages come on the screen, then they'll save themselves onta the hard disc. Just leave the thing switched on, an' check it doesna go wrong."

"Ah canna check it! An' what can go wrong? Might the bloody thing catch fire?"

He shrugged. "In that case, gerrl, call the brigade. Or do they call them operatives these days? See you in a week or so."

They embraced, and for a long moment everything was forgotten except their love for each other, and their imminent separation as the fishing-boat skipper, rugged and hardened beyond his fifty-three years, went out to face the hazards of the Norwegian Sea.

When the front door had slammed behind Archie, Helen McGovan had her own ritual for the next agonising hour or so. She had gone down to the docks only once, and vowed that the experience of watching her husband's ship sail out beyond the North Pier was something she would never repeat. She checked the house and made sure it was shipshape and secure for her, and for their daughter Marian, while Archie was away at sea. Only then could she relax.

The computer! She went through to check it and watched for a while in fascination, but total ignorance, as message after message came up on screen, then was sucked away to be stored somewhere inside the machine.

The messages seemed to be supporting a reunion of people who'd voted for the Referendum Party eight years back; endless names, addresses, and numbers: phone, fax or e-mail. She saw one which was from a man who claimed to have the complete RP database of some quarter-million members, with the suggestion that he be contacted at a Post Office box number. Helen jotted the details just as the screen went blank before the next message appeared.

She looked at the scribble on the scrap of paper and decided she would reply to the box number; judging by the steady flow of messages, Archie might take weeks before he got around to finding this one again.

The messages were still coming when she went to bed, but when she checked at breakfast time on Monday the screen was doing nothing: just a steely-grey, with those strange symbols around the edges. It was almost as if somebody had pulled a switch and stopped the flow — but that wasn't possible, was it? There was no change by midday so she traced the power cables back to the wall sockets and switched them off.

IT WAS A LITTLE after ten on a Monday morning at the end of August and Axel Teutoburger felt his heartbeat accelerate at the prospect of action, although he was no longer a brigadier-general in the Eurowerhmacht; it was politically too dangerous to have serving military officers in the Eurosicherheitsdienst now that more members of the European Commission were aware of the pan-European police force. He pressed two intercom buttons on his phone-fax and snapped: "Miss Bouderon, Mr Casbergen. In my office, if you please."

The head of criminal records (personnel) smiled cautiously as she entered, her honey-blonde hair bouncing on her shoulders. The head of electronic surveillance had a fixed expression that would melt in any direction he chose as soon as he knew what the boss had to say.

"Sit down, please," Teutoburger said quietly, waving to two chairs facing his desk. "You've sampled the material, Frans?" The Belgian nodded, permitting a slight smile to escape. "And you've shut it down?"

"Of course, sir. The moment you suggested it."

"And your opinions?"

"Seditious, sir. One could go further: treasonable. Somebody is planning an insurrection."

Bouderon glanced sideways at the head of electronic surveillance, her eyes opening as she realised the implications.

"In plain language, Frans — somebody is preparing to strike at the European Union?"

"Without a shadow of doubt, sir. At the moment it appears to be a one-man protest that will almost certainly come to nothing. However, I propose we watch events in case they escalate: the protest has certainly touched on sympathetic nerves across the Union."

"Good," Teutoburger smiled. Then he glanced at Bouderon and their eyes met briefly, flashing electricity. "Any movement on that other little problem, the bombing campaign against provincial governments?"

The French woman clenched her fists under the desk, aware that her authority was being put under scrutiny.

"Nothing has happened since Sergio Gonzáles went to the Basque country straight after the Copenhagen bomb, sir. We are still convinced the man... he had a strange name... was behind it, and we still have the case open."

"Bring him in," Teutoburger said with finality. "Bring him in and we'll sort him out."

"Without evidence, sir?," the beautiful eyes asked.

"Evidence? Damn the evidence, Bouderon. We have the authority of the European Commission to act on suspicion in cases of treason or suspected terrorism."

"*Bien fait*," she answered with a smile of concurrence. "But I think we have to look further afield for the computer conspiracy, sir. Frans will explain."

Casbergen nodded. "The one who's mailboxing that libellous letter comes from Liechtenstein. We've pinpointed him to a small area in the capital, Vaduz."

Teutoburger sighed. "Outside the Union, eh? Remind me, Frans — how do you shut him down and then manage to trace him?"

The head of electronic surveillance laughed. "Child's play, sir. You remember: it all began with the microchip implanted into cows during the bovine spongiform encepalopathy scare back in the eighties. Put a chip as big as your thumbnail under the animal's skin and you've got him tagged for life."

"Her," Bouderon corrected. "Cows are female."

"As I was saying, place a scanner on the cow and you can read off all her data. Parents, place and date of birth, and all the rest. Then came the updating microchip, which could diagnose the animal's health: whether she was developing BSE."

"I remember all this," Teutoburger nodded. "Then came the interactive chip, right?"

"Correct, sir. We could input instructions. Make the cow dance, BSE or not. By now the chips were so small you could put forty on a one-euro coin. That's when we started putting them in all televisions, computer modems, cars — as well as cows." Casbergen smiled. "It's not common knowledge, of course, but now they're down to five millimetres long and thinner than a pencil lead, we've started a programme to insert them in the brain stem of newborn babies. The chips are so thin they don't give a shadow on X-ray, and they certainly don't show on ultrasound."

"I'm well aware of it, Mr Casbergen." With a smile that said I-can-do-it-as-well-as-you-can, he said: "It all began with neural prosthetics. Implants to allow the deaf to hear, to control epilepsy, incontinence — that sort of problem. Then in Tübingen the Institute of Medical Psychology, I think it was, developed an implant that allowed humans to activate machinery by thought. Eh, Mr Casbergen?"

The Belgian nodded, a shade deflated. "So you know the ultimate development potential, sir? Interactivity?"

"Indeed. The chip will tell the human what to do. Human robots, eh? Robots who have been programmed not to question orders, but to obey. If only Hitler were alive to see his dream come true."

Christine Bouderon shut her eyes for a few seconds in horror. Implanting microchips in babies, without the parents' knowledge? She was twenty-seven, and time was getting a little short if she were to fulfil her natural instinct and become a mother. But she rebelled in total disgust at the idea of having her infant implanted so that it could be under lifelong surveillance and control. She suppressed a shiver as she wondered how she could ever have found this man sexually attractive. She had certainly made the right decision that day in Montmédy Castle. Still shocked, but not showing it, she looked up, a fixed smile on her mouth as Axel Teutoburger said: "Fine, Frans. Put our two great minds together and we have all questions answered, eh? Back on the computer module problem: you send out a microwave from the nearest mobile telephone transmitter mast and that de-activates the security microchip in the modem. Means he can't get into the Internet any more. I'm with you there, but I must confess I don't know how that locates the computer itself?"

Casbergen didn't know whether his boss was fooling, or not. "The chip's last act is to send out an ultra-high-frequency beep for a microsecond; it's automatically triangulated from the mobile phone masts and it's accurate to within fifty metres in ideal conditions. So we have him, sir."

"But it seems we have this one in Liechtenstein? He may as well be on the moon, man."

Casbergen smiled. "Tonight, sir. We'll pick him up tonight."

Bouderon shuddered. That meant her department would ultimately be in charge of questioning this man who was bold enough to challenge the Europäische Vereinigung on the Internet. Fair enough — but was the ESD justified in stepping over the border into foreign but friendly territory? She knew the service would claim justification if the means supplied the desired result. After all, transgressing another nation was minor, if the service was already considering invading and controlling the human mind from soon after birth. For the first time, she began to wonder if she was in the right job.

"And the other one?" Teutoburger asked. "The one who wants to have a reunion of Britain's Barmy Army?"

"Same story, sir. He's off the air. I hear he's been located to within four or five properties in Aberdeen, Region UKA4. Somebody will be going in there tonight, as well." Casbergen, knowing he was on totally safe ground, allowed his smile of complacency to stretch as wide as his face would allow. "Then we have both problems licked, sir."

FATHER ERICH ZIMMERMAN pondered over his faulty modem

while he conducted Mass. At mid-morning, in a gap between church duties, he disconnected the component and walked into Vaduz where he laid the part on the counter of his computer supplier. "Kaput, Hans. You have another?"

The computer engineer knitted his brows. "Modems don't usually give trouble." He stared at the priest for a moment. "Doesn't look familiar — did I sell you this?"

Zimmerman put his tongue in his cheek as he thought. "No, Hans, you didn't. I remember now. I was on a coach trip to Bavaria and I got it in Bregenz when we stopped for lunch. Why?"

Hans frowned. "Have you been doing anything the authorities wouldn't like?"

The priest clapped his hand to his heart as he felt its rhythm accelerate. "Which authorities, Hans? The European Union?"

"Got it in one. Watch." He dismantled the modem, the gizmo which connects a computer to a telephone and allows, among other things, access to the Internet. As the casing came apart the engineer pointed to a microchip half the size of a match head. "There it is."

Zimmerman peered at it through the offered magnifying glass. "What in God's Holy Name is that?"

"A bug. A surveillance bug. They're planted in all modems sold in the great and wonderful autocracy that surrounds us — I mean the European Union, if you didn't understand me."

"But why, Hans? Why?"

"Erich," the engineer said quietly. "You told me you've made a study of German history in the twentieth century." He looked around, checking that he couldn't be overheard although there was nobody else in the shop. "Whenever you have a government that is not answerable to the people through the ballot, that government gets a paranoia that somebody is planning to overthrow it. I needn't remind you about the Geheime Staatspolizei, the dear old Gestapo of Nazi times, need I? I needn't talk about the Soviets' KGB? The dictatorships in Chile and Argentina? Idi Amin in Uganda — remember him?"

"I remember him, Hans, and you needn't remind me."

"And I must stress, Erich, it's the governments at fault, not the people. The average German was as scared of Hitler as the occupied French were. And the Russians were terrified of the KGB."

"I know, Hans, I know. But we haven't gone that far, surely? Not in Europe — again?"

"Have you heard of the Eurosicherheitsdienst?"

Zimmerman gasped. "No. You must be joking."

"Indeed I am not, my dear Erich. And I'm not surprised it's news to you. It operates from Berlin, near the old Checkpoint Charlie, and it'll soon be just as bad as the Gestapo. I heard about it through contacts in the computer business, but..." He leaned closer. "...you never heard of it from me. Right?"

Zimmerman nodded, totally shaken. "What does this security service do?"

"Among other things, it has sections in every modem manufacturer and importer in the Union. It plants bugs, just like this." Hans used tiny cutters to snip the microchip free, then he soldered the cut wires together and reassembled the modem.

"Don't the manufacturers know?"

"Of course they do, but they have no option, and they're sworn to secrecy. No point in establishing a security force if it can't do its job, is there? There are bugs in other things, too. Phones, of course. I hear they're in car computers as well, but I've yet to find out why."

Zimmerman was learning fast. "So this little gadget cut off my access to the Internet? How?"

"How do you think, Erich?"

"You mean somebody must have activated it? Oh, my God! It doesn't bear thinking about. How do they do it?"

"Do you have a mobile phone, Father?"

"No."

"Plenty of people do. You've seen those transmitter masts all over the countryside?"

"My God — secret transmitters!"

Hans said quietly: "You don't fancy taking a little holiday, Father? Visit friends deep in Switzerland, perhaps? Leaving this afternoon?"

"But this is Liechtenstein! We're not in the Union!"

"Father, I thank God we're not."

Father Zimmerman hurried back to his comfortable home attached to St Maria's Church, scarcely able to contemplate the threat that now hung over him. But he knew the facts of Hitler's rise to power, and the knock that came on thousands of front doors at three in the morning. He knew that totalitarianism had happened in Europe within his lifetime: he was perhaps more prepared than many younger people for it to happen again. But he was eighty-seven, far too old to begin the life of a fugitive. Should he stay and wait for these new people, the security police, to pick him up? What would happen?

As he reached the former monastery holding the comfortable cell where he lived, he considered the possibilities. A friendly warning not to post seditious notices on the Internet? Hardly. Removal to another cell, one with bars on the windows and devoid of heating? No thanks, not with winter looming up. A slave labour camp? An extermination camp? Absolutely not — the autocracy could never have got that far down the road. But that was the ultimate: that was where governments not answerable to their citizens eventually went — if they survived long enough.

"No, Erich," he told himself. "You're going. You serve God, and this is not of God's creation. You had the sign, telling you to use the Internet. You would be defying God's will if you stayed around and waited to be arrested. Whatever you've stumbled on, it's far greater than your humble self. You must go away from here and continue God's work, whatever it may be, in whatever way God wills."

He reconnected the modem, logged onto the Internet, and within minutes another reply to his letter came up on screen.

He felt his hands and legs tremble with the realisation that there were still hundreds, maybe thousands, of people out there in the grasp of the Urian, who were seeking help, and as it stood he was perhaps their only salvation.

"Go," he told himself, but his conscience told him he could not ignore these cries for help. He went to the broom cupboard and threw everything aside until he found a large rucksack he'd last used twenty years ago. He thrust a blanket in the bottom, then switched off his computer and packed it, with its keyboard, display screen, and printer, then packed another blanket and spare clothes around it and on top. He snatched a smaller case and thrust more clothes and an assortment of canned and dried foods in it, finally adding some cutlery and a tin-opener — and a torch.

Then he left. No note, no farewell message to anybody in the church. Father Erich Zimmerman, aged eighty-seven, walked out of the door and into his self-imposed exile, leaving no trail at all.

He walked into the centre of Vaduz and took a bus northward, out of town. Two kilometers on, he got out, walked to the junction with Route 191 and caught the next bus into the village of Buchs, in Switzerland. By mid-afternoon he was in Zürich, anonymous and — he hoped — safe.

EIGHT

THEY CAME FOR Archie McGovan at three in the morning. The ESD was extending its tentacles across Europe, but it had no agents of its own north of Birmingham, which meant none at all in the Province of Scotland. Sergio Gonzáles, whose political section — spying on politicians and public figures across the Union — was also involved in liaison with Command Headquarters of the Eurowehrmacht in all the member provinces.

He had passed on a request, which was to be construed as an order, to Herr Oberkommandant, Hauptamt, Edinburg — in Spanish, el Señor Comandante, Cuartel General, Edimburgo, which didn't sound so terrifying. The recipient was the officer commanding the Euroarmy barracks in Edinburgh Castle, whose last British occupants had been the King's Own Scottish Borderers (the regiment had refused to change its name on threat of mutiny, claiming that the last 'king' had been a queen) but which were now home to the Brigada Blindada, a Spanish tank regiment. The request was to apprehend the operator of a computer which had logged onto the Internet. The e-mail address was given but, as it had no correlation to the postal address, it was useless. The location was given to within five bungalows in Fintry Street on the northern edge of Aberdeen, but there was no occupier's name.

There was a problem. The Brigada Blindada had only one officer who spoke English, and he was virtually incapable of understanding the Aberdonian dialect; the Edinburgh accent was bad enough.

The Comandante had only one way to tackle his problem. He took ten private soldiers from the Edinburgh Castle Barracks and sent them north, to arrive at Aberdeen at three o'clock on Tuesday morning. They knocked up all five households in Fintry Street simultaneously and the officer with a basic command of English was ready to apologise to four of them.

Three households were without computers when the troops searched and he apologised to them, without managing to calm their ire. Of the other two, one was without a modem, which left the guilty party exposed.

"What the bloody hell do ya mean, bangin' on the door at this hour o' the morrn?," Helen McGovan demanded, holding her dressing-gown across her chest.

The officer slapped the computer display unit. "You post letters on Internet," he stated. "Yes?"

"I post le'ers on Internet? Ach, man, Ah dinna ken what' you'rre talkin' about. Ah canna worrk the bloody thing, so ye can ge' out o' ma hoose this minute just."

The officer was adamant: he had the evidence before him, and he knew the penalty for failing to make an arrest. "Madam, I do not understand. You will come with me and we will talk in Edimburgo." He laid his hand on her shoulder.

Helen McGovan erupted. "Tak you'rre filthy hands off me, ye bloody Spanish git!" She stepped back and brought her knee up into the officer's groin with such force that he doubled and collapsed onto the floor, honking for breath like an asthmatic. The soldier left facing her was so astounded to see an apparently vulnerable woman in her middle years, fell a trained soldier with one blow, that he stepped back into the bungalow. "Gie out, ye scab, if..." she began, but she felt her left arm being grabbed and forced into a half-nelson hold; a man's arm went around her neck from behind, and a leg knocked her off balance. She fell heavily, face-down, onto the floor and had cuffs on her wrists before she could recover. Two soldiers dragged her to her feet.

"*Viene con nosotros, y viene tranquila,*" a soldier ordered, his tone leaving little doubt that he meant busines. As Mrs McGovan was dragged to the armoured personnel carried parked in the middle of the road, she called to her astounded neighbours: "Call the police! Ah've done nothin' wrong. This is supposed ta be a free country..."

Two other soldiers followed, carrying the computer and its attachments. None of the military noticed the terrified face of a young woman peering around the door of another bedroom. Only when the APC had roared away did the woman come forward and meet her neighbours in the front garden. "What's happened?" She cried. "Mother's never done anything wrong. Who were those men? They weren't Scots, or even English."

Eight shocked people in their night attire asked questions that none of them could answer. They were still wondering exactly what had happened when Marian McGovan dialled the emergency service and got the police.

"Help! Some soldiers have just broken in an' kidnapped me mam — an' taken me dad's computer..."

She paused, listening in stunned shock to the explanation on why the police couldn't intervene.

"Yeah, they were foreigners, Spanish, I think....Ye mean, *they have more authority here than you do*? What kind of a world is this? How long has this been the law?"

"It's a decree from Brussels, miss," a frustrated police voice tried to explain. "They're establishing a European police force, but they keep meeting opposition. In the meantime, the Euroarmy has powers of arrest, and we mustn't intervene."

"But why did they send bloody Spanish soldiers? What's wrong with Scottish troops? An' where've they taken my mam?"

"There are no Scottish troops in Scotland, miss," the police officer explained in a tired voice. "Nor English in England. They're all scattered around Europe and we've got pillocks from Greece and Finland and God knows where."

Marian, a secretary in a supermarket in the city, sank to the floor. "You're having me on."

"No, miss. It's been so for a fair while now. For donkeys' years French police haven't been able to serve where they're born. This is just the next stage on."

"But why weren't we *told?* They can't do this, surely..."

"When did Europe ever tell any of the ordinary people what it was going to do? Apart from the single currency and the federal state."

"But we had an opt-out from the single currency." She paused. "So how the mick did we get into it?"

"The famous Article 104c. Two years ago."

Marian shook her head. "I haven't been following politics. I just go along with what happens. Maybe I ought to find out what's going on before the Brussels mob wipes out Westminster."

The voice paused. "They already have, miss."

"*What?* No! You've got to be taking the piss. You can see it on the telly."

"I'm afraid you've got a lot to learn, miss. Westminster's still there, but it's got no more power than a town council. It's all a farce."

"God!" Marian sank lower until she was almost laying on the lounge carpet. She was aware of neighbours wandering in and out, and that her nightclothes were almost up to her waist. She wriggled. "I know the Queen went to New Zealand, but that was her own choice."

"If you throw a dog on a fire and tell it to jump off, it will. But do you call that free choice?"

"You mean — she had no choice?"

"She could have stayed as Mrs Windsor."

Marian shrugged. "Oh, well. Scotland would have gone republican anyway. Hey — where's my mam?"

"I expect somebody will be contacting you later in the morning, miss, but my guess is she'll be on her way to Edinburgh for questioning."

"Questioning? What for? She's done nothing!"

"Then they'll release her, won't they? I'm really sorry, miss, but when the Army gets involved, we have to stay clear."

Marion scrambled to her feet. "I'll write to my MP!"

"Not wishing to be disrespectful, miss, but you'd get as much result by complaining to your local fishmonger."

"Thanks," she snapped, and put the phone down. Her mind was in turmoil. What had happened to Scotland, to Britain, since those stupid euro notes came into use? If foreign soldiers could break into their home and arrest her mam, *for nothing,* what else could they do? She felt as if her world had ended. All the values she had come to learn and live by since childhood, were now meaningless. What was the point of going to work; could some faceless whizz-kid shut down the supermarket *for no reason?*

"If this is Europe, I don't want to know it," she whispered to herself, then stumbled to the front door to find some way of securing it for the night.

ON THE WAY to Edinburgh in the APC, Helen McGovan was thankful that nobody had spotted Marian; the girl would be scared witless, but would soon find a way of getting her mam out of whatever mess she was in.

And what in God's name was it all about? She knew it had to involve that message that Archie had put onto the Internet, but he was only asking for names and addresses. What was wrong in that? They had been coming in fast, as if Archie had tapped some reservoir. And now the soldiers had all the names — every one of them.

No, she thought. Not quite. She had seen one message that offered Archie the entire database of the Referendum Party, and she had replied to it — by post. She had no idea what was going on, but she was vaguely aware that her husband was organising some form of protest, and an even vaguer memory reminded her of some talk about a massive fine for criticising the Common Fishing Policy. And there was plenty to criticise, she knew: Britain had been robbed of her two hundred mile fishing zone...but Britain had been robbed naked of everything worth while. The British people were now economic slaves of Europe. But if Archie's action, whatever it had been, could get the Common Fisheries Policy scrapped, then she was with him all the way.

She hoped that somebody would get a message to the *Good Hope* to warn Archie what had happened. If he sailed blithely back into harbour, somebody was bound to be waiting for him.

THEY CAME FOR Erich Zimmerman at half past two — discreetly, as Vaduz is outside the Eupäische Vereinigung. Four men in civilian clothes and driving a private car but nonetheless acting on Casbergen's direct orders, came down from Feldkirch in Region

AT34, the Vorarlberg, and crossed the frontier into Liechtenstein a little after midnight. They had plenty of time.

They parked in the centre of the little capital city in the area already marked out on their large-scale map; they knew they were within fifty metres of the bugged modem.

As the city went to sleep, they looked about them. The target area was dominated by St Maria's Church, and a medieval building which looked like cloisters; there was also a corner of a small public square. Unless the computer operator had been sitting in the nave or in full view on the square, he had to be in the cloisters.

There were no lights in windows. A single street lamp cast an orange glow on the ancient stonework and in the two hours the men watched, they saw nobody at all on the streets. This quarter of Vaduz obviously went to bed very early.

It seemed pointless to wait until the witching hour of three so the quartet walked casually across to the cloisters and found what had to be the entrance a little to the left of the street light. A few steps led up to an imposing timber-studded door which, to their surprise, was unlocked. Inside, permanent security lights led them up further stairs to the first floor, which was obviously divided into apartments off a main passage.

They counted. Six apartments. And four men.

They took one apartment each, knocked cautiously on the door, waited, and knocked again. One by one the doors were opened and sleepy priests peered out at their visitors.

"I'm sorry to disturb you at this time of night, but somebody posted an urgent message on the Internet. Somebody in this building."

Two of the priests nodded. "Ah," said one. "Father Zimmerman. He's a wonder with computers, despite his age."

"Age?" asked the visitor.

"Nearly ninety. He's in apartment four, down on the left."

The visitors quietly made their way to apartment four as the other doors closed and the priests went back to bed. They stood by Zimmerman's door, two each side, and knocked quietly. Then louder. They knew if they hammered on the door the other priests would investigate, and there could be problems: the Eurosicherheitsdienst didn't go looking for trouble outside its territory.

They used two prising bars on the door and forced it open with no more than a loud squeak, then they were in.

The place was empty. There was an obvious space on a small table where the computer had stood, and there were packets of discs around. The mouse pad was in place, but everything else had gone.

Working in near silence the four took only minutes to search the small but smartly-furnished bachelor apartment. Bedding was missing, and there were kitchen shelves which showed distinct signs of having been plundered in a hurry.

The visitors left as quietly as they had arrived, and drove back to Region AT34.

SOME YEARS BEFORE the Eurosicherheitsdienst had spread its tentacles much beyond Berlin, Xavier Yzurdiaga knew that somebody was watching him and waiting for him to make a mistake: he guessed it was somebody from the Grupos Antiterroristas de Liberación. Several years had passed since he had thrown the bomb at the Folketing in Copenhagen, but he didn't fool himself that the file had been closed. He often recalled, usually with a shudder, the visit of that strange man who questioned him a little bit too closely for comfort and who seemed to be satisfied by the ridiculous excuse of the Scrabble competition.

It was impossible to be looking over one's shoulder all the time, metaphorically or literally, but Yzurdiaga never fooled himself that 'they' were not still watching. It would help if he knew who 'they' were.

A year ago, in 2004, he had taken the remaining 7.5kg of Semtex and the five detonators from their hiding place in the cylinder of the old coach engine and buried them, wrapped in thick plastic, in a blanket, in the remains of the original lead envelope, in a watertight steel chest, in its turn wrapped in plastic. He had chosen the location with meticulous care: it was in the French Province, just in case the border with Spain was ever under scrutiny; it was in ancient woodland that had never seen the ravages of mankind and, judging by the steepness of the gradient, would never see it in future — certainly not by mechanised felling practices. Access was from a nearby quarry, reached by an unmade road yet only half a kilometer from the tiny hamlet of Uxiat on the reasonable road from St Jean-Pied-de-Port down to Orthez, in the French département of Pyrénées-Atlantiques in Region FR61 (Aquitaine). It was at low altitude, no more than two hundred metres, so it would be accessible for almost all the year, and it was only 80km from Zarautz in a direct line. He considered he had done well to take such meticulous precautions.

And Eustaquio Arrieta was the only other person who knew where it was.

It was Staqui who saved him from the Servicio de Seguridad Europeo, the European Security Service. Staqui, now living in moderate luxury from a win on El Gordo, the Fat One — Spain's Provincial Lottery — was sitting on a street bench in Zarautz in the October sunshine on a Tuesday morning when he saw an armoured personnel carrier stop abruptly outside the offices of Carrozas XYZ. He was intrigued as he saw four men get out: men in the uniform of the Ejercito Europeo, the Euroarmy. Strange customers, he considered, and timed them. Seventeen minutes passed before they emerged, carrying what appeared to be, from a distance, a small filing cabinet.

Staqui never moved a muscle but emotionally he gave the soldiers full attention. Surely Xav would not be so stupid as to keep any written records of their exploits together, or of his own little bombing campaign? He waited several minutes before strolling over and finding the three young women in the office in a state of shock and panic.

"What did they want?" he asked as calmly as he could.

"Staqui! They wanted Señor Yzurdiaga. They wouldn't believe he's not here. They searched everywhere, and took away a filing cabinet."

With his heart beating faster, he asked: "What was in it — do you know?"

The woman who was recovering fastest nodded. "Nothing to worry about, Staqui. The boss wasn't that stupid. But they want him. Why, Staqui — why?"

"Who were they?"

"Soldiers. They were talking English, but I couldn't understand more than the odd word. Señor Yzurdiaga isn't here, honestly."

"Where is he?" Arrieta couldn't remember the woman's first name and he didn't want to raise her doubts by admitting it. "You know me, don't you?"

"Of course, Señor Arrieta. You're an old friend of Señor Yzurdiaga." She paused. "Can you help him, do you think?"

"Where is he?"

"On a coach coming back from Nice. He should be..." She glanced at a schedule sheet. "He'll be passing Biarritz in a couple of hours. On the autoroute."

Arrieta glanced at his watch. "He's got a mobile phone? The usual number?" The woman nodded. "I'll warn him. Leave it to me." He checked. "Is there anything else you ought to tell me?"

"Maybe I shouldn't say this, but... Well, he still dreams of Euzkadi independence. He's always talking about getting Euzkadi out of the European Union, only he calls it the east wind. I don't know why."

Arrieta frowned. "It's the poetry in his soul. Leave it to me."

He hurried home — it was not prudent to run — and took his Jaguar out of the garage. He threw a sleeping-bag, a can of water and a few packets of biscuits into the boot, kissed his bemused wife Lolita goodbye, and five minutes later was on the autopista heading for

Biarritz. He was doing the European maximum motorway speed of 120 kph when he crossed the open border with the French Province just sixteen minutes later. He left the motorway at junction two and took to the foothills of the Pyrenees, stopping a little short of the tiny village of Ahetze from where he could look down on the traffic hurtling along the Autoroute 63. Visibility was excellent, and telephone reception should be even better. He dialled Yzurdiaga's private number on his mobile and got nothing but static. If he were on schedule, Xav should still be fifty km away, near the French Basque village of Peyrehorade.

He dialled again a minute later, and decided to repeat the exercise every minute until Yzurdiaga answered or until the XYZ coach came into view beneath him.

On the third attempt, and with perfect reception, Yzurdiaga answered.

"Staqui here, Xav. Where are you?"

Yzurdiaga was elated. "Staqui, old friend...!"

"It's business, Xav. And remember, *las paredes oyen* — walls have ears. Where are you?"

"Twenty-five k east of Bayonne. Can you tell me what's the problem, old friend?"

"Go into the town centre. Leave your transport. I'll pick you up by the cathedral."

There was a pause. "Fine. I'll leave my car in the suburbs. Out."

Arrieta smiled. Xav knew that Staqui knew that Xav was in a coach, not a car, and that there was a fair chance that a selection of mobile calls would be monitored. Arrieta left his vantage point and drove down to the old *route nationale* 10, into Bayonne. There were parking restrictions around the elegant Gothic cathedral of Ste Marie, but he ignored them, staying in his Jaguar but keeping his eyes open for officials in blue uniforms. Moments later the XYZ coach pulled in, Yzurdiaga leaped from it, hauled his luggage from the underfloor rack, and stepped back as the coach pulled away. It was all over inside forty seconds.

Arrieta gave a quick *pip* on his horn and as soon as Yzurdiaga was aboard, he drove off. He parked at the first possible spot and explained the situation.

"The Ejercito Europeo? Acting for the Servicio de Seguridad, do you think?" Yzurdiaga bit his tongue. "If so, I'm not going back to Spain."

"What else can you do, Xav?"

Yzurdiaga felt sick at heart, yet he managed to raise a smile. "It's been planned for some years, old friend. I'm going to hide up in

Andorra, and I'm going to concentrate one hundred percent on getting rid of the European Union, if I die in the attempt."

"This is crazy, Xav. What about your family?"

"Victoria knows. José Antonio is only fifteen so he's not old enough."

"But... *Díos,* Xavier. You could be in hiding for years!"

"I don't think it'll be that long. If by any chance you feel inclined to drive me there, I'll tell you about it on the way."

"Drive you to *Andorra*? Now?"

"If you put your foot down you can be back home before dark."

A MID-AUTUMN DEPRESSION had moved south-east from Greenland, giving the fishermen in the northern European waters cause for concern. The depression passed over Iceland and into the Norwegian Sea, bringing westerly gales in sea areas Faroes and Fair Isle.

Archie McGovan had been watching the forecast charts coming from Inmarsat and EGNOS and had decided to head north for slightly calmer weather; he reckoned due east of Iceland would be about right.

The *Good Hope* caught the inner edge of the storm and for two days, with no nets out, it rode the weather. The 60-foot vessel was built to survive such conditions, with little consideration for comfort, but cold grey waves surging out from the west crashed over its bows for almost fifty hours. McGovan and his crew frequently wondered why anybody should be mad enough to choose this floating hell as a way of making a living, when fingers were permanently numb and feet always cold, even in September.

For two days voice communication with Aberdeen was ruined by atmospheric conditions, although satellite data came through and the European Global Navigation Overlay System showed his position on screen at any time of day or night. The same satellite could send the same information back to Aberdeen so that help could be at hand whenever needed.

Conversely, if he wanted to fish outside his designated territory, he could be caught on screen, and if the Fisheries Control in Aberdeen wanted to give him trouble it could send his receiver number to the European Union, which could cut him off from EGNOS and leave him to find his way home by the sun and the pole star — unless he had a sextant aboard.

Which meant the first crackly voice to come through to the *Good Hope* was on Friday, 17 October. "*Good Hope, Good Hope*, this is Fisheries Control Aberdeen, do you read me? Over."

McGovan fine-tuned his knobs. "Fisheries Control, this is *Good*

Hope receiving you strength four but with interference. Worst of storm gone. No damage. Over."

"I have a personal message for skipper McGovan."

There's nothing personal about a ship-to-shore radio message, McGovan thought as he heard the news that his wife Helen had been arrested and detained for forty-eight hours in the Castle Barracks in Edinburgh.

"On what charge? Where is she now?"

The communications officer of Fisheries Control told all he knew, that Mrs McGovan had been severely shocked by the arrest, in public, in the early hours, and by the inability of the police to intervene. She was at home but still shaken.

"What in God's name ha' we got here?" McGovan shouted. "A military dictatorship? Are we no better than a banana republic? I'll have my MP onto this, you marrk my words."

"Your daughter has already tried, *Good Hope*, but she understands there's nothing the MP can do. It's a European matter."

"My wife is a bloody European matter? We'll see about that!"

He listened to more details: the taking of the computer, and the verdict of a computer engineer in Aberdeen that the entire hard disc had been wiped clean — and the modem ruined. Even when a new system had been keyed in, the computer wouldn't access the Internet. In short, the computer was like a grand house, but somebody had stolen all the furniture.

"So what do I do now? Head back for Aberdeen an' write this trip off as a loss?"

The voice said, amid interference: "You face arrest if you return, *Good Hope*. Advise you make your plans with this in mind. Over."

McGovan handed over the wheel to the mate and stared out of the wheelhouse window, rolling with the waves but not seeing them. Arrest? It could only be over that message he'd put on the Net. Was it treason to talk about the Referendum Party now? Jimmy Goldsmith's mob had disbanded after the May 1977 election, but the organisation lived on, nibbling away at the Disunion. What had it achieved?, McGovan asked himself. It never won a seat — in the face of vast tactical voting, it never stood a chance of that — but it had pulled in almost 800,000 votes, enough to make the three main party leaders go public on the commitment of a referendum before Britain joined the single currency, and the promise that Britain wouldn't join a federal Europe.

But politicians are notorious for changing policies when the electorate isn't looking, and *everybody* was pussyfooting around the issue. Every politician knew that federalism was the only thing on offer from

Europe, and a referendum on the currency *alone* was a total waste of time. Goldsmith knew that at the outset, which was why he was pushing for the far bigger question: *Do you want to go into Europe all the way, or do you want a simple trading partnership?*

McGovan kicked the wheelhouse wall. The question should have been: *Do you want to go in all the way, or do you want to get right out of it — like Norway is?*

Since that last option wasn't there, either in Sir Jimmy's question or Europe's constitution, Britain had remained in the Union after 1997, while the new Prime Minister, Tony Blair, tried (or so he told the voters) to rebuild Europe with Britain's interests in view. There was no immediate threat of New Labour joining the single currency, so there was no referendum.

"Wha' a load o' bullshit!" McGovan swore. "Wi' fifteen other member states tryin' ta push you over the cliff, of course there was a threat! It was like clamberin' back up the waterslide against the current — bloody impossible!"

So New Labour pretended it was trying to negotiate the biggest back-pedal in history. But Europe wasn't interested in back-pedal deals. Europe had *never* been interested in anything but the steady march towards federalism, and all those politicians down the years who had talked of getting Britain's voice heard, were either nincompoops or liars. So Britain had remained a signatory to the Treaty of Maastricht. It had remained vulnerable to a single clause that was full of loopholes. McGovan had heard people talking about the clause: was it called 104c?

Dusk was falling and the storm abating when McGovan called the crew together in the tiny galley; only the mate was absent, still at the wheel, but he had heard what was coming.

"Lads," the skipper began. "If Ah go home, Ah'm under arrest. Ah've been playin' on the Internet an' that's now a hangin' matter, it seems. Ah've been sayin' things our dearly beloved leaders in Brussels don't like. Frankly, Ah'm fed up to the back teeth wi' Europe an' the Fisheries Policy. What Ah propose is that we fish up around latitude sixty-five an' ta hell wi' the muckin' quota system and EGNOS. Then we'll sell the whole catch in Bergen."

His five crewmen stared at him in amazement.

"An' then Ah'm goin' ashore. Ye can take the *Good Hope* back home, get what ye can for her, take your cut an' gie the rest to ma missus."

"Ye can't do that, Archie! What the hell will ye do in Norway?"

"Wait for ma family, then we'll all clear off to somewhere sunny. Ah've had it wi' Europe."

"Ye canna do it, Mac. Ye canna take money out o' the Disunion."

"Sod the Disunion! They tell me fifty million things Ah canna do. Before they tell me Ah canna even *breathe* wi'out their say-so, Ah'm gonna do just one thing of ma own volition. Any rate — who's to know?"

"Why don't we go to the Isle o' Bloody Man? That's no' in the Union, an' Helen an' Marian could get there easier."

"Aye." He looked at his crew. "But what' aboot you lads if we all end up in the Isle o' Man? You two ha' got wives."

The older crewmen looked at each other and made up their minds within seconds. "I'm with you, Archie. What is there for us back home? You know as well as I do — speak up against the Fisheries Policy an' you're fined up to fifty thousand quid. That's what they'll do you for, skip — fifty grand; sixty grand in Mickey Mouse money. Talk about free speech — it costs a bloody fortune! I wonder how many people who voted in the last real election, back in ninety-seven, knew the rules? How many knew about the police state? Tell 'em today, an' how many would believe you? *Fifty thousand quid for speakin' your own mind!*" He shook his head as if he could scarcely believe it, eight years later. "Our wives'll come with us anywhere we go, as long as it's out of this bloody Disunion."

The other married deckhand agreed. "An' if we can't stay in Mann, then we'll go somewhere else. Iceland..."

"Too bloody cold, mate. The Med."

"The Med? Half the shoreline's in the Disunion as it is. Malta an' Cyprus want to stick their flamin' heads in the noose, yet the stupid gits haven't had independence for five minutes. Make it North Africa."

"Sod that for a lark! Ghadaffiland? The Med's fished out worse'n the North Sea, any rate. The Spaniards have seen to that. You've either got to go down to Senegal..."

"Forget it. The Frenchies bought the fishin' rights in the nineties an' have sucked it clean. Gambia's your first stop, or go round to Ghana an' Nigeria."

"Oh aye? Would they let us in with all our sophisticated gear? An' where's the market? If we can't get a good price for the catch we may as well stay in Aberdeen. I tell you, lads — there's only one place to go: United States."

"United...?" The deckhand's voice rose to a falsetto protest. "Haven't you been followin' the news? The Grand Banks is fished out an' Cape Cod ought to be renamed Cape Sprat."

"So that's it," Archie McGoven summarised. "We canna stay here — well *Ah* canna — an' we canna go anywhere else. We may as well sink the bloody tub here an' now."

"We can fight," the youngest crewman suggested. "We can fight, skip."

McGovan nodded. "Aye. Ah said that myself, an' I posted that stupid letter on the Net. That's what fightin' did for me."

"No, but we can, skip. You know the Isle o' Man's sort of broken off diplomatic relations with Europe, don't ye?"

"Ah heard talk of it."

"So let's go join them."

McGovan shrugged. "Let's go join 'em. Just like that. An' what do we do? Fish out o' Douglas, if they'll let us? Or turn the tub into a gunboat an' go chargin' up the Mersey? It costs a small fortune to keep the *Good Hope* afloat, if you didna ken."

The skipper stormed out of the galley, up the swaying companionway and into the wheelhouse. The motion was subsiding but the Norwegian Sea was still in turmoil and far too rough to cast the nets. In a filthy mood, Archie McGovan thought of the money slipping through his fingers on fuel, tax, insurance, wages, maintenance, net repair, and a dozen more expenses — while the nets were inboard. He shouted at the mate: "Go below, Brucie. We been havin' a council of war. Round it up, call a vote, an' come an' tell me what ye all want ta do. Ah'll go along wi' it." The mate hesitated. "Go on, man! Git!"

He was in one of the filthiest moods as he thought of the injustices that had been heaped upon the British fishing industry since Prime Minister Edward Heath, the biggest Europhile in the heap, had glorified the truth and taken Britain into the wonderful pastures that adorned the route of no return which led, ultimately and inevitably, to the slaughterhouse of nations.

At that time Britain, with so many other nations, was negotiating 200-mile-wide territorial waters for its fishermen. This would have given Britain four-fifths of the fishing stock off the western coasts of Europe, in waters which had traditionally been British by custom and by common sense drawing of boundaries. If Britain had claimed — and received — fishing grounds on the same boundaries which divided the North Sea oilfields, then she would have had even more.

But Heath was also negotiating with Brussels, which didn't want Britain to seize such a prize. So the Common Market ministers quickly concocted a clause giving every member state equal access to all Common Market fishing grounds. They completed the clause and incorporated it into the Treaty of Rome just hours before Britain formally applied to join the club.

Britain was hooked — but its fish were there for other nations to hook.

A long, long way down the line from that incident was the 1997 report which still wrankled with him, eight years later. A Lincolnshire fisherman (it had yet to be enumerated UK33) had a quota for sprats, as the official line was that there were no more herring in the North Sea. Yet when the man hauled in his nets he found 50 tons of herring mixed with his sprats. Obeying the regulations on conservation of non-existent stock, he threw all the herring back — dead — and managed to catch sprats the next time he cast his nets. But herring and sprats have always swum together and there were still a few of the supposedly extinct fish in his catch.

When he landed the haul in Grimsby an official of the Ministry of Agriculture, Fisheries and Food inspected them and found a few of the herring. He insisted on sorting through one basket of the catch, taking two hours to identify the few herring by using the official sampling method: stroking the fishes' undersides, as herring are smoother than sprats.

The fisherman calculated it would have taken him 31 days and nights, working continuously, to go through his entire catch that way.

Treachery and mindless bureaucracy all the way, McGovan reminded himself bitterly. Right. He would fight. He and the crew of the *Good Hope* would go to war on Europe with whatever weapons they had: a sixty-foot fishing boat, and six angry voices.

BRUCIE THE MATE came back to the wheelhouse with the crew's decision. "We're behind ye all the way, Skip. We can see what's been happenin' to the fishin' industry an' we're as sick of it as you are."

"So?" McGovan rasped.

"It's your boat, Skip. You make the choice on what's best for you. Whatever it is we'll go along wi' it. An' if you're thinkin' of making a bloody big catch an' sellin' them in Bergen, then scootin' off to the Isle o' Man, we're with you. If you want to go to America, we'll give it a try. If you want to go to west Africa, it's okay by us. We'll get our families out later, to wherever it is we end up."

McGovan drew a very deep breath and turned away. Grown men don't cry, especially fishermen. "Thank ye, Brucie. You'll never know what this decision means to me."

The mate gave the skipper a friendly punch on the forearm. "You can do a hell of a lot wi' sixty thousand Mickey Mouses. Why give it to the bloody fiscal in fines?"

They fished where they were for three days, filling their hold with baskets of cod and herring, with a scattering of whiting and mackerel, then headed for Bergen in the sovereign state of Norway to sell them.

When they put to sea again they knew that personal arrest and impounding of the *Good Hope* were the best they could hope for, followed by the stiffest fine the sheriff's court could impose — for they knew they were being spied on. McGovan had done the unthinkable and criticised the Disunion on the Internet, and his wife had been arrested. Thanks to the marvels of EGNOS, the *Good Hope*'s every move was being watched.

They sailed west by south, going north of the Shetlands, where the EGNOS navigational information suddenly ceased. Somebody, somewhere, had cut off their direction-finding aid, condemning them to rely on the old-fashioned sextant and chronometer. But the *Good Hope* was well-fitted, and found its way past the Outer Hebrides and through the North Channel by the Global Positioning Satellite. The boat docked in Douglas, in the Isle of Man, and her crew became the first commercial fishing refugees from the European Disunion.

NINE

LISA AND I WERE in Castletown, only a few miles away from Douglas, but we knew nothing of Archie McGovan. We had walked from our rented home in Castletown, east to the hamlet of Derbyhaven, passing the turf where the seventh Earl of Derby began racing horses. We climbed the little tump of Hango Hill, where Illiam Dhône, William Christian, had been executed, and we looked across to the elegant architecture of King William's College. The king had given his name to the place because he couldn't afford to give anything else.

We turned north at Derbyhaven the hamlet and walked north along the edge of Derby Haven the tiny bay, with the low-water mudflats on our right and the back of Ronaldsway Airport on our left. The road originally ran on to Ballasalla, where Anthony Callan lived, but an extension to the runway had cut across it. This was where I would board Callan's Cherokee if ever I took the dubious offer of a flight to England.

Now, with the tourist season killed and with no commercial flights whatever to the mainland, the airport was strangely quiet. The only traffic was with the Channel Islands, Bergen, and Switzerland, the weekly flights travelling half empty.

"Somebody over there flying model aircraft." Lisa pointed to the end of the tarmac road. I watched a small high-winged monoplane buzzing around the end of the runway, and I quickly saw the man who was controlling it as he turned to keep it in view while he played with the radio controls.

"Doesn't it remind you of something?" I asked Lisa.

"Not the fire-bomb? I didn't see it, if you remember."

"It reminds *me*," I answered, and was aware that my heart was beating faster. We walked a little quicker towards the model aviator and eventually saw him bring the machine in to a perfect landing on the end of the road.

He waved to us. There could, I knew, be absolutely no connection between this cheerful man in Derbyhaven and that vicious bombing attack on our home, but I was angry that I had been reminded. I suppose I ought to be back in Clacton seeing about getting the window replaced and the room redecorated.

We reached the little aircraft, parked innocently in the middle of the road to nowhere, and I guessed it was about the same size as the one I had seen coming straight at me. But thousands of model aircraft were the same size.

"Is there a model aircraft club in the island?" I asked.

The man shrugged. "Used to be. The guy that ran it shut it down a couple of months or so ago." Our ground-based aviator was around sixty and as bald as Ronaldsway's main runway.

"Why was that?" I asked innocently.

"No idea. Probably something to do with this business of cutting ourselves off from Europe."

My curiosity was insatiable. "The guy who ran the club. Do you know his name?"

"Aye. Callan. Lives in Ballasalla. He owns that plane you can see over there — the full-sized one, I mean."

I don't know how we got back to the rented house but as soon as we had shut the front door I gasped to Lisa: "We're leaving."

"Leaving? Where? What?"

"The island. We're going to Guernsey."

"Why, Terry? What's got into you? Just because you see a man flying a model aircraft?"

"You heard what he said. Callan — the man I met at Rushen Abbey — used to run the club, but he shut it down a few months ago — loosely about the time some murderous maniac flew a model aircraft straight at our house."

Lisa tried to comfort me. "You're being paranoid. There are fifty-odd million people in Britain and the Isle of Man. Think about it — there's a fifty-million-to-one chance that this man Callan tried to kill us."

"Not so, my dear. You forget one vital thing: my face is very well known. I'm a sitting target to any pro-Europe nutter. That must boost the odds by half a million to one. The woman at the airport told me that Callan is a merchant banker and he often goes to the continent on business. That makes him one of the pro-Europe nutters, and that boosts your odds by a hundred to one. And that brings it out at evens."

"Rubbish!"

I waved my arms in exasperation. "Look. *Somebody* did it. Somebody who knows something about model aircraft. Somebody with a damned good motive. Somebody who knows my face. When I told Callan my name over the phone I could almost *see* him gasp for breath. When I asked for a lift in his plane he didn't want to let anybody know about it. Don't you see? He could have shoved me out the door in the middle of the Irish Sea and no questions asked!"

"You're paranoid!"

"And you're blind! Are you coming with me?"

"Where?"

"Guernsey."

"No, Terry, I'm not. We've got Cat here with us, we've got a nice place with an option to buy. Why should we uproot ourselves again? It's not as if we're spring chickens."

I flung myself on the settee, frustrated by her determination. "Alright," I conceded eventually. "Alright. I've got to go back to London soon. Will you promise me one thing?"

"Keep the door locked. Don't talk to strange men. Yes, Terry, I'll promise all that. Now — can I start the dinner?"

THE *VIKING MAIDEN* brought me back to start the television programme for CCC. We had two brainstorming days in the Soho Square office, and the studio hurriedly prepared specifically for the relaunch of *Tell Tel*, in an empty warehouse somewhere in Docklands — I shan't give the location even now — behind one of the most disgusting front doors you could imagine. Dried-up dog excrement, general street filth, dying weeds and used condoms littered the doorway, but we carefully stepped over them to preserve the image of dereliction. The door was very secure, but it looked as if it hid nothing, not even a good night's doss.

There were four of us: Philip Andrews, the cameraman-producer recruited as much a part of the deal as I was; Mark and Matt, the researchers, inevitably dubbed the Heavenly Twins; and me. CCC had offered another two but Philip and I turned them down in view of our cramped quarters, although we would be grateful of them later. The top brass insisted on one sex, to avoid complications, although the European Union might have objected. On the street we all dressed in dirty clothes and looked like hobos — but I had to be the one with a decent haircut and smooth cheeks — and we smartened up a bit once we were inside. And there was always one person on duty at any time, day or night.

The studio was small but smart, and had its own built-in edit suite; the office had a fax, three phone lines, and we had direct access to the Internet and to e-mail. There was a complete but simple kitchen capable of near-gourmet meals, a large clock to compensate for the total lack of daylight, and a curtained-off bed. "I'll grab that if I may," I said. "I haven't fixed up accommodation yet, and the less I'm seen on the streets the better it'll be."

And there was a solid steel door: the company had done wonders to get all this ready in the short time since signing me up.

"Expecting visitors?" I asked Philip as he showed me the security systems. I shuddered as I recalled seeing that model aircraft crash into my bedroom window and burst into flames — and the one we had seen in the Isle of Man.

"None we can't handle, but we're ready for anything short of nuclear war."

I smiled. "I don't think it'll come to that." I counted to five then added: "Yet."

In those two days we thrashed out a format: the programme would be unashamedly anti-Europe and there would be absolutely nothing sacred. "We've hit the jackpot for starters," Philip explained. "The Heavenly Twins have found two MEPs who must have had a revelation from Heaven. They're both anti-Europe and they want to sabotage the set-up from within. They've got mini-video-cameras so we should get some interesting footage. But we're going to mask their voices and avoid identifying them in any way." He punched me lightly on the arm. "In fact, Terry, we're not even telling you who they are."

My hair prickled. More and more, I had the impression that we were all preparing for some sort of war.

"CCC has decided that the first few programmes will set the scene. Tell us how we got from thinking the Common Market was great-aunt Millicent in mufti, to knowing the European Union is the most dangerous thing to strike the continent since the Black Death."

I raised my eyebrows.

"They both creep up on you when you're not looking," Philip explained.

Finally, we were ready.

We recorded the first programme in one unbroken take, which must be unique in the circumstances. I began by laying it squarely before the viewers. "Good evening. I'm Terry Mason. Welcome to this first edition of the new-style *Tell Tel*, the programme that does for the European Union what Adolf Hitler did for the Zionist Pensions Fund. In case you don't know, this is the programme that the European Union closed down a few weeks ago, but we're back again, courtesy of CCC, Central Cable Channel, although we're going out all over Europe by satellite — so Wilcommen, bem-vindo, bienvenido and welcome wherever you may be.

"Apparently we went too close to the forbidden zone of European politics in the first series. This new series of *Tell Tel* plans to go much closer to that forbidden zone. We intend to penetrate it wherever and however we can to bring you the truth — the shocking truth — about the nice little Common Market and how it became the fearsome Euromonster that now rules our lives."

That was enough of my face. We cut to a film sequence showing the exteriors of the major EU buildings, starting with the Council of the European Union at 175 rue de la Loi, Brussels. It is a glass-fronted building on a corner site, supported by concrete pillars. Once you can accept modern architecture, it's not ugly. The EU's own literature described the Council of Ministers, the common name, as having supranational and intergovernmental organization, where ministers from the provincial governments (for which we once read 'national' governments) discussed a wide range of subjects from economy and agriculture to transport and the environment. The blurb stressed the 'democratic' nature of the council as its member ministers are elected, but my voice-over stressed they are voted in only as members elected to — for instance — the Westminster provincial parliament, from where they are appointed to serve on the Council.

My voice also explained the community legislation passed in this glass maze: several hundred *regulations* each year which, even before the United States of Europe came into being, were binding on member states and bypassed their own parliaments. Then there are around fifty *directives* which the emasculated parliaments could polish up a bit, but certainly not ignore. And then there are *decisions* which must be obeyed by the persons to whomever they are addressed, and the victims range from an entire region to bodies such as the Confederation of Industry (the old Confederation of British Industry and its counterparts), or to private individuals, such as Richard Branson or the millionaire fishermen of Whalsay in the Shetland Islands.

I had to add that in recent years the council had opened its doors a tiny amount to the proleteriat: some documents were available and some debates were shown on CCTV, but old-style democracy was still treated like venereal disease.

I quoted again from the Union's own literature and held its little blue book for the camera to see. "It says that *mainly* decisions should be taken either by qualified majority voting or by unanimity. But note that word *mainly;* if you keep *mainly* all the foxes out of the chicken run, you may as well let them all in.

"The Council works at three levels; *pillars,* they call them. Pillar One deals with major issues such as agriculture, and the Council can either adopt the Commission's ideas, change them, or throw them out. The other two pillars cover security, justice and home affairs, where the council has some say in making policy. But note — *you,* the voter, have no say at all. You don't even know who's in the Council of Ministers. Do you?"

Next, the European Commission building further down Law Street at number 200. This is where the dreaded twenty rulers of the continent lived and breathed and had their being — with the Polish contingent yet to be nominated. These twenty generated enough legislation to keep a staff of 1,500 clerks busy, on subjects such as completing the single market back in 1993, and drafting the legislation for the single currency from 1999 on, with 300 of them doing nothing but translation.

My voice-over said: "Although the commissioners are appointed by the provinces — member states before Armageddon — for five years, they have always been obliged by oath to put Union interests before those of their home. They listen to comments from business and labour — but they are not compelled to act on what they hear. Their only loyalty is to their master, the Union. Remember the Westminster MPs who paid attention — well, quite often — to the people who voted them in? Happy days!

"Can you go into the public gallery and listen in, like you can at the Westminster provincial parliament? Oh, no! You may see some of the paperwork it spews out, and you may apply to go into the building, but that's all."

Then we showed the European Parliament with its three homes, the Palais de l'Europe in Strasbourg; the edifice at rue Belliard, Brussels, which looked like a giant art-deco wireless set with a glass frontage rising to a semicircle; and the newest creation in the city-centre Léopold complex — plus the Secretariat in Luxembourg. My voice-over explained that the two original homes were created to avoid favouritism, and the entire 626 members of the parliament, plus those due from Poland, shuttled from one home to the next several times a year, taking *everything,* down to the last filing cabinet. The cost is phenomenal.

I explained that the Parliament started off with as much power as a neutered rat, but it's now required to 'express an opinion' to the commissioners before they can start their cauldron boiling to produce some more magic potions. And in some areas of business, such as the Regional Development Fund — and you know what 'regional' means — it can suggest alterations to the Commission's proposals. There's also a co-decision arrangement with the Council of Ministers. And it has to agree the entry of more member states whose governments want to commit political suicide. Probably its greatest power is the appointing of the President for a five-year term of office.

"Oh, yes: we mere mortals can petition Parliament if we think we've been wronged — but nowhere in this little blue book does it say that MEPs actually *make* laws. They're the only people we can vote for — yet they can't make legislation. Wonderful, isn't it?"

My voice-over added: "In Russia the president is elected by the people. In the Euromonster, with a population of 370-odd million, he's nominated by six hundred or so people and voted in by just twenty others. Who would have thought that the world's most bigoted

Communist state could now be more democratic than the Union, yet democracy was born in the province that was once the Greek nation."

Then we showed some of the lesser buildings; the Secretariat, the European Court of Justice and the European Investment Bank, all in the north-eastern district of Luxembourg. And my commentary warned that there were thousands of minor buildings and offices scattered around the provinces.

I came back on camera. "It's going to come as a shock to you, but the last meaningful general election held in Britain was way back in 1992, shortly after Margaret Thatcher was evicted from Downing Street. Her anti-European stance is well-known from Dublin to Athens, but the pity is, the average person didn't know *why* she was so bitterly opposed to Brussels.

"It's another pity she never told the common people. But why should she — *no* prime minister had been truthful about Europe since Ted Heath took us in in 1972. And were we taken in!"

There were film clips of Heath telling the nation there was no threat to our sovereignty, of Maggie at Bruges saying "No, no, no!", of Major saying in 1991 "There will be no referendum," and in 1996 saying "I have made it clear to the House on previous occasions that I believe a referendum on joining a single European currency could be a necessary step."

"By the 1997 election," I said in close-up, "the Euromonster had spread its tentacles so far that Westminster was already bypassed. The European Commission — made up, you will remember, of unelected bureaucrats answerable only to Europe — concocted its regulations, directives and decisions, and sent them out to its provincial and regional offices around the Union. The main one in Britain is within shouting distance of Parliament, but the two work completely separately. And during that '97 election there were more than 250 offices from Lerwick to Truro, pumping out Union propaganda and trying to influence the election in Europe's favour. My God, we needed Jimmy Goldsmith's Barmy Army, didn't we?"

The camera zoomed in even closer. "And by provincial I really mean national. Don't ever forget we're not a nation any more. We have been conquered by ignorance, and given away by politicians who should be hanged for high treason."

After a film sequence of the Storey's Gate office in London, I came back. "Remember I was telling you about the diktats churned out by the Commission? They are sent to Commission offices in every province and region, from where they're forwarded to the true victims of the latest Brussels laws: county councils, doctors, farmers, plumbers, signwriters, library assistants, students, fishermen, fairground buskers, education authorities, you name them."

Now we decided to go for the jugular. Computer technology faded my face to a grotesque skull with fiery eyes. In a voice like that of a Dalek I said:

"And don't forget. Back in 1997 as now, that was the law. There had been no consultation. There was no appeal. Do it — or pay the penalty. Many of the diktats were cruel, unjust, stupid, unworkable — but they were the law. And — to quote the little blue book again — they had had 'a detailed examination by experts.'"

We showed film of abbatoir owners driven out of business, fishing boats being burned on the beaches, factories being closed.

My normal face was back. "Of course, we had some benefits as well. Firms moved their businesses to Britain from France and Germany. Inward investment boomed. Do you know why? Because the British Government managed to hold back the worst of the flood of the legislation. Germany and France didn't. They were hit even harder. It became almost impossible to sack anybody in Germany, so companies daren't employ people. Unemployment began rising. Soon the German economy was in crisis — and it got worse..."

I paused for a dramatic breath. "Do you realise that in Europe if a company couldn't afford to pay a manager twenty grand a year, and contrived to sack him at great expense — if that manager then got another job at ten grand, his old company was supposed to make up the difference? It couldn't afford to pay him twenty grand for working, so it was supposed to pay him ten grand for doing nothing at all."

We went on for another fifteen minutes, ramming home fact after fact, things that the average Briton had never had spelled out until that moment.

Towards the end I tried to get the story into perfect balance.

"We're not attacking the German people. The average German didn't want a federal state. We're not hitting the French people. They didn't want it either. We're hitting the governments across Europe. They were the only ones who knew the truth, and they took us all into this ghastly mess. And now we're stuck with it. As Chancellor Kohl said back in ninety-six, 'We will make the process of European integration irreversible.' He also said: 'Might is right in politics and war.'"

We cut to a map of Europe, with national boundaries shown, and old familiar names such as Portugal and Austria. Then it faded to a map of the European Union, showing regional boundaries and the designating numbers of each region — all 193 of them, including those in Africa, Asia, South America and North America. Then it highlighted the free areas within Europe: Switzerland and Liechtenstein, Monaco and San Marino, Andorra, Norway and Iceland, and the eastern republics from Prague, Budapest and Ljubljana to the Urals. Finally we pointed out yet again that Gibraltar was free but Spain had included it in its seventeen regions; Europe itself had shown the Isle of Man as part of England which it had never been in its entire history; and the French Region FR25, Basse-Normandie, was laying claim to the Channel Islands.

"But our main attack is at the European Union itself. It has become an empire and, like all empires throughout history, it is power-crazy and land-grabbing. The British Empire was tyrranical and corrupt as seen through the eyes of a Kenyan tribesman and a Malay peasant.

"Now we know how those people felt. The European Empire is just as tyrranical and corrupt — and we are the underdogs. We are the modern slaves of Europe." The word came to me in a flash of inspiration. It wasn't in the script, and I didn't know it was used in the Falklands. "We are the slaves of Euroslavia," I cried, as the map burst into flames and the programme faded to its few closing credits.

Philip thumped me on the back "Very good!" he said in his typical understatement. I felt the tears come, and I cried for several minutes.

I cried for Lisa and Cat, still within Callan's clutches; I cried for the threat to my life, for the damage to our house, for the insecurity and stress of my new job, but most of all I cried for Britain, and for a Europe enslaved yet again. I suppose I cried for all the people of Euroslavia.

TEN

THE NATIONAL PRESS... how in God's name can I say 'provincial' press: that means the Glasgow *Herald*, the Staffordshire *Sentinel* and others. I mean *national* — British national.

As I was saying. The national press — the *Daily Mail,* The *Times* — went as big as it dared on the *Tell Tel* programme. To go too big would be to risk a major fine or even temporary closure — remember: the fishermen already knew that there is no such thing as free speech any more.

Central Cable Channel was also getting inundated with requests to show the programme again, and to transmit it in other European languages. There was an offer from ČeskoTV in Prague to broadcast the programme terrestrially and via its own shared satellite, which was different from the one CCC was using; this would give coverage deep into eastern Europe, warning people living up to the Ural Mountains about the facts of life in Euroslavia.

CCC saw the potential, not so much from a cash point of view — although the company was to make a million or more euros from the deal — but in the interests of public service. Starting three days later that original programme was shown twelve hours a day on the newly-accessible ČeskoTV satellite back-to-back, non-stop, the English version alternating with its subtitled German, Polish, Finnish, Romanian, Serbo-Croat and Magyar versions. CCC itself subtitled it into French, Spanish, Portuguese and Italian, the languages of western Europe, so that *Tell Tel* became the most accessible programme in the history of television. The trouble was, the title didn't translate: it became *Oigame* in Spanish, and *Mit Tel Europa* in German. It meant, literally, 'With Tel Europe' but when the words were merged into one, Mitteleuropa, it meant 'Middle Europe', which aptly described German's location. If you think that was complex you should have had several of the other translations explained.

Before we were ready with the next week's programme we were receiving messages of support from all over the continent. CCC had deliveries of mail by the bagful at Soho Square and after the first delivery asked Europost, the former Royal Mail, to screen it all for possible explosives. Two letter bombs were found that first day, but thousands of letters — and I mean, quite literally, thousands — were in support of what we were doing from our Docklands studio.

Other messages of support came in by phone to Soho Square and were recorded. Soon people had found the company's fax number and e-mail address, and messages came in in a steady stream. Days later, CCC began receiving responses forwarded by ČeskoTV, many of them in languages which the CCC staff couldn't even recognise, let alone translate. A tiny selection of them all was sent down to us in the Docklands studio by unmarked courier.

"My God!" Philip gaped. "What have we started? Seems like half the country wants to get out of Euroslavia, Terry."

The Heavenly Twins started sorting for items worthy of inclusion in later editions of *Tell Tel*. "We've got the germ of a programme here, Phil," Mark suggested. "All these protests from all sections of society, and these are from Britain only. Opposition to Euroslavia is right across the spectrum: factory workers, farmers, fishermen, housewives, businessmen, professional types, redundant military, even some politicians. It's bloody incredible!"

"How many opposed?" Philip asked.

"Just look." Matthew pointed to a heap six feet in diameter and knee high. "They're in favour of getting out, if we can." He pointed to another heap which wouldn't fill a waste-paper basket. "They're Europhiles or don't know, or I can't bloody understand what they're saying."

Philip nudged with his toe at an even smaller pile. "What are these?"

"They back us, and they're worth following up." Matthew picked up a fax. "Listen to this. It's from the Chief Minister of the Manx Government. I'll read you a snatch: '...very pleased to learn somebody is at last prepared to organise a resistance to the European Union. You may like to know that the Sterling Zone islands are doing all they can...'"

He skimmed the next few lines, then: "'We are not aware that the British national press has reported that the Kingdom of Mann, the States of Guernsey, and the States of Jersey, received an ultimatum from Brussels demanding that all accounting be done in euros, effectively phasing sterling out of international trade. As a result these independent territories, plus Gibraltar and the Kingdom of the Falkland Islands, have refused to recognise the euro.'"

"I know," I said. "I had to use the *Viking Maiden* to get back to Britain."

"Hold it, Terry, there's more. 'You will be saddened to learn that the major oil companies will shortly suspend transporting crude oil from Saudi Arabia and the smaller Gulf states to the European Union, because of possible major faults in the supertanker fleets. It is suspected that metal fatigue may have made several steel plates in the hulls liable to fracture without warning. As a result, all major bulk carriers will be withdrawn from service to allow structural checks to be made.'"

"Wow!" I gasped. "So they've done it!"

"Done what?"

"Sorry. I'm talking out of turn."

"There's more. You want it? 'The Manx Government can also report that yesterday it was delighted to receive one billion US dollars of investment from the Kingdom of Saudi Arabia. It is understood that the two Channel Islands and Gibraltar are receiving similar investments, which have been withdrawn from the Bundesbank in Frankfurt and the European Investment Bank in Luxembourg.'"

Matthew drew in a deep breath. "I don't know what we've started with this little telly programme, but I have a feeling it's already too late to stop it. Saudi has declared economic war on Euroslavia: what the hell do you think brought that on?"

We called for some of that support which CCC had offered, and two youths came down, bringing their own sleeping bags and enough food and water for a fortnight. "Soho Square thinks it's too dangerous for anybody to be seen on the streets unless absolutely essential," one of them announced. "So we're here for the duration."

They had brought more letters, faxes, and e-mail printouts of support, from all around the British provinces and those on the continent. In the batch we found a fax from the Kingdom of the Falkland Islands, but it was in code. Hours later we found an e-mail with the key to the code, and we deciphered the main letter. Philip read it. "'...Ambassador has negotiated an agreement with the Royal Saudi Government and the major oil producing companies operating in that country to suspend sales of oil to the European Union unless payment for such sales can be made in sterling.'" He choked with laughter.

"That's rubbing salt into the wounds, isn't it?"

Philip read on. "'The Ambassador has negotiated similar agreements with Kuwait, with Bahrain and with the United Arab Emirates. It is also announced with regret that supplies of petroleum products will be interrupted due to the need for structural surveys to be made....' We know about that already." Philip gasped. "What do you make of all that?"

I said: "It's the best example I've ever heard of the biter being bitten. Good for Mister Ambassador!" Seriously, I added: "But it takes us back to 1974 and the oil embargo."

"Christ! I know that! But what effect is it going to have?"

"Hey, *you're* supposed to be the quiet one! Effect? It'll hit the euro economy hard. Very hard. Europe's only got about sixty million barrels of accessible reserves..." I met Philip's questioning gaze. "Alright.

EUROSLAVIA

I did some research on oil only a few weeks ago. So it's going to hit industry and transport. The euro's going to dive. There's going to be increased tension across the Union. Unemployment will rise..."

"And winter's on the horizon. People will die of cold. Transport will be hit..."

"Hey," I said. "Do we know *why?* Why are the gulf states turning off the taps? Surely it can't be anything that Falkland has said?"

"What about Falkland oil? We'll still get that, won't we?" one of the new researchers asked.

"Of course not. They'll probably come up with the defective tanker scare as well. It'd be interesting to know if tankers going to other parts of the world have these risky plates in their hulls. Frankly, I very much doubt it. Don't you see? This is the first turn of the screw to get Britain out of Euroslavia. We'll have to suffer like everybody else, but it'll be worth it to get our freedom."

"What about North Sea oil?"

"I've heard that the Falklands are sending some free petrol to Norway, as an inducement for the country to turn the taps off, although Euroslavia will still have Britain's share." I drummed my fingers on the desk. "This is ruddy good news, lads. But can we find out what's really behind it? That's where the real story is. And what about Iraq and Iran? Will they make up the shortfall? I can't imagine all the tanker fleets having problems."

Philip smiled, back in his usual good humour. "Don't forget, Terry — it's the oil companies that make the sales, not the producing countries. There'd be no point in the other Gulf states cutting supplies if Iraq and Iran could just take up the slack. Either that ambassador knows a thing or five, or he's managed to get the major producers on his side. Say — who is this the ambassador, anyway?"

Mark read the letter again. "Name's Hutchinson." He took the *Statesman's Year Book* off the shelf. "Hutchinson," he began, but I stopped him. "Hutchinson? Not Brian Hutchinson?"

"The very same."

"Ye Gods!" I snapped my fingers. "I went to school with him. Well — he was two years older. Brilliant lad. Got nine distinctions in School Certificate. Even took his own typewriter into class. Went to university to study Japanese, then joined the Foreign Office. He's a wog, like me."

"A wog?"

"Wisbech Old Grammarian. I came across him on his last posting when I was writing a guide book on Malta. He was something in the British diplomatic service there. How did he get to Port Stanley?"

Mark grinned. "Walked, by the sound of it." He consulted *Who's*

Who. "Retired to Jersey. That's the last we know." He dropped the book. "Feel like renewing old acquaintances? Maybe you could get the inside story?"

I laughed. "It's certainly worth a try."

WE MADE A HABIT of recording every incoming phone call, which proved vital the next day when CCC shunted through a call from Soho Square.

"Ah'm Archie McGovan," the voice said, and I'm sure we would have missed much without that recording. "Ah've just arrived in Douglas in mah boat, the *Good Hope*."

He told us what he knew: he had posted a letter on the Internet and as a result the Spanish Army had come up from Edinburgh Barracks and raided his home on his first night at sea. His wife had been detained in Edinburgh Castle but had later been allowed home. She was affronted, shocked and insulted by her treatment, and had waited anxiously for a letter she guessed was important.

"She's got it, the noo," McGovan shouted. "She's got the whole database o' the Referendum Party membership from the ninety-seven election."

"How, in God's name?" I asked.

"Dinna ask, an' ye'll hear no lies. The Referendum Party doesna know, but that's all Ah'm prepared to say."

"What are you going to do with this database, Archie?" I asked.

"Wha' do ye think, mon! Write ta them all an' suggest we lead a mass rally on Brussels. A hundred thousand people. Maybe two hundred thousand. Ye like the idea?"

I glanced around the room and saw that everybody was listening in on the loudspeaker. "I like the idea very much, Archie. A hundred thousand people marching..."

"Not marchin', mon. That's yesterday's talk. That's Jarrow, that's Aldermaston. We drive. We all go by car."

I whistled. "When?"

"Soon as I can post all the letters."

"You ought to be the first member of the public to know, Archie, that there's an oil embargo on the way. Most of the Gulf states are refusing to supply Euroslavia. You haven't got time to post out a hundred thousand letters. You'd better start your rally as soon as you can, and tell everybody to take spare cans of fuel."

We all heard his dismay.

"Ah cannae do it in the time. The bloody Dagos have pinched ma computer."

Philip nodded to me: I knew what he meant.

"Shall we do it for you, Archie? Make a story of it on the telly? We've got access to satellite all over Europe, certainly as far as Moscow, an' I guess they'll screen the programme all day."

"All *day?* Christ, man! I get chased by the Dago army for puttin' somethin' on the Internet — they'll crucify your lot if they catch 'em."

"Maybe," I said, and I had to acknowledge the truth in the fisherman's logic. "First, Archie — where are you calling from?"

"Douglas, Isle o' Man."

"Isle of Man! My wife's in Castle..." I stopped. This man sounded genuine, but I couldn't be too sure. "So you can speak your mind?"

"Aye, but if Ah ever set foot in Euroslavia — that's a damned good name, Mr Mason — Ah'm likely to be arrested for tellin' the truth. Sixty thousand fine in funny money."

"Okay, Archie. You stay out of Wonderland for a while. How's this: we tell your story — why you've quit fishing, why you posted what you did on the Web. Tell us some home truths about the fishing industry. Tell us why you want a hundred thousand motorists to drive to Brussels."

McGovan was on the point of exploding. "Christ, man! Don't you *know* why?"

"Sure I do. Why do you think we're doing this programme? But we want it in your words." I'd thought of something while I was talking. "Ever heard of the Festival of the Dead?"

"Only the tons o' dead fish Ah have to tip back into the sea."

"Festival of the Dead," I said again. "*Fête des Morts*. The French make a big thing of it. All Saints' Day, November first. Public holiday. A million people across the country — sorry, *province*; when will I learn? — a million of 'em go to the cemetery where their dear departed are buried. They make a day of it, maybe driving half way across France to get there. A million of them, all in their Sunday best and loaded down with children and grandchildren, and armfuls of flowers."

"So?"

"First of November. How about holding your Brussels rally on the same day?"

"But people won't be able to go to both events. Surely that defeats the object?"

"If your appeal gets a million motorists protesting about Euroslavia, nobody'll get to either event." I paused. "Think of it. Total chaos. It'd give Brussels something to think about."

McGovan grunted slow approval. "But could we get a million motorists to turn out?"

"Who knows? If your story's good enough; if they think it's worth the effort. If they're fed up to the eyeballs with Euroslavia..."

"Could be more than a million," he mused. "Could be half the motorists in Europe. God! That's millions!"

"I know."

"The last of 'em won't get within miles o' Brussels."

"I know that too. But it doesn't matter. It's the taking part that counts."

"God! It would make them European Commissioners shit scared."

"You'd better ask your drivers to bring food and drink for a week — no: make it a fortnight — just think of the disruption, man!"

"Ah am thinkin'. Either you're as mad as they come, Mr Mason, or it's a bloody good idea."

I smiled. "I agree with you."

"But wha' do these people want? Wha' are they goin' ta Brussels *for?*"

"What do *you* want, Archie?"

"Ah want an end ta the Common Fisheries Policy."

"Is that all?"

"Hell, no! Ah want ta get out o'... Euroslavia? Ah want ta stop bein' chased by Spanish ships at sea an' Spanish soldiers on land. Ah want ta keep the fish Ah catch, an' no' throw 'em back, dead. Ah want ta know there'll be a British fishing industry in five years' time, because the way things are lookin' now, there won't. The Eurobloody people want ta kill it off completely — every last boat, every last net. And for why? Do ya know?"

"I have an idea, but please tell me."

"Because they want ta replace it wi' a European fleet. That's why. Any fisherman sailin' out o' Britain will have ta fly one o' them *stupid* blue flags wi' all them gold stars on it. It's a bloody insult, man! An' Ah'll tell ye more. Ah want ma gerrl to grow up in a free country, like Ah did. An' Ah want it ta be the same country — Scotland. Britain."

"Where's your wife, Archie? Where's your daughter? Are they in Scotland?"

"Hell, no! Ah radioed 'em ta meet me in Oban, west o' Scotland, and Ah picked 'em up on ma way down ta Douglas, here. We're free o' Euroslavia, thank God."

"Right. How can we contact you, Archie? But be careful with your answer."

He gave me his ship's radiophone number, then rang off.

In the studio, we stared at each other as if we'd just won the British Lottery. Finally I spoke. "Can we really pull it off?"

"You mean, a mass protest drive to Brussels? A million cars blocking the city? Three million? *Ten* million? Have you thought of the downside?"

"I'm thinking. Emergency services couldn't get through. There'll be people die of heart attacks, old age, hypothermia."

"Dehydration."

"Not so much in November. There'll be babies born in cars. There'll be crashes, road rage, breakdowns. People will run out of food, cash, petrol."

"What about the people in Brussels who support Euroslavia? The majority of them do. Same in Luxembourg. It's only in France and Germany that you've got forty-odd percent opposition. The believers would probably barricade the autoroutes to keep the protesters out."

"Okay," I said. "So we don't block the city centre. We block all the access routes, five miles long — ten miles, maybe. *Fifty* miles. We keep them blocked for a fortnight. Will the government fall?"

Philip shook his head. "No way. Not if we barricaded it for a month. The faceless few aren't answerable to anybody. Long before two weeks are up they'd bring in the bulldozers and clear away the blockade. Then you'll have your millions of motorists without their cars, but still with the payments to keep up. You'd have riots."

I smiled. "Riots. Against Euroslavia? Not a bad idea. But don't forget — on top of this we have an oil embargo, the collapse of the euro, and the jewel in the crown: winter." I shrugged. "Can you think of anything better?"

Philip sighed. "Frankly, no. But I think Archie Whatsisname got it right — you're as mad as they come, Terry."

"Put it to the top brass in CCC. Let other people make the big decision."

THE TOP BRASS in the Eurosicherheitsdienst was so greatly concerned about the satellite relay of *Tell Tel* that he called his three heads of departments in for a special conference.

"We have to stop this at once," Teutoburger thundered, as if he were still a serving officer of the former Wehrmacht. "This is verging on treason and this Mason character is heading for extremely dangerous waters." He counted on his fingers. "There are several places to intercept the transmission. One, in the studio, but that could be anywhere in Europe."

"Or even outside it, sir," Casbergen suggested. "Such as Switzerland." Nobody queried his statement that Switzerland was not in Europe.

"Two, between the studio and the transmitter. The actual video tape could be sent by courier, or the thing could be sent digitally over land lines. Three, in the satellite station before it's beamed up. Four, there's a million-to-one chance of putting the satellite out of commission."

"Perhaps slightly drastic, sir?," the head of political surveillance suggested.

"Very drastic," Teutoburger agreed. "Five. The receiving television sets. They all need a scrambler device: could we immobilize them?"

Franz Casbergen, the Belgian-born head of security systems, shook his head. "They need to have the appropriate microchip, sir, like we have in computer modems and most telephones. There's nothing in satellite unscramblers. It's something we'll have to look at, sir."

"We have to act *now*, Casbergen."

"Then I suggest we knock out the earth station, sir."

Teutoburger stared at his head of section. "Are you *mad*, Casbergen? You can carry an earth station in the back of a car. Television news teams do it all the time. So where are you going to look? Every car park in the Union?"

"But it takes power, sir. If you're transmitting quality pictures all day, strong enough to be beamed back to a footprint half the size of the continent, you need power. You can't carry that in the boot of a car. And you can locate one that size by intercepting the beam."

"Then find the earth station, Casbergen! And put it out of action."

"Sir. I'll start work on it right away, sir."

Christine Bouderon, head of criminal records, felt sick at the casual way in which her boss could suggest yet another intrusion into the private lives of Eurocitizens. Wasn't it enough that the scheme to implant microchips into each newborn was well into its experimental stage?

She felt Teutoburger's eyes on her yet again. "Christine! Perhaps you have some bright suggestions on how to stop this catastrophic satellite transmission?"

"My field is criminal records, sir, not spy in the sky. But surely the best way is to stop it at source? Give this Mason a warning he'll never forget."

The President of the Eurosicherheitsdienst nodded slowly. "Yes, Christine. Prevention is better than cure. But it would have to be more than a warning. We would need to eliminate this Mason, but would some other fanatic spring up in his place?"

Bouderon felt herself shudder. She hadn't meant political assassination.

"We know the company which is broadcasting him. CCC. We know everything there is to know about the company, down to its issued share capital. But we don't know which studio it's using."

"Why not?"

"I'm working on that, sir. Our office in Centre Point in London is trying to infiltrate CCC, but it's not easy."

"Tell them they *must* come up with results. Then all it needs is a well-placed bullet or a bomb."

Bouderon closed her eyes. She had started the groundwork but she didn't want to be responsible for this Mason's death — *my* death. For all she knew, this Mason was just some mutt who had been talked into issuing all this anti-Europe propaganda. But surely, she thought, he had a right to his views?

"Follow it up, Christine," Teutoburger smirked. "And you other gentlemen, follow your own lines of investigation. But get one thing clear: we stopped this programme once before. It must be stopped again — permanently, this time. If necessary, Mason must be killed."

THE AMBASSADOR to the Sterling Zone bowed to the waist as he was ushered into the presence of the President of Iraq, Chairman of the Revolutionary Committee and Council, and Prime Minister — Saddam Hussein.

The president continued writing at his desk, apparently oblivious of his visitor standing loosely to attention in front of him. The Ambassador had seen it all before, notably in the Far East, and he spread his balance evenly, switched his mind to his home in Jersey, and waited. He could wait half a day if needed, without showing strain.

Eventually it was Saddam Hussein who lost his patience. "So," he said in Arabic, bringing his interpreter hurrying forward. "You wish to present a petition?"

Brian Hutchinson said: "I wish to offer my greetings and best wishes to you, Mr President and Chairman, as this is the first time I have had the honour of greeting you." And that, the ambassador thought, is about all I can offer you; there is no way I can talk about reciprocal deals involving technology to make fuel from hydrogen. And if I could, I wouldn't.

"Indeed it is. Pray continue." Saddam Hussein lounged back in his chair and looked up at his visitor, standing beside the guest chair but making no move to occupy it without invitation.

The formalities would be a repetition of his approach in Saudi Arabia, Hutchinson knew, and wondered how people in high office could find so much time to waste. When it came to discussing facts, he began: "The European Union is facing economic crisis, Mr President."

"So?"

"If your country has any funds invested in Frankfurt..."

Saddam Hussein leaned forward, still not inviting his guest to sit. "Do you think I am stupid enough to let those Nazranis get their hands on any of my money? I well remember how they treated the poor and sick of my country after our mercy expedition into Kuwait."

"Of course, Mr President." But the Ambassador recalled a hint that the Saudi Minister for Petroleum and Mineral Resources, Sheikh Ibn-al-Houri, had passed onto him in a later phone call. Iraq, said the sheikh, still had a billion US dollars in Frankfurt. It was not much, but it was more than Saddam Hussein could afford to jeopardise. "However, as my duties take me around the Gulf states, I felt it incumbent upon me..." He saw the interpreter hesitate, and said instead: "I thought I should warn you, Mr President."

"And why, Ambassador, do you choose to warn my government about your government's financial position?"

"No, sir. If I may explain, I do not represent Britain. I have no connections whatever with the European Union."

"No?" Saddam Hussein leaned forward. "None at all?"

"None at all, sir. I may add I am personally saddened that my country has been swallowed by Frankfurt and Brussels. I represent the small islands of the mid Atlantic which still trade in sterling." He paused. "In fact, Mr President, I can tell you that these countries, though small, are sovereign states, and are among the world's leading financial centres. Douglas. St Helier. St Peter Port. Gibraltar. Port Stanley. You have heard of them, of course."

"Of course. And Grand Cayman."

"You will, no doubt, be aware of the strength and stability of sterling." It was a statement; the Ambassador daren't infer that Saddam Hussein was ignorant of anything.

"Indeed. So where does that involve me, Mr Ambassador?"

"Not one of these sovereign states was involved in the trouble with Kuwait." And that was true, he thought; none had a single soldier of its own. Britain handled their defences.

"So?"

"We all speak English but we are all independent of Britain and Europe. We are inviting investments from the Arab World, the oil producers, the growing economies of the Pacific rim, Mr President. We are able to offer much better results than Frankfurt can, as our little nations specialise in financial services — except for the Kingdom of the Falkland Islands which, as you will know, is rich in oil and fish. Frankfurt's financial services are subject to many competing influences, such as the major unemployment problems of the European Union."

"I had heard of those problems," Saddam Hussein murmured, and the Ambassador thought he saw a cynical grin.

"I can arrange for some of our financial advisers to discuss any problems any potential investor nations may have, or any loans they may contemplate."

It's damned hard work talking to this character, the Ambassador told himself. I'm glad I wasn't part of his human shield.

"I will consider your suggestions, Mr Ambassador, but for now you must excuse me. As you see, I am very busy." Abruptly, the audience was over and Ambassador Hutchinson realised he was going away with nothing. There would be no Iraqi oil embargo against the European Union. Saddam Hussein picked up his pen and continued writing. The interpreter backed away, unsure of what to do until a servant came in, bowed to the President without receiving acknowledgement, and escorted the Ambassador out of the presidential presence.

Damn! Brian Hutchinson thought as he emerged into the open air once more.

I PHONED THE House of Keys in Douglas and asked for a contact for my former schoolmate, Brian Hutchinson, and received a string of numbers. I tried the Falkland Islands first and a clerk in the government suggested I concentrate on Saudi Arabia.

I did. On the third call I located the Ambassador's home in Riyadh and left a message. Two days later his secretary called me back to state that the Ambassador didn't remember me at school and could not speak directly to any member of the Press; all questions should be directed to Port Stanley.

I went back there and the original clerk said she thought she might be able to tell me something, sometime. I'd had that kind of response many times during my career in journalism and recognised that it meant whatever you wanted it to mean.

Two days later she surprised me by phoning the number I'd given her, in the Dockland studios of *Tell Tel*.

"Mr Mason? I can tell you officially, on behalf of the Government of the Falkland Islands, that Bahrain and Kuwait have told us through our ambassador that they've given notice to the Deutsche Bundesbank and the European Investment Bank that they're withdrawing all investments — I repeat, *all* investments — and currency from the European Union."

"God Almighty! Thanks. Can I use this on television?"

"That's why I'm telling you, Mr Mason."

"Thanks again. Hey — I just remembered. One of the Investment Bank's jobs is to make sure Europe gets its energy. Somebody there must be messing his pants at this news. Do you happen to know where the money's going?"

"The Sterling Zone and the Cayman Islands," she said, and the smirk was detectable seven thousand miles away. "Best of luck."

"Thanks very much, Miss... Keep us informed, will you?" But the line clicked dead. I turned to the studio. "Wow! We're really on our way!"

I phoned the Isle of Man again and spoke to Lisa in Castletown, but she wasn't as interested in international finance as she was in the skipper of the *Good Hope* who was making the news in the *Manx Courier* and on Manx Radio. "He wants to lead a motorcade on Brussels and block the city's roads until Euroslavia collapses. By the way, darling, that's a lovely name. Did you think of it?"

"Until Euroslavia *collapses*? He didn't get that from us: does he realise he'll have to wait a hundred years?"

"But it's a good idea," she protested. "You should get together."

"It is and we have. We're pushing it for all it's worth this week, but it's only one battle. I don't see it's going to win the war. There'll be lots of battles before that happy day."

"Talking of battles, do you know who bombed the house? Do you still think Callan was involved?"

"I'm working on it, darling," I lied.

KEYSMAN ANTHONY CALLAN landed his Piper Cherokee at a private airstrip near Uttoxeter and used his mobile phone to report his arrival to the local police; he was, in the eyes of the European Union, coming from abroad. "But not for much longer, I hope," he told himself. Then he called the local taxi service and was ferried to the town centre. He got out by a stone water conduit which marked the spot where the old Dr Samuel Johnson had stood bareheaded in the rain as a self-imposed penance for refusing to stand on that same spot as a boy, and help serve at his father's bookstall.

Callan was wearing an old raincoat and a battered trilby hat, as far from the expected attire of a wealthy merchant banker as he could contrive. The man he met was dressed slightly shabbier, but not too disreputable as to attract the attention that neither man wanted.

"Robinson," Callan murmured in greeting; neither shook hands, nor looked each other in the eye.

"Mr Callan," Robinson acknowledged as they strolled off into the backstreets of the small Staffordshire town. Everywhere was quiet as Callan had been careful to avoid a day when Uttoxeter was in the racing calendar.

"So what went wrong, Robinson?"

"Wrong, Mr Callan? Nothing went wrong. I chose a time when he was home. The aircraft went straight through a bedroom window an' exploded. Hell of a mess. I wonder the house didn't catch fire."

"And then?" Callan probed, his voice harsh.

"Mason and his missus came bursing out the front door. I was about a couple of hundred feet away. They jumped into their car an' came straight at me."

Callan never varied his pace, nor turned his head. "Straight at you, man? What do you mean? He tried to run you down?"

"Yeah. You could say that. So I had no choice, did I?"

"No choice about what?"

"I shot him."

"*What?*" Callan stopped, but continued walking a moment later; there must be nothing about this meeting to raise the slightest interest in any casual passer-by. "You shot him?"

"Had to do something. He tried to kill me."

"So you tried to kill him instead. And, luckily for you, you missed."

"How do you know that, Mr Callan?"

"Because Mason has been to see me."

Robinson stopped. "How could he? I never spoke to him. I never told him anything. How could he link you an' me?"

"Keep walking, man. I never said he did link us. I said he came to see me. He obviously hadn't the remotest idea I was behind the affair. And it must stay that way, Robinson — do you understand?"

"Yes, Mr Callan. But he *is* a menace. He's back on the telly again, goin' on about Europe. Euroslavia, he calls it."

"I know. I've seen the programme. So you failed, Robinson. You failed dismally."

"Failed, boss?"

"The idea was to scare him off. But you failed. Now he's back again and doing a hell of a lot more damage than he was doing before you started."

"I was only following your orders, boss."

"I did *not* order you to shoot him. I have no intention of being an accessory to grievous bodily harm, or to murder. Is that understood?"

Robinson sighed. "Understood, Mr Callan. You're the paymaster."

"And don't you ever forget it. Now, I'm calling the whole thing off. I'll look after Mason myself. He's taken his wife and family pet to live in Castletown. The irony of it is, Robinson, you didn't scare him enough to quit his propaganda; you only succeeded in scaring him out of Clacton. You scared him right into my clutches in the Isle of Man."

"Christ! What a coincidence!"

EUROSLAVIA

"Coincidence nothing. He felt threatened within the European Union, and quite rightly. He didn't know who was attacking him; it could have been the Security Service for all he knew."

"Security Service, boss? Who runs that?"

"Never you mind. He did the most sensible thing from his point of view: he got out of Europe. The Channel Islands are rather expensive, so he opted for the only other place going. And he found himself a house right on the edge of the airport."

"But the airport's closed, isn't it, Mr Callan?"

"Only for a while. They'll see their folly pretty soon, and open it again."

"But the Falklands have stepped in, haven't they? Sending oil and cash to these little places?"

Callan steered their route so that they would return to their starting point by Samuel Johnson's faucet. "And part of that is Mason's doing. As you rightly say, Robinson, the man is a menace. But I have ways of stopping him, far more effective than your bungling."

"How, boss, if I might ask?"

"His wife. He'll do anything for her."

Robinson smiled. "Ah! You want any help?"

"No! Not from a trigger-happy maniac like you. Your orders are to pull out. I don't want to see or hear from you ever again." Callan had been watching the backstreets and as they passed a car-parking bay that was not overlooked, he snatched Robinson's right arm and twisted it behind the man. "You scream and I'll break your wrist."

"I ain't screamin'," Robinson moaned as he was bundled into the recess. Callan used his free hand to give Robinson a thorough frisking but he found nothing.

"I don't normally carry a gun, Mr Callan."

"It's the tape recorder I'm thinking about." Finally he found it in Robinson's trouser pocket and pulled it out. "So. You believe in insurance, do you? So do I. Your payoff's here, two thousand euros in mint-condition fifties, and you won't find a single fingerprint on them."

Still holding Robinson's arm, Callan pulled a manila envelope from his overcoat pocket, held it by the corner and waved it above his head, scattering rust-coloured banknotes around the parking bay. As they fluttered to the ground, Callan put his foot to Robinson's bum and sent him staggering forward. The Keysman's last sight of his former accomplice was of Robinson sprawling onto rough tarmac.

He took a taxi from Johnson's conduit to the airstrip and touched down at Ronaldsway Airport eighty-five minutes later.

EUROSLAVIA

I CALLED THE House of Keys again and got through to the Chief Minister. After the introductions I told him the news about Kuwait and Bahrain and stunned him into silence.

"Sir John? Are you there?"

"Yes. But this is fantastic, Mr Mason. You know there's a load of petrol on its way from Morocco? And the people down there in the Falklands have offered us financial help for the loss of trade and tourism? But more Gulf States! This is wonderful news indeed."

"The name's Terry, by the way. It's not going to be too much money to handle, is it?"

"How much is involved, do you know?"

I laughed. "How long is a piece of string, especially when you stretch it from earth to the moon? But what about this Archie McGovan? Does the House of Keys go along with his campaign to block the streets of Brussels?"

"If he can help restore democratic government, and take power back to the people, we support him."

"Thanks, Sir John. I hope you can watch the next edition of *Tell Tel*."

WE OPENED THE PROGRAMME with the now standard greeting, "Wilcommen, bem-vindo, bienvenido and welcome," which led into an update of the news. After the story of Bahrain and Kuwait's notice to withdraw all funds from Frankfurt, I said: "The Japanese Government learned of Saudi's move and announced in the past hour that it is also pulling out all its investments in Frankfurt. This obviously doesn't mean it's moving its car factories out of Britain — that's impossible. It means that Japan is taking back all its capital held in reserve in the Investment Bank, and is slowly selling its Eurostocks."

We showed the usual picture of the gaunt concrete exterior of the Bundesbank in Frankfurt, and the EIB in Luxembourg, looking like a concrete-and-glass layer cake.

"You will remember that Saudi Arabia was the first country to announce its withdrawal of funds. The money markets are notoriously fickle and suspicious, and any move like this is watched extremely carefully around the world. Now that two more oil states have decided to follow, this may well bring about a worldwide rush to get cash out of Euroslavia. It's a pity that people and countries can't be pulled out with the same speed."

We cut to a short clip of people running around the EIB's corridors, looking like tellers on the London Stock Market before it went computerised, and then emasculated when Britain's foreign reserves took that one-way journey to Frankfurt. Then came a clip from dear old Hengst Berghofer, the financial commissioner whose letter to the Sterling Zone had started the collapse: but this was official film and amounted for little. I should explain that we had to borrow the film from the BBC. You would expect Berghofer to say it was only a temporary run, a blip, and nobody should worry.

And then came the guts of the broadcast. We threw in an interview with skipper Archie McGovan and his wife Helen aboard the *Good Hope*. Lisa in Castletown had set it up, and actually done the filming with a borrowed digital camera but without a tripod, which explained some of the camera shake. Then McGovan had sailed to Llandudno to deliver the cassettee to the wife of one of CCC's production team, who had driven with it to London. CCC had made a copy before sending the digital pictures by land line to our undercover studio in the docks area.

It was worth all the effort. The skipper stood on the foredeck of the *Good Hope* and said in his poshest accent, cutting out much of the Aberdonian brogue: "I'm now goin' to risk a fine of sixty thousand euros, fifty thousand pounds in real money, for speakin' out an' tellin' the truth. I say the bloody Common Fisheries Policy is aimed at bringin' the British fishing industry to an end. There — that's worth fifty thousand quid in anybody's money."

The camera pulled back to show a box of fish at his feet. "When I was fishin' out of Aberdeen I had my set quotas, an' I had my set fishing grounds. There are so many rules an' regulations that it's damned impossible to go to sea an' not break at least one.

"F'rinstance, I catch one cod — *one flamin' cod* — more than my quota, an' I bring it ashore. The fisheries inspectors are there waitin' for me. They find I'm over quota an' take me to the sheriff's court. An' I'm fined fifty thousand. Pounds, not that other trash."

There was a library shot of a Scottish sheriff's court, the equivalent of an English magistrate's court.

"Or I falsify my ship's log. I dinna — do not — mean to do it, but it just happens. It's a tiny thing — I miss loggin' that we got a radio call from the fisheries inspectorate. When I get back, the inspectors are there. They go through the log an' find that I didna log in the call — an' I'm up before the sheriff. Fifty thousand again. But *why* are the fisheries inspectors waitin'? Because I spoke out against Euroslavia's fishin' policy, that's why. So if I want to stay in business, I keep my mouth shut. Now, you tell me if that's a restriction on freedom o' speech?"

Lisa, bless her, cut to Helen McGovan. "Most fishermen have mortgages on their boats. They have heavy bills to pay. If they canna pay the fines, the bloody bailiffs seize their boats or their homes. Can you imagine it? Families an' kids out on the street, an' with winter comin'?"

Back to McGovan. "The Spanish are the worst. They rake up everything in the sea — they've been doin' so for years: it's why the Med's empty. But when they get back to Vigo or wherever — no fishin' officers. They're all in bloody Madrid, miles from the sea. So the fishermen land fifty tons of over-quota cod an' nobody bats an eyelid." He leered. "Ah guess that's another fifty thousand quid?"

We had a shot of the *Good Hope* from the quayside, then McGovan added: "The Spaniards mortgage their boat in the Bahamas, let's say. They live in Spain. They have a Bahamas limited company to cover everything. They go over-quota but they needn't cart it back to Spain. Suppose they land their catch in Britain. They're taken to court. Ah! But the skipper doesna own the boat! The company does — and the mortgage people. An' they're in the Bahamas as well. There's nothin' the bailiffs can seize. So the Spaniards get awa' with it." He paused for effect. "An' if I stand in Liverpool an' say what I've just said — that's *another* fifty thousand quid."

The camera cut back to me, pretending I was talking live to McGovan. "So what do you want to do, Mr McGovan?"

An edited bit of film replied: "I want ta get out of Euroslavia. Right out. If a farmer criticises the Agricultural Policy, he doesn't get a fine. Not yet, at least; it may come. If a reporter criticises anything, they call it investigative journalism. As long as it's not Europe he's having a go at. But we fishermen have ta shut our mouths or we're clobbered. Is that fair?"

"It certainly isn't, Mr McGovan," I said. "And how to you propose to get out of Euroslavia?"

Lisa had been feeding McGovan a few questions; we edited his answers to make it seem he was answering my live query.

"I want to make Brussels an' Luxembourg — an' Frankfurt, for that matter — sit up an' tak' notice. I want to have a protest march. But not a march on foot — that's history. I want people to go in their cars to Brussels and them places. Take enough food an' water an' bedding an' petrol to last a fortnight, at least. It'll take that long."

"A protest by motorcade?" I suggested. "How many cars?"

"We might get a hundred thousand cars. We might get a million. We might get half the motorists in Euroslavia. But it'll show them unelected bureaucrats just what the ordinary person thinks."

"And when do you want to do this?"

"Start out the middle of October. Got to allow plenty o' time ta get to Brussels. And we've got ta remember that, the more cars we get, the less the chance o' gettin' all the way. But that doesna matter. If ye get stuck in a queue of protesters twenty miles from Brussels, that says a hell of a lot more than if ye could drive right into the city centre."

"Certainly does," I agreed.

"Mid October, then. Wherever you come from, aim to get to Brussels or Luxembourg on Hallowe'en, the night the witches roam. Couldn't choose a better time. An' then bring the place to a standstill on All Saints' Day."

"Many places will be closed," I cut in. "It's a public holiday in most of Europe. It's the Festival of the Dead in France and Wallonia. It's *Allerheiligen* in Germany and *Todos los Santos* in Spain — All Saints' Day."

"An' we'll be as holy as the rest of them," McGovan boomed. "If we can sit it out for a week, or two weeks, or longer, it'll show them buggers in Brussels what we think."

"Will you be there?"

"I'll be there. I'll risk bein' arrested an taken to the sheriff's court. The most they can take is the hoose; I've got the boat an' the family an' all our cash in the Isle o' Man, where it's stayin' as long as Scotland's a bloody province o' Brussels."

We cut off the interview there and I faced the camera to ram home the challenge.

"There! McGovan's Motorcade. The target is three million cars. Three million private cars descending on the Euro capitals. We'll block the roads. We'll bring the cities to a standstill. It certainly won't be enough to bring down Euroslavia, but it'll be a start. People power can do wonders; it helped bring down the Berlin Wall, to end Communism in Russia, to stop the Chinese plundering Hong Kong. Let's see what it can do to bring down the Brussels autocracy and bring democracy back to Europe!

"If you can make it, plan your arrival at least a day early; two or three days early may not be pushing it too much, because the roads will be jam-packed, not only with the motorcade but with the Festival of the Dead. And bring absolutely everything you need — food, water, clothes, and above all, plenty of fuel for the car. You can expect the price of petrol to double when the service station people see the crowds — and don't forget how we opened the programme. There's an oil crisis on the way. Above all, remember that winter's coming. It could get very cold. We'll be covering McGovan's Motorcade on *Tell Tel*, so I hope to see you there."

As we went off air I had a massive presentiment of evil descend on me. Within hours, Euroslavia would know what was coming, and could prepare against it.

Producer Philip Andrews managed a weak smile. "We're sitting on the cliff-edge of history, Terry. Is the cliff going to give way, or shall we have a wonderful view of events that may change the world?"

I punched him lightly on the shoulder. "Don't get so ruddy poetic. People are going to *die* out there in McGovan's Motorcade."

ORSON WELLES TERRIFIED the United States with his radio broadcast of *The War Of The Worlds*. Millions of British viewers saw the Coronation in 1953. Millions more watched the first moon landings. Yet the satellite broadcasts from CCC's earth station somewhere in the English Province, and from ČeskoTV's earth station near Prague of the second programme in the new *Tell Tel* series must have had the highest viewing figures ever known in Europe — even allowing that the Czech programme was again screened back-to-back, with subtitled translations in the eastern European languages, complementing our versions in the languages of the west.

I like to think the viewing figures were two hundred and fifty to three hundred million within Euroslavia, counting multiple viewings as one. I know that most of the Europhobes across the continent wanted to do something positive to tear their nations from the grip of Brussels.

There were protests everywhere, from small villages in Greece to a spontaneous rally that blocked Trafalgar Square for hours. There were marches in many cities, some collapsing into riots as supporters of Euroslavia battled with opponents.

It is impossible to list every protest because nobody could have counted them, but later estimates said maybe ten million people took to the streets that day, and more than four hundred of them died or were injured in the protests.

We sat in our bunker-studio shocked into silence as we heard reports coming in by radio and on CCC's phones and video links from Soho Square. None of us could have dreamed there was so much pent-up resistance, despite what the opinion polls had been hinting until they were officially silenced. We knew only one thing for certain: from now on, Euroslavia's days were numbered.

AXEL TEUTOBURGER WONDERED if he had already gone to hell. Casbergen's team of electronic surveillance experts had been waiting for several days for the next appearance of *Tell Tel* and within minutes of its appearance they were tracking the source of the transmission. Soon Casbergen's team showed him a map of Prague and pinpointed a village to the north.

"Čakovice, sir. That's where it is. Somewhere within a hundred metres of here." The team leader made a neat pencil cross on the map.

"You're sure?" Casbergen snapped, but without waiting for an answer he hurried into Teutoburger's office. He pushed past Christine Bouderon and thrust his map on the cluttered desk. "There, sir. Čakovice."

Teutoburger glanced up at him. "Then shut it down."

"How, sir? It's in the Czech Rep..."

"I don't care if it's on the moon, man — shut it down! Bombs, guns, bows and arrows if you like, but *shut it down!*"

Casbergen stepped back. "Sir."

Teutoburger answered yet another phone call. "Yes! We've just located it, commissioner. Čakovice, just outside Prague....Yes, sir. We're going in with a team." He put the phone down and glanced up as Bouderon, with her honey-blonde hair hanging down beside her beautiful face, came into his office. "Ah, Christine. This man Mason. Isn't it time you were ready to move your men in?"

"CCC is no newcomer to the security business, sir. Our people in London have tried infiltrating, they've tried bugging the phones, tapping the lines, using directional microphones from across the street. They've got plenty coming out, sir, but not a mention of this Mason."

"What are you getting, then?"

"Scheduling discussions, budgets, holiday arrangements for Christmas, office chit-chat. If this Mason's being talked about at all, it's confined to a soundproof studio, sir."

"Then you'll have to find a way of getting into it, won't you? What have you been doing all week, woman — sitting there with your fingers in your knickers?"

"We are dealing with experts in the espionage business, sir."

"No, Bouderon — *we* are the experts. Everybody else is an amateur compared with us. Find the English earth station — where they transmit to their satellite. Find Mason's studio. Put a tail on every person who leaves CCC's office, day or night. Kidnap one of the staff and threaten to tear her guts out. Put a bomb under the MD's car. Christ, woman! Use your imagination! Stir the *Scheize* in Centre Point."

"In person, sir?"

"In person, Christine. Catch the next flight to London, and put the fear of God in those pimps you call agents. I want *results*. If I see this Mason on the screens once more I'll drag you by your knickers from here to Helsinki." He closed his eyes as the illusion sank home: he couldn't imagine a more pleasant way to spend a day. When he opened them again, she had gone.

He answered two more phone calls then told his secretary not to route any more through unless they were from the President of the

Commission himself. Then he sat back to think: up to now he had been chasing events; he had to get in front of them if he were to check the flood of protest.

He played our *Tell Tel* broadcast again and thumped his desk when he saw me advocating three million motorists to converge on Brussels. "Got you!" he shouted. Then he pressed the intercom to summon his immediate staff. "Casbergen! Come here at the double!"

A frightened voice answered: "Mr Casbergen has gone, sir. He said he was going to Prague."

"Damn." Another intercom button. "*Bouderon!*"

The executive in command of criminal records hurried in. "Sir?"

"Before you go to London, see that a statement is issued to all media in Brussels and Luxembourg. Press, radio, television. And the Internet — why not?"

"But that's not my department, sir..."

"This is an emergency. If I say it's your department, it's your department. This statement: from 2200 hours Europamittelzeit on Sunday October 30 to 0200 hours EMZ on October 31, and again from Monday October 31 to Tuesday November 1, *Allerheilige, Fête des Morts*, all vehicles in Brussels city, Brabant, Hainaut and Namur, in Luxembourg region and province, and in Champagne and Lorraine, are to have their batteries disconnected. That's regions BE1, BE31, 32, 34 and 35; LU; and FR21 and 41. Got that?"

She stared at him, wondering if he had tipped over the edge into insanity. "Order people to disconnect their car batteries, sir? Might I ask why?"

"No, Bouderon, you may not. You're not paid to query my orders. See to it right away."

She paused. "But..."

"*Do it!*"

Still she paused. "Disconnect batteries, sir? People are going to wonder why. Can we give them any hint...?"

Teutoburger bared his teeth in a swelling fit of rage. "Tell them anything you like. Tell them the Martians are coming, for all I care. And think up some suitable penalty for every motorist who doesn't immobilise his vehicle."

"Sir." She clicked her heels in arrogance, mocking the Nazi salute. "I'm sorry, sir. That order does not come within my competence, and I query, sir, that you have the authority to issue such an order that — if you'll forgive my saying so, sir — has no apparent purpose."

Teutoburger's face turned purple. "Insolence! Insubordination! That order is full of purpose but it is not for my juniors to question my moves. And of course I have the authority. I *am* the

Eurosicherheitsdienst. I am not answerable to Parliament, or to the Council of Ministers. I am answerable only to the President of the Commission, as we all are, and I already have his orders to quell these riots by whatever means I deem suitable. Now — go!"

She paused, staring into his eyes for an eternity which stretched to five seconds. Then she subsided. "Yes, sir. But I must register that I do it under protest."

"Protest noted. Just get the job done."

XAVIER YZURDIAGA WATCHED *Tell Tel* in Spanish on the television in his luxury home in Sant Julià de Loria in the tiny principality of Andorra, and felt his heart pounding with excitement. A motorcade of protest to converge on Brussels and Luxembourg! Brilliant! He guessed he could fill three XYZ coaches of Basques who were desperate for liberation from two masters.

He wrote a brief note on his computer and faxed it to his office in Zarautz; it was the most secure way of communication, but nothing was secure these days. And, much as he liked Andorra, he felt imprisoned in this tiny country of just under five hundred square kilometers — a hundred and ninety square miles — where the only road climbed from eight hundred metres at the Spanish border to 2,407 m at the watershed of the Pyrenees.

Andorra had been independent since the Middle Ages but until the close of World War Two it had been an insignificant place.

The all-weather road changed all that. Tourists began pouring in, and hotels and shops began serving them, still without taxes. Until 1970 the vote was restricted to third generation males aged twenty-five and more, and thereafter there was a quota system for Spanish and French nationals who wished to work there. Yzurdiaga applied for permission for himself and his wife Victoria in 1986, thinking he may need to escape the anti-terrorist organisation. But Victoria hadn't joined him as she found the mountains too oppressive.

By 2000 the little land had all the trappings of civilization, such as two embassies, its own police and post office, and its General Council of 28 members. The 17,000 Andorrans were overwhelmed by 45,000 foreigners — but the Valls d'Andorra stayed outside Euroslavia and so served Xavier Yzurdiaga.

For the eighteen months since Staqui Arrieta had driven him into this hideout, over that watershed from France, Yzurdiaga had been running his company by computer and fax from the relative safety of this most southerly village in the country. He daren't present himself at the Spanish frontier just two kilometers downhill, for fear of being arrested; neither dare he enter France. Only once since he had arrived had he left the tax-haven, and then it was by hiking over the Port de Cabús and down to the tiny hamlet of Tor in Spain. And he didn't want to repeat that experience.

He watched my programme until he could almost recite it; the comments about Spanish fishermen didn't please him, but he had to admit they were truthful. He wasn't surprised that *Tell Tel — Oigame* in Spanish — would stir up public sympathy, but he was not expecting to hear of protests in the streets so soon.

Spain, especially the industrial regions of Euzkadi, ES21, Cantabria, ES13, and Catalunya, ES51, had led the disruptions. The television showed crowds of men and youths, with a scattering of women, marching down Las Ramblas in the heart of Barcelona, shouting *Abajo Europa!* and *Sin Trabajo!* — Down With Europe and Jobless.

He tuned into French television and learned of riots in regions FR81, Perpignan; and FR62, Toulouse and Carcassonne. Men were carrying banners and placards protesting against high income tax and the loss of hundreds of jobs in the aerospace industry. And some had slogans in English proclaiming *Down with Europe,* obviously playing to the worldwide television audience.

When he read the fax from Zarautz, he nodded. His staff confirmed they could certainly fill at least two coaches of protesters to Brussels, carrying all their food and luggage beneath the floor. Yzurdiaga nodded again. This time he would risk border crossings and join the protest; perhaps he would collect the Semtex and have a party, but he certainly wanted to be there if it were going to be the end of Euroslavia.

FATHER ERICH ZIMMERMAN was horrified to see the television pictures of popular unrest. He knew it had to happen, but he had thought it would be after his time. Now it was back again, as it had been through recent history, especially when that Austrian corporal was building his empire on hatred, revenge, and the desire to seize other people's territory.

And he knew very well the factor which was common through every protest: the will of the people was being denied. Chancellor Kohl had refused the German population the chance to vote on the *Einheitswährung,* the single currency, and his successors were reaping the harvest.

Wir wollen Freiheit! roared the crowds in Munich, and on the television in Zimmerman's rented room in Zürich. "We want freedom!"

An old man was drawn from the crowd to the microphone. "What freedom do you want?"

"The freedom to run our own country without interference from other people. Why should Italy and Spain tell us how to do things? What does Greece know about fishing in the Baltic? And why can't we have our Mark back, instead of this euro?"

"Do you realise that many other people in Europe accuse Germany of ruling everybody else?"

"I know they do, but it's rubbish. We feel like an occupied territory again, just like in 1945. We want Germany to be German!"

"Will you take your car and drive to blockade Brussels?"

"Haven't got a car anymore, otherwise I would."

The interviewer found a young woman. "What are you protesting about?"

"It's impossible to get a job. The employers have to pay almost as much in taxes as they pay their staff, and if business goes down they can't afford the redundancy pay. So they don't hire us at the start. We should be like Britain was."

"You can move to another part of the Union and find a job?"

The girl laughed. "Have you tried it? Too many unemployed in Spain — you wouldn't get a job there. Same in Italy, same in France. Any case, I can only speak German and English. Forget it."

"So why are you protesting?"

She leaned towards the microphone as the background noise intensified. "I don't want to be a second-class citizen in my own country. Years ago we brought in thousands of Turks to work in the factories. Looks like I may have to go to Turkey to work in the tourist trade. Why should I? Germany was once great. Now we have to share everything with everybody else — but there's not enough to go round."

"Will you drive to Brussels?"

She nodded. "There's a party of us going, yes."

Father Zimmerman switched off the television and stared at the blank walls surrounding him. He was now eighty-eight, sitting in a grim little room and waiting for death to creep up on him with its blessed relief.

"I'm going too," he whispered. The words didn't shock him so he said them again, louder: "I'm going, too! I'm going to march on Brussels and if it is God's will I'll help bring down the Devil, the *Urian*, Euroslavia."

ELEVEN

"I'M GOING TO BRUSSELS," Annette Dugard shouted in French as she saw television coverage of riots and street demonstrations across the continent. "I'm wasting my time in Alderney; I should be back in France, where I belong."

But how to get there?

Sitting in her rented apartment in Château à l'Etoc on Alderney's northernmost tip, she looked out of her window and saw the smudge of France's Cotentin Peninsula on the horizon, almost hidden under grey early-October skies. The urge grew; she had to do what she could to help France in her hour of need.

She phoned the Mesuriers in St Anne and got Fiona. "Have you seen the television?"

"I'm watching it now. I don't know whether to laugh or cry — do you?"

"I'm going to do both, to make sure," the French girl sobbed. "There — it's tears first. But I'm crying happiness if it's going to be the end of Euroslavia." She paused. "I'm going home, Fiona."

"To France?"

"To Montmédy. To La Meuse. To Region Forty-one."

"Why, Annette? What can you do?"

"First, I'm going to join the...what's it called? McGovan Motorcade? I don't know what I'll do yet. If I'm lucky I'll be like another girl from La Meuse — Jeanne d'Arc. She fought for her country."

"She died. Pretty horribly, too."

"Maybe I'll die also, Fiona, but it's a cause worth dying for. Don't you feel it in your heart?"

"Yes, but not that much."

"France has surrendered to Germany three times in a hundred years: 1870, 1914, and 1940. Now it has done it a fourth time, but it happened so slowly we can't give a date. France is *France* — it is not Europe! It is not Denmark, nor Finland, nor Greece. I'm going, Fiona. Wish me luck."

Fiona le Mesurier, the Hampshire lass who had married into Alderney society, asked: "How will you get there? Who will you go with?"

"I don't know yet."

"Come and talk it over with John, and Peter Carteret."

"He's the other island man on the States of Guernsey?"

"Maybe there'll be other people wanting to go from here, or St Peter Port. Maybe from Jersey. You can't just rush off. For a start, how will you get to Cherbourg — swim?"

"But I *must* go. I want to be there on the outskirts of Brussels by Hallowe'en. By the *Fête des Morts*."

FRANS CASBERGEN HAD no military background, yet he was under orders to put the ČeskoTV television earth station in Čakovice out of action. He asked around his staff in the electronics surveillance department until somebody suggested he recruit a small detachment of Austrian troops from the two battalions stationed in the Tempelhof area. He made the arrangements by phone then took an unmarked minibus from the ESD motor pool under the mock church beside the Kristallkoffer in the Friedrichstrasse.

The detachment was waiting, ten soldiers dressed in casual civilian clothes and looking like a group of youths about to go raping old ladies or starting a riot at a football match. The officer in charge was an *Unterleutnant* named Fischer. It took two minutes for Casbergen to realise the sub-lieutenant had seen no active service at all and resented the idea of infiltrating a friendly foreign country to commit an act of sabotage.

"We've got to take out one building, that's all, Lieutenant," Casbergen explained as the soldiers reluctantly clambered aboard the minibus, dragging miscellaneous canvas bags with them. "What's all that stuff?," he added, pointing.

"You don't want us to *push* it over, sir? How big is this place? What does it do?"

"Size — no idea. Pretty small, I guess. It's an earth station. It beams television images to a satellite."

The lieutenant stared at him and his unfriendly manner changed to hostility. "Not *Mit Tel Europa?*" He gave the German title for *Tell Tel*.

"Yes," Casbergen agreed.

"Sir." He clicked his heels, the closest he dare come to imitating the Nazi salute to a senior officer.

Casbergen felt his temper rising. "Your insolence and insubordination are noted, Unterleutnant Fischer. You will be hearing more of this incident. The Eurosicherheitsdienst demands that this building be put out of action, and you are under orders to carry out the mission. That is all."

"Because it is speaking the truth, sir?"

Casbergen grew livid. "Truth? This ČeskoTV is filling the airspace with malicious lies and so it must be silenced — do you understand?

You are an officer who has sworn loyalty to the European Union, are you not? I am a senior officer of that Union. I command you to follow orders."

The Lieutenant slowly rose to his full height, clicked his heels again and this time gave the Nazi salute. "*Zu befehl, Herr Oberst*," he snapped, mocking the subservience of German officers during the Hitler regime.

Casbergen's vision faded briefly as his anger rose to fever heat. He felt his right hand balling into a fist, but he managed to control himself. "You are a traitor to your nation, Leutnant Fischer. Now move!"

"My nation is Austria, sir. Vienna. Region AT13, as the Europeans insist on calling it. I cannot be loyal to a power which usurps my nation. My grandparents lived through the first *Anschluss*, now I have experienced the second. I will obey your orders, sir, but I do not agree with them."

"My God, man, I'll have you strung up for insubordination!"

"As you wish, sir. May I ask for your instructions?"

"Get this show on the road. While we're heading south, work out a way to immobilise this building."

The lieutenant looked from his tactical survey map which marked Čakovice as a village just north of Prague, then up into Casbergen's eyes with an expression full of resignation. "Is it in open country, sir? Is it in a village? Is it guarded?"

Casbergen realised the difficulties he faced. Teutoburger, with his military experience, would have been able to blow up a building, but Teutoburger was overwhelmed with security problems from a Europe in crisis. "I don't know, Leutnant. I don't know. Just let's get going."

They heard the sounds of street disturbances as they passed the Schönefeld district of southern Berlin, then the autobahn was clear. Casbergen was worried because the lieutenant appeared to be giving no further thought to their task as they approached Dresden.

Dresden was in turmoil.

They came in from the north and saw smoke rising from the city centre. Casbergen wondered if it was like this in February 1945 when British and American bombers destroyed the historic city and killed 35,000 people, but common sense told him this was minuscule in comparison. They drove cautiously into Neustadt, the New Town of the Communist era, where Casbergen felt sick at heart at the scores of uniform blocks of apartments. He could imagine himself growing up into a hooligan if this was all he had to look at. He wasn't surprised to see gangs of youths fighting each other in the no-man's-land that surrounded these concrete monstrosities. Probably they weren't fighting over Europe; they could have been fighting just to relieve the monotony of ghetto life, or the hopelessness of unemployment.

They tried to cross the Elbe by the Marienbrücke, but the banners being waved like weapons showed them that this was, indeed, a battle over Europe.

"Turn around," the lieutenant shouted to his driver, but suddenly the minibus was caught in the turmoil. As sticks and fists hammered on the bodywork and the soldiers inside dropped onto the floor, the driver reversed out of the crowd, an awful lurch telling them all that they had driven over somebody.

The driver stopped, but Casbergen yelled: "Keep going! They asked for it!"

Leutnant Fischer looked in disgust at Casbergen as he refused to let the driver investigate. And then the mob was chasing them, and reverse gear was not fast enough. The driver swung the steering wheel in an attempt at a handbrake turn, almost overturning, and smashing sideways into a car whose driver was also trying to escape.

They were back in Neustadt. As the soldiers stayed on the floor, the driver was navigating by instinct as he hurled the minibus around corners until he shot out onto the Dimitroffbrücke, the bridge leading to the city centre.

Casbergen saw the road was clear, as riot police were keeping the gangs at bay in opposing sidestreets. Then a burning bus forced its way through screaming crowds and lurched into the main road, where its fuel tank exploded. The lieutenant saw an opening on their left and screamed at it; the driver swung the wheel and headed for an alley beside the restored Hofkirche, the royal cathedral.

It took them onto the Neumarkt, the New Market, littered with burning vehicles. The driver knew his life may depend on getting out of that place so he raced across the open market place, bouncing over kerbstones and crunching on glass bottles. They scarcely saw the Frauenkirche, the Church of Our Lady left as rubble from that day in 1945 until restored to its original at the end of the Twentieth Century with the aid of virtual imagery.

Tyres screamed as they took a wrong turn in Leninplatz before heading south on the Wienerstrasse.

When they were once more in open country, heading into the Erzgebirge — the Ore Mountains — and the frontier with the Czech Republic, the soldiers clambered back onto their seats, looking nervous. Casbergen took the opportunity to give a brief lecture.

"You saw that? That's what's likely to happen all over Europe if we don't destroy this building. It's spreading propaganda all over the continent."

"Sir, it's allowing the voice of democracy to be heard," the lieutenant said loudly enough for everybody to hear. "Why has the European Union always denied freedom to other opinions? Why is it afraid of truth? Why does it follow so slavishly in the footsteps of Nazional Socialismus — *sir*? Why has Germany not allowed a referendum?"

"For the same reason that your country didn't!" Casbergen snapped.

"The truth might come out, sir? At least, you grant that Austria is still a *country*. Sir."

The road climbed the wooded slopes of the Ore range and at the crest they came slowly to a stop at the frontier crossing, where a Union customs officer and a Czech customs and immigration officer shared the moderately-quiet border post.

"Been here before?" Casbergen asked the driver.

"First time, sir."

They were all expecting trouble if anybody should ask to look in the canvas holdalls that lay beneath the seats.

The Union man waved them through. "Trouble in Dresden?" the Czech officer asked casually.

The lieutenant nodded. "Riots in the streets. Cars on fire. We got caught in the thick of it."

"Terrible shame," the Czech replied. "It's a pity to see the European Union go that way."

"What do you mean?"

"It was designed to end wars, wasn't it? Now it looks as if it's starting one." He checked all passports and waved the bus through.

They rolled down the Ore Mountains, bearing the first dusting of winter's snow on the Czech side. "What exactly is in those bags?" Casbergen asked Lieutenant Fischer.

"Grenades. And two Beretta 12S submachine guns with four magazines of forty rounds. Do they meet with your approval, sir?"

"As long as they stay out of sight, Leutnant."

In the late afternoon the smoky skyline ahead hinted of Prague's industrial zones, still not completely clean although the Communist era ended fifteen years ago.

"Go to the town centre," the lieutenant told the driver, giving Casbergen a sideways glance as if inviting him to countermand the order. "Then we'll look for the E48 to Stettin — Szczecin, or however it's pronounced."

The Hradčany area in the city centre looked like a chocolate box come to life. They saw the ninth-century castle on its hill, and were amazed at the one-third scale Eiffel Tower which — they were not to know — was built just two years after the masterpiece in Paris. And then they were in the industrial suburbs where gaunt factories and even more gaunt housing blocks stood side by side for mile after dismal mile.

They came to Čakovice at dusk. It was once a charming village but it had fallen under the Communist hand of heavy industry, and all beauty was gone.

"So where is this television earth station, sir?" Unterleutnant Fischer asked with a hint of insubordination as he waved the driver to stop on a strip of derelict land beside the road. "What are we looking for? The conventional satellite dish pointing at the sky?"

"I imagine so."

"And where in the town is it, sir? Or shall I tell the soldiers to fan out individually and look?"

Casbergen could scarcely contain his fury. "That would be the better idea, wouldn't you think? It might test the capabilities of your military skills to their limits."

"Eurosicherheitsdienst!" the lieutenant mumbled sarcastically as he ordered his detachment to get out. "Slouch," he said quietly. "We're civilians. Wander round and look for this ČeskoTV place. Come back within half an hour — and not all at once." He turned to Casbergen. "You surely can't hide a satellite dish," he said.

"YOU SURELY CAN'T hide a television studio," Christine Bouderon told the staff of the European Security Service in their luxurious office suite in Centre Point, the tower block which rises from the northern end of London's Charing Cross Road.

"We've been searching for a week," the head of department explained. He was Malcolm Hawes, a rugged man with an industrial background and now two years short of retirement. "We're limited by practical as well as legal constraints, madam."

Bouderon nodded, recalling the authoritarian manner that her boss Teutoburger had adopted. "And quite right too," she agreed. "So, to sum up: you know everything there is to know about Central Cable Channel, to the rent it pays on its offices. And you know everything about every one of the thirty-seven staff from the chairman to the tea lady. You have snitch photos..." She paused. "Snitch or snatch?"

"Snatch, madam," Hawes confirmed.

"Snatch photos of each one of them, except the chairman, and you have rebuilt a curriculum vitae of each?"

"That's correct, madam."

"And *yet* you cannot find a single talk of this Mason? Are you certain you have the right company?

"The CCC logo is on every *Tell Tel* programme, ma'm."

Bouderon paused. "But you cannot infiltrate a spy into the offices?"

"Not a hope, ma'm. The company's small enough not to want too many recruits, and it isn't going to hire strangers at a time like this."

"Then cannot you turn one of the present employees? I can authorise you a ten thousand euro bribe."

"Not enough, madam, by a long way. This Europe issue's very big with the British these days. I doubt we could buy inside information for half a million."

Bouderon gasped. "Half a million euros? Are the English so loyal to a dead cause?"

Hawes never flinched as the words *dead cause* hit him. How could this foreign woman understand a Briton's desire for independence, for the return of the country that had been stolen? He could trace his ancestry back six generations down an Anglo-Saxon line: indeed, he *had* traced it back as a gift to his daughter-in-law when she presented him with his first grandchild. He had been an ardent Europhile for years, but his enthusiasm had begun to wane after Britain was forcibly shown the advantages of joining the single currency during Blair's term of residence at 10 Downing St, midway in the Presidency of Neil Kinnock in Brussels. Hawes had seen the results of the loss of sterling at first hand: the collapse of the City of London as a financial trading centre: the demise of the yuppies, the bankruptcy of Lloyds and the closure of that monstrous office block which looked like an oil refinery. Perhaps, he thought, that was the only advantage of joining the euro. He had noted the closure of pubs and wine bars, of sandwich bars and cafes, and seen the FLAT TO LEASE signs go up in the Barbican — and stay there.

And when Tony Blair was himself appointed as the English Province's Commissioner to Europe, Malcolm Hawes knew that his loyalty to the European Union had taken its final blow.

Yet he had to keep up a pretence of loyalty; at his age he would never find another job at even a tenth of the salary, for if he left the ESD he would be a marked man. He was keeping his chair warm until retirement, and dreading that somebody might suddenly pull it out from under him.

"We know, ma'm, that everything to do with *Tell Tel* is done behind locked doors — security-locked — and nobody mentions a word of it outside that door."

"Does Mason operate behind that locked door?"

"We're absolutely convinced that Mason never comes near Soho Square, ma'm. He, and the production team, are operating from some studio quite some distance away. And there's the problem."

"And there, also, is the weak link, Mr Hawes. There *must* be somebody who goes from the square to this studio. Find him, or her, and you find Mason."

Hawes shook his head. "Not so easy, ma'am. Once or twice a week, at random times, half a dozen people will come out of CCC's doors all at once. They're all carrying a briefcase chained to their wrist and they all walk off in different directions."

"So follow them. One at a time if need be."

"We've followed all six, ma'am. We've got nowhere. They turn back as soon as they realise we're on to them."

"You're security service people, for God's sake! If you can't follow a suspect..."

Hawes raised a finger. "What do you do, ma'am, when your suspect suddenly turns around and comes back at you? Then does the same five minutes later? Your cover's blown."

"We *must* find this Mason. It's desperately vital." But even Bouderon found the doubts growing in her mind. This company had gone to extreme lengths to protect the presenter of its top show. Was it doing so purely for financial reasons — or because it believed that Europe was a monster that should be destroyed?

I CALLED ARCHIE McGOVAN on his ship's radiophone and asked him to call me back on a safer landline. He returned the call within ten minutes, full of excitement.

"It's gonna worrk, isn't it, Terry?"

"What is?"

"The motorcade, man! Ah've been in touch wi' the Channel Tunnel boys an' they'll give priority ta anybody goin' ta Brussels."

"Archie — two points. Can you talk like you did when my wife videoed you, so I can understand? And why should Eurostar go out of its way to help?"

"Duty free sales, man!"

"It never had them before."

"If we get rid of Euroslavia an' go back to bein' Britain again, mebbe it can get duty frees. Clever thinkin'. The ferries'll help as well. They'll put on extra sailings from the middle o' the month. I'm gettin' plenty o' calls from people that's goin'."

"How the hell can people call you? How do they know your number?"

"Your lady was good enough ta let the name *Good Hope* show on the screen. There's a radio-phone directory. How do people contact you?"

"With great difficulty and only through CCC. I've still got a price on my head."

McGovan laughed. "Aye! An' so have I! Fifty thousand quid — sixty-two thousand five hundred euros, to be precise. On each count o' speakin' my mind."

"My price is higher than that," I said. "My life."

"God, man. Ah didna ken."

"So when does the Motorcade start rolling?"

"Some have gone already. They want a ringside seat. There'll be more of them set off next week, then we should start to see it take off — I hope. Soon as I know how it's goin' my boys are gonna load three or four cars on the deck o' the *Good Hope* an' ship 'em over to Wales by night. There's several Manx people goin'."

"Who?"

"One carload from the Gov'ment here. Faulds — he's the Prime Minister, sort of. There's a Bridget Norris. Runs a shop — ran a shop, I should say. Got a chest like the figurehead o' the Cutty Sark, an' then some. Some guy called Callan. Couple more whose names I canna remember. Don't know any o' the others."

"Callan?" I felt my heartbeat increase. "A Keysman?"

"That's him. Know him, Terry?"

"I've met him," I said, with a tone that tried to send him a warning. "Look, Archie. I know next to nothing about the man, but he doesn't need to travel with you. He's got his own aircraft at Ronaldsway Airport."

"Oh. Mister Moneybags, eh?"

"Probably more than that. Mind if I give you some advice? Don't ever turn your back on him."

Archie laughed. "He doesna look like one o' them!"

"For God's sake — he's not gay! It's just that I wouldn't trust him as far as I can spit with my mouth closed."

"Point taken, lad."

"And another thing. If you're taking Callan, whatever else you do, Archie, don't let my wife step aboard the *Good Hope*."

"Oh. He's a ladies' man. Sorry I got it wrong."

"You've *still* got it wrong. In plain English, I think he's the one who put a price on my head. Now do you get it?"

"My God, Terry, I do. I'll watch him like a hawk."

As I put the phone down on McGovan, Philip answered the red phone, the hot line from Soho Square. Staff there had been scanning all satellite transmissions from whatever source, as we expected Euroslavia to respond to the menace of McGovan's Motorcade. Now Philip snapped the phone down and logged one of the computers onto the Internet.

Philip knew just what he wanted and within moments we were watching a film. After a few flickers we saw a smart woman behind a news desk, talking what I knew to be Dutch, although I couldn't understand it. There was a picture of a car, then a big red cross was superimposed, and the sound faded to the Euroslavian anthem, Beethoven's *Ode To Joy*.

Then came that awful blue flag with those dozen gold stars, and we caught the start of the announcement in French given by a different woman. I translated as it went along.

"Certain forces who are opposed to the European Union's democratic way of life — that's rich! — are planning a demonstration, major, for the end of this month. They are urging people — innocent, law-abiding — to drive to Brussels and Luxembourg and stop the circulation — traffic, that is.

"Do not be misguided. This protestation is against the law. This message is for all motorists in regions BE1, BE24, BE31, BE34, BE35, in LU, and in FR21 and FR42. Between 2200 hours European mean time on the 30 October and 0200 hours on the 31 October, and the same hours on the night following, the 31 October to the first November, all vehicles must be off the public highway and must have the battery..." I hesitated, waited until the announcement had finished, then continued with my translation: "I think she said disconnected, but it's a new word to me. Then she said anybody who doesn't do it is under pain of a fine of a thousand euros, according to section something of some directive."

"What on earth are they up to?" Philip asked. "Disconnect your batteries? You sure you've translated it right, Terry?"

"Not exactly. Unless it's to make sure that cars in the Brussels area can't be moved overnight. Maybe moving cars are protesters, stationary cars are supporters. There'll be plenty of stationary cars in Benelux, at that rate. It's the only part of Euroslavia that really *ought* to have one currency and one government."

"But they're not even asking loyal supporters of Europe to block the roads against the besiegers. Surely that would make sense?"

"WE'VE FOUND IT, SIR," Unterleutnant Fischer reported to Frans Casbergen. "ČeskoTV. The satellite dish is about five meters across and there's nobody on guard. It'll be easy — even though it's done under protest."

"Your sentiment is noted once again, Leutnant," Casbergen snapped. "Get on with the job or I'll have you court-martialled."

Lt Fischer conferred with his men, and each loaded three grenades in their pockets but left the Berettas in the minibus. Casbergen picked up a single grenade and followed the detachment as one of the soldiers led them to the earth station, marked by an upturned saucer pointing skywards. But it was sited on the flat roof of a building about the size of three domestic garages, some three metres and a bit above ground. A thick chain-link fence three metres high, with a razor-wire overhang, surrounded the complex.

Casbergen looked around for some identification. "Are you sure this is the right place? This is Czech Television?"

"How many people have something like this in their back garden, sir?" Fischer asked as if talking to a child.

"And how do we get through that?" Casbergen hissed, pointing to the fence.

"Unstitch it," the lieutenant hissed back. He took a wire-cutter from his pocket and snicked one of the vertical zig-zagging wires at ground level; he traced it to head-height, cut it again, then twisted the loosened wire clockwise until he had unstitched the fence, as if he were a seamstress unpicking a seam. Within a minute there was a gap wide enough to squeeze through, with no snagging ends.

"Marvellous!" Casbergen breathed as the soldiers began sliding into the compound.

The lieutenant looked up at the satellite dish, a jet black object against a paler black sky. He could now see that it was made of mesh, but it was tilted so near the vertical that, if it were solid, it would hold rainwater. So it would hold hand grenades.

"Toss two grenades in," he ordered in a loud whisper. "Keep the pins in." He lobbed his own up, and heard them land on the mesh. "Like that." A volley of loose grenades, each the size of a large grapefruit, shot skyward, with only one bouncing out and landing on the roof.

"How do we detonate them?" Casbergen asked.

Unterleutnant Fischer did not answer directly. "Everybody out and back to the bus," he hissed. As the last soldier slipped through the fence, the officer turned to Casbergen. "You shall have the honour of detonating it, *sir*. In the name of democracy and the Europäische Vereinigung. Please give me your grenade."

He took it and held it in his hands with his own remaining explosive. "When I pull the pin out, there are thirty seconds before detonation. Throw your first grenade in, *sir,* and if it misses the target, prime the second and throw that. Look, I'll prime the first one for you."

Casbergen frowned, fazed by the officer's apparent change of tone. The lieutenant held both grenades in the poor light and with thumb and forefinger made a show of pulling out the priming pin; he threw it away. "Your grenade, sir. Twenty-five seconds. *Throw it!*"

As Casbergen lobbed the primed bomb into the air, the lieutenant backed away, then ran for the fence. As soon as he was through the hole he threw himself onto the ground and buried his head in his arms.

The explosion was phenomenal as twenty-four grenades released their energy within a fraction of a second. The satellite dish shattered into uncountable fragments which were hurled hundreds of meters. The flat roof of the outbuilding was crushed to the ground, leaving the outer walls exposed to the blast; chunks of masonry hit the chain-link fencing and lodged in it.

Casbergen's spare grenade exploded a microsecond after the main blast, hurling his shattered body in all directions.

Unterleutnant Fischer struggled to his feet and ran as if the Devil were after him. He hurled himself into the minibus and croaked: "Get out of here!"

"Where's the boss man, sir?"

"Warming his hands by the fire," Fischer gasped. "He went too close."

As the bus raced out of Čakovice towards Prague, the lieutenant relived the past few moments. He had counted on Casbergen knowing that a single grenade burst was small, and not mentally multiplying the blast by twenty-four. The final grenade was Fischer's insurance, and he had gambled that Casbergen would not notice he had pulled *both* pins.

"Slow down," he shouted to the driver. "We're not fugitives on the run!" They reached the northern limits of Prague with its miles of dreary industry. "Head straight into the city and take the road south..."

"South, sir?"

"South. To the Austrian border, to Linz."

"Why, sir?"

"You realise what we've done? We've invaded a neutral country and destroyed vital communications. That, by anybody's reckoning, is an act of war."

"But we were under orders, sir."

"Whose orders? That lunatic Casbergen, who wants to stamp out the last gasp of freedom? He's no better than Himmler was. And whose orders was he following? The Eurosicherheitsdienst. Have you ever heard of it, soldier?"

"No, sir."

"I'm not surprised. So what are you going to tell the top brass when we can't produce friend Casbergen?" The soldier never replied. "Precisely. Your word against theirs: who's going to be believed?" Unterleutnant Fischer glanced up at the floodlit buildings of the Hradčany and began to think about the next stage in his life, as an army officer on the run.

TWELVE

NEWS TRAVELS FAST, and bad news travels even faster. CCC's head office learned of the bombing of ČeskoTV's transmitter before midnight, and we in the bunker studio in Docklands learned about it within minutes.

"We're looking for an alternative access point in eastern Europe," the head of production said. "I don't think there'll be much of a problem; the programme's pulling in the viewers."

"Any idea who planted the bomb?" Philip asked.

"None at the moment, although one of them got himself killed. There was plum jam splashed all over."

"Plum jam?" Philip asked, then he understood. "Good God!"

"How's your food supply down there?"

"Holding out," Philip answered. "Must you ask about food straight after talking about plum jam? Your association of ideas..."

The head of production gave a short laugh. "Don't be so squeamish. By the way, we must stress it's absolutely essential that Terry doesn't show himself outside the studio — send the Heavenly Twins out if you must go shopping. We've got spies outside the office, waiting for us to lead them straight to you."

"Spies? How do you know?"

"We're not exactly stupid. By the way, we'll send the courier over tomorrow. It'll be Felicity, but if she thinks she's being tailed she'll make a dud run."

"It's not essential. We can manage."

"She's got a special delivery for you. Something we can't fax or e-mail."

"GOOD AFTERNOON, Mrs MASON," the tall, dark stranger said as my wife Lisa answered the front door of our home in Castletown. "Can you spare me a few moments?"

She hesitated, keeping the security chain attached. "Who are you and what do you want?"

"Callan. Anthony Callan. I'm a representative in the House of Keys — the Manx Parliament."

"I know what the House of Keys is, Mr Callan," Lisa answered rather frostily. "And I've heard of you from my husband."

"Ah, yes. The man who wants everybody to confide in him. May I come inside for a few moments?"

Lisa hesitated. Callan looked reasonably handsome and far from menacing, but she shook her head. "Sorry. Not while I'm on my own."

"But I won't hurt you."

"Somebody set fire to our house a little while ago. My husband seems to think you know something about it, so I'll be obliged if you'll take your business elsewhere." She began closing the door but Callan thrust his fingers in the gap, trusting that Lisa wouldn't crush them. She didn't.

"If you won't have me inside, may I talk to you outside?"

"What about?"

"Common sense. And ultimately, money. A lot of it."

"We don't need your money, thanks."

"But you'd like to be able to buy this house, wouldn't you?"

"We have an option to buy." Suddenly she began realising there were questions she should ask. "How did you know who I am? And where we live? And that we're renting this place?"

"Come outside, Mrs Mason, and I'll tell you. You're perfectly safe — there are people in the street."

"Stand well back," she said. She unhooked the chain, checked that Cat was inside, then went out, locking the door behind her. She slipped the keys into a tiny pocket in the waist of her skirt. "Start talking, Mr Callan."

"Your husband came to see me, Mrs Mason. I must admit I was surprised to see such a famous face in Rushen Abbey. He said you were both renting a place in Castletown, so it was no problem for me to search the land registry. There was no sale recorded, so you had to be renting. Copies of all lease agreements are kept in Douglas: need I say more?"

Lisa walked towards the centre of the little town. "Why did you want to know all this?"

"Because I have a proposition to make to you and your husband."

"Money?"

"If money is what you want, yes."

"What for? You want to buy his silence — is that it?" They reached the little Nautical Museum overlooking the estuary of the Silver Burn. A small bridge led across the burn to Parliament Square and an older House of Keys.

"The Isle of Man cannot possibly continue using sterling, particularly now the European Union refuses to accept it."

"If Europe refuses to acknowledge it, that's all the more reason for us to keep it. We're fighting for our independence, if you don't realise it."

"Independence? It's a global market these days. It's time for a global economy. Sovereignty means little in 2005."

EUROSLAVIA

Lisa looked at him. "Sovereignty meant a great deal to the Falklanders when the Argentinians invaded, and to the Gibraltarians when Spain put the pressure on. It's a terrible shame the Hong Kong people couldn't have their own sovereignty. Don't talk to me or my husband about giving up your nationality — or having it stolen. How much are you offering, anyway?"

"Up to a million."

"A *million*? Pounds or euros? It doesn't matter — we wouldn't touch a penny of it. Terry's not for sale. Nor am I."

"I could make things very difficult for you."

Lisa laughed. "Difficult? We've already been burned out, shot at, had threatening letters, and had the show pulled out from under us. How could you make it any more difficult?"

"You could disappear, for one thing." There was no menace in Callan's voice, but the threat was implicit. "Or your husband could."

Lisa chilled, realising that my fears had been genuine. "If I disappeared," she said icily, "the police would know exactly where to look. My husband has written up what he knows and left it with CCC's chief exec. If anything happens to either of us, that letter gets opened." She moved away from him. "In any event, Terry's out of your reach. Nobody can get to him — not even me. Not until the series finishes."

"*Tell Tel*? How long do you think that will go on? A week or two at the most. Europe won't tolerate it."

"And that's precisely why CCC is broadcasting it. We're fighting for democracy, freedom, independence. I don't suppose you know the meaning of the words. Now I'm going back home, and if you follow me I'll scream like hell."

Callan reached and touched Lisa's arm; she snatched it away as if his fingers were red hot. "I have a multi-million pound deal riding on the Isle of Man accepting the euro. If your husband changes his tune and comes out pro-Europe in his next broadcast, you can have a quarter-million pounds within the week, and I'll make it up to a million the moment the deal is signed." He paused. "If not, your face will be so ugly you won't dare look at yourself in the mirror." His eyes met Lisa's and she realised it was no idle threat.

Lisa gently rubbed her arm. "Mr Callan, we wouldn't touch your filthy money if it were the only thing between us and starvation. Now, good day."

"One final thing. You have one week to convince your husband he should change his ideas on Europe. And if you or he breathe one word of this conversation to anybody else, you know what will happen to your beautiful face." He stroked his cheeks.

"You *did* send that flying bomb," she whispered.

"No. But I know who did. Don't forget, Mrs Mason: your face or your fortune. You have a week."

McGOVAN'S MOTORCADE NEVER had a beginning. It just happened. Gradually, people across Euroslavia began to notice more traffic than usual going in one direction. In northern Spain, regions ES11 to ES41, and in Madrid, Region ES63, it was east; and in ES61, Andalucia, it was north-east. There was none from the fleet of Carrozas XYZ of Zarautz in the first exodus.

The motorists in Region ES63, Gibraltar, bitterly resented having been classified ES, which means España, as they were neither Spanish nor in Euroslavia, and they had a thousand protesters distributed around every available coach on The Rock. Among them were some dockyard workers who had helped offload several thousand tons of free fuel from Morocco and two members of the Gibraltar Lower House who knew where some of the billions of dollars of oil money pulled from Frankfurt had been reinvested.

Traffic was on the move north-eastwards from France's Region FR61, Les Landes; from FR81, the Languedoc; and from FR52, Brittany. In Italy's eighteen mainland regions and in Sicily, Region ITB, the traffic headed north; in Germany, from Region DE6, Hamburg, to DE3, Berlin, and from most of the other thirty-seven regions, the direction was south-west or west; in Sweden, from Region SE04, Malmø, to SE08, Lappland, it was south, and very heavy relative to the population. The Swedes wanted to get rid of Euroslavia as much as the British did, and for the same reason: they were dragooned into the single currency by Article 104c, the same one that had caught the United Kingdom.

Very few came from Greece's nine mainland regions, and none at all from Region GR42, Rhodes; and Region 43, Crete. Opposition to Euroslavia was sufficiently vocal, but the distances were great, there were still problems in driving through what had been Yugoslavia, and many Greeks feared the northern European winter.

In Britain the first vehicles headed south from Region UKA1, covering the area from the Scottish Borders to Tayside; and from UKA2, Dumfries through Glasgow to Oban: they had further to go. Later, cars and vans and coaches began leaving regions UK82 and UK84, Manchester and Liverpool; UK73, the West Midlands; and the region with the greatest population in Euroslavia, UK55, Greater London.

We'd had a call from Archie McGovan confirming he was joining the motorcade with Callan's team, but Callan had a bit of unfinished business and wouldn't be ready to leave for a couple of days.

The Irish Republic, whose population was happy living in

Euroslavia, never bothered to move, and there was plenty of time for the Dutch to think of driving out of their twelve regions, including NL42, Limburg, which held Maastricht. Similarly the motorists of the ten regions which surrounded BE1, Brussels, were no more inclined to protest than were those in Region LU, Luxembourg. Furthermore, many of them had been threatened with a fine if they didn't disconnect their car batteries overnight. They didn't understand the reasoning, but they accepted that all the laws coming from Brussels had a purpose...eventually.

The news media could not ignore such a mass movement of private vehicles, which promised to build up into the largest motorcade the world had ever known. On the first day, every news programme featured it large, and mostly with sympathy. Only the Irish dismissed it as a publicity stunt, while the Dutch, Belgian and Luxemburger stations gave it scathing treatment. These, they said, were motorists from the further reaches of the Europeaan Vereiniging who wanted to damage or destroy the greatest institution the continent had ever seen. Why could they not see how beneficial it was to have just one currency in commerce and industry, instead of juggling with up to four?

What was all the argument about sovereignty, gold reserves, vast financial centres, and what to do with the last of the colonies? The Belgians scarcely remembered their huge territories in the Congo basin and the Dutch had forgotten their empire stretching from Java to Surinam. As for fishing, Luxembourg had no fleet, and the Dutch and Belgians were very happy with the Common Fisheries Policy now that they could fish anywhere in the North Sea.

We at CCC watched and listened as long as there was transmission on the motorcade, and we recorded hours of footage. We saw roadside film of cars crossing the Spanish Meseta, already winter-bleak; we had a passenger's-eye-view of the journey up the Via Cassia from Rome, which would have fitted nicely into a travelogue; and aerial views of a convoy leaving Munich. And then we had interviews with drivers and passengers: why were they undertaking such lengthy journeys at such a bad time of the year? There was one word we noticed in almost every answer: libertat, libertad, liberté, libertà, liberdade, freedom, Freiheit, frihed, frihet, vrijheid, eleftheria, vapaus, wolność, and even the cry from a Welsh woman: rhyddid.

Philip and I exchanged long looks. "For the first time in my life," he choked, "I feel I am doing something really worthwhile. I'm fighting for the freedom of a continent. If I die now, I'll have achieved something with my life."

While we were still watching the motorcade I had a call from Lisa. "I had a visit from that Keysman Callan. He as good as admitted he was behind the firebombing."

"God! I thought as much! Get out of there at once, Lisa. Today."

"I will. But he wants me to tell you he'll make a mess of my face if you don't back down on Europe."

I didn't answer. What was I to do? Risk my wife's disfigurement, or continue my campaign for freedom for three hundred and seventy million people — not all of whom wanted to be freed.

"You've got to carry on, Terry," she said almost at once. "I've put Cat in a cattery and I've packed enough gear to see me settled in somewhere. I'm catching the next flight out of the island and I don't care where I'm going."

"I heard from McGovan. He's travelling with Callan's lot but they're not leaving for a day or so. Apparently Callan has some unfinished business."

Lisa caught her breath. "I think I know what it is."

"Look, Lisa. Get to the airport. Stay there until you can get away. Then call me the moment you're safe. Love you."

CHRISTINE BOUDERON HAD ordered Malcolm Hawes, head of the European Security Service's London bureau at Centre Point, to choose his three best surveillance agents and drum into their thick skulls the absolute urgency of finding the anchor-man on *Tell Tel* — in other words, me. "I'm not expert in surveillance, but I could certainly do better that you have managed so far."

Hawes nodded. "We've hired a theatrical agent to give us better disguises, ma'am. The agents are dressing now, before going out on patrol. Would you like to see them?"

She paused. "I certainly would." When, a little later, the trio drifted into her temporary office, Bouderon inspected them carefully, and was impressed. "I must say, some thought has at last gone into this project. You two are what — Concert engineers?"

She had almost said 'British Telecom' but at the last moment had remembered the company's new name, which had taken it conveniently out of the politically-correct spotlight aimed at reducing the emphasis on nationalism. As British Petroleum, BP, had been known as Benzin Petrol for decades in Germany, so Deutsche Telekom had changed to DT Telekom.

"Yes, ma'am. Me an' Gord. We'll be hidin' in a striped tent until they come out of the offices."

"And you?" Bouderon pointed to a woman in a navy blue skirt and jacket with yellow trim, and a peaked cap to match. "What are you?"

"Traffic warden, ma'am. Legitimate business to be walking around Soho Square all day."

"Won't there be a real traffic warden?"

"We've thought of that, ma'am. We've made arrangements with the police; he won't be doing the square today. And I'll be a real warden. I shall be giving out parking tickets."

"And for the evening shift we have a prostitute and a drunken man."

Bouderon laughed. "Excellent! You seem to have put some thought into it this time. If this does not work, nothing will work. Now, you know what we must do. You will all be on the street, but not too close to the studios. When the suspects come out, you will each follow one. Your orders are to follow to where you are led, to note the address and a description of the building, but not to go in. Is that understood? *Bonne chance.*"

The three agents left Centre Point separately to begin their surveillance of the CCC offices in Soho Square, a few streets away.

Bouderon borrowed a small staff car from the garage lost amid Centre Point's foundations and drove around the square three times until she gave up looking for a vacant parking meter and parked on double yellow lines within view of Central Cable Channel. She lifted the bonnet to signify a breakdown — but not too high to obstruct her vision of CCC — and decided to accept every parking ticket that her ESD agent must issue. She saw the two Concert men erect their tent over over an inspection point, and she nodded to the parking warden as the woman made a note of her number.

"I must give you a ticket next time, ma'am."

"Of course you must," Bouderon agreed. She quickly realised the difficulty the agents had as there was a steady flow of pedestrian traffic around the square. A taxi pulled up outside CCC and Bouderon saw a tall man with spindly legs clamber out and go into the television office. He looked exactly like a character she had seen years back in the film *Un Poisson Nommé Wanda*.

After an hour she used the carphone to summon Hawes, the head of the bureau, to come out and pretend to repair her engine. In the meantime she was becoming aware of a middle-aged man in a grey suit who was wandering around the square, clipboard in hand, making notes at each address. Hawes had his head under the bonnet and was protesting about this waste of his valuable time when Bouderon, standing by the front wheel, hissed: "There! He is coming again. Who is he?"

Hawes slowly looked up and saw Clipboard stroll past. "Some council official."

"That is his third time around. He is no council official — he is also watching CCC."

Hawes frowned. "He's certainly not one of ours."

"Then we must watch him as well."

"But we can't stay here all day. It's a dead giveaway."

"Then you must pretend to repair the engine and I will drive away."

Half an hour later, having parked the car under Centre Point, Bouderon strolled around Soho Square, now wearing a dark coat. She looked at the brass nameplate on each door and quietly checked on the two Concert agents (she wondered why that didn't sound quite as she planned) as she passed their tent. The traffic warden was still on her rounds, but there was no sign of Clipboard. She saw a trio dressed like pop stars flood out of a taxi as if they had an audience of ten thousand screaming fans, and crash noisily up the steps into CCC's offices.

She stood at a corner of the square, studying a map of London, when she saw three people come purposefully out of the offices. She glanced up. They were youngish men wearing dark suits, and each carried a black briefcase. Bouderon realised one of these must be the courier to Mason's hideout — but which one?

The trio split on the pavement, one walking towards her, another going away, while the third set off around the fenced gardens in the centre of the square. Bouderon studied her map as the man hurried past her, then she followed. She realised almost at once what a difficult task she had: she was forced to walk so fast that she was making herself conspicuous.

She saw the traffic warden glance at her, and Bouderon nodded at her quarry. Instantly the warden took off her uniform jacket and turned it inside out. She thrust her peaked cap into a floppy handbag that appeared from a pocket, and shook out her shoulder-length brunette hair. She took over from Bouderon a little way down Greek Street, allowing the French woman to hurry back to the square.

The Concert tent was empty — but she gradually became aware of a man painting the iron railings circling the gardens. It was Clipboard, but without his board. And he wasn't going anywhere.

Intrigued, Bouderon walked as casually as she could until she had put some of the gardens between herself and Clipboard, but still allowing herself to see the steps to the front door of Central Cable Channel. She took out her map of London for want of a better reason for standing there.

Half an hour passed. She saw the man with the long spindly legs leave CCC, and recognised him as John Cleese, then minutes later a woman with her own version of long legs also came out of CCC. She was carrying a briefcase and she turned quickly on the pavement, hurried to the far corner of the square where it joined Frith Street, and hailed a taxi.

Bouderon had seen Clipboard's immediate interest. He dropped his paint pot and brush through the railings and ran to a car parked by a meter near the Frith Street corner; its windscreen wiper had several parking tickets thrust under it.

Bouderon mouthed some French expletives as she realised all her efforts had been useless: Clipboard had obviously been there before and knew what to expect. She walked back to the Security Service bureau wondering who else was on my tail, and why.

CLIPBOARD SCREECHED HIS car out of Soho Square into Soho Street, following the taxi. All traffic had to turn left into Oxford Street and he joined the crawl. He took the opportunity to put on a light mackintosh to cover his overalls. "What the bloody hell do you mean by falling asleep on the job?" he shouted at the youth who was untangling himself from a blanket on the front passenger seat and slowly clipping his seat belt.

"I feel a nerd sitting there watching that warden stick all those tickets under the wiper. Besides, it was cold. Who're we following, Mister Robinson?"

"That taxi."

"Which taxi? The road's full of taxis."

"It doesn't matter. Hey — where's she going?" The cab with the girl from CCC took the next turning left — Dean Street — and headed south. "Christ — she's going back again."

Traffic was much lighter on this lesser road and Robinson, the man who earlier had been carrying the clipboard, let two other cars get between himself and his quarry. He saw the cab take another left into Compton Street, then left again into the bustling, crawling fuming jam of Charing Cross Road.

"She's leading us a pretty dance, Mister Robinson," the youth groaned. "That's four left turns. We're going back where we started."

The cab stopped for traffic lights at St Giles Circus, with the skyscraper of Centre Point, the base for the head of bureau of the English Provincial sector of Eurosicherheitsdienst, rising on its right.

"She's getting out," Robinson snapped. "Take the car back home."

Robinson hurled himself from the driving seat and raced after the woman, seeing her hurry into Tottenham Court Road Underground Station. He pushed his way rudely through the crowd and reached the ticket office three places behind his quarry. "Hainault, single," he snapped at the cashier, thrusting a ten-euro note under the glass screen and pocketing his change without counting it.

He stuck with her on the Central Line to Bank station, and through a change of trains to the Docklands Light Railway during which he took off his mack and carried it over his arm. He noticed the young woman was paying careful attention to her fellow passengers, but she never appeared to notice him. When she came to the surface in Docklands and hurried to a derelict area that had not seen redevelopment in the Canary Wharf phase, he was still trailing her.

He stopped when she stopped, two hundred yards ahead. When she looked around her, he flattened himself into a warehouse doorway; he put one eye around the corner of the brickwork and saw her disappear through a wall.

He hurried forward, stopped within twenty feet of where he had last seen her, ostensibly to light a cigarette, and noticed an ordinary wooden door let into a brick wall. Keeping his head movement to a minimum he swivelled his eyes until he was reasonably sure he was not being watched, then he took several casual steps towards the door. At first it looked as if it had not been opened for months, but then he saw there was a distinct crack between the wood of the door and the dust and soil where last summer's dead weeds still stood.

He risked a smile before hurrying away. At the next corner he pulled a dog-eared copy of *London A-Z* from his coat pocket and put a red felt-tip cross marking the site of the doorway. Then he took a mobile phone from his other pocket, dialled, and said: "Boss? I think I've found Mason for you."

Callan's voice answered. "Robinson? Are you an imbecile? I told you I'm no longer interested in doing business with your friend."

"But I've got him."

"Then lose him. I'm not in the least interested in what he has to offer, now or in the future." The phone clicked dead and Robinson stared at it for a moment before shrugging his shoulders. Callan may not be interested, but he knew somebody else who would be.

TEUTOBURGER SUMMONED CASBERGEN into his office, but the deputy head of electronic surveillance hurried to answer the demand.

Teutoburger had lost his military bearing and was more visibly fraying at the edges the longer this crisis continued. "Where's Casbergen?" he bellowed.

"Not back yet, sir."

"Not back? He's been gone two days — where the hell does he think he is?" He didn't wait for an answer. "You're Andersen, aren't you? Listen, Andersen. Time's come to start pulling in known activists. Get hold of Bouderon..."

"She's not back either, sir."

The president of the Sicherheitsdienst slammed his fists onto his desk. "Are we running a kindergarten here? Get somebody in her section. Get the lists of all known activists and find out exactly what they're up to. We've got to get some positive movement showing around here or the President of the Commission is going to want some heads to roll. Move, man!"

Kris Andersen from Uppsala in Sweden, Region SE02, had been a conscientious employee of the European Security Service since he had been head-hunted from his job in the Swedish Civil Service, and he was an ardent supporter of the Union. He had made a point of asking Mlle. Bouderon about her surveillance on dissidents, and he now went in search of her deputy, Frenchman Marcel Cervaux. He left Cervaux's office and went back to his own with a bulky file of computer print-outs which he began to study.

He quickly realised that every name on the list was associated with a company, which inevitably meant that every name had access to a computer. Almost every company computer these days could log into the World Wide Web, and for that it needed a modem. And he knew that every modem in the Union had a bug. And the latest development of bugs could be ordered to do all sorts of clever tricks from killing itself to intercepting all traffic passing through its modem, be it voice, fax or visual imagery, and transmitting it back to the nearest line interchange where it could be beamed to a satellite, and so received in the incident room in the Kristallkoffer, the head office of Eurosicherheitsdienst on the Friedrichstrasse in Berlin.

The amount of traffic generated if all the bugs in the Union were activated, would reach astronomic figures. The amount of traffic intercepted from the list of known activists would be phenomenal, would employ at least sixty people in each of three shifts around the clock, and would still not guarantee complete surveillance. But Bouderon had put a star against a small number of names on the list, and Cervaux decided he would start with those. Three shifts of ten could manage that workload.

ONE MORNING IN mid-October, Xavier Yzurdiaga wrote a message in Basque on his computer in his small apartment in Sant Julià de Loria, in Valls d'Andorra, and faxed it over to Carrozas XYZ's office in Zarautz. It said: *Am joining McGovan Motorcade in rented car. How many coaches going? Send itinerary. Is Staqui going?*

Simultaneous with its transmission from Andorra, it was printed out in the coach operator's office in Euzkadi. But the phone number of Yzurdiaga's Andorran office was not on Bouderon's list, so her deputy Kris Andersen had not activated it. Even if he had, the microchip in Yzurdiaga's modem could merely send a copy of the message to the telephone exchange in the village capital of the tiny state, where it would have died as nobody had managed to infiltrate the Andorran telecommunications system. Twenty years earlier, when France and Spain ran competing businesses in Andorra-la-Vella, the *PTT* and the *Teléfonos,* it would have been ridiculously easy to bug both offices.

But the *telefonica* in Zarautz had been bugged, so within a fraction of a second of the incoming fax being handled by the modem in XYZ's office, it was being transmitted to the European Global Navigational Overlay System geostationary satellite, from where it was beamed down to the Kristallkoffer in Berlin, with a precise bearing on the receiving modem, accurate to within twenty metres.

The trouble came at the Kristallkoffer where human intelligence was required to read and interpret every communication, and that wasted hours. As the message from Zarautz was in Basque, it was mid-afternoon on that day before a Basque-speaking translator could be found. She decided the message was of sufficient importance for her to forward the translation to Kris Andersen, who skimmed through his boss's database until he found the XYZ coach company, headed by one Xavier Yzurdiaga.

Soon Andersen realised he had struck paydirt. Yzurdiaga had been a suspect in the bombing raids in five provincial capitals, and had been questioned after the Copenhagen bombing, significantly the last in the series.

"We'll have you, *copain*," he gritted. "We'll have you this time!"

He keyed up the standard Instruction to Apprehend form on his computer and filled in the gaps, in German. EGNOS bearing; postal address from the older files, Carrozas XYZ, Zarautz; name, Xavier Yzurdiaga; the other information such as passport number, social security number, credit rating, convictions and the rest, didn't seem worth digging from other files: they'd be on his Eurocard, anyway. He filled in the last space with *terrorism and murder*.

Then he faxed it to the Burgos bureau of the Eurosicherheitsdienst; the modems on the transmitting and receiving computers in the Kristallkoffer were, of course, not bugged. It was eleven past four when the message went through, and six minutes later he received the translated reply from Carrozas XYZ to Yzurdiaga, holed up in Andorra. The scrutineer had intercepted it only because the few words were in an unintelligible language.

It said: *Three. S on one. Depart Z 07002810.*

Andersen put both messages together, and instantly understood the second, which replied to the first. Three XYZ coaches were going on the motorcade, and the man named Staqui was travelling on one of them. They were leaving Zarautz at 0700 hours on 28th October — ten days hence.

He sat back and thought for a moment. Yzurdiaga was presumably hiding in Andorra and would head for Brussels from there. But how? By hire car? There was no hint of where he would rent the vehicle — in Andorra, Spain or France. Or would he go in one of his own coaches? But that would surely be too obvious? Neither was there any hint of where or how he would cross the Andorran border. There was, in fact, no way of tracking him. He could reach the European Parliament with an enormous bomb in his car, unless he were picked up by chance.

Andersen keyed another Instruction to Apprehend putting in what little information he had: suspect's first name Staqui, probably abbreviated from Eustaqui. Surname unknown. Associates with XYZ coaches. In the last blank he put *accessory to terrorism and murder*, and sent it on its way to Bilbao.

OUR HIDDEN STUDIO took another phone call from the Falkland Islands. "Mr Mason? The Royal Falklands Parliament has recently learned through its ambassador in the Far East that Japan is pulling out all its gold from Frankfurt, and it's given notice that it wants all its currency reserves out as soon as possible. It's even willing to take up a small penalty for early withdrawal."

I put my loudspeaker on so everybody could share the news. "That's wonderful! Do you know how much is involved, and where it's going?"

"Billions of US dollars, that's all we can say. And it's going to the Sterling Zone, the Cayman Islands and Wall Street."

"This is going to start a run on Europe, isn't it?"

"Sure is. We hear the Gulf States will be announcing their own withdrawal tomorrow. After that, the euro will be in free fall."

"Jolly good news. Thanks a million."

The young woman's voice took on a sadder note. "But you're in Europe. You're going to feel the pinch as well, and with winter coming on. It's not going to be pleasant."

"We don't mind. Can we put this out on the air?"

"Sure. The press agencies are being notified but we wanted you to be the first to know. It's all official."

A few minutes later Philip took another call which threw us all into even greater exhilaration. "We've got the option of another satellite link in Europe. In fact, Soho Square says we've got three offers. We'll be back on air in a few days, lads. You want the bad news as well?"

"Why not?" one of the Heavenly Twins groaned.

"There were bits of clothing and bone found in the wreckage of the ČeskoTV station. So it was sabotage, apparently."

THE *GOOD HOPE* sailed from Castletown in the Isle of Man with a smart 1987 Jaguar as deck cargo. The passengers for this voyage across to Holyhead on the Isle of Anglesey were the Chief Minister of the House of Keys, Sir John Faulds; Sir John's mistress, Keyswoman Bridget Norris; the owner of the Jaguar, Keysman Anthony Callan; and the owner of the *Good Hope,* deep-sea fisherman Archie McGovan, whose own car was in Douglas.

LISA CALLED ME from Flesland Airport, Bergen, in Norway. "I've just landed, Terry."

"Landed? In Norway? Where in God's name are you going from there?"

"I don't know. I thought I'd head south..."

"But there's McGovan's Motorcade coming. Don't get caught up in that. Why not keep out of Euroslavia altogether?"

"But I can't stay in Norway, with winter coming on. I could fly to Tunisia or Cyprus or the Med, somewhere. Can't talk now, darling — money's running..."

The money ran out.

THE OLD AUSTIN J4 van had driven onto the *Trondenes* cargo-ship at the Old Jetty in Alderney's Braye Bay, and three hours later had driven ashore at Carteret on the Cotentin Peninsula in France's Region 25. The passengers aboard it were John and Fiona le Mesurier; Annette Dugard, the artist who had been living at Château à l'Etoc but who was now going home to Montmédy; and Guernseyman John Doyle, looking sprightly for his seventy-three years. They had sleeping bags and enough supplies to last them for two weeks, which filled the remaining space in the van.

They had expected to meet opposition from the French authorities, but the local *gendarme* asked: "Brussels? Good luck — wish I could come with you."

They had a week to get to their destination and on that first half-day they took an easy route through Bayeux and Caen. They spent their first night on the edge of a vineyard near the tiny village of Moult, the women sleeping side by side in the rear of the van, while the men slept at the front. The nights were cold and they slept nearly fully-clothed, anticipating the possibility of an interruption during the dark hours.

EUROSLAVIA

Annette Dugard felt the thrill of being back in her native country once again and thought of her sketchy plans to go home to Montmédy after the Brussels protest, and join whatever resistance there was to Euroslavia. If there wasn't any now, she guessed there soon would be.

On the second day, Sunday, they made an easy run to the lowest crossing-point on the Seine, giving Rouen a wide berth. Despite federalism, France had managed to retain its law banning the movement of lorries on Sundays, but the road east from Le Havre was busy with cars, almost all heading east and almost all loaded with people and luggage.

McGovan's Motorcade was drawing the crowds.

The Alderney party was forced to find a pull-off for Monday night long before dusk, and chose a set-aside field by Neufchâtel-en-Bray, a little market town devoted to the sale of cheese. Every available field gateway and lay-by was filled with members of the motorcade, and the Alderney contingent was surprised to see the number of children and dogs — even the odd cat. Then Annette remembered. "Some will be celebrating the *Fête des Morts,* but that's next Tuesday, a week away. Do they think the roads are going to be that busy?"

XAVIER YZURDIAGA DECIDED to leave Andorra on Saturday on foot, by the route he'd sworn never to use again, over the 2,300-metre Port de Cabús and down the mule-track to the tiny village of Tor. The option was to walk over the crest of the mountains into France, but the passes were several hundred metres higher, and the snowline was already down to 1,500 metres. He dressed for the journey, carrying his sleeping-bag and rations for three days, and after a night at Tor he hitched a lift in a Land-Rover Santana down to civilization at Ribera de Cardos. By bus down the beautiful valley of the Noguera Pallaresa, then back up the next valley, the Noguera Ribagorçana in another bus. A second night at Vilaller. Through the nerve-wracking nine-kilometre Túnel de Vielha and then downhill all the way, to the border twenty-six km further on.

Thanks to the Schengen Agreement there were no frontier controls between France and Spain, and the bus with Yzurdiaga aboard, reached Tarbes in safety a little after dark. He chose a smart hotel near the Jardin Mussey, looking sad for itself in early winter, and on the Monday morning he rented a car without any problems.

There was shopping to do: plenty of food, a camping stove, and whatever he may need to rig up a car bomb. He was out of timing devices so he added three small alarm clocks and three powerful torch batteries to the list. Plus a sturdy spade: he had 7.5kg of Semtex to dig up, and some very big bangs to make.

And then he headed west for the tiny hamlet of Uxiat, and his cache of explosives. Pau. The roads were noticeably busy with cars, mostly heading for Toulouse and — he presumed — the route north to Brussels. Orthez. Beautiful little town famous for its fortified bridge, and for the castle of the Count of Foix, one of the early co-princes of Andorra. South-west, gradually climbing towards the distant snow-capped Pyrenees.

He was watching for Uxiat, then for the turning to the quarry, now abandoned. He parked, lowered the window and sat — waiting, watching. There was no noise from the forest climbing the steep hillside; no alarm calls from birds, no crashing of *sanglier* — wild boar — through the undergrowth. Monday was not one of the days of *la chasse,* when Frenchmen armed themselves with ferocious firearms and tried to decimate the local fauna.

He slid out of the car and clambered slowly up the slope, hauling his way from tree to tree and sending a pigeon flapping through the pines, warning all the wildlife. The light was poor under the conifer cover but he knew he was on the right track.

That was when a man in a flak suit stepped out from behind a tree and raised a large gun at him. Yzurdiaga was not to know it was an AK47 Kalashnikov.

"*Stop! Manos arriba!*"

Yzurdiaga did as he was ordered, raising his hands slowly and dropping the spade. Another man in a flak suit slithered down the slope, holding another Kalashnikov, and Yzurdiaga heard others behind him. Before he had time to wonder what had happened two more men slid down through the pine-needles. Yzurdiaga recognised the one with his hands cuffed in front of him.

"*Staqui!* What in God's name...?"

Eustaqui Arrieta was crying. "I'm sorry, Xav. They caught me. They started torturing my daughter. You remember Carmen? She's twenty-six, and eight months pregnant. They made me tell. I'm so very sorry, Xav."

Staqui's guard kicked him at the base of the spine. "So you identify this man as Xavier Yzurdiaga?" Staqui nodded in silence, staring at the ground in shame and humiliation.

The first man aimed the Kalashnikov at Yzurdiaga's heart. "Servicio de seguridad europeo. You are under arrest for acts of terrorism and murder. I don't think you'll see much of Brussels for the next twenty years."

FATHER ERICH ZIMMERMAN was as excited as a stag at rutting time. A motorcade on Brussels! This was as good as the surrender at

Compiègne in 1918, the Normandy landings in 1944, the first crossing of the Rhine at Remagen, the Russians and Americans meeting on the Elbe, the fall of the Nazi Reich.

This was the might of the German Government being put in its place — again. Never mind that the *seat* of Euroslavia (he loved that word) was in tiny Belgium and even tinier Luxembourg, the power itself still rested in German hands. Germany had 99 of the 626 Members of Parliament while Luxembourg had six, and it had ten of the Council of Ministers' 87 votes. While nationalism in the old sense was officially suppressed by Euroslavian policy, Germany had thirty-nine regions to attract its peoples' loyalty, and England had just twenty-seven.

"*Ich fahre gegen Brüssel,*" he sang, parodising a wartime song that he hoped he'd forgotten. He had no idea how he would get there without a car, but what matter? He left his computer and books in store and packed only his bedding, spare clothes, and as much food as he could carry on his sturdy but ageing body.

The Swiss weren't bothered about McGovan's Motorcade as they had stayed, sensibly, out of all European conflicts for a century. It meant there would be no extra border traffic to distract vigilant inspectors, but he'd risk it. He doubted that he'd ever make his way south again. "*Ich fahre gegen Brüssel,*" he sang as he hefted his worldly goods, walked into Zürich city centre and bought a coach ticket for Paris.

CHRISTINE BOUDERON FACED the assembled European Security Service staff in their Centre Point office. "Truly, I am disgusted that you have not be able to apprehend a man whose face has been seen on every television from Aberdeen to Athens. If you think this is the way the Security Service operates, then you have much to learn. I will make a full report in Berlin and I know that some of you will search for other employs — unless you find Mason for me by when I reach the Friedrichstrasse." She turned to Malcolm Hawes. "You among all. You must show initiative. I expect it of you."

Hawes felt seething anger as she criticised him in front of the lesser staff. He had been in various aspects of security most of his working life and he had never before been ripped off in public, nor by a woman, a foreign one at that.

"Madam," he said slowly. "Until Mason shows himself on the streets, we are powerless. You've seen how clever those CCC people are."

She sighed. "I know, Mr Hawes. I know the problems you have. I agree that Mason can stay free for years if he is diligent. But when I get back to Berlin, who will face the reprimand — you or me?"

"I appreciate your problem, ma'am," he said with a touch of sympathy. "Perhaps you would like to stay another twenty-four hours?"

"I cannot. I must be back before this motorcade reaches Brussels." She turned away from the gathered staff and amazed herself by mentally framing the question: *why?* Why did she need to go back to Berlin, to a president who was either leering at her body or bawling orders at her? Teutoburger, she saw, was carrying a workload beyond his capacity and he was heading for a breakdown. Add to that her deep suspicions that he was going beyond his duties; he had no mandate whatever to send Casbergen into the Czech Republic on a search-and-destroy mission; she doubted that he had a mandate to conduct experiments on planting microchips into new-born babies — and if he had, then the Eurosicherheitsdienst was an evil entity and she had no place in it.

She felt as if some other force had taken control of her mind and body as she heard herself saying: "Very well, Mr Hawes. I will stay another day. We have one more day to find this Mason."

THIRTEEN

SITTING IN OUR bunker, we had a splendid overview of McGovan's Motorcade as we monitored every satellite transmission beamed down upon Europe.

Philip could not contain his pleasure. "Who'd've thought the Euro policy was to clamp down on criticism and bad press? Yet this is the worst press Euroslavia has ever seen — millions of motorists driving on Brussels to shut down the powerhouses of autocracy!"

"Would you like to work that quote into the next broadcast?" I asked.

"At least, we know there'll be another broadcast. It's a toss-up now which earth station we'll use."

"Couldn't we use them all? Switzerland, Poland and Norway?"

"Good idea, but it all costs money. We'll have to leave it to Soho Square to decide, as usual."

I went back to the bank of newly-installed monitors, brought in at dead of night, and watched Europe heading for the biggest people-power demonstration the world had ever seen. It was Thursday in the last week in October, with five days to go before the assembly was due to reach the vital organs of the Euromonster.

And I had not heard a word from Lisa since she arrived in Norway. Where was she? Still in Bergen? Travelling south and getting involved in the motorcade? Or sunning herself in north Africa?

I switched my thoughts back to the motorcade. Aerial views showed a steady stream of traffic, almost all of them private cars, heading towards Brussels. Lyons, in the Rhône valley, had the biggest snarl-up in its history as the autoroutes from Paris, Genève and Marseille met in the built-up area, and fed the *routes nationales* to Clermont-Ferrand, Mâcon, St Etienne, Grenoble and Valence. This, mixed with the city's own traffic, the northbound motorcade, and the traffic for the Festival of the Dead, had created one tailback to Rive-de-Gier and another half way down to Valence.

The French Riviera was blocked as traffic surged up the west coast of Italy, anxious to avoid the Alpine snows. Paris was chaos, but that was nothing new.

Germany's eastern regions were disgorging steady streams of traffic but the countryside was open enough to absorb them. Magdeburg showed a more sinister approach to the Euroslavian protest as columns of black smoke rose from the city centre, although peace had returned to Dresden.

EUROSLAVIA

The car ferries from Sweden's Region SE04 to Denmark, one of the three former nations that had not been regionalised, were working around the clock to carry the protesting motorists southward. Helsingborg, Landskrona and Malmø had long queues building at the ferry terminals while Göteborg and Varberg could just cope.

Occasionally the intruding television cameras went in much closer. We saw a load of protesters whose old coach had broken down on the bridge linking Sjaelland with Fyn in Denmark; they were trying to hitch lifts and were shouting abuse to fellow-motorists who didn't stop.

An accident in Zaragoza had turned into a fight, and the *policía* had become involved when a protester from one car had slit the throat of a passenger in the other vehicle.

"It could turn out to be very dangerous," I observed. "There'll certainly be riots when they all get seized up for days — and it's going to happen. I just hope it doesn't start a civil war."

Philip frowned. "I dread to think it, but if we got a million people around Brussels fighting to get their countries back, how long would Euroslavia last?"

"Not long. Probably no more than fifty years." I shrugged. "Remember the Hungarian uprising, when the people screamed for the West to go and help? And we did sod all. Remember the Prague Spring of 1968? It's going to take a hell of a lot more than McGovan's Motorcade to finish Euroslavia. By the way, have we heard how McGovan himself is getting on?"

ARCHIE McGOVAN WAS finding it difficult to believe that a simple idea was having such a major impact on the lives of millions of people. "A bloody motorcade to Brussels?" he told Sir John Faulds as he turned up the volume on the Jaguar's radio and heard news of events on the continent. "Ah thought Ah'd be lucky ta get ten thousand mugs ta support me. Shows just how many people want ta get out o' Euroslavia."

Anthony Callan, at the wheel of his car, nodded. He believed he had been working in Britain's interests when he had reinterpreted Clause 104c. It made sense to have one currency among trading partners; one currency meant one tax rate, one interest rate, one economic policy. And why not? The United States had been doing it for years. But as he drove across England to the ferry at Harwich, he was beginning to have doubts. The Americans had democracy coming out of their ears: they voted for judges, sheriffs, mayors, councillors, senators, congressmen, and the president himself.

But Europe hadn't worked out that way. Europeans voted only for members of that impersonal Parliament in Brussels or Strasbourg, and that was all. And the twenty-odd commissioners, safe in their ivory tower, pulled all the strings of government.

If the passengers in his car realised that he — *he* — had started the movement which had robbed Britain of her nine hundred and forty years of independence, then maybe lynching would be back in favour.

Beyond Nottingham, in Region UK31, he asked over his shoulder: "Remind me — why is Europe split into these regions?" He knew the answer; he wanted to have his opinions reinforced.

Mrs Bridget Norris, sitting in the back with the Manx Chief Minister, Sir John, said: Why do you call it Europe, Anthony? Can't you get your tongue around Euroslavia?"

Callan shrugged. "Euroslavia," he said, for the first time. He still didn't like the word.

Mrs Norris continued. "Easy. The Brussels lot want to kill off nationalism, so they invented regionalism. Tynesiders can be loyal to Region Thirteen because they live there. London doesn't count."

"It certainly doesn't count now," Sir John added. "And that's why the Labour Party was so keen to give Scotland and Wales their own assemblies — for what they're worth today."

"How do you mean, John?" Mrs Norris asked.

"Because they had to break up the Union — the British Union. The United Kingdom. Euroslavia is the new union, the new nation. You can have *provinces* called France and Spain, with people loyal to their regions. But you can't have a *province* called the United *Kingdom,* can you? Scotland, yes. Wales, yes. England, yes."

"The clever bastards," Archie McGovan gritted. "An' ta think Ah voted for 'em!"

Callan had to admit that Sir John's argument was right. Nobody but a lunatic could be expected to be loyal to Brussels, but loyalty to one's region was a natural thing. Substitute that regional support for the outdated loyalty to nation state, and Europe... Euroslavia... was in business.

Callan had also listened to McGovan's interminable criticisms of the Common Fisheries Policy, and much to his dismay he had to admit that the fisherman had sound reasons for his bitterness. Maybe the European Union wasn't such a good thing after all? He had also been thinking long about his debate with Lisa, my wife. Lisa had been adamant in her opposition to the rule of the Brussels autocrats and he admired her refusal of a bribe to persuade me to change my mind. Why did she have such strong allegiance to the old idea of nationhood? The Castletown house was locked and empty when he had called the next day to tell her his threat was all bluff. Callan could order some hit man to start a scare campaign, but it wasn't in him to cause actual bodily harm to anybody, least of all to a woman.

He thought again of that surprise call on his mobile phone back in the Isle of Man. Robinson wanted to report that he had trailed a woman from CCC's offices in Soho to the hidden studio in Dockland, and he had found Mason in the process. But Callan was no longer interested in me: he was having serious doubts about his committment to Europe.

YZURDIAGA WAS STILL in shock as the four Servicio de Seguridad agents began the descent to the quarry, but he realised the best time for him to strike for freedom was now. The prospect of years in prison had been looming for a decade, but only as a bad dream in the background. Now it was real, and he decided he would rather die fighting that rot in jail.

He could hear his own guard just behind him, struggling with the carpet of pine needles on the steep slope. *Now!* He swung around, knocked the guard's nearer leg from under, and as the man fell, Yzurdiaga lunged for the gun with his shackled hands. He caught it, bringing it down heavily on the back of the guard's head as the man fell forward onto the ground.

The Basque lunged forward, coming to rest on the uphill side of the dazed man, with the other three Seguridad agents, and poor Staqui, in front of him, downhill, and with their backs to him.

Yzurdiaga had a second to think, to weigh the consequences: life in prison or a life on the run. There was no choice: he aimed the Kalashnikov and brought down the first two agents with a shot each. The third threw himself to the ground and had his gun aimed uphill before Yzurdiaga could draw a bearing on him.

Yzurdiaga paused. He had only seconds before his human shield would regain consciousness. "Staqui — no!" he yelled, although his friend was standing motionless, deep in his humiliation. But the agent turned his head, and Yzurdiaga shot him in the temple.

Now his human shield began moaning. Yzurdiaga thought about putting a bullet in his brain, but that would be murder. He pulled the man's belt from his trousers, tied his wrists together behind the man's back, and secured him to a small tree. It wouldn't hold for long, but long enough.

He felt in the man's tunic pockets and whooped with joy when he pulled out a bunch of keys. "Staqui — unlock these handcuffs." In the seconds that it took his friend to fumble the correct key into the lock, Yzurdiaga found himself thinking of the ironies of the Castillian Spanish language, which had the same word for 'handcuff' and for 'wife' — *esposa*.

While he released Staqui's bonds, his super-active mind was already on other problems. "Where's their car? Were there only four?"

Staqui pointed to the two men stretched out on the ground. "Are they dead?"

"Haven't time to find out. Leave that to number four." He pointed to the man bound to the tree. "Why did you do it, old friend? Why did you tell them? And how long have you been waiting for me, for God's sake?"

"Two days."

"Two *days?*"

"Shoot me, Xav. I deserve it. Shoot me. I can't live with myself any more. Go on, or I'll do it myself."

"Don't be so stupid, Staqui. Is the Semtex still there?"

"They didn't find it."

"Right, then. You've got a choice, Staqui. Are you coming with me to Brussels or are you going home to Lolita?"

"You know I can't go home. If I don't shoot myself I'm with you, Xav. And God only knows what the future holds."

"It holds my fist on your nose if you don't help me find that Semtex and get out of here before people start investigating those gunshots. Come on."

ON FRIDAY, OCTOBER 28, the Norwegian Government announced to the major news agencies that it was withdrawing all short-term investments with the European Investment Bank as of that moment; this public announcement of financial transactions was a totally modern trend to open up the workings of the markets and so avoid loss of confidence by rumour and innuendo, but when country after country made similar statements there was inevitably a growing feeling that the euro was no longer holding its value. Within minutes, Switzerland joined the pull-out. Then came the Czech Republic, which also gave notice that it would lodge an official complaint against the European Union for destroying a satellite transmitter station at Čakovice. Iceland and the Bahamas announced their withdrawal of funds soon after, and it was obvious to the world that the Union currency was in severe trouble.

Two hours later, when the United States publicly declared its loss of confidence, the euro was sliding uncontrollably. Late on that Friday afternoon, 28 October, 2005, the EIB and the Bundesbank would begin their struggle to save the currency, secretly thankful that the weekend would give them thinking time. But before trading closed, the Bundesbank announced that interest rates, which had started the day at 7.5% and had risen in two stages to 10% were hiked up to 14%.

CHRISTINE BOUDERON WAS determined that tomorrow, Saturday 29 October, her last day in London, she would find me. That Friday evening she went around the nearest charity shop in Charing Cross Road and bought the most sombre, unappealing, non-eye-catching clothes she could find. On her final morning, dressed to be inconspicuous and with her hair curled under a woollen bonnet, she borrowed a wheelchair from Centre Point's emergency stores and pushed it to Soho Square where she was determined to alternately sit and stand all day — except for answering the calls of nature — until she saw that courier again. Maybe a Saturday would be better than a weekday? She had no cover story: she thought her action was sufficiently bizarre for passers-by to assume she was perhaps mentally deranged and so leave her alone.

Her telephone repair men and her female traffic warden were off the job, and she smiled at the regular male warden as he came around noting car numbers. His reaction to the smile satisfied her that she was portraying the right image: she was ninety cents to the euro.

She noticed two or three celebrities come and go at CCC's offices, but the clipboard man was absent: maybe he had found out all he needed? And then, around half past eleven, he arrived.

He wasn't carrying the clipboard, nor did he show any interest in retrieving his can of paint. He walked cautiously up to Bouderon and paused in front of her.

"You were here yesterday," he said. It was a statement of fact, not a question. "You're still looking for him."

Bouderon frowned. "Looking for whom?"

"Mason."

"I do not know what you mean. Please go away."

Robinson shrugged. "Please yourself. I can tell you you won't find him in a month of wet Wednesdays. But I can take you to him."

Bouderon rose from her chair. "Why do you think I am looking for someone?"

"Sod me, woman — it's obvious! You an' that traffic warden who kept sticking parking tickets under my bloody windscreen." He paused. "You want him? This is your last chance." He turned to go.

"Of course I want him."

"How bad? Five grand?"

"Five grand what?" Bouderon puckered her brows.

"Don't play the innocent with me, miss. Five thousand euros. In cash. Within the hour."

"I don't carry that quantity of money upon me," Bouderon said in her slightly stilted English. "Will you come with me to my office and I'll give it to you."

"And where may your office be, miss?"

"Centre Point."

Robinson guffawed. "You wouldn't get me in that place! Tell you what, though — I'll wait for you by the fountain outside."

Twenty minutes later Bouderon was back in St Giles Circus outside the Centre Point high-rise. She held her arms wide, signalling to Robinson that she had a package but nothing else that may cause him to run. And she was alone.

Robinson — Clipboard — rose cautiously to his feet and waited for her to come to him. He took her packet at arm's length, opened it and counted the money.

"Now your part of the deal. Where do I find Mason?"

He grinned. "You should have kept your car in Soho Square a little longer. I followed that woman to Docklands. Derelict warehouse; looks as if nobody's been through the door for months. Mind if I reach inside my coat?"

Bouderon glanced around. Nobody would risk a shooting in such a public place. "Slowly."

He pulled out the tattered *A-Z* and carefully passed it. "You'll see a big red cross where the door is. Mind if I ask why you want this guy?"

"Politics. Why did you want him?"

"Money. My boss paid well." He waved the wad of euros. "But not this well." He backed away until he was lost in the crowd, then ran. Bouderon studied the cross then went down to the ESD car pool. Her mission in London was almost at an end.

WE HEARD A DULL thumping on our steel outer door, and stared at each other. "Expecting visitors today?" I asked.

Philip shrugged. "Felicity came yesterday with the special present." The present, which we had been warned could not be faxed or e-mailed, was a revolver. One of the Heavenly Twins had recognised it as a Smith & Wesson 2100 which fired 9mm cartridges. He wondered how Soho Square could have procured such a weapon after the consequences of the Dunblane massacre.

Now Philip picked up the pistol and walked to the heavy steel door. "Who is it?" he called, then looked through the peephole. "It's a bimbo," he said to us. "What shall I do?"

I shrugged. "Let her in with her hands up?"

Seconds later the young woman entered, arms erect in the surrender gesture and with Philip aiming the Smith & Wesson at her midriff.

"Who are you?" he repeated. Everybody in the studio was watching her as she lowered her arms and smoothed her honey-blonde hair. When she smiled we could all appreciate her beauty, despite the charity-shop clothes.

"Mister Terry Mason," she said with a smile, advancing and offering me her hand. "I have been looking for you."

"Now you've found me." I took the hand carefully. "And who are you?"

"Miss Christine Bouderon, head of the criminal records department of the European Security Service."

We all jumped back a pace or two and grasped whatever was handy as weapons.

She smiled. "Have no fear. I have been sent from Berlin to arrest you, dead or alive, but I question the validity of my orders. You are totally opposed to the European Union, Mr Mason, are you not?"

"Up to here," I answered, with a slicing gesture across my throat, but I never took my eyes off her for a second. "We all are, in this room."

"I have been trained to believe that the European Union is right in everything it does, without question. But maybe I am misled. Things are happening now, in the Eurosicherheitsdienst, which I know are wrong. May I sit down?"

She had taken us completely off guard. Philip beckoned her to a seat but still kept the pistol aimed at her. She went on: "There are many millions like you, across Europe. Who is telling the truth — the people who want to end the Union, or the people who have spent their lives creating it?"

I stared at her. "Are you real? I'm not dreaming, am I? You're really head of criminal records at this Security Service place? Where is it, by the way?"

She explained briefly where the Kristallkoffer was situated. "I am real. And am I dreaming too? Are you really Terry Mason, the man whose face has been on every television screen across Europe?"

I relaxed. "I guess we're both awake." Philip and I met each other's gaze, and we exchanged subtle nods.

Philip said: "We're going to trust you, Miss Bouderon, but first I'm going to frisk you. I regret..."

"*Frisk* me? You want to *jump* on me? What is this?"

"Look for hidden guns. I regret we have no female staff here, and it will be a careful search."

She shrugged. "I understand. At least, you apologise. My boss, Axel Teutoburger, would just jump."

Some half an hour later, when we were certain she was unarmed and she was relaxing with coffee and biscuits, I said: "So let's go through this again. You want to hear our argument, why Euroslavia could lead to the Third World War? And then, if you think we're right, you'll do *what*?"

"I will work with you. I will be your informer inside the Kristallkoffer. You will have much need of me, I think."

"Indeed. But why this change of heart? I find it as believable as if the Pope converted to Islam. And aren't you putting your life at risk?"

"I suppose so. Let me tell you something I have not told anybody at the Kristallkoffer. I am born in Montmédy, a little town in La Meuse, France, near the bottom part of Belgium. My grandfather was a poor farmer whose wife kept a bar, a bistro, to make enough money. He saw Germany invade in 1940. He saw the bridges blown, the horses taken, the women raped. He hated the Germans, but when the war was over and they went home, they were only a hundred kilometers away."

I nodded.

"His father, my great-grandfather, was born in Montmédy in the first year of the twentieth century — a hundred and five years since. He was a soldier in the first war, and the things he saw were too horrible to understand. Men being tied to cartwheels and taken into battle. Men who could not run to face the Germans as they knew they would die, so our own officers shot them in cold blood. It was the mass slaughter of the innocent. Men dying of...." She stopped. "No. I cannot tell you."

"I guess we already know," Philip said. "We've all seen it on the telly. In fact, I bitterly resent those inscriptions on First World War memorials: 'gave their lives for their country.' Rubbish. They were robbed. They were dead whatever they did."

I could see that Philip was getting morose on one of his favourite topics. I chipped in: "So you were glad when this Monnet fellow tried to stop France and Germany fighting again?"

Bouderon nodded. "My great-grandfather died when I was twelve and he was a few months from his ninety. He told me the European Union would be the best thing ever to happen in the continent."

"And you believed him?"

"Why not?" She shook her head. "But I do not think it is good what I see and hear now. Microchips put in new-born babies. Twenty men and women in Brussels who rule three hundred and seventy million people by decree. A madman who sends soldiers into another country. A security police answerable to nobody."

"You mean the Eurosicherheitsdienst?"

"I do."

"Who is it answerable to? Who's your boss?"

"The very top man is the President of the European Commission. Only he can tell us what not to do."

I gasped. "What *not* to do? Then who in God's name tells you what you *can* do?"

"I think it is my boss, President Teutoburger. I think he is in total control, and the more I think it, the more scared I am. He sent a man into Prague to destroy your satellite transmitter."

We exchanged glances again. "Don't we know it. You may like to know we've now got the choice of three dishes."

She smiled. "I am glad — I think. But the Sicherheitsdienst — the more it begins to look like the Gestapo, the Schutzstaffel. Next we will be having concentration camps."

"God! You don't honestly think so?"

"What is to stop it?" She sat in that chair so innocently, yet she was voicing opinions that I had not dared even think about. "What is there to stop it?" she repeated. "The people have no say. They do not even *know*. The people of the Soviet Union had no say, and millions died. The people of the Third Reich had no say, and millions died. The people of Euroslavia, I think you call it, have no say."

"And millions will die in the fight to have a voice?"

"Perhaps. I hope not. But trouble always comes when the German people are taken where they do not want to go."

"And many of them didn't want this Mickey Mouse money."

"A majority. As in France, also. So it must surely be wrong."

"Grandfather made a mistake?"

"Not at all," she argued. "The idea of a European Union is excellent. You do not have Texas fighting Oklahoma, and you should not have France fighting Germany. But the desire must come from the ordinary people, not from the governments."

"And that will never happen. We are all too different."

"Far too different, Mr Mason. Race, language, culture, climate, religion. What we eat. How we play. Britain and Spain look out to the Atlantic. Germany looks to the east, for *Lebensraum* — even today. In Spain it is *mañana*. In Germany it is always *now*."

"Europe will *never* be one state at heart," Philip protested. "For a start, which one language would it use? English?"

Bouderon actually laughed. "The French would never agree. We have spent too much time protecting our language from the American influence."

"It's because of you French that we have this stupid rule of labelling all ingredients in Latin. *Aqua* for water's not too bad, but why *paraffinum liquidum* when the Ancient Romans never knew the stuff? And *lardum* for bacon? Crazy."

"Spain would not agree, either."

"Germany certainly wouldn't, although logically, the common language should be English."

"Why, please?"

"It's the unofficial world language, and its parents are French and German. It's tailor-made."

The conversation developed and Philip and I abandoned our plans for the afternoon in order to try to convince this refugee from the heart of Euroslavia that she was wrong and we were right, although the rest of the staff continued watching the monitors and working on the next *Tell Tel*. Finally Bouderon shook us both by the hand and admitted defeat.

"*Vive l'Europe libre!* Down with Euroslavia!"

I could scarcely believe my ears, although I had seen which way things were going. The Pope bowed to Mecca. Pigs could fly. The sun would rise over the North Pole.

"And now?" I asked. "You go back to Berlin?"

"And I will help your cause, when I can. It will only be once, because I shall be exposed and forced to flee. But I *will* help."

We shook hands all round, and escorted her through the steel bulkhead to the street door growing among its weeds. When she drove off, Philip and I faced reality. "I'm going to call Soho Square," Philip snapped. "We're getting out of here right now — all of us, and all this gear."

"Don't you trust her?"

Philip snapped again: "I trusted Edward Heath, and look where it got us. But I'll tell you one thing, Terry — I've got it all on tape."

"*What?*"

"Every word she said after the frisking. Two cameras, one sound recorder. Everything!"

"You're not going to use it?"

"That depends on whether she keeps her word. But just in case she's a bloody good actress and she took us all for a load of suckers, we're getting out."

WE HAD A REMOVAL van outside the emergency studios within two hours and we moved *Tell Tel* to a derelict chicken farm in Essex, Region UK54, locking the steel door as we left.

That night a bomb exploded outside that door and the entire masonry was destroyed. Philip swore it was Bouderon's work and he wanted to broadcast her heartfelt confessions across the continent. I managed to persuade him to give her the benefit of the doubt; I suspected Callan may have had something to do with it.

And that Saturday night, as we settled down in new sleeping bags in the corner of a long-empty packing shed, I wondered where Lisa was. She couldn't call me, because we wouldn't get the phones transferred until the next day.

BY SUNDAY OCTOBER 30, the first vehicles of McGovan's Motorcade had reached the urban limits to Brussels and Luxembourg and were being stopped by police road blocks. The protesters raised no objections, parking in their hundreds and then their thousands on the hard shoulder of motorways and in the outer lane of other dual-carriageways. The traffic jam was as effective as had been French farmer's strikes when they brought out thousands of tractors, but on this first day it was not as catastrophic as the French lorry-drivers' strike of 1996 when major routes across the country had been blocked for days.

The protesters set up camp where they were, prepared to live in their cars for days, if needed: they had all brought adequate food, bedding and water, and almost all had enough fuel to get them at least half way home.

Vehicle registrations showed how far some of the cars had come. There were SE prefixes from Sevilla in Region ES61 mixing with number plates stating *Roma* in IT6; there were cars with 05 for the Ariège département in Region FR62, parked by HH from the Hansestadt Hamburg in DE6. There were Fiats and Fords, Seats and Volvos, Rolls-Royces and Renaults.

And still they came. Passengers in window seats in jet airliners coming in to land at Charles de Gaulle saw the serpentine stream on the great Boulevard Péréphérique. People in Dover watched cars queueing for the ferries as if it were the height of the holiday season.

On that Sunday night, the battered Austin from Alderney parked in a backstreet in Mons as all farm gateways had been filled for miles back. Father Erich Zimmerman was in the back of an old Renault van with several other hitchers of mixed ages and gender, a few miles away near Valenciennes.

Xavier Yzurdiaga and his companion Eustaqui Arrieta in their rented car were conscious that the Servicio de Seguridad — the Eurosicherheitsdienst in these parts — was on the lookout for them, and almost certainly the normal police would be interested in the two Basques — and the parcel of Semtex and five detonators that lay under the spare wheel. With these complications in mind they made a habit of finding a campsite well before dark; on this night they had driven up a woodsman's track through the trees on a hillslope in the Ardennes and had found an old sandstone quarry overhung by tall trees. Behind them lay the little French town of Montmédy, which meant absolutely nothing to them; behind, but only five hundred metres away, lay the village of Torgny, the southernmost settlement in the Province of Belgium.

Callan had shipped his Jaguar on the ferry from Harwich to Hoek van Holland and was a few miles short of Antwerp. Protest traffic was much lighter on this route, but local traffic and a major road accident had delayed the party. Archie McGovan had been overwhelmed by the response to the appeal that he had started, and had sought refuge in silence. Callan was silent to prevent condemning himself by ill-chosen words.

BOUDERON DIDN'T MAKE it back to Berlin on that Saturday for the simple reason that all flights were full and her security credentials didn't qualify her to have some other passenger kicked off. She called the Kristallkoffer and reported to Teutoburger's office, amazed to learn that he was still in the building.

She landed at Berlin's Schonefeld Airport late on Sunday and took the Schwebebahn, the 'hanging railway' to the Friedrichstrasse station. She walked to the Kristallkoffer, arriving a little after 2100 and, on the instructions of the security guard, went to Teutoburger in the incident room, a high-security chamber one wall of which held a bank of video screens.

"You are *still* on duty, sir?"

"Why not? Crime and sabotage have no weekend breaks. You have come to report that you have eliminated Mason?"

"Mason cannot be found, sir," she said.

Teutoburger swung from the video wall on his swivel chair, and screamed at her. "And that's *it?* That's your report? Mason cannot be found? You've been over in London for God knows how long, and all you can say is this *kerl* cannot be found?"

"Yes, sir." She had told herself she would need to stand to attention for a good ten minutes while the President of the European Security Service ranted at her. It must now be obvious to anyone, she reasoned, that Teutoburger could not cope. He was well on the way to a major mental breakdown, or a massive heart-attack.

The diatribe was less than she anticipated because her boss collapsed in a bout of coughing and dismissed her. Once he had recovered he turned back to his screens in the incident room, a smallish chamber that never saw the light of day and had twenty-four video monitors in a solid bank on one wall. They could be programmed to receive signals from a wide range of locations from Seville to Stockholm, or to form a mosaic of just one picture. Or they could be used as computer screens controlled by the keyboard and mouse on the long desk.

At the moment, as it was night across Europe, they were blank, but alive and shimmering. Yet Teutoburger dare not leave them for many minutes in case something should happen; he had been in the incident room for twenty continuous hours except for answering the calls of nature, and he anticipated he would be here, day and night, until the crisis was over.

So far, the crisis had gone as he had anticipated — no; as he had planned. All local traffic had been ordered to have batteries disconnected from 2200 on this night — just a few minutes away — until 0200 tomorrow, and the same again tomorrow night, as directed by the emergency programme on local television and the Internet: Bouderon had done her job, despite her protest. Therefore all the traffic on the autoroutes, highways, roads and lanes in Brabant, Namur, Hainaut and Luxembourg, as well as Brussels itself, in the former Duchy of Luxembourg, and in Champagne, Ardenne and Lorraine; must be involved in the protest. Or in the *Fê des Morts*.

Simple.

But from here on he was going to do it himself. Casbergen had gone to Prague and got himself killed. Bouderon had gone to London and failed miserably: she should be charged with incompetence. González was a Spaniard and as much a buffoon as the rest of his tribe.

Teutoburger would do it himself; he had always planned it that way, ever since the system was installed. It was truly a wonderful toy, one to be proud of. And as he *was* the Eurosicherheitsdienst, he could take all the glory; it was his responsibility, his duty, his honour, to operate the system. He was not aware of his pounding heart as he played with his keyboard in front of the bank of flickering screens, bringing up on one the outline maps of the provinces of Brabant, Hainaut, Luxembourg and Namur, which made south and central Belgium. His heart pounded and his fingers rattled over other keys until he brought up the map of what had been the Duchy of Luxembourg and was now the Luxembourg Region. Finally, and with a severe pain gripping his chest, he called up the map of the Champagne and Lorraine regions of north-east France. The three maps were on separate screens; he now repeated the process, superimposing the highway system, then he accessed the locations of every mobile phone transmitter mast in the eight regions and overlaid them as pulsing red dots on the composite map.

Pausing while a severe shaft of pain struck him in the sternum, he then brought up a questionnaire on screen. His heart pounded; he knew he was having a heart attack, but duty came before all else. He thumped himself on the chest. There was no time to waste. He answered, in English, the questions in front of the four boxes. *Regions?* ALL. *Time/Date start?* 2359, 301005 , *Time/Date Stop?* 0001 311005. Then he did it all again for the night of 311005 to 011105.

The last question asked OPERATE? Y/N. He pressed Y as the heart attack struck, the fiery pain forcing him to slide off his chair and onto the floor.

ERICH ZIMMERMAN WOKE slowly on Monday morning, 31 October, troubled by a sharp chill in the air and strange noises. Not the gentle snoring of the other Euroslavia protesters in the back of the old Renault van; it was more like a moaning, a groaning, with the hint of something approaching a scream.

Zimmerman eased himself from his sleeping-bag and pulled his trousers up from knee-level: all his money and documents were in those pockets and he wasn't risking losing them.

He stepped outside, crunching on the hoar-frosted grass of the wide verge, with the lights of Valenciennes competing with the dawn in a cloudless, cold sky. In the faint light he could see other vehicles parked randomly, their owners and passengers en route to the world's biggest protest rally.

The moaning was coming from somebody in the nearest car, a smart white Citroen, and in the gloom Zimmerman could make out somebody else in the driving seat, trying to coax an unresponsive engine into life.

He walked over. "Can I help?" he asked in French.

The man in the driving seat grasped his arm. "Help? We would be so grateful. My wife is in labour, but the engine won't start. I don't understand it — it was perfect yesterday."

"It's been a cold night," Zimmerman observed.

"That is not the problem. Where is your car?"

"The old van," Zimmerman nodded. "You want to get your wife to hospital?"

"Please. If you could help. Her waters have broken."

The old priest stumbled back to the van and roused the driver, stretched across the front bench seats. "Emergency. Woman needs the hospital in Valenciennes."

"If there is one," the driver moaned, but within five minutes all the passengers were awake and the couple from the smart Citroen were on the van's front seat.

There was no time to sort out motor problems as the old Renault cruised into Valenciennes, a town that had suffered severely from the Luftwaffe half a century earlier, then again when the coalfields became uneconomic. They found a small hospital and left the grateful couple.

"No point in going back," the driver yawned. "We'll pull up in the town square until daylight."

JOHN LE MESURIER, nominal owner of the old Austin van, woke when he heard the first sounds of the new day drifting across the town square at Mons. After a cold breakfast, he scraped the frost off the windscreen, started the engine and eased slowly onto the road. Several other parties of motorcade protesters were standing around their vehicles as if waiting for Christmas or Armageddon; a number of them cast envious eyes at the old van.

Le Mesurier called out of his opened window: *"Qu'est-ce qui passe?"*

"Le moteur. Il ne marche pas."

"Dommage."

He drove on. "Can't get their cars started," he commented although everyone in the van had fluent French.

"Plenty of them," Annette Dugard commented. "Something terrible's happened. Euroslavia has found a way to strike back. Or was it the frost? It was pretty cold in the night."

"Don't be stupid," the old Guernseyman John Doyle grunted. "How can they stop every motor in town just by waving a wand? And it certainly wasn't the cold, if this old truck could start up."

"I don't know what's happened, John, but your magic wand is as good a guess as any. Every car has had a breakdown."

"Not everybody," Fiona Le Mesurier said. "There's a car up ahead. It's moving."

"Don't stop our engine!" Dugard cried. "Whatever witchcraft it is, we don't want to be stuck in Mons!"

They drove on slowly, heading north for Brussels on a road that had very little moving traffic, so vastly different from the previous day. They passed dozens of vehicles, seeing drivers frantically trying to open bonnets that refused to budge, seeing others trying to push-start, or coasting downhill to a chaos that was not going anywhere. Soon people were starting to wave them down, to call out to them for help.

"We can't stop!" Le Mesurier called from his window.

He felt detached from the scene all around them; he felt as if he were standing in some amusement arcade wearing a virtual reality mask which was trying to convince him his was one of only a few vehicles able to move, and he didn't understand it.

But his wife did. "The only things moving are old," she observed. "Does that make sense?"

CALLAN AND HIS PARTY were awake before daybreak. Callan had had a miserable night, tortured by guilt and tormented by cold feet. According to the news on the car radio, McGovan's Motorcade had brought protesters out in their millions. Why? Why was the European Union so unpopular? It had brought economic stability to the continent for the first time in history; many Germans alive today remembered when a bucketload of banknotes wouldn't buy a loaf. Many Italians remembered their lire in freefall. Sterling had had more downs than ups. The French franc had been devalued by 99% in the 1950s. Nowadays there was stability — so why didn't people want it?

He turned on the car radio and got a part of his answer. With the financial markets back at work after the weekend, the euro was facing an even greater loss of confidence and the base interest rate had already been kicked up to 15%. Callan guessed it would rise again before the day was out.

His need to reach Brussels was even greater, but he dreaded getting there. It was going to be one of the turning-points in his life, but he didn't yet know which way he would turn.

As a frosty dawn revealed the flat landscape he noticed the traffic was building up fast, mostly heading south and several of them taking masochistic pleasure in overtaking his Jaguar. The 1987-vintage Jag, he knew, was too old to compete with modern motor technology.

Soon after leaving the region of Antwerpen, which was also designated BE21, he began noticing motorists having trouble with their cars. They were pushing, hammering their fists on bonnets, kicking tyres in frustration.

Very slowly he remembered what Commissioner Boeke had hinted to him; there was a development under way which would allow car engines to be immobilised by remote control. It seemed to Callan at that moment that the system was already highly developed.

Then he began to relax. The system involved the tiny in-built computers in all modern cars. A Jaguar built 18 years ago had no such refinements. He was safe.

LISA TOOK THE train from Bergen, over the snow-covered Kolen Mountains, the backbone of Scandinavia, and dropped down the fantastically scenic Hallingdal into Oslo. Another train took her down the coast to Hälsingborg in the Swedish Province, and across The Sound on the crowded car ferry to Helsingör, Shakespeare's Elsinor, in the

Province of Denmark, where she spent the night. She tried phoning me but the line was dead: the outside line still had not been rigged up to the chicken sheds.

People were asking her if she was heading for Brussels or Luxembourg to join McGovan's Motorcade, but she told them she was trying to keep clear of it. She was cautious enough not to mention me, or even that her name was Mason.

"But you should come. You are British? Surely you do not like Euroslavia? Why not come?"

"I do not like Euroslavia," she explained, "but I do not wish to join the protest. I have no car."

The next day she took another train down to Hamburg and across the plains of Saxony to Köln, more concerned with why she couldn't contact me than with the obvious air of doom and excitement that seemed to permeate the carriage.

"British?" an elderly woman asked. "Zen vy do you not go to Brussels? Zis *Einheitswährung*, zis single money, is all wronk. Ve Chermans are sufferink. Ve haf been sufferink since Polen ask to choin. No — since long before. And now ze money is sinking like ze *Titanic*."

"Pardon?" Lisa asked.

The woman's male companion interrupted. "Crisis of confidence in the euro. Europe has too much unemployment. You know it is thirteen prozent in Germany, and more than twelve prozent now in England. Greece is bad. It has more than twenty prozent — we go to Corfu each year for our holiday. But Spain is terrible. Thirty-two point four prozent! No wonder Spanish economists are screaming insults at Frankfurt, claiming that a fifteen prozent interest rate is politically motivated for Germany and will bring total disaster for small businesses in Catalunya, and will cause half the people of Andalucía to leave the region."

"Fifteen percent?" Lisa asked. "What's fifteen percent?"

"Have you not heard? Bank interest rate. It goes up one punkt today and it is likely to go higher. Soon we must bring out the wheelbarrows again, no? Ah — this Europe! We are supposed to work for the common good, but while Frankfurt controls the money, Frankfurt will have policies only for Germany. We should — how do you say in England? — call it a day."

YZURDIAGA AND ARRIETA also woke before daybreak. In the chill air they boiled coffee over a camping stove, grateful for the privacy granted by the fold of hills around them.

"Well, Xav, is it still going to be Brussels? We're much nearer

Luxembourg. And we must remember what's under the spare wheel."

Yzurdiaga sucked his top lip. "Luxembourg? Council of Ministers, building empty this time of year. Court of Justice, open. Court of Auditors and Investment Bank, both open. Second-rate targets but easier to make a first-rate strike. Okay, Staqui, Luxembourg it is."

"Do you really think you'll be able to bomb one of them? I mean, the city's going to be packed with protesters, and security will be as tight as a bull's arse in August. We don't want another brush with the Servicio de Seguridad, even if it's only to ask the time."

"True, old friend. We'll review the situation as we go along."

They set out a little after daylight, using a Michelin map to navigate along a backroad through little villages: Lamorteau, Harnoncourt, St Mard.

"Must have been pretty cold in the night," Staqui commented. "Plenty of cars that won't start." He pointed out vehicles with registrations from all parts of France and a few from Spain, but not one of them was moving.

"Local traffic's not affected," Yzurdiaga said, nodding to an older car with Belgian plates.

A kilometer on, they slowed for a distraught motorist who blocked their path. "Can you help, please? We are desperate to get to Luxembourg."

"Don't switch off," Staqui hissed as Yzurdiaga used the central locking system to secure all doors. He shook his head sadly and inched forward, but the stranded driver leaped onto the bonnet. Yzurdiaga hit the brake pedal, shooting the man off the front; he reversed a few metres then slid into bottom gear and drove around the still-protesting driver. Both men felt their heartbeat increase with the sudden stress.

"Local traffic *is* affected," Staqui protested as they passed a man using a crowbar to open the bonnet of a frost-covered car on his front drive. Then he saw the connection. "It's new vehicles, Xav. Something's happened to them all and they won't start. Old cars are OK."

"Then how come we managed to start this morning? This car's only a year old."

They drove through St Rémy and Signeulx, almost scraping the unmarked border with France as well as squeezing past long rows of immobilised vehicles.

"This is like some nightmare," Yzurdiaga groaned. "I get the feeling that if we stop, we'll never start again." As he spoke they saw a villager walk into his opened garage and take sacking off the engine of his newish car, exposed to the chill of night as the bonnet was up.

Yzurdiaga stopped to see what would happen. The man leaned over the engine, his right elbow moved as he wielded a spanner, then he slammed the bonnet and drove slowly onto his forecourt. Yzurdiaga moved on. "Not all local traffic is affected. Not all protest traffic, either."

They were on the main N88 road to Luxembourg, and France was only a hundred yards away, when Arrieta noticed a mobile telephone transmitter mast in the corner of a field.

"Xav," he said moments later. "I think I've got it. We were in a hollow last night. You wouldn't have got reception on your mobile."

"I didn't bring it."

"That's not the point! Somebody sent out some sort of signal that's blocked the ignition on all cars — all newish ones at any rate. And we didn't receive it because we were out of range."

"That's science-fiction, Staqui!"

"But it fits the circumstances. People can't open their bonnets, either. Open ours, Xav, before you stop the engine."

Under protest, Yzurdiaga pulled onto the verge and unclipped the bonnet latch; the lid opened easily. "So?"

Staqui reached across and cut the ignition, then restarted it. "We're in the clear. Let's get going."

AXEL TEUTOBURGER RECOVERED sufficiently to know that he'd suffered a coronary attack. He flexed the fingers of both hands and found them functioning, although he had no sense of touch in the left hand. His legs and feet worked, and he could move his mouth. He was grateful he'd had the warning and he summoned the staff doctor to the incident room even though it was barely three o'clock in the morning.

"It's hospital for you," the doctor ordered, but Teutoburger shouted him down.

"Pills. Give me whatever pills I need to keep me going. I've got the biggest crisis since the Normandy landings, and I'm in charge."

"If you don't..."

"And if *you* don't give me the pills I'll see you in hell. Now — where are they?"

The doctor took a small bottle from his case and put it on the president's desk. "That'll do you for now. I'll be back in an hour, if you're still alive..."

"I will be. Just hope that you are, doctor." Teutoburger crunched all four pills, winced, and turned to face his shimmering video wall with all screens blank.

He slept, waking when the doctor came back with more pills. "No more than one an hour, or you're on a short cut to Paradise."

"Clear off, doc. Thanks."

He slept again, rousing at six when he began calling up live pictures from a selection of surveillance cameras across the European Union. Brussels city centre: the leisurely start of what would soon be the rush to work on this last day of October. Paris: plenty of cars parked in the streets, but that was normal. Luxembourg: streets almost empty. The former frontier post on the E17, the Lille to Brussels autoroute: a knot of about a dozen cars parked on the hard shoulder on the eastbound carriageway, with signs of activity.

Teutoburger moved his mouse and the camera zoomed in a little until he could see men arguing, trying to force open bonnets, and actually turning one car onto its side. He laughed. "Fools! Imbeciles! You try to damage the European Union, but we are cleverer than you! It will take an authorised motor distributor with the right computer software to get you out of that mess. Maybe sometime next week, eh?"

Doornik, what the French called Tournai: the town centre was blocked solid with cars, and Teutoburger saw two caravans caught up in the snarl. Nothing was moving; nothing *could* move.

As the light grew, he began selecting more rural cameras. Brussels city limits, autoroute 3 from Liège. Last night the first two miles had been lined by orderly-parked cars prohibited entry to the city. Now, as a frosty dawn broke, he could see hundreds of people scurrying around like ants. Teutoburger knew they had all realised that not one vehicle in the queue could be started. All the engines were as dead as a scrapyard. Not one bonnet clip could be released. Not one heater would work. The people would either stay there and freeze, or they would see sense and go home. On foot.

"So much for McGovan's Motorcade!"

When the daylight grew better, Teutoburger ordered a light aircraft to fly over Region BE1, the chief city of the Belgian regions and the capital city of the European Union. He called Bouderon and Gonzáles in, and Kris Andersen who had temporarily taken over Casbergen's duties, and allowed their immediate heads of unit to join them, so there were ten people watching the display, with all 24 monitors keyed in to make one giant moving picture.

It was awesome. It was terrifying. It was humbling. It was exhilarating. It all depended on one's mental outlook.

The spotter aircraft showed the city centre, within the orbital autoroute, to be operating normally, and the Autoroute 201 to the airport was clear. Beyond the orbital, where police had stopped the protesters' vehicles, total chaos reigned. Every inbound carriageway was blocked solid, as far back as one could see on this crystal-clear morning. Almost every vehicle was where it had been parked the previous evening, but a few — notably the old cars — had started and their drivers had tried to manoeuvre clear of the blockage.

As the plane flew lower, the audience saw the problem; the cars had been parked bumper-to-bumper and there was very little chance of escape.

Christine Bouderon covered her mouth in typical feminine style as she saw thousands of people milling around on the roads, arguing, fighting, staring up at the aircraft and waving their fists. People were forcing open the bonnets with tyre levers; they were tipping some cars on their side to get at the engine. Other protesters were resigned to their fate and were boiling kettles on gas stoves on the edge of the hard shoulder, scraping the frost from the windscreens, or thrashing their arms across their chests to generate warmth.

Between traffic movements at the airport, the spotter plane flew higher, crossing the city centre where there was almost normal local commuter traffic, plus commercial vehicles, and the giant earthmovers on the roadworks south of the centre where the orbital motorway was being completed. Then it banked and came within sight of the suburbs outside the orbital. From around three hundred metres it was giving a panoramic view of a giant, mechanical still-life. Car roofs were glinting in the sunshine on all six autoroutes, the eight main trunk roads, and every minor road leading into the city — and none of it was moving. Queues stretched in most instances as far as could be seen, and on this micro scale little ant-like dots were drifting around, mirroring the human tragedies that they had seen on the macro scale.

Bouderon was deeply shocked. All these people, and many hundreds of thousands more, had made the effort to leave their homes and drive half across the continent to protest at Euroslavia. She knew their motivation must be great, and she began to appreciate even deeper, their bitterness, anger, frustration and downright disgust with their elected leaders, who had led them blindly, over many years, into a political and economic union of incompatible states under non-approachable, inaccessible, unrepresentative leaders.

In those moments she knew she was committed, heart and soul, to the cause of resistance.

"Wonderful sight, isn't it?" Teutoburger gleamed. There was no longer a pain in his chest, merely a grumbling sensation that told him the kraken was resting. "They thought they could destroy us, but they cannot. The Union is irreversible, and will last a thousand years!"

Bouderon recalled where her grandfather had first heard those words and who had spoken them. Kohl had said some, Hitler the others, with two generations between them.

Even Kris Andersen, Casbergen's Europhobe replacement, was shocked. "What are you going to do, sir?"

"Do? Nothing. There is much worse to come. Give them another night and another few days."

"I didn't see any police or anybody else controlling the crowds, sir."

"Of course you didn't. They're in reserve. Our protesters are more worried about their precious cars; half of them are bought on finance. There's no need for crowd control."

The giant video wall showed a bright red blob of flame topped by a rapidly-growing cloud of oil smoke, and the tracker plane turned towards it. The picture was lost for a minute then the aircraft banked and the inferno came into view. The area was immediately recognisable as the place where the plane had passed low overhead, but now a dozen or more vehicles were burning furiously and protesters were desperately manhandling cars out of the solid line in order to create a firebreak. Hundreds waved their fists skywards; many were jumping in their fury, and some were even hurling bottles and car jacks at the aircraft.

Teutoburger laughed. "Slipstream must have blown those gas stoves over." Bouderon hurried out of the incident room before she was sick.

THINGS WERE HAPPENING fast at CCC. The chicken sheds were proving very difficult to convert at such short notice; there were problems with electricity supply, communications links with Soho Square, and the ordinary telephone line was still not connected. I could imagine Lisa's fears and worries as she tried to call and failed to make a connection. Was I ill? Or dead? I was worrying about her as well. Where was she? Safe in Norway, or heading for the problems of a Euroslavia threatened with a major traffic snarl-up, with an oil crisis, with its currency tumbling steadily against the dollar and the yen. And against the dear old pound in the Sterling Zone.

From that day, the last day of October and the day before the Festival of the Dead, *Tell Tel* was broadcasting around the clock on cable in Britain, direct to a satellite from CCC's own station hidden deep in a fold of the Chiltern Hills, and from the Polish and Swiss satellite stations in Europe. Quality had gone plunging down in return for quantity, and even now I cannot think how we managed to put it together from inside a derelict chicken farm on the edge of a field in Essex, with improvised landlines from Soho Square, with overhead electricity vulnerable to the weather, with absolutely no security beyond our total isolation, and with our living quarters still in the packing shed. If we hadn't been so devoted to our cause of bringing down the European Union, we would all have gone on strike for better working conditions.

And the pictures we were beaming up? They were a compilation of live pictures from any available source — and there was no shortage of choice — with some particularly graphic sequences being repeated, such as the coachload of protesters which plunged off a bridge in Koblenz and drifted down the Rhine while slowly sinking. Tucked away in our derelict chicken farm in Essex, we were seeing the film immediately before it was sent by land line to the transmitters, and Philip and I were adding live commentary, some of it purely guesswork. I managed to put in a bit of spontaneous French, otherwise it was all English.

When we learned from the Bracknell Weather Centre that a mass of cold air was drifting westward from Russia, and there had been a particularly hard frost the previous night in eastern Germany as well as all of Scandinavia, we threw in the weather charts as well.

They looked ominous. Snow was on its way; it was falling in Helsinki, Stockholm and Berlin by midday and was forecast to reach Brussels by midnight, the midnight which would see not only the main thrust of McGovan's Motorcade protesting against Euroslavia, but also herald in the great French tribute to the dead, the *Fête des Morts*.

CCC was not, of course, the only station broadcasting live coverage of McGovan's Motorcade on this day. I suppose almost every station in the world was giving nearly wall-to-wall pictures of the greatest display of people power that the planet had ever seen, and certainly the largest gathering of motor vehicles since Mr Rolls met Mr Royce. CNN was beating us hollow by the depth of its interviews, research and coverage, but we didn't mind; it was the expert at this sort of thing — and *we* had started it.

All over France the Festival of the Dead was drawing motorists to congregate at the cemeteries, as families gathered from all parts of the country, and from other parts of Euroslavia, to honour their ancestors. Almost every shop in the country was closed in respect of the dear departed, the sole exceptions being florists and out-of-town bistros and restaurants.

Every year the *Fête des Morts* caused traffic jams in the larger cities, particularly in Toulouse, Marseille, Bordeaux, Lyon, Paris, and the industrial cities in the north-east.

This year, however, the northern cities were being overwhelmed by the motorcade, and Philip and I were hard-pressed to keep up a commentary.

"It's total gridlock," I remember saying of an aerial shot of Lille and Roubaix and into Kortrijk in Belgium. "Miles of stationary cars. Every road leading to Brussels is snarled up, and those coming away from Brussels aren't much better. It's incredible to think that mankind could build so many cars, and that everybody should want to drive on the same stretch of tarmac at the same time. It's an absolute madhouse."

"Look at that," Philip took over on my signal, and as the picture cut to a helicopter shot of two coaches which had been in head-on collision north of Arras. "Probably one going north to Brussels, the other coming south to a Festival of the Dead. And now there are more dead stretched out on the road. I wonder if our chopper is going down to pick up the injured? No — there's a paramedic chopper coming in on the right of your picture. It's a fact that the only shots we're going to get of grim scenes like this are from the air. Cars that are moving aren't going walking pace, and half of them aren't going anywhere at all."

The weather chart came on again, showing that snow was still due to reach Brussels by midnight.

"I really admire the guts of these hundreds of thousands of people — millions, there must be — who've come out to voice their objections. It's a sight that the rest of the world must be taking to its heart very seriously indeed. It shows that you can lead most of the people some of the time, but when they realise they're being led where they don't want to go, they let their opinions be known in the only way they can, as Euroslavia hasn't had an effective democratic government since it began."

"Hard words, Philip," I commented.

"But true, Terry. If the people of the old Soviet Union had had the chance to protest without being gunned down, Communism would have vanished decades earlier. It's only ignorance, fostered by lying politicians in every country, that allowed Euroslavia to get such a hold on the continent of Europe. Now we're all reaping the whirlwind."

I had had a message from Soho Square in my earphone, and I planted the question that was suggested. "Do you think this is the beginning of the end of autocratic government? I understand we've performed a small miracle and we have a video link with Teresa Gorman, the former Westminster MP for Billericay and a leading Eurosceptic in the nineties. Mrs Gorman — is this the end of the European Union?"

The screen shimmered briefly as it cut to one of Britain's most likeable former members of Parliament. "I think it will take much more than a protest," she said, "even one on this scale. It must surely be the world's largest gathering, don't you think? But even if the whole system collapses tomorrow, every member state has the vast majority of its cash locked away in the European Investment Bank and the Bundesbank. By the way, I've just heard something on the BBC radio news. Can I tell you? It's OPEC — you know, the oil producing and exporting countries, based in Vienna. Apparently it's just announced a total oil embargo on the European Union. The radio stressed *total*. I heard it say even Iraq has joined in. Saddam Hussein said something about the miles of stationary traffic around Brussels reminded him of the long lines of Iraqi troops pulling out of Kuwait, before the Americans bombed them."

"Total?" I could scarcely believe it, and it terrified me. "Where are the oil producing companies in this? Do they go along with it?"

Mrs Gorman said: "I'm only guessing here, but could it be something to do with people power? If millions of ordinary people make the effort to drive to Brussels to protest, then many more millions must have the same idea. Tens of millions, maybe half the population of the Union."

"That's more than a hundred and fifty million."

Mrs Gorman brought the commonsense feminine angle into perspective. "I know if I were in charge of a major company, I'd listen very carefully to what my customers wanted. If one oil company decided to come out in favour of the people, could the others stay behind?"

"Possible, possible. The timing's ideal, with the euro still sinking. I'll bet Euroslavia would love to be able to pay in pounds sterling now. Or even Falklands pounds."

She smiled. "Now, wouldn't that be lovely? As it is, virtually every country in the world which has got money or gold invested in Frankfurt, wants it out. Who can blame them? They want to withdraw every penny they can. You remember the dear old penny, Terry? Twelve to the shilling? Of course, that had to go."

"I remember the dear old half-crown, too. And the farthing — how about that? Do you think other countries want to see the collapse of Euroslavia?"

Mrs Gorman nodded. "It's too big. It's far too unmanageable. And it's dangerous. We've been preaching democracy to the poorer countries for years, then we went and ditched it. How can they believe anything we say, after that? Euroslavia? My God, it's been a pig's dinner from the start. And it's been a white elephant. Can you have those metaphors together? Yes, I think most countries will be pleased to see it collapse. I know I will."

THE PICTURES FROM CNN were picked up clearly in Port Stanley, the capital of the Kingdom of the Falkland Islands. Sir Claude Warner, the Vicereine, called the Chief Executive of the islands' parliament, Sir Tom Smith. "Seen the box, Tom?"

"Bloody good news, isn't it?"

"Shall we make it a public holiday?"

"What, today? Too late — half the day's gone already."

"No, I meant tomorrow — Tuesday. All Saints' Day. Announce it today."

"Could do, Cloudy. Or we could wait until Euroslavia collapses — it can't be long."

"What?" Sir Claude was suddenly serious. "Why do you think so? You're much more positive than people in Britain."

"Look at the evidence, sir. Oil embargo announced. Run on the Mickey Mouse money. Now this mass protest of millions of motorists. If it were a democracy it would be forced to the polls."

"But it isn't a democracy."

"You remember how the Berlin Wall and the Iron Curtain came down? The Commies couldn't exert enough authority. How people power brought down the Shah of Iran? People power brought down Ferdinand Marcos in the Philippines? It'll be the same in Europe, only the bloody fools in their ivory towers don't know it yet, or if they do, they'll hang on to the bitter end. Okay, sir — call a public holiday for tomorrow, then another one for when the castle of cards collapses. I'm with you all the way."

"And what about the Emergency Committee for the Oil Embargo?"

"It's days are numbered, Sir Claude. It's days are strictly numbered. Mark my words, this is the beginning of the end for Euroslavia — but I don't see it collapsing just yet."

HER MAJESTY QUEEN Elizabeth of New Zealand watched television avidly on that last Friday in October, 2005, in the private lounge of Eden Palace on the fringe of Auckland. She was delighted to see that the downtrodden peoples of Europe were making a stand for freedom, but she was aghast at the size of the protests. She had no idea that the European Union was that unpopular.

But it gave her deep satisfaction to know that, once again, her subjects in the United Kingdom were in the forefront of the movement: the Aberdeen fisherman, Archie McGovan; members of the island governments in Douglas, St Helier and St Peter Port; and that queer fellow who had caught the public imagination with his blatantly anti-Europe programme, *Tell Tel*.

She began to wonder whether she was really watching the beginning of the end of Euroslavia — oh, what a highly emotive and descriptive word that was! — and whether she could begin dreaming of her return to London as monarch and head of state.

She knew that if it were to happen, there would be many changes. The Monarchy would be much smaller. She would almost certainly lose Balmoral if Scotland didn't want her as queen. She sensed that Buckingham Palace would be turned into an ultra-smart hotel or a tourist attraction, or both, and she had few regrets: the place was too big in any event. And, after the experience of Euroslavia, personal freedom would be a major issue; people would be thrilled to become British citizens once again, but the term British *subject* had had its day.

Yes, it would be so nice to go back to London — but she must never forget that New Zealand had given her asylum when she needed it; she would return here as often as her ageing bones would allow.

Long live Britannia!

EUROSLAVIA

FOURTEEN

IF THE ROADS around Brussels and Luxembourg had been in chaos on Monday morning, by Monday afternoon they had been brought to a total shutdown. Carloads of incoming protesters whose engines had not been immobilised the previous night, because they were outside the control regions, had advanced on Brussels in their hundreds of thousands. Teutoburger, seated in front of his video wall in the incident room, was watching his empire seize up despite his efforts.

Aerial views of the Brussels approach routes showed the inbound carriageway of Euroroute 411 blocked solid with stationary traffic, some of it immobilised the night before but the majority having come in today, the day before McGovan's Motorcade was due to make its impact on the city. At Oudergem on the city limits, police had formed a solid block across the road with their patrol cars, Land-Rovers, and now were reinforced with riot squads using the ubiquitous plastic shields.

But still the traffic surged in. People had destroyed the central barrier and were driving through onto the outbound carriageway, risking head-on collision with other vehicles. A steady stream of cars, with a few vans and coaches among them, was penetrating the city centre.

Teutoburger jammed his fist on the intercom button and yelled: "Gonzáles! Get in here at the double! Gonzáles! Where are you, man?"

The Spanish-born head of political surveillance, whose duties had been suspended during this crisis, hurried in. "Your wife is in reception, sir. She asks to see you, urgently."

"Wife?" Teutoburger thumped his chest as another pain struck; he threw two more pills into his mouth, ignoring the recommended dosage. "Got no time for wives. How the hell did she get past security? Tell her to go away." He pointed to a close-up aerial shot in the top left quadrant of the video wall. "Bloody protesters pouring through like a flood tide. Stop them, Sergio!"

"How, sir?"

"Get hold of the ESD office in Brussels. Tell them to send in the military."

"The military, sir?"

"You heard what I said, dammit!" He crumpled under another jab of pain, wondering how long he could endure the agony. But the honour of the Eurosicherheitsdienst came first. "Send in tanks, APCs, scout cars. Send in those giant earthmovers from the roadworks. Send in whatever's available — *but stop this bloody haemorrhaging!*"

"Have we the authority, sir?"

"Don't *you* start! I have the authority. I *am* the Eurosicherheitsdienst. And don't just stop at the E four-hundred-eleven. It must be happening all around the city. *I want Brussels sealed so tight not even a cockroach can get in!*"

"Sir. At once. And your wife, sir?"

"To hell with my wife!"

THE COLD AIR mass surged relentlessly westward from Poland and the Russian Steppes. In our derelict chicken farm in Essex we continued taking it in turn to add a voice-over. Following the latest weather chart, which showed vast areas of deep blue for the Arctic conditions, we had live pictures from some Russian television station; I could recognise the Cyrillic script but the commentary was meaningless. A brief shot of the Kremlin prompted me to assume we were looking at Moscow, but it was a Moscow unlike anything I had ever seen on any screen. Snow was laying thigh deep across Red Square, where giant snowploughs were beginning to thrust it aside to make access for vehicles and pedestrians.

Philip added a commentary on aerial shots of the open countryside, where farm animals were noticeable by their absence. "The people still take their livestock into the farmhouse, as they've done for generations. All the fodder is inside, and the animals' body heat is a cheap alternative to central heating." His eyebrows asked me if that were still correct, and I shrugged in reply.

"If this weather comes any further west," he said, "there are going to be some major problems for the motorcade. Temperatures inside the cars will drop below freezing. Children and old people will be at risk. Water supplies will freeze, and probably there are thousands of people without enough bedding."

"And if the cars are stuck for a week or more, there are going to be some terrible sanitary problems," I added.

I daren't say it on the air but I wanted to scream: "*Lisa! Where are you? Call me, for God's sake!*"

THE MILITARY ARRIVED during the afternoon and sealed off Brussels city centre from the rest of the world. No vehicle, not even a cycle, was allowed to penetrate in through the *cordon sanitaire*. Within the city, thousands of protestors who had already infiltrated the blockade began looking for convenient parking places, and fights were beginning between them and the residents; Teutoburger saw a news sequence shot at street level in which two parties were fighting it out with their cars, until both were wrecks left blocking the centre of the road.

And then the first of the earthmovers from the southern ring road moved ponderously in, scooping away all cars that were in its path, locals as well as from the motorcade. The slow process of clearing the city centre of immobile metal, had begun.

Lorries, coaches and private cars trying to leave the city were beginning to back up behind the military barrier, but they had no hope of passing as the incoming traffic blocked all carriageways and was tailing back a mile, two miles, sometimes more, on the wrong side of the road.

The airport remained open, and trains continued to use the Centraal Station and the station at Jubelpark south of the Vijfteeeuw Park, the fifth-centenary park.

LISA REACHED COLOGNE in late afternoon and tried to call me from the station; she had tried the phone in the train but couldn't make sense of the instructions. Still no answer.

She could feel the weather growing noticeably colder and she was glad she had left Norway. Yet Köln was going to be particularly cold tonight, as October came to a close. She walked into the city to find a hotel room, but there was nothing available.

"Sorry, madam," the receptionist at the third hotel explained. "I think you will not find anything in the city. It is the Euroslavia protest, the motorcade."

"But I can't sleep out on the street!"

"I agree, madam."

"Then where can I sleep?"

"In the coach station, perhaps? In the rail station?"

"I've just come from there." She felt the tears of frustration, mixed with a touch of fear, burning the back of her eyes.

"Perhaps take a sleeper train south — away from Brussels?"

It seemed the only logical action, but the booking office could offer her nothing except trains east- or northbound, to Berlin, Hamburg, and back where she had come from.

In the end, in sheer desperation, she decided to stay in the buffet until it closed, then try to sleep in the ladies' lavatories.

IN BRITAIN, BUSINESS was coming to a standstill as people were crowding towards the nearest television set to keep updated with the most rewarding yet terrifying news most people had seen; its impact was far greater than that of the Second Gulf War when Kuwait was liberated, because it was so much closer to home.

Soho Square told us that our non-stop coverage would continue until six p.m., when we would alternate half-hour on air and half-hour off, until nine p.m. The breaks would give us chance to pack up all our personal gear because we were moving out.

"Out?" Philip queried. "Where now?"

"We don't know yet. But you'll leave all the studio gear. We'll arrange to collect that later."

CALLAN AND HIS party from the Isle of Man came to a halt near the village of Houtem when they caught the end of the tailback on Euroroute 19 from Amsterdam. Despite the excellent start, it had taken Callan half the day to advance thirty-five km, and now there seemed little prospect of going further.

"I'm going into Brussels, even if I have to walk it," he gritted. "I've some unfinished business with the European Commission."

"What about the car?," Bridget Norris wanted to know.

"Ah'm comin' wie ye," Archie McGovan snapped. "This motorcade was all my idea an' I'm goin' to see it through. Don't ye realise, man, if I do nothin' else till my dyin' day, this is the greatest thing Ah've ever done. I'm goin' to bring Euroslavia to its knees."

"Sorry, Archie. I've got more important business."

The fisherman stared at him open-mouthed. "More important? More important than freein' three hundred an' seventy million people from autocratic tyrrany? Ye canna be talkin' sense, man! This is the greatest mass protest that mankind has ever made — an' you've got *more important* business?"

Callan had undergone a conversion almost as dramatic as if the voice of God had spoken from out of the sky to the world's most confirmed atheist. He had known that the European Union was right: it offered peace, prosperity and conformity. But millions of people were rejecting it so forcefully that he had had, with extreme reluctance, to convince himself that — perhaps — the masses were right and he, Callan, was wrong. If the peoples of Europe preferred to resume living in a scattering of individual countries with ridiculous borders, speaking a dozen languages, having different bank holidays, different customs, different and sometimes incompatible religions — then who was he to convince them otherwise?

It was a terrible blow to him, personally. The Sterling Zone would go its idiosyncratic way and probably make an outstanding success of it. Mann would have its own little government for another thousand years. And there would never be a motor industry on the island, paying him a vast fortune for arranging a tax haven within the euro currency zone. It *could* have worked: London had allowed sterling tax havens, so Brussels and Frankfurt could have done the same for the euro.

But it was starkly obvious that the average European — setting aside the people of the old Benelux states — didn't want to be European. He or she wanted to be Catalan, Welsh, Alsatian, Languedocqien. Callan had been wasting his time.

And that meant he had some old scores to settle in Brussels. And *that* meant he had to reach the centre of the city. And when he reached it, McGovan would see just how important his business was.

"They're smashing down the central barrier ahead," Sir John Faulds pointed. "Can we get through, Tony?"

"We'll make it. We have to." Callan watched in uncontrollable anxiety as, two hundred yards ahead, a group of men began rocking the crash barriers side to side, slowly loosening their foundations in the soil. "Can't wait for them," Callan snapped, getting out of the Jaguar and beginning to rock the barrier a mere five yards ahead. Within seconds other men had joined him and before they had any noticeable movement thousands of men and many women were shaking the barrier in synchrony as far as they could see in both directions.

Archie McGovan, adding his weight to the cause, paused to wave his fist at a Cessna which flew low overhead, a television camera plainly visible in the passenger's window.

When the barrier was lifted from the ground on the backs of straining men, the motorcade began to bounce across. Several small cars snagged their silencers but continued, the roar of their engines adding to the cacophony of blaring horns and voices screaming in their success.

Sir John thought the scene must be familiar to many continentals, who had helped liberate their land from Nazi suppression — or who had helped defend it from the advancing Allies. The European Union had been created to prevent a repeat of scenes such as this, yet it had spawned the greatest mass protest in the history of the human race.

The road ahead was open. Callan took his place in the surge to where the euroroute ended on the bank of the Canal of Willebroek. The N1 road took them slowly inwards, passing the Koninklijk Kasteel, the now-disused Royal Castle.

"Park in there!" McGovan shouted. "We shan't get anywhere better!"

Callan swung his steering wheel and joined another queue, crossing the canal and surging into the Royal Domaine, a vast grassy park with ornamental lakes; two soldiers stood by the entrance, unable to stop the flood of motorists despite the rifles they carried.

"People power!" Bridget Norris shouted at them.

An hour before sunset they found a suitable parking spot on the edge of the mass of thousands of other vehicles; Callan was concerned that, if more motors were immobilised in the night by whatever means Euroslavia had developed, then he must have a clear run out of the park. Only after that could they set about making themselves comfortable for the night.

There was, of course, no public toilet capable of serving such a crowd. Bridget bobbed down at the back of the car, conscious of other women doing the same, while the men did what they had done for generations, and urinated anywhere.

While Bridget and Sir John prepared a hot dinner over the camping stove, Callan suggested to the driver of the neighbouring car that he disconnect his battery.

"Why? We will run the motor in the night to keep warm."

"Your motor will not work in the morning. It will be immobilised by some radio transmission. You saw all those cars by the roadside? They will not move for days, perhaps weeks. Disconnect your battery, please, and tell your neighbour to do the same."

The motorist shrugged, looked at Callan as if the Manxman were crazy, and carried on with what he was doing.

"So be it," Callan told himself. "At least, you're not blocking our exit."

PROBABLY A MILLION people had set out to reach a specific cemetery in France, to honour the family dead in the *Fête des Morts* on All Saints' Day, but in the north-east quadrant of the province, Region FR3, Pas-de-Calais and Nord; Region FR22, Picardie; Region FR21, Champagne and Ardenne; and Region FR42, Lorraine, few had arrived by nightfall on the last day of October, which the Britons were celebrating as Hallowe'en, All Hallows' Eve.

Few motorists were equipped with adequate provisions such as sleeping bags, camping-stoves, and suitable food. Many were going no more than 150 km and they knew they could cover that distance comfortably in three hours, even with delays from this motorcade. Most forgot about the return journey. Now, all across the north-east, families had abandoned their slow progress in order to find accommodation for the night, but despite the prices having doubled or tripled, every room was taken. Thousands of people would find themselves trying to sleep in their cars, many of them still seized in traffic jams.

XAVIER YZURDIAGA HAD unwittingly made a good decision when he opted for Luxembourg instead of Brussels. He had driven to Aubange, crawled along to Athus, inched the hire car over the uncontrolled border into the Province of Luxembourg, and picked up the main N5 at Rodange. From there on, there were frequent delays to Dippach, twelve km from the city centre, but there was always movement.

"Let's take the back roads," Staqui suggested, and navigated through Sprickange and Reckange, getting within five km of the city by mid-afternoon.

"Now we start breaking the rules, old friend," Yzurdiaga said. Ahead, the traffic heading into Luxembourg was a solid line with scarcely a hint of movement. He eased the car out of the queue and drove slowly on the wrong side of the road, squeezing onto the verge to allow oncoming traffic to pass. Motorists in the queue hooted indignantly, but Yzurdiaga ignored them. He drove under the E25 autoroute bypassing Luxembourg city to the west, and cautiously passed a line of stationary vehicles in the suburb of Cessange, until he came to a T-junction by the church, at dusk. Here a knot of policemen had held up their right hands hours ago, and the traffic had obediently stopped, forming the tail-back that had caused Yzurdiaga his problems.

"Oh, God, Xav. It's started to snow. We don't want to get stuck here all night."

"We're not going to — hold on," Yzurdiaga cried as he slid the gear lever into second and shot the car forward. He had no intention of hitting anybody, and he swung the car wide, grazing a house wall. But they were through, and round the bend. He raced ahead on an empty road, and realized they had entered one of the strongholds of Euroslavia almost without a hitch.

"Most people must have gone to Brussels," Arrieta suggested. "By the way. All those village names, Xav. What does 'ange' mean?"

"Angel, but not in this context." Yzurdiaga grinned. "I don't know, though — maybe our angels are watching over us." He drove on a hundred metres until they could see a wooded gorge plunging away on their right. "The Alzette River. And we must be in the city centre — there's a giant statue of Jacques Santer in front of the Ducal Palace." They stopped, surprised that the city was so quiet. Why had no other motorist challenged the authority of the policemen's upraised hands?

"Xav. Remember what's under the spare wheel? What are you planning to do with it?"

Yzurdiaga looked at the statue. "I'd love to shove it up Santer's arse, but prudence dictates otherwise." He paused, aware of the noise of engines behind them. He was ready to shoot off when he saw in the mirror a sports car, chased by an assortment of other cars. He also noticed that the snow was falling thicker, with the promise of plenty to come.

Arrieta gasped. "Surely they've not been waiting there all day for some nut case like you to show them the way?"

The cars streamed past, and continued streaming. "I reckon they have, old friend. I guess three things prompted them to move — us, the snow, and nightfall. Oh, well — let's join the crowd. We've got to find somewhere to park. Looks like we're in for another cold night."

"Park? In Luxembourg? With that Semtex in the boot? Can't you get rid of it, Xav? Throw it away if you have to."

Yzurdiaga stared at him. "Throw it away? After what I did to lay my hands on it again? And you don't just go along and stick a wad of Semtex on your target. You've got to put a detonator in it, wire it up to a timer and a battery, pack it so it doesn't look like what it is, then you have to plant it very carefully. We don't want to kill anybody." He remembered the three victims of his bombs of a few years ago to add to the toll of dead left in the Pyrenees. Was he responsible for six deaths? Not even Andorra would be a safe haven for him now. He dismissed the problem for the moment, knowing it would never go away. "And then you've got to locate your target and put the bomb in the best possible place. The Court of Justice or the Court of Auditors, or the Investment Bank — these places are going to be guarded to the hilt with all this protesting going on."

"You've got your target," Arrieta said nonchalantly. "And it's not guarded."

"Got it? Where?"

"Jacques Santer, straight in front of you. If you stand on my shoulders you can shove your bomb between his feet. The snow won't affect it, will it?"

"Jacques Santer," Yzurdiaga mused. "You're right, old friend. Then we'd better get out of Luxembourg before he topples from his plinth."

The cars streamed by as Yzurdiaga retrieved a half-kilo pack of explosive and a detonator from the boot. "You want to take a walk, old friend?" he asked Staqui.

"No. I haven't got much to go home for either, have I?"

Yzurdiaga ignored the *either* as he worked under the faint glow of the courtesy light, building his bomb while Arrieta, under protest, went out of range. The cars were travelling much slower and the snow was falling thicker as Yzurdiaga stood on his friend's shoulders to plant the sixth bomb made from the Czech Semtex on the statue of the man who had masterminded the Maastricht Treaty. "A most fitting end for you," Yzurdiaga said as he jumped down. "Right, Staqui. Let's get out of town."

"How long did you give it?"

"An hour."

Leaving Luxembourg city was far easier than entering it. They drove past the Ducal Palace, turned right over the Alzette Gorge and took the road south, towards Thionville in France — Region FR41. Just short of the border they turned east and headed into a fierce snowstorm. By Mondorf-les-Bains driving was difficult and most traffic had ceased, although the road edges were lined with thousands of cars, most apparently holding protestors in McGovan's Motorcade. The Basques struggled on through another village and then as they saw a sign bearing the too-familiar symbol of a dozen golden stars set in a field of dark blue, they realised they were approaching the uncontrolled border with Region DEC, the Saarland.

A strong burst of snow forced Yzurdiaga off the road, and he pulled up on the crowded market place in the centre of a smallish village. "This is as far as we go tonight, Staqui. Where are we — do you know?"

Arrieta peered at the map. "France a kilometer on our right. The Moselle dead ahead. We're in a place called Schengen."

Yzurdiaga sat up straight. "*Shengen*, did you say?"

"Why?"

"My God! This is the village where they signed that accord. You know — the one that opened all the borders and let all the drug smugglers and illegal immigrants through."

Arrieta smiled. "Not to mention a few people carrying Semtex."

FIFTEEN

THE OLD RENAULT van that carried Erich Zimmerman and a miscellany of other hikers, progressed slowly from the centre of Valenciennes, but all day it was delayed by the immobilised vehicles along the roadside, and by the new input of cars heading for Brussels.

Sitting in the solid-sided back, Zimmerman had no peripheral view and could see little from the front or the rear. He was aware mainly of a stop-start progress, with the vehicle standing motionless for minutes at a time, many times during the day. The only enlightenment came from commentaries by passengers with a more privileged view, and then the news was usually that 'I can't see the end of the queue.'

It was a cold and miserable day and the carnival atmosphere he had expected, was not there. Around midday an argument broke out among the passengers, speaking in French with some German and Italian input. "We're not going to do it. We may as well turn back."

"Rubbish! Pessimism gets you nowhere."

"Neither does this van. I wish I'd brought my cycle."

"Why don't we go on by train?"

"Who's got the fare? And what do you do in Brussels with all the hotels full?"

"We can't abandon this old bus — somebody would steal it."

"I can't think who'd want it."

"At least, it started this morning. Thousands of newer cars didn't."

"Wonder why that was? Did they put something in the petrol?"

"We run on the same stuff. No, it's witchcraft."

"*Witchcraft?* Listen to this guy — he's nuts. That does it for me. Drop me off in Mons and I'll catch the train."

"Sure, me too. I could walk it faster than this."

And so, when they were within walking distance of Mons, the driver treble-parked on a building-site and took out the van's rotor arm, although he didn't expect to see the vehicle again.

Mons-Bergen station was just as chaotic as the roads, but without the vehicles. The renamed *Chemins de Fer Belgiques Provinciales* had abandoned the battle to control passenger numbers and sold tickets to anybody who had the cash. Zimmerman drifted away from his party on the platform and, despite his age, was prepared to make some effort to get aboard the train.

Twenty minutes later he achieved his goal, although he was sandwiched in the crowd with no hope of lifting his arms to his face, far less of finding a seat. The sea of miserable humanity surged back and forth like water in a bucket as the train accelerated out of Mons then stopped at Soignies to allow a few more passengers to squeeze aboard. Zimmerman could imagine the carnage that would follow if this thing were derailed.

The old priest half-expected there to be a check on the outskirts of the Belgian chief city, and everybody forced out, but the train rolled into the Centraal Station with no problem. As Zimmerman was carried by the crowd onto the platform and out into the city centre, he realised he had achieved one ambition: he had come to Brussels to join the vast crowds protesting about Euroslavia.

But he had come without a vehicle. He was not part of the motorcade. And now he was here, he had no idea what to do beyond the basic requirements of self-preservation.

THE OLD AUSTIN van started with reluctance on that Monday morning in Mons, but almost all other vehicles parked around it were as dead as if their engines had been sold for scrap.

John le Mesurier drove away with a deep sense of guilt, the ice on the windscreen slowly thawing as his mood improved. Progress north was painfully slow, although Brussels was only fifty kilometers away.

They entered Soignies in early afternoon and, like Zimmerman's party, realised that they would never reach Brussels at this rate.

"But we knew all along that we'd probably never get within fifty miles of the place." Fiona le Mesurier was philosophic. "That's surely not the purpose. The reason for the motorcade is to make a protest, and we're doing just that. If we sit on the road at Soignies for a week, we've made our statement."

Annette Dugard agreed. "If there are three million cars on this jamboree, then it's physically impossible to get them all into Brussels even if you pack them solid in every street. It'd be a tight squeeze to get three million *people* in the streets. We're here — that's all we can expect."

"I'm going to Brussels," John le Mesurier stated. "I'll walk all night if I have to. I'll find somewhere to park the van and I'll come back for you as soon as I can." He called over his shoulder. "What about you, John?"

John Doyle, the Guernsey conseiller sighed. "I didn't expect to get to Brussels, but if you're walking it, so am I. As long as the ladies don't mind being left alone."

"Looks like we're all going. I don't fancy being left here with no man around."

"Then how are we going to do it? We're certainly not going to drive all the way."

Dugard was studying the Michelin map. "There's a canal running from Charleroi, south of us, into Brussels. Maybe we could get a boat?"

"Maybe pigs could fly."

"Well, it's worth a try. There's a turning just ahead that leads straight to the canal."

"And does it mark the boathouses? What are we looking for — canoes or a river cruiser?" Le Mesurier drove forward another fifty yards.

"We just might find a barge."

Three hours later they found the canal, and managed to reverse the old Austin van into a thicket of blackthorn. While le Mesurier was taking out the rotor arm from the distributor head, and removing a spark plug, his wife saw a barge coming around a bend in the southern distance.

"We have found a barge," she cried. "And it's going in the right direction."

"How do you know he'll take us?"

She pointed to a footbridge further along the canal, its raised passageway accessed at each end by steps. "He won't have the option."

Doyle looked at the bridge with apprehension. "If you think I'm going to drop from that..."

"You can always look after the van, John. We'll send you a postcard from Brussels."

They stuffed their pockets with as much food as they could carry, and walked onto the central span of the footbridge as the barge approached. Traffic still crawled across the road bridge as McGovan's Motorcade and the *Fête des Morts* competed for space. The bargee saw his intending passengers, put his engine into reverse and nosed his sixty-foot-long cargo-carrier towards the bank, crunching through inch-thick ice; Dugard led the chase and all four were aboard before the wake began to surge again at the stern.

"Brussels?" the bargee called. *"Parlez français?"*

"Bien sûr," Dugard replied, and listened to a recital of the man's problems.

"He's French," she translated. "Comes from Chaumont in the Haute-Marne — Region 21. Been on the canals for years but never seen so much paperwork as he has now. All of it from Brussels. He's so *bouché* — fed up with it — that he takes us to Brussels to protest. He'll bring us back if we like, in a few days' time."

Smiles appeared for the first time that day. "Good fellow!" Le Mesurier went forward and shook the bargee's hand.

"And if you have trouble in Brussels and you want to hide from the authorities, come to my barge. You are welcome. Now, you would like to go below? You will find a dozen other protestors in the little saloon." He paused. "Brussels? We are there by eight this evening. And then tonight it will snow."

TEUTOBURGER STRUGGLED THROUGH the day, leaving his swivel chair in the incident room only to urinate. The video wall had become his entire life, and his sole purpose in living was to keep the arteries open. Not his own arteries, which were restricting the flow of blood to his heart so that he needed the continual stimulant of drugs, not only those he took orally but those the doctor was now injecting directly into his veins.

"You are killing yourself. If you have any respect for your body you'll get away from this desk right now."

"I'm dead anyway. Just let me go in my own time."

"Your wife's still outside, waiting and crying..."

"I asked you before, how did she get past security?"

"I vouched for her. She's in a terrible state, man. Have you no thought for her? She knows I'm here with you, and I'm damned certain she knows why. You owe it to her..."

"I owe nothing to anybody, doctor. Now leave me alone."

Teutoburger at once threw all his emotional and mental effort into winning the living chess game that was dominating the enormous map on the video wall. White king was besieged in Brussels with queen, queen's bishop and seven pawns. King's bishop, king's castle and a knight were holed up in Luxembourg. The black king with almost all his army was attacking Brussels, leaving only a bishop and a pawn to strike Luxemburg.

White king advanced, clearing a single square of space around him, then black king counter-attacked and the ground was lost again.

In reality, the police and a few detachments of the Euroarmy — mostly an Italian artillery regiment — were holding the approaches to Brussels on the outer ring road, but there were several haemorrhages, such as on the E19 coming south from Antwerp, when several thousand cars slipped past the authorities by breaking through the central barrier and advancing along both carriageways, effectively sealing off the exit route. The south was his greatest problem, from Ukkel to Oudergem, where the ring road was still being built and so there were no natural defences.

If he could hold the onslaught until tonight, he would win, because once again the transmissions were due to be sent out from the mobile phone masts, activating the mini-computers built into the cars. The computers would draw on the battery power to burn the cable to the starter motor, and also to weld the bonnet lock, preventing access to the engine. And all those hundreds of thousands of Fiats and Fords, Vauxhalls and Volvos, Daewoos and Toyotas, would be useless.

He couldn't send the transmissions before midnight or he would catch hundreds of thousands of local cars, whose drivers were ardent supporters of the federal Europe and who wouldn't yet have disconnected their batteries.

It was a war of attrition but, knowing about his secret midnight weapon, Teutoburger was confident of victory. If only he could hold on...

WE LEARNED MUCH later that Teutoburger's grasp was far weaker than anybody had thought. If only Christine Bouderon had known then what she came to learn later, she may have saved so many lives — but maybe victory could be achieved only at such a price.

That afternoon, the last day of October, the European Commission was in emergency session; normally it met once a week. The only information to emerge after the events, came from some of the minutes recorded with extra items from a few of the commissioners, but it appears the main — perhaps the only — subject on the agenda was maintaining law and order in the face of the mass demonstration by motorists.

Axel Teutoburger's actions were evidently under strict scrutiny, with a number of commissioners expressing shock that the Eurosicherheitsdienst could not only have been created without their knowledge, but could have reached such strength.

TEUTOBURGER HIMSELF REALISED the extreme predicament he was in. If he failed to save Brussels from invasion by the mob, not only was he finished but so was his dream child, the Sicherheitsdienst. He surveyed his video wall, noticing that the giant earthmovers on the roadworks to the south of the city were being parked. They would not be working over the Allerheiligen holiday.

"This is treason! I ordered them into the city to clear the roads! I want *all* of them into the Grote Markt," he shouted, balling his fists and provoking another shaft of pain in his chest. "The earthmovers!" He pushed the buttons on his speakerphone and, from the Kristallkoffer in Berlin, ordered Sicherheitsdienst staff in Brussels to commandeer the remaining earthmovers and have the machines at their disposal from daybreak on Allerheiligen — All Saints' Day.

PHILIP AND I WERE worn out. Not so much physically as emotionally. All day we had sat watching the monitor screen and adding a live, instant, commentary to it. There was no time to correct any mistakes; before we had spoken three more words the blunder had been sent back to London, dubbed onto the pictures, beamed up to our geostat sat and bounced back again or sent by landline to the continental stations for beaming, to be received anywhere in the footprint from Lisbon to Lappland, Dublin to Dnepropetrovsk.

We had updated traffic news wherever we could, telling of the Festival of the Dead chaos superimposed on the Motorcade melodrama. We had thrown in the weather forecasts, with increasingly dire warnings of untimely snow sweeping in from the east. And feedback was telling us that, until six p.m. when we had gone off air for thirty minutes every hour, it was one of the most successful programmes we had done at CCC, despite the competition from CNN and a dozen other networks. By afternoon those in the know were estimating more Britons were watching television at that moment than ever before, and the same was apparently true throughout Euroslavia with the sole exception of Greece.

Now we were waiting for news of our own future. We were packed and waiting to go.

A few minutes after nine, the call came. I was desperately hoping it was from Lisa but I knew the only phone links we had were still from Soho Square.

Philip answered and put the speaker on.

"There's a truck on its way, gentlemen. It should be with you in half an hour. It'll take you to Stansted where we have seats on a chartered jet. Take off at 2200 sharp, so don't be late."

"Where are we going?" Philip asked.

"Brussels."

"*Brussels?* We're broadcasting *Tell Tel* from the middle of Brussels? You're joking!"

"Not from the city centre. From the airport. Euroslavia has rigged up a special studio for all the British-based television channels. Other countries apparently will be using their own special studios in the same block."

I called: "Do they realise the kind of programme we're putting out? It's as anti-Europe as we can make it. This looks like a trap, to me."

"They know. Provided you're putting out the truth you can be as sceptic as you like — that's part of the deal."

"What's the rest of the deal? They slit our throats in the dead of night? I don't trust them — I don't feel happy broadcasting from Euroslavia."

"You're doing it now, Terry. Your chicken shed's as much part of Euroslavia as Brussels Town Hall is. By the way..."

"Yes?"

"We've had a call from Lisa. We explained why she couldn't get through to you directly and we've told her you're on your way to Brussels."

"Thanks for nothing! That'll worry her sick."

"I doubt it. She was calling from the railway station in Cologne."

SNOW WAS FALLING heavily as we landed at Brussels. I guessed that at this rate the airport would be closed by daybreak. Our party of rival networks — Telefis Eiran, CCC, ITN, BBC, C5, Sky, Old Uncle Tom Cobbley an' all — temporarily united in a single cause, was escorted to a special studio suite with all the appearance of being hastily prepared, but certainly not as hastily as the chicken sheds we had just vacated.

Recalling the security we had needed while that madman had been stalking me — and we still didn't know if he'd had his pound of flesh — I asked one of our escorts whom he worked for. When he answered "Service de Sécurité Européen," the hair on the back of my neck tingled.

We saw crews of other news networks — RAI, Antenne 2, Deutsche Rundfunk and others — settling into neighbouring studios and we all nestled down as quickly as possible at our edit suites. Most other networks had kept to their schedules during the move, but CCC, of course, had lost its commentary. We were due to pick it up at first light.

None of us could sleep for long, and around five a.m. we were watching the monitors and wishing we had our own camera crew to send onto the streets. No such luck: we all had to share what was offered from the official camera team. It was censorship right enough.

"What about our spies in the Parliament?" I asked Philip. "We haven't heard much from them."

"I think that was being over-optimistic. I doubt if we'll ever hear from our friend Bouderon again, either."

"You've still got the tape?"

He patted his pocket. "But it might be too dangerous to broadcast it from the heart of enemy territory. I doubt we'd be able to get it on air; I have a feeling that all we'll be able to show is heavily-censored pap."

The first pictures showed a scene of total horror. During the night around thirty centimetres of snow had fallen — that's a foot in grandfather's language — and those approach roads that we saw were blocked by mounds of the stuff, each presumably hiding a car. In the glare of floodlights the individual mounds merged into one solid mass, stretching as far as the dimmer street lights could penetrate. There was not a sound coming from the lines of thousands of carloads of protesters, and there was only one person visible, a man urinating in the roadway.

We were appalled. "People are going to die in this," Philip whispered; the pictures seemed to demand a reverend hush. "McGovan's Motorcade has gone terribly wrong. If none of those cars can run its engine, people will be dying of hypothermia and exposure in their thousands."

"The authorities will have to do something," I suggested, "but for the life of me I can't think what. They'll have to get access first, and how the devil are they going to do that?"

We saw a weather chart of northern Europe, which told us the belt of snow was moving westward and would reach London in late afternoon. Behind it, an Arctic air mass was drifting in under clear skies, which promised some of the lowest November temperatures since records began. I had always thought that talk of global warming was nonsense.

Another monitor showed the centre of Brussels, with nothing moving. Then the camera itself began tracking forward and we quickly realised that it was mounted about ten feet above ground on a large vehicle which was scooping up the snow in front of itself, swinging sideways, then backing off, allowing us to see what had been dumped. From the imprint in the compacted snow we thought we were viewing from the cab of a giant bulldozer.

"The Grote Markt," one of the other TV researchers said aloud. "The old market square in the city centre."

The mechanical giant went back to its task, next time shovelling its bucketload into the mouth of a sidestreet. Soon other metal monsters were appearing on screen and we guessed our vehicle was built to the same design. If so, it was an earthmover with a centrally-mounted grading blade and a front-mounted scoop. Our rival researcher began describing the scenes he recognised, particularly when the earthmovers were in sight of the Euroslavia buildings.

"They're a hell of a size," Philip commented. "Why should Brussels have them? They don't get all that much snow here."

Gradually the truth began to hit us. "They're from the roadworks on the ring road. And... oh, my God! They're going to clear the access roads!" I gasped.

"No!"

"I bet you twenty euros they are. God! This'll be manslaughter on a massive scale. Call Soho Square an' tip 'em off."

"You're crazy, Terry. They wouldn't dare!"

"Just watch." As the daylight strengthened and Philip made his connection to London, we again saw the view ahead from that camera mounted on a 'dozer. It was a wide road running through an unrecognisable residential area, and the machine was making good progress, pushing the snow then swerving to the side and dumping it, pushing ahead again and sidesweeping. Soon we could see the Euroarmy vehicles that had formed the blockade across the autoroutes; they were manoeuvring back and forth, vacating their positions.

"You're damned right!" Philip gasped.

From our abstract viewpoint on top of a giant earthmoving bulldozer we could see hundreds of specks scurrying around the immobilized motorcade as people cleaned their windscreens, tried to heat up some food, and defecated.

Philip said: "They'll stop. They're clearing the snow, that's all."

But they didn't stop. We had a grandstand viewpoint atop the earthmover as it drove on, pushed ten tons of snow at the first cars in the stalled column, swerved, and pushed the load onto the sloping ground at the edge of the autoroute; I presumed it was a grassy bank.

As the earthmover pulled back again we saw somebody clamber in terror out of the front of the crumpled car, where the windscreen had been until a few seconds earlier, then the sway of the earthmover took the car out of view and the giant machine slid forward again, crushing two cars, side by side, this time. Again it dumped them on the slope, paying no regard whatever to the vehicles or to any people inside them.

The soundtrack was shockingly authentic: screams, and the sickening crunch of cars being crumpled like plastic bottles. But no blare from car horns.

The phone on my desk flashed its light; whoever had prepared these studios knew his job. "Commentary! We're on air! Give us some commentary, for God's sake! Are we seeing what we think we're seeing?"

"You bloody are!" I snapped, then began doing the job for which they paid me. I tried to describe the scene, but it was difficult as I could scarcely believe my eyes. "Tens of thousands of cars in McGovan's Motorcade have been immobilised on the approach roads to Brussels. The motorcade has been a thundering success because these queues stretch back for mile after mile. But it's not all success, as these cars aren't going anywhere for the foreseeable future. We don't know how they've been stopped, but not one of them can start its engine and not one of them can lift the bonnet to have a look underneath," It wasn't particularly grammatical, but who cared?

"And now the authorities — again, we don't know which ones —

are coming in with these giant earthmovers and shoving the cars aside as if they were toys. They're dumping them by the roadside, with the people still inside them. It's unbelievable! The snow's around a foot deep, and it must be cold enough out there to freeze a bottle of water solid, even inside the cars. And remember, they can't start the engines to get any warmth. This is carnage!"

A genuine snow-clearer must have made some impact on the airport runway as we began seeing aerial shots of the city. Philip cut them into our transmission and I switched my commentary to describing the snowbound city with very few people around. It was, of course, the first of November, and it was also the Festival of the Dead.

"Look. From our studio here in the airport we can't recognise any of the roads, but you can see that these ruddy great earthmovers are working on several at once. Somebody, somewhere, has got to answer some very serious questions — preferably right now. This is barbarous action. It's ruthless. Oh, God, I'm lost for words — come in, Philip."

I turned away from the screens, my mind racked with questions. Had we been brought over to Brussels to witness scenes such as this? Was it official policy to mount a camera up there and show the world the carnage that was going on?

Or had one of the MEPs we'd heard about, one who'd got a spy camera, done it to disgrace the Union? If so, how did he or she know what was going to happen? And how long before somebody else put a stop to it?

THE BARGE HAD moored in the Haven just north of the city centre and the party from Alderney came ashore at eight, after an English-style breakfast which the bargee prepared. "You do not know where your next meal is," he warned. "And if the canal freezes I do not know when I go south again. I try for maybe two days, if you all want to escape from the madhouse."

Brussels under a foot of snow was nothing like what they had expected. They trudged south, joined by a stream of pedestrians from the grounds of the Koninklijk Kasteel just to the north; they heard yet more stories of car engines that would not start.

"Where are we going?" Dugard asked le Mesurier. "European Commission first?"

"Rue de la Loi. We'd better ask the way."

Another party of four was trudging along: a tall man dressed smartly, and with sensible calf-length boots; a middle-aged man wearing a Russian Cossack hat; a burly, weatherbeaten man dressed in seaman's yellow oilskins but with landsman's boots made for walking; and a woman in her early forties who, despite having slept in a car with three men, was wearing full make-up. John le Mesurier asked the party at large the way to rue de la Loi.

"The Commission?" Callan answered. "We're going that way ourselves. Tag on if you like."

As they walked they exchanged experiences and learned that both parties came from those smaller parts of the British Isles which were still using sterling.

McGovan could not keep his silence. "Ye see all these cars? These thousands an' thousands of cars from all over the place? Well, it was my idea. It was all my idea. They put it on the telly, an' this is what has happened."

"You're Mr McGovan?" Dugard was awed. "Now I can see you better, I recognise your face. Congratulations! I'm honoured to meet you — you must be thrilled to bits about all this."

"Not exactly," Archie McGovan added. "Too many people. A lot of 'em are goin' to die. That makes me awfu' sad."

"Die? Why?"

"The weather. Fights. Accidents. Natural causes." He shrugged. "But mebbe it's all in a good cause. The end of Euroslavia."

ERICH ZIMMERMAN HAD spent the night with thousands of other protesters in the Centraal Station. Shivering, hungry, he had watched an earthmover clear the snow from the front of the station, then he had begun his solitary march to the European Commission building on rue de la Loi.

Solitary he may have been, but he certainly wasn't alone. At daybreak the protesters were outnumbering the citizens of Brussels as they set out for their destinations, any of the Euroslavian buildings within the city limits.

XAVIER YZURDIAGA SWORE profusely when the rental car wouldn't start.

"We've been clobbered," Eustaqui Arrieta concluded. "We forgot to disconnect the battery when we pulled up."

"*Hombre!* It was snowing a truckload! We could be forgiven for forgetting the Holy Mother's birthday last night."

"So what are we going to do now? Walk back to Euzkadi?"

"I'm not a bus mechanic for nothing, old friend. I'm going to get this thing working if it kills me."

He searched in the boot for anything of use, and studied the aluminium tubing of the haversack he'd carried with him over the Port de Cabús from Andorra to Spain. He pushed the frame into the gap between the radiator grille and the bonnet, and levered. Sweat began breaking on his face but before the tubing collapsed, the buckled and twisted bonnet clicked free.

He studied the battery; it was sound. He traced as much of the electrics system as he could, and found a wire that had burned at the starter motor; that, plus the welding of the bonnet catch, had overloaded the circuit and blown the main fuse. He improvised with wire torn from the courtesy light and with adhesive plaster from his simple first-aid kit, and finally he switched on the ignition. The engine started.

"You deserve a medal, Xav."

"As long as you pin it on me, Staqui."

"What now — home?"

"Home? In this snow? And with seven kilos of Semtex looking for a job? As soon as it's cleared I want to go and see what damage we did to Jacques Santer in Luxembourg."

WE'VE GOT RIOTS in the streets!" Philip was describing the scenes as they came up on our monitors, trying to keep his commentary relating to the picture that was being beamed up to the satellite. "We've got six giant earthmovers clearing the autoroutes and main roads, and they must have dumped hundreds of cars. We know there have been a few deaths because we've seen bundles in the snow with terrible bloodstains. That's what's sparked the riots. You can see it — thousands of people; I don't know, maybe it's tens of thousands — are abandoning their cars and streaming into the city on foot. They're hurling gas stoves and car jacks at the crews of the earthscrapers, but they're surging on past and flooding into the city like a tidal wave."

The phone flashed. One of our small team went to the control panel, played with the knobs, and brought up a low-quality picture. He snatched up his phone again and nodded. "Got it. It's the what? My God — thanks."

Philip continued. "It's like the centre of Rome when the Pope gives his blessing. It's like the crowds from fifty football matches. It's like Piccadilly Circus on New Year's Eve — but all of this thrown together. It's terrible. It's menacing. And it's not stopping. As the people pour into the city, so there are more coming in from behind."

On cue, I took over the commentary as the blurry image was fed into the system. "We're now receiving pictures live from the heart of the European Commission," I snapped. "These are being fed to us from a spy camera and we don't know how long they'll last. We gather the Commission has been in session since early this morning, and we can certainly guess what's on the agenda. It's a pretty rowdy meeting as you can see, but I'm afraid I can't hear much over the shouting." I paused.

"Let me remind you that these twenty people are the driving force of the European Union. They're nominated by the member provinces — two from what was the United Kingdom — and they're appointed by the European Parliament, but it's pretty much a rubber-stamping affair. Once they're here, they forget any loyalty to their home country; they're under oath to act only in the interests of the European Union." That wasn't controversial; the last thirteen words came from the Euroslavian blue book.

I beckoned to Philip, who picked up another pamphlet and began defining subsidiarity and the Committee of the Regions. "This committee is made up of 222 people, mostly mayors and heads of councils — and every one of them is nominated. They automatically sit in this committee for four years, presumably even if they're unseated back home. If there's something that a region can do better than the Union can, like local sport..."

All the screens went blank. Philip paused, then reverted to his opinions on the vast crowds flooding into the city. "It's a sight I've never seen before. It's frightening. I'm sorry about the loss of pictures, by the way; we're doing all we can to restore them. It's like millions of wildebeest on migration in the Serengeti, if you've ever seen that on television. They're being driven on by some primeval urge, and I don't know what I'm talking about any more. In fact, I don't even know whether I'm talking to myself..."

The phone flashed again. "You are," I told Philip. "The news isn't what Euroslavia wants to see, I guess, so somebody has pulled the plug."

I doubted if we'd ever be able to prove anything, but I was convinced our disillusioned MEPs had found an excellent way to use their cameras.

THE EUROPEAN COMMISSION was in turmoil. The commissioners had realised the awful truth: that they had inadequate control over their own physical protection. While an unruly army of angry citizens was advancing upon them on foot, they realised they had no adequate defense to offer.

The European dream had been created by politicians hungry for power; Bismark's dream of empire had been political with strong military backing. Hitler's actual but short-lived empire had been political with a superb military force to keep it in power: the SS, the Gestapo, the Wehrmacht, the Luftwaffe.

Euroslavia had had no military support at all. Chancellor Kohl's suggestion back in 1996 that there be a continent-wide police force had been the closest the politicians had come, and from that faint suggestion had emerged the Eurosicherheitsdienst.

Euroslavia mainly relied for its protection on the Eurosicherheitsdienst. And the Eurosicherheitsdienst was the virtual creation of one man, Axel Teutoburger. And Teutoburger was proving, with every moment that passed, that he was incapable of controlling the monster he had created.

Only in the past two years had the Euroarmy and the Euroluftwaffe been formed, but they were of second-rate troops, those who had been willing to forego their allegiance to their native country. The commissioners were realising that the Euroarmy was a rabble whose members had no sense of loyalty to the region where they served. Austrians were in Swedish Lappland, Finns were in Portugal, Scotsmen in Greece.

The commissioners had been watching all the satellite television broadcasts of the mess that Teutoburger had created, and they were divided on the issue of what to do. Half were shouting that only a madman would scoop up cars with people still in them, but the other half were pleading: who else but Teutoburger could save the Union? The Euroarmy was a farce.

But when they saw *themselves* on the CCC channel, their fury was beyond control. It took only a few moments to find the camera, hidden in a bag placed on the table in their assembly chamber and wired in to an ordinary telephone socket: the tiny camera was sending pictures by landline to the airport studio from where they were beamed to the satellite and so broadcast all across Europe.

"Get that studio off the air and arrest everybody in it! It should never have been allowed in the first place!"

"Who planted the camera? Whose bag is it?"

Several commissioners remembered that a member of the European Parliament had come into the chamber, but none could remember who he — or she — was.

WHEN THE SCREENS went blank everybody was momentarily stunned. Then the reality dawned. "Let's get outa here! Our job's finished — let's move!"

There was a mad rush for the door, with CCC's people as desperate as the others to get away. Our situation was obvious to us all: we had been commenting on pictures of the European authorities clearing snowbound roads *with no consideration for human life*. It was unavoidable that people had been injured and almost certainly killed in the barbaric incident, which was still going on as far as we were to know.

If ordinary citizens were expendable, what safeguard had newspeople who had been passing scathing comment on the scenes?

I joined the rush for the door and into the snow. The small charter plane which had brought us all in from Stansted was still on the tarmac, with other charter planes that had brought news teams in from the other provinces of Euroslavia. I fell headlong into deep, virgin snow, and when I pulled myself up again I saw maybe a hundred and twenty people floundering to the aircraft. But the machines were all snowcovered and wouldn't be going anywhere for quite a while.

Philip and our gang had gone. I was alone outside the studio we had occupied for less than twelve hours. I clambered to my feet, but paused to let my mind catch up.

The runway at Brussels Airport had been cleared enough to allow a single light aircraft to take off and film the city. There was no prospect of commercial jets landing for hours. The charter jets were small and perhaps could make a getaway — but they needed aircrew, fuel, and all the snow cleared from their wings and fuselage. They were going nowhere for several hours.

Meantime, Lisa knew I was at Brussels Airport. Would she try to join me here? I *couldn't* run away and abandon her, after she'd made that solo trek south from Norway.

I walked slowly back into the studio and shut the door behind me.

CHRISTINE BOUDERON BURST into Teutoburger's incident room as soon as she heard that the cars in the motorcade were being scooped up and dumped. She seized Teutoburger by the hair and tried to pull him from his chair.

"You're mad! You're a monster! How can you crush people to death in their cars? Stop this murder at once!"

Teutoburger swung around in his chair. "You're too late, darling Christine. The order has gone, and nobody can countermand it."

"*You* can, you maniac! Where are the controls? Which phone did you use? What's the number? *Tell me!*" She pulled his chair backwards, away from the controls in front of the video wall, which was showing the clearing-up process from the air and tracking in towards the city: we later learned that these aerial shots had been fed into the satellite transmissions, presumably by one of those two rebel MEPs. Bouderon found it difficult to recall that she and her boss were off the Friedrichstrasse in Berlin while the carnage they were seeing was in Brussels, four hundred miles to the west.

Suddenly Teutoburger crashed forward in pain, staggering out of the chair. He was gasping, choking, in the throes of another heart attack. His right hand scrabbled in his pocket for the life-saving pills, but Bouderon kicked them from his grasp.

"Suffer, you madman. Die. Or tell me how to cancel that order."

Teutoburger writhed, and Bouderon wondered how any man could survive the agony. Then she detected a faint nod, and appeal for help in her boss's eyes. She opened the container and gave him one pill.

"Four," he gasped.

"One."

A faint nod. She heaved him to his knees and managed to slide him into his chair. She gave him one further pill, pushing it between his lips so that he could crush it with his teeth. She noticed that his left hand and arm were now useless and guessed that the next major stroke would be his last. But she couldn't afford to let him die.

She pushed him to the console. "I've had time to think. I know it's the ESD bureau in Brussels. I even know the number. But the order is coming from *you*. Or you die waiting for the next two pills."

Slowly Teutoburger's right hand reached out for a phone handset. "Dial the number," he whispered. "You say you know it."

She keyed in the code, waited, and heard her boss say in a voice distorted by a partially-paralysed tongue: "Enough. Stop the snow clearance. Stop destroying the cars. Pull back to the Grote Markt."

She snatched the phone. "Hello? This is Bouderon, director of criminal records and second-in-command to Brigadier-General Teutoburger. I have further orders for you. Stand down all Euro forces in the regions under your command. I repeat, stand down all Euro forces. Euro forces are not to intervene in civil disorders under any circumstances whatever. You will repeat that." She paused while she heard her words echoed, and saw Teutoburger's right eyebrow raise in inquiry. "The brigadier-general will confirm that order if you wish; he's standing right beside me, but he's injured his mouth. No? You're happy? Fine."

She put down the phone, thinking that she had at last been able to honour her promise to that queer fellow on the television. She gave Teutoburger his remaining two tablets then said: "And now you will resign as President of the Eurosicherheitsdienst."

"Never! I have told you many times, Bouderon, I *am* the Eurosicherheitsdienst."

"You can't even say the word. You will tender your resignation to the President of the European Commission now."

"Never." He glared defiantly at her.

"I shall take you to Brussels where you will tender your resignation in person."

"Never."

"We shall see. In the meantime..." She called for the medical officer, and when he reported to the incident room she said forcefully: "Mr Teutoburger and I are going to Brussels to confer with the Commission. Mr Teutoburger has just had another heart attack — frankly, I wonder how he manages to survive. Could you please do what you can for him, and sedate him for the flight?"

The doctor nodded to her, then nodded towards the door. Bouderon saw a strangely familiar woman hesitantly entering the incident room. "Mrs Teutoburger?"

The woman nodded, her lips tightly drawn. "What's happened to my husband?"

"I'm afraid he's had another heart attack. He has to go to Brussels now; the doctor is giving him a sedative."

Louise Teutoburger exploded. "My husband's half dead, and you're taking him to *Brussels*? Have you no heart?"

Bouderon dropped her eyes. "I'm sorry. He has to speak to the President of the European Commission in person." Maybe she was being callous, she thought, but nothing short of a heart transplant could keep this man alive. "He'll be under sedation through the flight."

"If he goes, I'm coming with him."

Bouderon nodded. "With pleasure, madam. The flight will leave as soon as it can be made ready."

She went to the phone again and ordered the service's Cessna Citation jet aircraft to be prepared and the main runway cleared of snow sufficient for take-off. "And while you're about it, make certain that the runway at Brussels is also cleared. Is that understood?"

This particular Citation was a seven-seat version which cost well over $4,000,000 eighteen months earlier. It had a flight crew of two and could fly at a maximum speed of 260 knots at 30,000 feet, with a range of 2,759km — much more than enough to take it to Brussels and back.

She heard Teutoburger slur to his long-suffering wife: "The lovely Christine with the honey-blonde hair is taking me to Brussels, my dear."

Bouderon turned around. "We leave as soon as possible — they estimate an hour. I suggest we take a four-by-four to Tempelhof if we don't want to get stuck in the snow." As she followed the others from the incident room she took a last look at the video wall. The earth-movers had retired from their road-clearing duties in Brussels, but an aerial shot showed hundreds of protesters gathered around, and on, one of the giant machines. If that should fall into the hands of the motorcade mobs, she thought, then Euroslavia is in severe trouble. But maybe that was just wishful thinking?

CALLAN AND HIS party heard the noise of tens of thousands of voices raised in protest as the earthmovers went to work all around them, and they hastened their step. John Doyle, trying to keep up, slipped on some polished ice and fell. A tallish man who was obviously several years older, stepped from the passing crowd and helped him to his feet. They found French a common language when Doyle said: "Thanks. Must keep up with my party."

"Where are you going?"

"Where else but the Commission?"

"I do not know the way," the older man said. "May I join you?"

"I don't know it either, but he in front, he does. Where are you from?"

"Liechtenstein," said Father Erich Zimmerman. "It is not in Euroslavia."

"Neither is Alderney. Nor the Isle of Man. Come on."

Callan had firmed up on his decision. He knew exactly what he wanted, but he hadn't the remotest idea of how to put it into practise. For a start, it meant getting in through the front door, and that would prove impossible under these conditions.

Brussels city was rapidly filling with an unruly mob, tens of thousands strong. They were there to protest to the unelected autocrats who had ruled their lives with increasing dogmatism for the past decade, and they armed themselves however they could: a road sign, a cobble from a minor road repair. They had no argument with the ordinary citizens of Brussels, even though they were presumably pro-European, so there was extremely little vandalism against private property.

The party of nine reached the European Commission building at 200 rue de la Loi and, as Callan had expected, it was guarded by around fifty police armed with riot shields, helmets and batons, and with CS gas pistols at their waists. Formidable, Callan thought, but if the mob gets rough, they'll crumble. Already several hundred protesters were outside the building, held back by a respect for the range of the gas canisters.

Callan had his strategy worked out as well as he possibly could: all he could do was put it into effect and hope it worked. He drew Archie McGovan, Sir John Faulds and John le Mesurier aside. "I have a plan that just might get me through that door. If it does, I have some private business to attend to. When I come back I'll try to keep the door open long enough for you to rush it."

"Haven't you seen the riot squad? How do you propose we get

through them? Or is that all part of your private business?"

"Haven't you seen the crowds? Their fingers are just itching to get their hands on something."

"And what do we do if we manage to get in?"

Callan smiled. "Have you never seen pictures of crowds looting government offices?" He paused, then gave instructions.

"We've got to hit you? We should have had that *Tell Tel* guy here — by all accounts he'd love to smash you through a brick wall."

"Pity he isn't here. Just try doing his work for him, eh? You're going to lynch me, right? The cops let me in to save my life."

McGovan cackled in derision. "It'd never work, man. We haven't got the motive to make it look real."

Callan turned on them. "Oh, but you have. You're the one who thought of this motorcade, McGovan, but I'm the one who sold Britain down the river. I'm the one who told the commissioners Britain was ripe for take-over. Blair didn't have the guts to say no when they threw Article 104c at him. *I'm the one who got you into this mess!*"

McGovan landed a punch on Callan's chin, which sent him sprawling in the snow. As Callan stumbled to his feet, the fisherman, in genuine fury, advanced on him again ready to knock him back to the ground.

Two of the policemen came forward menacingly, and Callan stumbled towards them, blood pouring from his mouth. McGovan checked, then hurried back to the party.

"You needn't have been so realistic," le Mesurier cautioned.

"Realistic? Man, Ah meant it! Ah'd have willingly killed him!"

"Still," le Mesurier said. "It's working. Look."

Callan, with genuine blood running down his chin, pleaded with the riot police to let him inside the building. "They'll kill me if you don't. I've got urgent news for Commissioner Gisbert Boeke, environment. Tell him it's Callan from Amsterdam outside. Quick!"

Two policemen took Callan to the door but kept him outside while the message was fed in; many in the uneasy crowd saw a doorman pick up a phone, wait, then open the door just wide enough for Callan to squeeze in.

"What now?" Dugard asked as they told the women about the plot.

"We wait. I just hope he was lying about Article 104," le Mesurier said.

Sir John Faulds, chief minister of the House of Keys, drew in a deep breath. "My God, so do I. So do I."

THE FIRST OF the charter jets took off from Brussels a little before noon, to my total amazement; there had been so much activity on the airport that one could think God was due in on the next flight. The aircrews had spent the night in the airport lounge, and airport staff whose normal duties were suspended had come out to help clear snow off the waiting machines.

"Why the hell aren't you coming?" Philip demanded.

"Because Lisa may be on her way. I can't abandon her."

"But you're sticking your neck out, man. Can't you see? We were supposed to be showing censored film — why else have us here? — but somebody who knows the job back to front was feeding in that hot stuff from the earthmovers. And we were thinking it was official and adding our commentary! If they can scoop up innocent motorists, what can they do to guilty broadcasters? And you still don't know who firebombed your house? Come *on*, man!"

"I'm staying. See you in London, Philip. Best of luck."

I felt sick in the stomach as our own jet took off amid a cloud of blown snow, banked, and headed westward to Stansted. Soon all the charter jets had gone and the only activity was the spotter plane: the big jets were still grounded.

And then I saw another small executive-type jet coming in from the east. I could see it was small and fast, with two engines slung in pods on its rear fuselage, but I wouldn't have recognised it as a Cessna Citation.

Bouderon's flight from Tempelhof landed at Brussels's Nationaal Luchthaven from a dazzlingly bright noonday sky and taxied towards the cluster of outbuildings which housed our television studios, among other things.

I watched, shivering, as a black saloon collected three people and took them to the terminal, dashing my hopes that one of them may have been Lisa. There was no way of knowing they were Christine Bouderon, Axel Teutoburger and Louise Teutoburger. In fact, with the television input still dead, I, the one remaining idiot from the broadcasting teams, knew nothing about what was going on in Euroslavia.

Minutes later a helicopter rose from near the terminal buildings and I guessed how my unidentified VIPs would reach their destination, which was presumably the rooftop of one of the EU buildings.

SIXTEEN

AS THE HELICOPTER came in to land on the roof of 200 rue de la Loi, the European Commission building, Bouderon felt the hair prickle on the back of her neck. The entire city centre was seething with tiny dots, all drifting towards the main Union buildings. She saw the earthmovers that had been scooping up cars and their human occupants, and she could appreciate the anger that was seething within each one of those protesters. She realised that the big machines were also on the move, hampered by the human mass.

"But you ordered them to stop," she said, half turning to Teutoburger before she realised that they were no longer destroying cars. They were now in the hands of the protesters; her wishful thinking had become a reality.

The helicopter landed on the top of the Commission building and Bouderon ordered the pilot to wait until she came back. Leaving Teutoburger with his wife, she shuffled through the snow to the lift shaft, and so down into the building.

She had been here many times, but it never ceased to intimidate her. She got off on the Presidential floor and hurried into the vast reception lobby. "I have the president of the Eurosicherheitsdienst waiting on the roof," she snapped to the first receptionist. "He wishes to give his resignation to the President of the Union, in person."

"Please wait one moment, Miss...?"

"Bouderon." She knew the routine: not a raised eyebrow, and three more receptionists to see. She knew this day was almost certainly the most traumatic the Union had ever experienced, but she had left Teutoburger and he was so disorientated that there was no telling what he may do, once the sedative wore off. Finally she was ushered into the most holy place in Euroslavia, with the possible exception of the Holy See — she had never been able to learn whether the Vatican City was in the Union.

LISA HAD HAD the worst night of her life. After she had tried Intereuropean Directory Inquiries, had spoken to a night receptionist at CCC and learned I was about to fly to Brussels, she knew she had to meet me there. But there was nothing she could do that night, with the weather so bitterly cold and her knowledge of German only rudimentary.

Still only with the clothes she was wearing when she left the Isle of Man, she stayed in the station buffet until it closed at midnight, then she passed several miserable hours trying to sleep in a cubicle in the ladies' lavatory.

She was back in the buffet shortly after it opened at six, for a hot coffee and an *Apfeltorte* before facing the outside world.

As she left the station she was appalled to see several inches of snow on the streets, but the snowploughs were already at work. It was a Tuesday morning, but as it was the Allerheiligen public holiday the streets were quiet: the Festival of the Dead was purely a French thing.

Lisa clambered over the ridged snow in the street gutters and hailed one of the few taxis. "You speak English? Can you take me to the airport?"

"Can do, but no flights until the runways are cleared."

"When will that be?"

"Late morning, it says on the radio."

"I'll try my luck, all the same."

As she clambered in the driver asked: "Where d'you want to fly to?" and gave away his American accent.

"Brussels."

He whistled. "The airport there is closed as well. Snow, and McGovan's Motorcade."

"Closed? How do you know?"

"You mean how does a cab driver in Cologne know that Brussels Airport is closed? Car radio. It's permanently closed to commercial aircraft until further notice. You still want to go?"

"I can't get there by train. I certainly can't get there by road. I've just *got* to get there — at least, to the airport. My husband's there."

"He's in aviation?"

"He's a journalist."

"Covering McGovan's Motorcade? God! Who'd have thought it! Millions of people coming out to protest over this Europe business! Shows the state of public feeling. You seen it on television?"

"Not for the past two days. I've been travelling down from Norway."

The driver stuck to the cleared roads and soon was heading southeast on Autobahn 59 for the Köln-Bonn Airport. "At one time I was all in favour of this European Union," he said. "But not any more. How can you make one nation out of Swedes, Portuguese and Greeks, let alone all the others? Did you see that *Tell Tel* programme on the box a week or so ago? Subtitles in a dozen languages, but I watched the English version mostly. That guy — Mason, is it? — really puts it over."

Lisa smiled. "Thanks. I'll tell him you said so."

"Say — do you know him?"

"I've been married to him for thirty years. That's why I want to get to Brussels Airport — that's where he is."

There was silence for a few moments, allowing Lisa to look at the countryside of the Rhine valley. It was bleak under this untimely snowfall. The main roads were cleared but she could see that traffic in many of the side roads was having a hard time.

"I think I can help you, lady," the driver said. "Would you mind flying in a small aircraft?"

"Not at all."

The driver stopped while he dialled a number on his car phone, then spoke in German for a few moments.

"You're in luck," he told Lisa. "Friend of mine — cabbies make loads of friends. This guy is in a pressure group, trying to force the break-up of...say: your husband calls it Euroslavia, doesn't he? A Europe of slaves? I like it. Anyway, this guy is flying over to Brussels as soon as he can get clearance, to see what's happening. He says he'll be highly honoured to take the wife of Tel Mason. Free."

"That's kind of him, but I can pay."

"Never look a gift horse, lady. Airport coming up: I'll see you get paged through to him. His name's Müller, by the way. Heinz Müller."

The cab driver pulled up in the taxi park and hurried Lisa through to the information desk from where the public address system called for Heinz Müller, who turned out to be typically Teutonic: tall, blond, square-jawed, and with a built-in smile. His aircraft wasn't quite so suave; it was a Piper Cherokee 104 with four seats and a low wing that obstructed much of the scenery and was similar to Callan's aircraft. Despite that, Lisa had an excellent view forward of the snow-covered countryside and was anticipating touchdown at Brussels in mid-afternoon.

ANTHONY CALLAN WAS shown into a private office at 200 rue de la Loi and asked to wait; nobody had paid any attention to his damaged mouth. He was surprised at how quickly his contact came to meet him. "Ah, Callan. How nice to see you again." The voice lacked conviction and sincerity, and the handshake was as limp as it had been when the two last met, in the VIP lounge at Schipol Airport. "My word, what have you done to your lips? You should get that seen to." Without pausing for an answer he went on: "You have something to report to me about the Isle of Man wishing to join the common currency? It looks very much as if your first analysis was mistaken, doesn't it?"

"Other people have intervened. Notably that Mason with his *Tell Tel* programme. He's made plenty of people think again about

Europe."

"And so has your McGovan, the man who thought up this highly dangerous motorcade. I would dearly love to get my hands on him."

"Would you, now?" Callan's eyes lit up. "It so happens he's downstairs. He did this to my mouth." Callan avoided adding that it was by his own request, although he had never expected such a forceful attack.

"You will deliver him to me, perhaps?"

"What's in it for me?" Callan had made his personal vow and there was no way he would betray McGovan now.

"I can tell you where Mason is."

"Can you, by God? Then it's a deal. Where is he?"

Boeke smiled. "At the Nationaal Luchthaven. Brussels Airport. All the television people are there, by special invitation. But we've stopped their broadcasting and they'll all be arrested soon. If you want your man, you'd better go quickly. Now — McGovan?"

Callan stared at the gross figure before him and thought how revolting this former occupant of an orphanage now looked.

"I must just tell you this. My analysis on the Manx Government joining the single currency was wrong," Callan explained. "Many of my analyses have been wrong. First, I thought the European Union was a wonderful idea. I still think it is, but not the way it's worked out. Second, I thought I was doing the best for Britain by getting her into the single currency, but there are *millions* of people out there who don't want it. Who's right — me, or them? And third, I picked up this smashed mouth for my trouble to make Article 104c a reality. I got it from Achie McGovan. I don't want it, so I'm passing it on to you with his compliments."

The punch, delivered with all his strength, was totally unexpected and caught Boeke on the side of the jaw. He was hurled backwards onto the floor and as Callan turned to make his escape, he saw he'd drawn blood — plenty of it.

He knew his chances of escape were slim; he was prepared for that as part of his penance. He hurried from the office to the lift shafts and pressed the button to go *up*: that would fool them. The lift breathed to a stop within seconds and he was gliding skywards before anybody knew what had happened to Commissioner Boeke. He stepped out onto the snow-covered roof of the building and saw a helicopter standing nearby, its rotor blades still turning.

He ran to the machine and accepted a helping hand from a woman. "What is happening?" she asked in German, looking at his mouth. "There is trouble?"

Callan nodded. "There is much trouble. To the airport — go, go, go!"

EUROSLAVIA

THE PRESIDENT OF the European Union hurried in, straight from the Commission meeting still in session on another floor. "Miss Bouderon? I believe you have Mr Teutoburger on the roof?"

"And you'd better come quickly, sir, before he dies."

"I'm with you." He snapped his fingers and three unobtrusive men followed him. Bodyguards, Bouderon wondered. They reached the roof and stepped out onto the snow, but the helicopter was already chopping its way into the distance, heading for the airport.

"HE'S NOT COMING BACK," Annette Dugard shouted over the roar of thousands of voices. "He's done a deal with them. I wouldn't be surprised he was in that helicopter."

Sir John Faulds felt as if he had been hit in the solar plexus. "First he's an honourable Keysman, then he's a traitor for Euroslavia, now he's back with his masters."

"An' he's got the bloody car keys," McGovan shouted. "Ah should ha' knocked him flat, the bugger."

"So what do we do now? We can't stay here — the crowd's pushing us closer to those riot police. We must get away."

A slow surge, like a Mexican wave at a football match, travelled through the crowd, compacting it and forcing it to the very walls of the Commission building. The eight-strong party felt itself being smeared along the wall, and McGovan used all his strength to prevent Father Zimmerman being crushed. It was now a question of personal survival and very few people saw the riot police pushed back to the door, which opened, allowing them to escape inside. Several protesters were squeezed in as well, against their wishes.

John Doyle began to think his last minutes had come. He stuck his elbows out to give his chest space to expand and prevent his being suffocated. Sir John thrust both hands against the wall, protecting Bridget Norris in the space he could keep clear.

"John — don't let it end like this," she shouted in his ear. "I love you, John. I must tell you."

"I know. I love you, Bridgie. If we have to go, let's go together."

The relentless pressure pushed his body sideways and he rolled against the wall, like a little eddy, bringing Bridget out into the crowd. And then they eddied again and he was once more shielding her.

Erich Zimmerman was squeezed several feet from the wall. He clenched his fists in front of his chest, forcing his elbows out, and he lifted his feet from the flattened snow, allowing himself to be carried by the crowd as a drowning man would be carried in the current.

The two Mesuriers and Annette Dugard linked arms and stayed together, and it was the man in the group who saw the upper structure of the giant earthmover slowly making its way through the crowd. He screamed in the sudden realisation that people must be fighting to escape from the caterpillar tracks, and so causing this Mexican wave. Scores of protesters had found their escape by clambering aboard, and were standing in comparative safety as the earthmover headed, painfully slowly, towards the glass front of the Commission building.

"TELL THE PILOT I want to go to the airport," Callan shouted to Teutoburger, who was sprawled in one of the four seats, strapped securely in place.

"Leave my husband alone," Louisa screamed at him. "Can't you see he's ill? I have to get him to hospital."

Callan pointed to the city beneath them, where dense crowds filled every available space and the earthmovers were finding it verging on the impossible to advance on the other Union buildings. "We'll never land in that lot! Get him to the airport. Fly him out to London — they do some wonderful transplant ops there."

Teutoburger saw the pilot looking to him for instructions. "Airport," he confirmed. "Fast." The president of the Eurosicherheitsdienst looked imploringly at his wife and knew, with inner conviction, that he would never have a heart transplant. He was dying; his left side was paralysed and it was only the pills that kept his heart functioning. And he had just enough pills to last until midnight. He closed his eyes and the image of Louisa faded, replaced by the beautiful features and the long, honey-blonde hair of Christine, Christine Bouderon. But Bouderon had turned out to be a traitor while Louisa had remained staunchly faithful to him. His mouth played with words and Louisa leaned closer to hear them.

"I've never been unfaithful to you, my dear. I love you very much. You deserved somebody better than me. Forgive me, please."

She hugged him, her tears washing onto his cheeks. "There's nothing to forgive, my *Liebchen*. If only this Eurosicherheitsdienst had not come between us."

"The Eurosicherheitsdienst is almost finished. The people do not want political and economic union, so the Eurosicherheitsdienst has no role to play."

"Coming in to the airport," the pilot announced. "Where shall I put down?"

Callan called: "Where's the television studio? I want to talk to that Terry Mason."

Teutoburger looked suddenly interested. "Is that here? Is that Mason man here as well?"

"He's here, right enough. I want to see him."

"So do I." Teutoburger gave a lopsided smile. "So do I."

THE FIRST EUROSLAVIAN building to fall was the Parliament on rue Belliard. A giant earthmover crawled through the parting crowds and continued crawling, smashing through the glass and steel portals as if going through a back-garden greenhouse. The crowd went wild with joy and surged in through the gap, while the roadbuilding machine trundled slowly on, grinding through the ground floor reception suites.

The second victim was the unfinished Parliament extension building, which was announced in 1997 at an estimated cost of E765,000,000, which was around £615,000,000.

The third was the European Commission on rue de la Loi. The driver, whose car had been scooped up and dumped by this very leviathan, paused to let the crowds disperse from the narrowing gap between the massive bucket and the front of the building. Then he moved forward. The shouts and screams from the crowd, which filled Law Street from side to side and stretched back to the Grote Market, were so loud that the crunching and grinding of breaking glass and the screaming of tearing and twisting metal, could not be heard.

The machine paused once it had breached security. The driver inched backwards, indicating his intentions to the crowds behind him. As they fought their way to safety the machine pulled clear of the gap, and the crowds poured in.

While the earthmover slowly turned, to begin its advance on the home of the Council of Ministers further along rue de la Loi, the party from Alderney and the Isle of Man, with the old priest from Liechtenstein, was sucked inside the Commission edifice like autumn leaves being carried on a mountain stream.

Nobody had control over his or her movements: it was the relentless force of seething humanity which thrust those in the front ever deeper into the building. Many were injured on obstructions such as reception desks, others were toppled like falling trees and fell victim to the surge behind them; there was no way that these people could survive the trampling and the weight of the feet that were forced to follow the mass.

Father Erich Zimmerman was one such. Archie McGovan had the priest by his arms, but Zimmerman was pushed over, his legs were pinioned by the weight of humanity, and McGovan could not haul him free. The fisherman's last glance of the priest was as the old man went down, like someone being swallowed by the quicksands. And then the flood of feet squeezed out the last breath of life, and McGovan found himself fighting for his own survival.

EUROSLAVIA

Old John Doyle from Guernsey was made of stronger stuff. He squeezed himself from the tide of flesh and managed to find temporary sanctuary on an island — the top of a reception desk. As he felt it groan under the one-sided strain, he rolled across, dropped to the floor, and found refuge beneath the great counter. He was to hide there for hours.

Annette Dugard managed to stay with the two Mesuriers. They were carried up the open staircase, horribly aware that they were walking on bodies, living or dead. John le Mesurier had a vision of the First Battle of the Somme in the spring of 1916 when almost a million men on both sides were killed. Towards the end, soldiers were fighting on carpets made of their own comrades' bodies.

This was similar, yet so different. This was on a far, far smaller scale, everybody was on the same side in the conflict, and there were more Germans than Britons in the crowd. This was a battle where Europeans fought Europe.

Bridget Norris felt herself being torn from Sir John Faulds's grasp. "Come back, John! I love you!"

"We'll be together again," he promised as he found himself being swept along the ground floor corridors, while Bridget was carried up those stairs, only yards behind the Alderney party.

Archie McGovan was swept against a column and to avoid being crushed beside it he hauled himself up, on the shoulders of some unknown person, until he could clamber out of danger, like a young seaman learning to shin up the mast. As he surveyed the scene beneath him, with faces in anguish looking at him and appealing for help, he began praying. This wasn't what he had had in mind. This was not the way to bring Euroslavia to its knees.

THE HEAD OF the small Eurosicherheitsdienst office in the heart of Brussels had been standing by his fourth-storey window for an hour, since he had received the shocking message from Mlle Bouderon in Berlin. *Stand down all Euro forces under your command.* What did the order mean? All *Eurosicherheitsdienst* forces? He didn't have many: two at the Centraal Station, six at the Luchthaven, two who patrolled the river and the little port, and two in this office keeping the paperwork under control. Twelve.

Or did Euro forces mean the *Euroarmee*? There were several thousand in the Belgian regions. There were the Germans with their tanks, a miniature version of the Panzers, whom he had called on to prevent the motorcade from overwhelming the city. There were Greeks in a signals regiment who were worse than useless because they knew nothing but their own language. There were Portuguese sappers and

Irish catering staff; Finnish infantry highly trained in Arctic warfare; British artillerymen and a detachment of Scout helicopters based at Lintkasteel near the Caterpiller tractor works north of Brussels. There were a few Italian paratroopers, and some Scottish military police but, following Union policy, there were no troops from the Belgian regions. He had five thousand three hundred soldiers of all nationalities... No. He corrected his thoughts. Regionalities. We are all European Union *nationals*. A mere fifty-three hundred to protect all of the Belgian regions — but from whom?

From fellow Union nationals? Scarcely. From this mob now in control of the city? But they *were* Union nationals — and it would take far more than fifty-three hundred men and women to bring them under control.

And he had been ordered to stand down all the forces. They were not to leave barracks. He shook his head. When he was a cadet, *stand down* meant go off duty; it did not mean being confined to barracks. Could he send them home? They were certainly doing no good here.

Once again he tried phoning the Eurosicherheitsdienst headquarters in Berlin, and once again he was told that no decisions could be taken as the president and all the deputies were absent.

He tried the European Commission complex, but the line was still dead. He tried other Union offices in the city, but they were just as dead. He was on his own, and the city was in turmoil. Suppose the turmoil extended to the barracks, and the troops had to stand and fight, or flee for their safety: *he* was responsible.

It wasn't as if there were a proper chain of command. The Franco-German Brigade had been formed in the 1980s and run on a small scale, but the Euroarmee and the Euroluftwaffe had been formed very recently, and command had gone by default to the Security Service, which meant ultimately that a former Brigadegeneral was nominally in command of the entire defences of three hundred and seventy million citizens of Europe. A Brigadegeneral controlled the Eurofighter squadrons, the warships of the English Navy, the remnants of the French *Légion Etranger* and the Greek *evzones* in their pretty blue-and-white skirts and fluffy boots. It wasn't too outlandish when you considered that twenty unelected bureaucrats ruled everything else.

He called in his two clerical assistants. "Send e-mails to all military detachments within the Belgian regions. Cancel all previous orders. All troops are to put on civilian clothing and vacate their quarters forthwith. They are to go home if they wish — if they can get through the snow. They can use military transport to get them to rail stations, but for their own safety they are not to offer any resistance if challenged by anybody. You have that, both of you?"

His assistants could scarcely believe what they had heard, but the head of the Brussels Security Services pointed out of the window. "Would you have believed that, yesterday? Go on — do it."

A SNOWPLOUGH CAME THROUGH Schengen in mid-morning, and Xavier Yzurdiaga joined in the queue of vehicles crawling along behind it, towards Luxembourg. The snowplough was stopped many times by abandoned vehicles, and was obliged to nudge them aside, invariably doing serious damage to the bodywork.

Eustaquio Arrieta grumbled. "It'll all be over by the time we get there, Xav."

"Good. Then we can go home with a clear conscience." But Xavier Yzurdiaga already knew that he could never go home. Not with six deaths to account for.

AXEL TEUTOBURGER HAD ordered the helicopter pilot to contact Air Traffic Control at Brussels Airport and demand the Eurosicherheitsdienst detachment to await his arrival with a wheelchair. They were to carry sidearms.

Now, as the helicopter landed, the four Security Service men and two women were waiting for him, dressed in an assortment of clothing; because of its security work, the service did not issue uniforms.

"Women!" Teutoburger moaned as Callan and the pilot helped him down the top two steps, but when his left leg began fouling every move, Callan picked up the head of the European Security Service and carried him down to the snow-covered tarmac and sat him with dignity in the wheelchair.

Teutoburger was in control once more. "Where is this television studio?" he asked, aware that his minions were either staring at his mouth or looking well away. He pointed with his right arm to one of the women. "Give me your gun. Lead on."

I had seen the building from the outside only in the darkness when we arrived before the snow fell the previous evening, and I therefore didn't know it was an office in modules with a wide wheelchair ramp. Callan pushed Teutoburger through the uncleared snow up the ramp then paused, reading the nameboards. The security chief pointed to the one reading *British Provincial Television*. "That way." He slid the pistol into his coat and quickly chewed more pills as he was wheeled along the corridor to the door crudely marked *UKTV*. Somebody had struck a note for independence.

He looked at the four men with guns in their shoulder holsters, bulging through their jackets. "You four, and the woman; we're arresting everybody in this studio. Do not let anybody escape."

Louisa Teutoburger cried out. "No! You're going to hospital! Can't you forget the job, before it kills you?"

THERE WAS NO way of preventing the crowd surging up the stairs and into the debating chamber of the European Commission. Normally the twenty rulers of the majority of the European continent met once a week, but they had met in emergency session the day before and were still in session on that Tuesday morning, November first, the day of the Festival of the Dead.

French, German, Spanish, Swedish, Austrian, Italian, British, Portuguese, Greek, Danish, and even a few Belgians, Irish and Dutch, the protesters poured in without cease, having come to demand their countries back. Flemish, Catalan, Tyrolean, Sicilian, Pomeranian, Thuringian, Breton, Corsican, Scottish, Aragonese, Piedmontese, Macedonians, Welsh, Basque, Andaluz, Alsatians, Normans, Walloons, Saxons, Londoners, Lapps, they came to reject the ideas of regionalism and subsidiarity in a European Union. They wanted either their former nation returned to them, or to have autonomy within their own region. They did *not* want a United States of Europe.

And they came to make their point clear.

They swept into the great debating chamber, pushing everything and everybody aside, like an avalanche coursing down a mountainside. Some commissioners managed to jump onto the enormous oval table, twenty feet across at its narrowest; two threw themselves under it.

The multitude knew it had reached its goal. Here were the autocrats, the unelected rulers of a continent, the assembly which had given them value added tax, high unemployment, and a host of similar ills, and had taken their fishing rights, their national currency, their pensions, their foreign reserves, and their pride. This was the assembly — or its successor assembly: who cared? — which had fed them lies and overburdened them with bureaucracy and stupidity, while hiding behind the officialdom of a non-elected demagoguery.

And the people knew what to do. Feet and fists became weapons as the vast chamber was systematically smashed, its chairs, its enormous table, its office equipment being reduced to rubbish.

There were screams and shouts and moans as the demolition continued. Windows were shattered, regardless of the crowds on the road beneath. The despised blue flag with its gold stars was torn to shreds and trodden under a hundred feet.

Inevitably, people were being injured. They were falling onto jagged timbers, broken glass, each other. And they were being beaten up. Mankind's basic instincts in the twenty-first century are little changed from the Middle Ages, and the easiest thing to do with a symbol of oppression was to smash it, whether it be male or female.

An unwritten, unspoken code of honour had taken the protesters into that building and up to that floor, but from there on the law of the jungle took over. Kill or be killed. If it shows fear, kill it. If it begs for mercy, kill it. If it's not dressed for the outdoors, kill it. If it moves, kill it.

Kill it!

Gradually the noise abated, and there were no more people pushing in through the door. Slowly, the demonstrators in the debating chamber could stroll or stagger out, and down the stairs to the entrance hall. In every room and office and hall in the Commission building, the demonstrators had done what they had come to do. They had demonstrated. But as they drifted into the rue de la Loi, where the vast pressure of thrusting bodies had been removed, they realised they had all done far more than demonstrate. They had used the only power available to them. And the results lay on every floor.

Soon, the people by the Commission building heard rumours that the same thing had happened at the European Parliament, at the Council of Ministers, even at the home of the Economic and Social Committee on rue Ravenstein, and the Committee of the Regions, also in rue Belliard.

There was a loud crunch in the Grote Markt as the giant statue of Jacques Santer crashed head-first into the snow, and there were lesser crunches around the city as Neil Kinnock, Konrad Adenauer, Edward Heath, Helmut Kohl and Raymond Barre crashed to the ground.

Slowly, the people's army realised that on the day of the Festival of the Dead, Euroslavia itself had died.

But would it stay dead?

SEVENTEEN

I KNEW NOTHING of the approaching menace until the studio door was kicked in and a strange man was pushed into view in a wheelchair. It is odd, but even in that first fraction of a second I realised he was paralysed down the left side. But his right hand held a small gun which swept the studio before settling on me.

"You are all under arrest," he slurred in German, "especially Mason."

"That's fine," I said. "I'm the only fool here."

"Where is everybody else?"

I wasn't feeling brave, with that gun pointing at my intestines, but I shrugged. "Gone home, I suppose."

Several other people poured in behind him, four or five with guns, which ruled out any hope of resistance. I noticed two of the party were women, and I guessed one was married to the invalid.

"Arrest, you said? First — who are you? Second — what is the charge?"

"You know well enough. I am Axel Teutoburger, president of the Eurosicherheitsdienst, and you are on a charge of spreading seditious libel."

I swallowed. I had had an inkling this might happen, once we were all on hostile soil — not that Britain would have defended us any better — and now I realised I really was the fool for staying behind when all the others fled. But Lisa was almost certainly on her way to find me — could I have abandoned her?

"Herr Teutoburger," I said. "I have done nothing wrong. I have reported facts as they are. Euroslavia recognises some freedoms of the Press, *nicht wahr*?"

"Of course. Freedom to publish the truth. But you have been broadcasting lies, Herr Mason. Subversion! Distortion! Incitement to civil disobedience! And what is this name Euroslavia? I could have you for treason as well!"

I was terrified, but determined not to show it — as long as I could hold out. "Congratulations on your English, Mr Titoburger. I could have half the politicians in Europe for treason, if I could find an honest court to try them. So what do you want?"

"Teutoburger. Under the authority I hold as President of the European Security Service, I am placing you under close arrest. The charges will be made later, Mr Mason, but you may be sure they will be serious. Some may carry the death penalty."

Death? If he was threatening me with death, what did I have to lose? "You stupid, precocious pig!" I spat at him. "The death penalty doesn't apply in Euroslavia. Just economic slavery for life."

"I *am* the Eurosicherheitsdienst," he snarled, with difficulty. "I make the rules."

"And you're judge and jury too, I suppose? Are you one of Hitler's leftovers?" I was rapidly losing control of my anger but some of the people with small-arms seized me by the wrists. I knew I was in the most serious predicament of my life, but I thought that if I could hold out long enough, this maniac would drop dead. And that sobered me instantly. I had completely forgotten about Lisa.

I looked up at the man who had pushed in the wheelchair and who had taken no part in the action since, and I was shocked to recognise Anthony Callan, the Keysman from Castle Rushen in the Isle of Man. I thought I saw him give me a slow wink, but I dismissed it as one of those softening-up techniques I'd read about in war thrillers. He'd give me hope, then Teutoburger would take it away. I wasn't going to play their game.

"I am judge, jury, executioner," Teutoburger said menacingly quietly. And from what I'd heard of this Eurosicherheitsdienst, I could believe him. "And now we will go. All of you."

"Where?" I asked.

"Nowhere!" The woman whom I suspected was Frau Teutoburger, grasped the invalid's serviceable right arm. "I want you to go to hospital, Axel." I don't know why she was speaking French, but a linguistic pudding-bowl was one of the few good things to emerge from Euroslavia. "Every second counts, my dear."

"Give me more pills and I will be alright." He waved his pistol and everybody obeyed. One of the armed men found some cuffs and clipped them on my wrists, then I was led out of the studio and onto the snow. As if his mind were working in slow motion Teutoburger answered the question of where we were going. "Montmédy," he said. "We are going to bury Mason in the dungeons of Montmédy, where nobody will find him." When I saw the helicopter with its rotors turning idly, my stomach sank. If this maniac got me on his own, I was as good as dead now, without waiting to be thrown in some dungeons in this place I'd never heard of.

The pilot shouted something, held up four fingers, and my stomach sank again.

Teutoburger pointed to his wife, me, and one of the armed men, whom I now assumed was one of the Security Service minions. "Four."

"And me," Callan protested. "I know Mr Mason quite well." Again he tipped me the wink.

Teutoburger hesitated. "Okay. You can carry me on your own. You may come." He held his hand out to the other man. "I'll have your gun."

It was a bizarre departure. Callan carried Teutoburger aboard, his wife and I followed, and the door was shut. On the ground, four armed people, one of them a woman, watched as our helicopter rotor blades began churning the air faster, and they turned away only when the blown snow became intolerable.

TWENTY MINUTES LATER the Piper Cherokee with my wife Lisa aboard, landed at Brussels from Cologne and taxied to a dispersal point as conventional airport snowploughs were still clearing the vast expanse of tarmac by the terminal, with each big jet having to be towed out of the way first.

Heinz Müller spoke to the air traffic controllers on his radio. "I understand some television journalists are in the airport compound?"

"They were. They all took off some while ago, as soon as we cleared the runway."

"Have they all gone?"

After a pause the metallic voice said: "We have no information on that, but a helicopter landed by the studios a few minutes ago. You could ask there." The voice gave them instructions on how to reach the temporary buildings.

They walked across the cleared tarmac to the studios and saw three men and a woman closing a door in what they assumed was the television studio. As they drew closer Lisa managed to read the notice: *British Provincial Television*. "Is a Mr Mason around?" she asked in English.

The woman pointed skywards. "He has left not many minutes since."

"Where has he gone?" Müller asked.

"You should ask Herr Präsident. He is under arrest."

Lisa gasped. "Arrest? What for?"

The woman shook her head and turned away, beginning to walk towards their truck. One of the men said casually: "The Präsident said they are going to Momedy."

"Where? Which president?"

"Momedy. I do not know where it is. You must ask Präsident Teutoburger of the Eurosicherheitsdienst."

Lisa turned away. "If I hear that ghastly word once more I shall go raving mad!" To Müller she moaned: "Momedy. Do you know of it? Is my husband in danger, do you think?"

The handsome pilot nodded. "I believe he is. We must go at once to this place." He led the way back to the Cherokee and pulled out a detailed road atlas of western Europe. The index soon yielded *Montmédy* and the map showed the little town to be 160km south-south-east. "There's an airfield not too far away at Douzy, near Sedan." He spoke to the air traffic controllers and added: "It's open. It's only a small place; we'll have to get there before it's dark."

"Can we?"

"I want to fly over Brussels first, to see what's going on. Then we'll head for Douzy. We'll make it, Mrs Mason, have no worry."

CALLAN, THE TEUTOBURGERS and I took off amid a minor snowstorm.

"Why were the broadcasts stopped, Mr Teutoburger?"

The disabled man slurred: "It was not my doing." He wasn't going to admit that he had no knowledge of the invitation being made to the media people of the continent; he assumed the President of the European Commission had authorised the move. "But we cannot tolerate the lies and misinformation you were all broadcasting. You and your friend Archie McGovan."

"You want *McGovan*? Why?"

"Because you two are trying to destroy the European Union. But you will not succeed. Helmut Kohl said, years ago, that it is indestructible and irreversible. You are wasting your time, Mr Mason, and giving many people unnecessary work."

"Starting with you." I paused, then glanced at Callan. "And you too, I assume, Mr Callan? Do you still want to kill me?"

Before Callan could answer, Teutoburger grunted. "This is interesting. Why do you want to kill Mr Mason?"

Callan paused. Again, he winked at me, and I still couldn't understand why — unless he were trying to reassure me. But he was obviously going to play along with Teutoburger. "For the same reason as you, but for different motives. I am the one who saw the time was ripe to take Britain into the single currency. I have business interests that'll suffer if the rest of the sterling zone doesn't surrender to the euro."

Teutoburger tried to frown. "There is no sterling zone."

"But there is. The Isle of Man, the Channel Islands, Gibraltar, and down the mid-Atlantic Ridge to the Falkland Islands. And it's quite strong. I tried to get them in, but I failed. Mr Mason, here, was too clever."

That moment was probably the lowest in my life. I realised that two separate people wanted me dead, for separate reasons. And both were sitting with me in this infernal helicopter going to God knows where.

Where, indeed? I looked out of the starboard window, into the sun. It was early afternoon in November, so I calculated that in the broadest terms we were heading south, probably with a hint of east. Then I looked again. I saw Brussels lying down there, maybe a thousand feet below. I could see the city centre, its streets blackened by uncountable people. But I also saw something else, and if the pilot noticed, he was saying nothing about it.

There was thick smoke soaring skyward from a number of buildings. I guessed that Euroslavia was dead, and its remains were being cremated. I felt that I had a remote chance of survival.

WHEN THE MASS of humanity was thrusting into the European Commission building, John le Mesurier was torn from his wife's arms and carried by the mob towards the great debating chamber. He managed to haul himself up on some heavy drapes just inside the large doorway, so protecting himself from being crushed, and giving him a sickening view of what was to happen when the blood lust broke out.

Fiona le Mesurier and Annette Dugard clung to each other and found themselves carried up the stairs until they reached the top floor. Up here, the lung-crushing pressure weakened, but the panic-fed urge to escape the crowd was no less. They saw a small relief stairway angling up from beside the lift-shaft, and ran up it. Seconds later they pushed open a crash-barrier door and found themselves on the roof; only then did Dugard realise that she had lost both her boots.

"We've done it — we're alone!" Mrs le Mesurier breathed with relief. "But where's John?"

"Who's she?" Dugard pointed to another woman, not wearing outer garments, standing beside the lift shafts. Having escaped from the mêlée below, she felt lighthearted and frivolous. "Excuse me," she asked the strange woman in French, "does the number forty-seven bus pass this way?"

Christine Bouderon turned. "Bus? I just lost a helicopter."

"Helicopter? That's good. We came here on a barge."

Bouderon was in no mood for weird humour. "I'm serious. We're in danger on this roof. We must escape."

Dugard became serious as well. "I know. We can just go down when the crowd gets thinner."

"And when that happens," Bouderon cried, "it will be too late. You know what they'll do?"

Suddenly Fiona le Mesurier realised. "Fire?"

THE E-MAIL INSTRUCTIONS reached the Euroarmée camps and

barracks around the Belgian regions, bringing mixed responses. The Irish catering corpsmen — and women — were ardent Europhiles, aware that their small country had benefited enormously from economic aid from Brussels. They wanted to stay where they were. The Finns had had enough of bureaucracy; the Portuguese and Italians wanted to get home out of this Arctic weather. The Brits had been on the verge of rebellion ever since they learned that their buddies who had not sworn allegiance to Europe, had been offered places in the Royal Falklands Army and RFAF. To a man, they felt they had been tricked into surrendering to the enemy: they were painfully aware that German speakers considered them the Eurowehrmacht and the Euroluftwaffe.

The artillery regiment burned their uniforms on the parade ground, took what transport they needed, and headed for Calais. Damn the snow.

At the Lintkasteel Airport near Grimbergen on Brussels's northern rim, the officer in command of the Muntjack detachment of six scout helicopters, called his troops for a meeting in the hangar. He put it to them squarely that he could authorise them to use military transport to get them to a railhead, from where they could go home. "I take it that this means you can elect for demobilisation from the Eurowehrmacht. Hands in favour?" He scarcely needed to pause. "Unanimous? I also take it that you'd like to use the Puma Gazelles as military transport? And what railhead do you choose?"

"Birmingham," one pilot called, and the issue was settled.

OUR FLIGHT SEEMED to last forever, but I later learned we travelled a hundred miles, across regions BE24, BE25 and BE34.

I asked Teutoburger to repeat where we were going, but he refused to answer. I also counted that he took two doses of tablets to keep his heart beating. He must have been in a bad way.

I had a moderately decent view of the landscape on this sunny Festival of the Dead, and I couldn't fail to notice that there was scarcely a vehicle moving. For miles south of Brussels the northbound carriageway of the autoroute we were following — I presume now it was Euroroute 411 — was blocked by parked vehicles.

It was a truly horrifying sight if one let one's imagination play a little. Down there were thousands upon thousands of motorists, every one stranded for days or even weeks to come. All windscreens had been cleared of snow, and there were some with their bonnets opened. Hundreds of people had abandoned their cars and were walking through the deep snow, either south to some city I couldn't know, or north into Brussels.

EUROSLAVIA

McGovan's Motorcade had been an overwhelming success, but I was certain the fisherman had never visualised it drawing supporters on this vast scale. And now came the misery. Hundreds, maybe thousands, would die of hypothermia, perhaps of hunger, of stress-induced heart attacks, and a few from aggression. But the motorcade had worked. Judging by the fires in the city, Euroslavia was on its knees, if not dead.

Occasionally I saw a service vehicle of some sort on the open carriageway; one appeared to be a van whose driver was probably selling food at some exorbitant price — and risking being robbed. Another was definitely an ambulance. Further south, where a snowplough had cleared the southbound carriageway, I began to see taxis using it, and assumed stranded motorists had used their mobile phones to call for help. It was ironic that mobile phone technology had landed the motorists in this mess at the outset.

The countryside was becoming hillier and I knew these must be the Ardennes. Soon there was plenty of woodland visible and in the distance I saw a little hilltop town with what appeared to be a castle. Then the helicopter banked a little and I realised we were approaching our destination. I lost sight of the town until its market square came into view beneath us, and we descended. There was little to see amid the blizzard blown up by the rotor, but I had the impression of a gaunt, part-derelict castle standing on the edge of an empty market square.

So this was to be my prison, perhaps the scene of my execution.

NUMBER TWO FLIGHT, 23E Squadron, Euro Air Force — the E signified England — filed a flight plan for six scout helicopters from Lintkasteel to Brugge — they could carry on from there across the southern North Sea — and they took off as soon as the machines were fuelled. Each of the six carried its maximum payload in groundcrew and luggage.

At five hundred feet the smoke over Brussels became obvious and the pilot of one machine radioed: "Lima two-zero. Just going to take a look. I'll climb to flight level one to keep out of range of trigger-happy johnnies."

He banked, peeled away, and headed south, over the Royal Park now filled with abandoned cars, direct to the nearest smoking building. Almost at once he saw several figures on the rooftop, waving desperately at him.

"This is Lima two-zero. There are people trapped on the roofs. Suggest you all come and give a hand." The pilot flashed his landing light as acknowledgement, then turned through a hundred and eighty degrees, back to the Royal Park. His passengers hurled their luggage out and jumped after it, lightening the load; the Gazelle was away again as the other five machines came in.

The lead Gazelle came in nose-low to the rooftop of the European Commission building, then pulled its nose up and landed. Six people ran forward; Bouderon, Dugard without her boots, Fiona le Mesurier, and three other people who had escaped to a dubious future on the roof.

"Can you take six?" Bouderon called in French.

"Certainly can," the pilot answered in English. When they were aboard he lifted off carefully then moved off cautiously to the Royal Park.

"Are you dropping us here?" one of the newcomers asked. "How can I get back to London?"

"London? How many of you?"

"Just me. I lost my car and all my luggage. I'll make it worth your while."

The pilot calculated. "One only. You're on, sir. A hundred euros for the flight of your life, but I'm picking up my buddies first."

"Please," Bouderon begged. "Can you take me to the Nationaal Luchthaven? A thousand euros?"

The pilot hesitated only a second. "I'm getting out of this bloody Wehrmacht today. Somebody in the Security Service authorised it, so I shall need some cash to tide me over in civvy street. You're on, miss. Cash — no plastic nonsense."

"Cash. Can we go to the airport first?"

A pause. "Okay." The helicopter banked slightly and headed over the stricken city.

Bouderon asked, as we flew over the chaos: "Do you know who in the Security Service authorised you to leave the armed forces?"

"Search me."

"I did." The pilot turned and stared at her. "You? Sure — and I built the Eiffel Tower."

"I'm serious. I am — was — deputy president, specifically in charge of criminal records. But when I saw what was happening down there, I changed my mind. I ordered it all to stop, and the armed forces to stand down."

The pilot hesitated. "Sounds credible, miss. So where's the boss?"

"He left me stranded on the roof. I think he's gone to the airport, probably planning to fly back to Berlin. If he's not dead already."

"Dead?" The pilot swallowed. "How come?"

"Coronary. As simple as that." Bouderon sensed a new-found respect among the other passengers. "I was a firm believer in the European Union," she explained at large, "but I totally abhor the way it has developed. I have pledged myself to help destroy it, and I think I have done my bit. Now I have to catch my boss before he tries a resurrection."

"Airport ahead, miss. Is that the Berlin plane on the edge of the apron? That Citation?"

Clearance work was continuing around the terminal but the airport had not reopened for commercial flights by the big jets; the seven-seater Citation that had brought Bouderon and Teutoburger in from Tempelhof was the only one that appeared ready for flight.

"He hasn't gone," Bouderon murmured. Then she noticed that the helicopter was missing.

The Gazelle touched down near the Eurosicherheitsdienst office and Bouderon ran all the way to it. Minutes later she was back. "Gone!" she cried. "Only one man there. He says it definitely was Mason they took but he doesn't remember where, and we ought to ask the other people who're looking for him. Who the hell could they be?" She clambered back aboard, updating the pilot on the latest developments. "I thought Axel was half dead, yet he can still pull a trick like this!"

"So where now? I have to get rid of these people."

"Okay, okay," she snapped, racking her brains. Where could Teutoburger, paralysed down his left side and keeping himself alive on a diet of heart pills, have taken his hostage? And why?

As the Gazelle slowly gained altitude and headed west for the Koninklijk Kasteel and thousands of immoblised cars, Bouderon tried to project her mind into her boss's. He had arrested that television presenter, the one whose broadcasts had started this motorcade madness. And, according to the Security Service staff at the airport, Mrs Teutoburger and another man were with him. While that was so, Mason was safe, but when Teutoburger had his man alone, anything could happen. Teutoburger must know his time was limited, and Bouderon knew that she had to act fast.

And then she remembered that visit she had made to her parents' home, and she had been exploring one of the playgrounds of her childhood when Teutoburger had found her. She remembered the guided tour she had given him of those grim dungeons in Montmédy's old castle, and her boss's reaction to them. The best place to hide a kidnap victim: a disused jail where nobody went, but which was easily accessible. She was certain she knew where the ESD boss had taken her prisoner for execution.

The helicopter was coming in heavily to the Royal Castle in Brussel's northern district. "You owe me a thousand Mickey Mice, miss," the pilot reminded her.

She had taken the cash from her money belt, and waited until he had landed before handing it to him. "I'll make it ten thousand if you take me to Montmédy," she offered.

Fiona le Mesurier was already out of the machine, with the other refugees from the roof-top, but Annette Dugard checked. "Montmédy? You're going there?"

"If this friendly, handsome pilot will take me, yes. Look," she said, addressing the pilot directly. "You're getting out of the Euroluftwaffe. The European Union is on its knees. I want to make damned sure it never picks itself up again. Doesn't that mean something to you?"

"It certainly does, miss. And if you're the deputy whatsit of the Gestapo, I guess you're the one to stop it. Okay, again. Ten thousand Mickey Mouses." The aircrew were stumbling towards the Gazelle, lugging their kit. One man threw his bergen aboard, but the pilot pushed it out with his feet. "Fare's gone up to ten thousand Mickey Mices each. If you haven't got the ready — hard cheese." He advanced the controls and the machine, now much lighter, lifted into the air.

"Three aboard," the pilot called. "Is that right? The guy who wants to get back to London for a hundred bits of mouse cheese — boy, have you got a bargain! The woman who's paying a fortune to go to God knows where — and who's the other?"

"Me," said Annette Dugard. "You're going to Montmédy? Can I come along?"

"Sure. If you split the fare with me. I can't pay ten thousand euros in cash."

"Why are you going to Montmédy?" Dugard asked.

"Easy. It's an old fortified town just over the border from Belgium. It has a castle on the top of the hill — Mons Medius. It has some disused dungeons, and that's where I'm certain my boss Teutoburger has taken his hostage."

Dugard blinked. "But why should he go there? How on earth would he know about it?"

Bouderon smiled. "Because I showed him around the place in the summer. I was born there. What's your interest?"

Annette Dugard also smiled. "I was born there as well."

Seven minutes later the helicopter engine started to lose power. The pilot fought the controls but quickly realised he had no option but to make a controlled emergency landing; they came down into thick snow in an open field a few miles east of Waterloo.

"Sorry, folks. Journey's over."

CALLAN CARRIED TEUTOBURGER from the helicopter. "Put me down," Teutoburger ordered. "You, pilot. Lock this thing up to keep the local kids out of it, then help Callan here take me to the dungeons. Mason, you go ahead, and don't forget — I may have just one hand but I've got two guns."

With his wife following, the disabled boss of the Eurosicherheitsdienst directed the way into the castle, his slurring voice giving a commentary.

"This is why we formed the European Union — to stop wars. This place was in Belgium when it was built. My friend Christine Bouderon — she was born in this town, you know — tells me Louis Fourteen captured the castle in the seventeenth century. Since then the Prussians have taken it once and the Germans twice. Down these steps."

The gloom closed around us as we slowly descended a dank flight of stone steps, worn hollow by countless soldiers' tread.

"You've been here before?" Frau Teutoburger asked with ice in her voice. "With that woman?"

"Only once."

I felt the emotional atmosphere tightening along with the physical sensation of doom and gloom. Behind me were two men, each vowing to kill me, with one nearly having succeeded; behind me, too, a domestic incident was coming to the boil.

At the bottom of the steps the air struck chill and dank, and voices echoed eerily. There was no indication that any local person ever entered this godforsaken fortress. The late afternoon light was dim, with the sun nearly setting, but down in the bowels we were in near total darkness — until Callan took a pencil torch from his pocket. "Borrowed it from the Jag," he explained.

In its feeble light we could see a passage leading away to our left, with a barred glassless window at the end, allowing in the only natural light. I knew I was going to be incarcerated here and I wondered how long I could survive in solitary confinement, in darkness, and in this dank and chilly tomb. Would death come from hypothermia, from starvation, or from a bullet between the eyes?

I was nudged roughly along the passage and soon I saw in Callan's feeble torchlight, the first of the cells. Thank God the details eluded me, but I could see it was no bigger than a bathroom and it had nothing, not even a bunk bed or a blanket. It was simply a stone cell, a sarcophagus for the living. A centuries-old metal grille was inset into slots in each side wall and I realised I was looking at a portcullis, the sliding door of medieval times.

"She showed me how it works," Teutoburger said. "There's the chain, Callan — haul it up. I'll hold your torch."

Callan appeared very reluctant to obey but the boss of the security service, grasping the pencil torch and his firearm in the same hand, waved them together. Callan reached to head-height for a large iron ring on the end of a heavy chain that had rusted over the years but was still intact. He heaved until the grill started to rise, the heavy, dull, rumbling noise sounding like the gates of Hell grinding open, and when the portcullis was two feet clear of the ground, Teutoburger called for him to stop. "Paul and ratchet; it won't come down. Mason can squeeze under there. Or how about the next dungeon — shall we put him in that one?"

We all moved on; Callan was already sweating with exertion and I was beginning to perspire from fear, regardless of the chill. Callan tried the next grille but it refused to budge. Persuaded by the pistol he hauled the third portcullis to knee-height and let it fall back an inch until it engaged the ratchet and stopped.

Teutoburger tried to laugh, but it came out more as a cough. "Well, Tel Mason. The choice is yours. But make it quick."

I realised there was no point in resisting so I lay down on the damp stone and rolled under the first portcullis. Callan, on orders, pulled on the chain again, released the ratchet, and the grill crashed to the floor, imprisoning me.

Callan pointed to the chain. "He can reach through the grill and pull that down."

Teutoburger held his mouth open to his wife and she thrust more pills in. As he chewed he murmured: "No way. He must climb up the grill to reach. From inside he cannot pull up the metal as well as his own weight. He is trapped. I doubt he will see the light of day again." Relying on the helicopter pilot for support he aimed the gun and torch at Callan. "Now you go in the next dungeon."

"Like hell I will..."

Teutoburger pulled the trigger and a bullet struck the stonework beside Callan. "You wanted to kill our friend Mason. You have all night to figure out how. Now — get in."

I felt relieved as I saw Callan's shadow sink to the floor and disappear into his own cell. I was pleased for the company, but I was also glad there was an empty chamber between us.

Teutoburger turned to his wife. "Louisa, *mein Liebchen*, please release the rachet so Mr Callan can make himself comfortable."

Frau Teutoburger obeyed. The second portcullis crunched down into the bedrock, and Callan began his incarceration. The woman stepped back, then suddenly turned on her husband and knocked the gun and the torch from his only working hand. She snatched them up from the floor and pointed them at her husband, one in each hand.

"I've had enough. You've been here with that woman. Did you

make love down here? Did you want a cheap thrill at my expense? Did you bring blankets, or did you do it standing up?"

"*Liebchen.* I have never been unfaithful to you. I swear..."

"You've been unfaithful to me ever since you became President of your own little Gestapo. You've lived for your job, and for that woman. You have no time for me at all. And now you've lost it all. The Eurosicherheitsdienst is collapsing along with the Europäische Vereinigung. So you can take the next dungeon and rot here with your friends. Pilot! Open the next cell, if you please."

The helicopter pilot obliged, pausing when the grill was at knee-height; he felt it settle back on the ratchet.

"Push him under. I don't want to see him ever again. Push him under, for God's sake."

Teutoburger's tall figure looked shrivelled as the helicopter pilot pushed him without dignity into the cell, then stood back. Frau Teutoburger stepped forward to take a last look at her husband, then felt the cool muzzle of a gun pushing into her temple.

"And I have had enough of all of you." The pilot reached his left arm around her and took the torch. "You will give me your gun, Frau Teutoburger, and roll under that grill to join your husband."

"Where did you get that weapon?"

"From your husband's pocket when I helped him down the steps." He released the safety catch, knowing she would hear the faint click. She gave him her gun, knelt on the cold stones, and rolled into her husband's dungeon. "You can't leave us here — we'll die of cold."

The pilot smiled. "This is the neatest job I've ever done. And now I couldn't care if I never set eyes on any of you ever again."

Moments later we heard the roar of the rotor blades, and then, gradually, there was nothing but the silence, the darkness, and the numbingly-cold air.

THE PIPER CHEROKEE flew over the centre of Brussels, giving Heinz Müller and my wife Lisa an excellent view of the devastation. "It's finished, it's finished," Müller shouted. "No government can pick itself up out of this sort of mess. It's finished, my dear friend! Thanks to you and your husband and all the millions of people in McGovan's Motorcade! Now, once again, we can try to put Europe together — but in little pieces next time, not one big blob. Seen enough? Then we're off to Montmédy."

The plane approached Douzy Airport, eight km east of Sedan, as the daylight was fading. Somebody had splashed yellow dye on the snow to pick out the cleared landing strip and the descent was perfect, with Müller putting his plane down so smoothly Lisa didn't even notice it.

He taxied along a single snow-plough alley towards the terminal, but it was only when they were out of the aircraft that they saw how deep the snow was. "Almost a metre," the air traffic controller confirmed as he shut down his tower for the night. "There's absolutely nothing moving on the roads."

"Nothing?" Lisa cried: her French is better than her German. "I have to get to Montmédy."

"The only way is to fly over the place and bale out — come down by parachute," the controller explained as Lisa looked puzzled. When she understood she turned to her pilot.

"No way!" he snapped. "We'll get a lift into the village, find rooms, and get out to Montmédy tomorrow. Will the road be cleared?"

"They'll be working on it all night, I hear, but there are so many abandoned cars on it. Village is blocked with cars that won't start, as well. Don't understand what happened. No rooms to rent — people from the cars have taken everything and they're even sleeping in people's homes. Don't know what things are coming to. Road's done east of Carignan — that's twelve km away, so they'll be here in the morning. But you won't get a taxi — Henri never disconnected his battery when they told him to."

"Can we sleep in the terminal?"

"If you don't mind sharing with fifty others."

It was a second miserable night, but in the early hours she roused as she heard the snowplough move through the village. Lisa and Müller floundered through the snow of the side road as soon as it was daylight, and they found the railway station, with eighty refugees from McGovan's Motorcade and the Festival of the Dead. The train pulled in at ten past nine and took everybody aboard although there was scarcely room to stand. Shortly before ten the train stopped at Montmédy and Lisa and Müller struggled to get out before yet more refugees crowded aboard.

"Well," Müller groaned. "Here we are. What now?"

JOHN LE MESURIER was distraught when fire broke out in the European Commission building. He was on the snow-covered tarmac of rue de la Loi, searching for a familiar face, particularly his wife's. He shouted her name, but the sound was lost in hundreds of other names being called. During the evacuation of the building the death toll had become impossible to ignore; there were dozens of crumpled and suffocated bodies, and dozens more with broken legs, crushed ribs and similar injuries.

From the moment when the flames took hold on the first floor, there was no chance of taking out the dead; rescuing the living had been difficult enough.

He helped haul several of the injured to safety, always looking for somebody he knew yet hoping not to find him or her among the dead or crippled.

As the flames burst through the windows and dense smoke surged into the clear sky, he heard a cry from the crowd as a helicopter came in, then banked and flew away. It was back several minutes later and put down onto the roof, and when it took off it was obviously heavily laden.

Le Mesurier tried running after it until he realised the stupidity of such an action, so he went back to the Commission and waited.

The sun was nearing the skyline and the air was distinctly cold when he saw Archie McGovan and Sir John Faulds greeting each other on the roadway. He joined them and the trio hugged each other in relief, then began comparing notes. From the Manx party, Bridget Norris and Tony Callan were missing. From the Alderney party, Fiona le Mesurier, Annette Dugard and John Doyle, the old Guernseyman. And there was no sign of the old priest from Liechtenstein. What was his name — Zimmerman? Carpenter in German.

There were sudden shouts from the ruins of the entrance hall as a group of men pulled away the debris of the main reception desk, and John Doyle staggered out to a round of applause.

"Ah'm sorry," McGovan said. "Ah'm so sorry. Ah didna want it to end like this. Oh, God — can I ever be forgiven?"

"But it worked!" Sir John Faulds thumped him on the back. "Look at all this! Euroslavia is dead, man. Every one of those commissioners got the short straw. Oh, that was terrible, but you can't make an omelette without smashing eggs. At least, it'll teach the world a lesson. You can only lead the people where they want to go. It was a *success*, man. Don't ever forget that. And now, we'd better find some shelter for the night. I guess we can all squeeze up in Callan's car, if we can get into the damned thing."

Le Mesurier shared a glance with Doyle. "The barge?"

"We can give it a try. With any luck we can get out of the city on it tomorrow."

With any luck, le Mesurier thought, Fiona might be waiting there for me. Or Annette Dugard might be there with news.

BUT NEITHER FIONA nor Annette was there. Annette Dugard was preparing to spend the night in a downed Gazelle helicopter in open fields near Waterloo, with the deputy boss of the Eurosicherheitsdienst, the British pilot, and a man who was hoping to hitch a lift back to London. Four citizens of the European Union who wanted to go back to being two French women and two British men. Ships that pass in the night, she thought. Refugees along the highway of life.

The temperature was dropping, and she knew it would be a bitterly cold night. They had little food: a tin of corned beef, three apples and a packet of biscuits. They were even worse off for bedding: the pilot's bergen had one single-size sleeping bag, Bouderon had left Berlin without a hat and coat, and Dugard had lost her boots in the Commission building.

The Gazelle had some rubber mats, which the pilot dropped out onto the snow. "Stand on them to do whatever you have to do, under the chopper. Then we'll all have to cuddle up real tight. I think we'll know each other a bit better by morning."

THE TWO BASQUES reached Euroroute 9 at Frisange, one of the southernmost communities in the Province of Luxembourg, following the snowplough from Schengen. Yzurdiaga was looking for the turn north to the city when Arrieta pointed to a new sign. *Accès à la cité interdite. Eintritt zum Stadt strengst verboten.* No entry to Luxembourg city.

"Well, that's that," Arrieta said. "Somebody didn't like what we did to Monsieur Santer, the local lad who made it to the top. Let's go home."

Yzurdiaga shook his head. "It's not as easy as that, old friend. You go home if you like, but I'm staying here."

Staqui felt the hairs on his neck tingle. "Staying here? In Luxembourg? Why? How long?"

"I shall be staying in Luxembourg. I don't know how long, but I guess I shall end my days here. Why? Because I still have one bomb to plant."

"Where's it going?" But Arrieta had already guessed.

"Where I said right at the start of our campaign. In the heart of one of the East Wind's main buildings, the Investment Bank. A giant deposit of seven kilos of Semtex."

"That'll make a massive..."

"Yes, Staqui. It will make one monstrous explosion. I promise you I shan't feel a thing." He paused, beckoning the motorist behind him to overtake.

Staqui looked at the sign. *No entry to Luxembourg city.* "You may need help to get into the city, Xav. We've been friends for so long, we can't break it up now."

Yzurdiaga said: "You do know exactly what we're going to do?

EUROSLAVIA

You do realise you're not wanted for any crime back home, whereas I'm wanted for six killings?"

"I came with you from the Semtex dump."

"No, Staqui. I abducted you."

Arrieta said indignantly: "Stop talking such nonsense and get going."

The journey was frustratingly difficult, with useless cars lining the northbound edge of the road for most of the journey, many of them still serving as temporary homes for their drivers and passengers.

"It looks like a gigantic squatter camp," Arrieta murmured. "And we could have been like them if you hadn't worked on the engine." But they were finding sections where enterprising mechanics had improvised repairs and cleared fifty or more vehicles, and they passed several mechanics still at work, prising open the bonnets and patching up the wiring.

"People are going to be driving cars with battered bonnets for several years," Yzurdiaga commented. "I wonder if it'll become a fashion? 'I was in McGovan's Motorcade'?"

"Even if it doesn't, there'll be plenty of mechanics come out of this week as millionaires."

They reached Fentange and Hesperange, the southern suburbs to the once-ducal city, without finding any obstruction and they guessed the sign was a bluff. Route de Thionville took them into the city and its one-way system, partially blocked by contractors removing the statue of Jacques Santer from the roadway.

"Oh, dear," Yzurdiaga smiled. "The poor man has had a fall."

There was far less evidence of mass protest in Luxembourg than there was in Brussels, for the smaller city wasn't held in such hatred by the average Europrotestor. Abandoned cars littered the sidestreets, most still covered in snow, and Yzurdiaga drove their battered rental car into one such street.

"Now we prepare the bomb," he said.

"*Caramba!* We should have done that kilometers back!"

"And risk an early bang? Not me. Go for a little walk, old friend, and keep people away."

"People? What people? A bitterly cold public holiday morning in November — what people? The protesters aren't walking the streets."

Yzurdiaga switched his mind to the final task at hand. He took the remaining seven kg of Semtex and two detonators, and put them on the floor behind the driver's seat. Working very carefully, he planted both detonators and wired them in parallel to the car jack, which he placed under his seat. Another cable ran from the car's fusebox to the wheel brace, which he carefully sited an inch or so behind the jack.

When he braked hard, or when the car hit a solid object, both lumps of metal would collide, so joining the circuit. This time there was no need for a timing device.

"Ready, Staqui," he called. They both climbed aboard and Yzurdiaga did a careful turn in the sidestreet before following signs to the *Institutions Européennes*. They drove down a steep road still slippery with snow, which made Yzurdiaga dread a premature braking and a misplaced explosion, but the road flattened and led them into a kind of garden city on Luxembourg's north-eastern fringe.

Here were many of the buildings from the early days of the Iron and Steel Community through to its emergence as the European Union.

"Here's where the people are," Staqui said. "Hundreds of them."

"Boulevard Konrad Adenauer." Yzurdiaga nodded at a road sign. "The Investment Bank is somewhere along here. It looks like a three-layer milk-chocolate sandwich cake. We'll find it, drive past, then come back again, shall we?"

Staqui nodded. Suddenly he felt that his voice was inadequate.

"There it is," Yzurdiaga said. "Guards keeping people away, but no chain link fences. No troubles at all. Protesters looking as if they're out for a Sunday morning stroll."

Staqui nodded again. Suddenly Yzurdiaga changed into lower gear, accelerated, and headed for the snow-covered lawns surrounding the European Bank. He held his finger on the horn button and protesters scattered. Staqui, realising what was happening, gripped his seat and held on as the car slithered through the snow. Then they were through the crowds and heading straight for the bank's main entrance. Yzurdiaga never changed gear. His foot was pushing the accelerator pedal onto the floor as he steered his path to destiny.

The final events took place within a fraction of a second. The car crashed into the front wall but before it could finish crumpling, the wheel brace hit the jack and sent an electric current to the seven kilos of Semtex. The explosion was small compared with the Oklahoma bombing or the Canary Wharf explosion, but it ripped the flat roof off the building and penetrated deep into the interior.

There was total shock among the crowds, but when the smoke and dust settled, everybody could see that the European Investment Bank was in ruins.

One rear wheel of the car was sent hurtling skywards and landed on the elevated Autoroute du Kirchberg, half a kilometer away. Nothing was ever found of the two Basques, Eustaqui Arrieta and Xavier Yzurdiaga.

WALKING UP AND DOWN in the dungeons of what I learned was a

medieval castle in a little town called Montmédy, I knew it was going to be a hellish night. I had left the derelict chicken farm in Region UK54 — hell: Euroslavia was dead. It was Essex again — with only an anorak for outer wear, and I was wearing ordinary shoes. I guessed I would have to keep moving all night or die of the cold. Teutoburger wouldn't last long, and I doubted if his wife would be alive by morning. Only Callan, the man with the inexplicable wink, was dressed for survival.

"Callan," I called as I began walking three paces, turning, and walking three paces back.

"Yes?"

"Was it really you who sent a model aircraft loaded with explosives through my bedroom window?"

"No. It wasn't. I was in the Isle of Man. But it did happen on my orders, I must confess. And it was one of my best model aircraft."

"You bastard! So you really did want to kill me?"

"Not at all. I'm not a murderer. I wanted to scare you off, that's all. The shooting was certainly not on my orders. The guy I hired got somewhat carried away."

"I thought it was me he wanted to be carried away. And what about the bomb? That was a bloody dangerous way to scare me off."

"It was only a small incendiary."

"Incendiary!" I stopped pacing for a moment. "It damn near blew the studio to bits!"

Callan gasped. "What are you talking about? Did Robinson try blowing up CCC's hidden studio?"

"He didn't just try. He succeeded. Luckily we got out a few hours before." Then the doubts returned. "It *was* your man, wasn't it? Or could it have been that Bouderon woman from the Security Service?"

Frau Teutoburger called from the next cell. "Will you please stop arguing and help my husband?"

"Why doesn't he help us for a change? Did he know anything about that bomb attack in Docklands? Ask him, woman."

"He's shaking his head. He says he sent Bouderon to London but he doesn't know about a bomb. You *must* help him."

"Help him? How can we — by telepathy? What's wrong?"

"He's had another heart attack."

"That was inevitable, woman. You put him in the cell, don't forget."

"I did not expect to be here with him."

"Would you believe it, Frau Teutoburger, but I didn't expect to spent the evening of the Fête des Morts in a French jail, either? I don't know how your husband has kept going. He must be stressed to hell."

EUROSLAVIA

"Give him some more pills," Callan suggested.

"I have. He can't chew them."

"Then I'm sorry," I shouted. "I don't wish death on anybody, but he didn't wish a long life on me, so why should I cry?" I turned my attention back to Callan. "How did you know your Robinson type found us?"

"My man was watching your head office in Soho Square. He was damned good at that side of the surveillance business, but after I had a good talk with your wife I began to have severe doubts about Europe. Then when I saw McGovan's Motorcade I knew I was wrong. If millions of people feel that strongly, it's got to be wrong. So I'm sorry for all I've done, Mr Mason, and I'll do whatever I can to put matters right."

"That's easy. Get me out of here."

"It was easier to get Britain into the single currency."

"Callan — was it *really* you who pushed Britain into the common currency?"

"All the pieces were there. Clause 104c had been in the Maastricht Treaty for several years. It was only when the Labour Government started hinting that it might have to put up taxes, that it all fell into place. Tony Blair could have told Europe to go to hell, but he knuckled under instead."

"But that happened some while ago. Why did you want to hurt me now?"

"I wanted the rest of the Sterling Zone to join the single currency. I had a major business deal resting on it. A fortune. If we got the Isle of Man into the euro zone but kept it out of the Union, it could operate as a tax haven. It could have had it made. Car assembly plants. It could have quadrupled its financial services. It could have been a Euro tax haven. The film industry could have moved in at low tax. The prospects were endless. But then you started interfering and I could see you would tip the balance. That's why I tried to silence you. If it's any consolation, I bitterly regret it now. That's why I tried to tip you the wink. I had come over to your side. I'm still on your side. If I could get myself out of this pigsty I really would take you with me."

"You do realise it wouldn't have worked? If Europe grabbed the Isle of Man into its single currency, it wouldn't have stopped there. It couldn't. Empires don't work like that. It would have grabbed the island and put Euro laws in place. It would have killed the golden goose."

From a distance Frau Teutoburger's voice spoke, but showed no emotion; she could have been buying a bag of apples. "My husband is dead."

"I'm sorry," I called, but I didn't know whether I meant it.

"And I am freezing to death!" she called, her voice full of fear for herself.

"So are we all, Mrs T." I scoffed at Callan. "You imbecile! Once Brussels got its filthy little fingers into you, it wouldn't stop until it had pinched every penny — every eurocent — you'd got. You did it to Britain with 104c; they'd try it on you with some other clause from Amsterdam."

"I know, Tel. I can see that now."

Up and down, up and down. Ten times, twenty, thirty.

"Don't call me Tel. I hate the name."

The cold was slowly being driven from my bones. I paused, leaned against the stone wall, but within minutes the chill was penetrating me once again. Up and down, up and down, and I guessed we hadn't been here an hour yet. And there was all the rest of our lives in front of us.

That was when I began to realise I certainly couldn't survive a second night without warmth, without food, without hope. I might not even survive this first night.

"How many people come here, Mister Eurosicherheitsdienst man?"

Up and down, up and down.

"I told you. My husband is dead. And I am dying. Help me, please."

"Do what we're doing — exercise."

Exercise — or pull the chain. I clambered up three rungs of my grille, reached through, and fumbled for the iron ring that Callan had hauled on. It was there. I pulled, but nothing happened. I took my feet off the grille, letting all my weight hang on my hands and on that ring. I felt a slight vibration that thrilled me as if I'd won the Golden Rose of Montreux, but that was all. I realised the chain had to be pulled slightly outwards as well as downwards, and I couldn't do that from inside the cell.

I rested, then up and down again.

"Frau Teutoburger," I called.

Minutes later: "Yes."

"Can you lift your husband? Can you stand him against the portcullis?"

Long minutes, with a faint scuffle. "I've done it. Now what?"

"Can you put his arms around your shoulders?"

Up and down, up and down. There was a touch of sweat on my brow, but the cold was eating slowly into my body.

"Yes."

"Are his feet on the ground?"

"Of course. I can't lift a dead weight."

"Can you climb the grille with him still on your back? So all his weight is on your shoulders?"

"I see what you mean. I will try."

God, if only Callan and I could help her! But then we wouldn't be behind these bars. Maybe half an hour later: "I have done it. I have climbed the squares and reached the ring."

"*Wunderbar!*"

We heard the grating of iron on stone, groans of exertion and frustration. "But I cannot do it!"

"You cannot do what?" I called. "You cannot use your husband's weight to pull down the chain?"

"It is asking too much. I'm sorry, but I *cannot!*"

So there was no hope of escape. I found a scrap of paper in one anorak pocket, and a ballpoint pen in another. In the darkness I had no way of knowing whether the paper was printed on, or whether the pen had ink — but, at least, I could make an impression on the paper.

I stood in the middle of my cell, away from the chilling walls, and wrote my farewell letter to Lisa.

I was not ready to die, but I knew I had no choice.

FIONA LE MESURIER had escaped from the burning Commission building through a rear door. Without thinking about a rendezvous in the front of the building she walked back to the little barge haven on the Canal de Charleroi north of Brussels's city centre and stayed there until the other members of the party arrived.

Bridget Norris made her way back to Callan's Jaguar in the Royal park and smashed the window to get in when she realised nobody else was coming back.

Five Aerospatiale Gazelle helicopters rescued around twenty people on the rooftops of burning buildings in Brussels, offloaded them in the grounds of the Royal Castle, then headed in convoy west-north-west towards Brugge, and on over the Strait of Dover towards Manston in Kent, where they landed, near the limits of their range. Three refugees from McGovan's Motorcade who had begged passage, clambered out into the chill night air.

"Freedom! And bugger Europe!," one of the pilots shouted.

THE SIXTH HELICOPTER was grounded in a field west of Waterloo. Dugard had stood on the rubber mat and studied the thirty-centimetre-deep snow, catching the pink rays of the setting sun. She knew that she would risk frostbite if she walked three miles without boots.

The four of them huddled up as closely as they could, Dugard's feet wrapped in the pilot's spare shirt, and all with feet and legs in his bergen. They sat together on the front seating, trying to share their body warmth as darkness crept over them.

"Are you really the deputy boss of the Security Service?" the pilot asked.

"Absolutely. Bouderon's the name. Christine. What's your name?"

"Hollis — William. From Norwich. And you really are from this Montmédy place, where you think your boss has gone?"

"Ex-boss, please. I switched my allegiance a few days ago when I met Terry Mason in London. He's the man who made those television programmes."

"I saw some. Hard-hitting stuff. Is it all true?"

"As far as I know. Euroslavia — wonderful name — was set up almost like a secret society. The Eurosicherheitsdienst really *is* a secret society within the main one. It's absolutely wrong. Do you know, they've started a programme to insert microchips in new-born babies? In a few years time there'll be no way of escaping surveillance unless you go down a mineshaft. They've rewritten a lot of the school history books, too, so that Hitler was misguided and Napoleon was a hero."

"He tried to conquer Europe, like this lot we've just kicked out!"

Bouderon nodded. "And you realise where we are? On the site of the Battle of Waterloo."

I PLANNED TO GO down fighting. I would not lay down and surrender to the cold. I would walk all night, up and down, and shout out to Callan and Frau Teutoburger from time to time.

Up and down, up and down. My mind wandered onto a limitless range of topics as I trudged, turned, trudged — then woke, lying on the stone floor and trembling with a penetrating chill.

"Callan!"

"I'm here."

I staggered to my feet. "I fell asleep."

"So did I. Glad you woke me. Frau Teutoburger — can you hear me?" Silence. He shouted again, his voice echoing off the grim stone walls. "Frau Teutoburger!"

"*Ich bin hier.*"

"On your feet! Walk!"

Up and down. I heard Callan stamping his feet as he walked. But there was no response from the third cell. "Frau Teutoburger! Speak to me! *Sprechen Sie mir!*"

"I am here. I am so cold I cannot walk."

"Walk or die. We can't help you."

God: what was the time? Wasn't it even midnight? Up and down...

I collapsed into sleep several times in the night, on the last time waking dreadfully slowly. I now know what it is like to drift into sleep and slide from there into death. I heard a noise in the distance and gradually realised it was Callan shouting.

"Mason! Wake up, for God's sake, man!"

"I'm here." As soon as consciousness hit, the trembling started. It was uncontrollable. Everything that could vibrate, was vibrating: hands, arms, feet, legs, and across my shoulders.

"Get up, man!"

My fingers were so cold they wouldn't move. I was on my belly, so I rolled onto my side and began propping myself up on my elbows. Then the knees, all the time answering Callan's urges. If this man still wanted to kill me, he was going about it a strange way. Then I threw my weight back and staggered to my feet, shaking uncontrollably.

"Frau Teutoburger?" I tried to shout, but my lips wouldn't function.

"No answer. I think she's dead."

"I was asleep. You saved my life."

"Then keep walking."

"I will." Up and down, flinging my arms across my chest. I was tired, unbelievably cold, thirsty, and hungry. How long could I go on?

"Listen!" Callan shouted half an eternity later. "Helicopter!"

"You're dreaming."

But I stopped walking and listened. The noise rapidly grew recognisable, then louder, and I shouted: "It's coming here!"

The sounds told their own story. A helicopter, lighter than the one we had come in, settled onto the square in the castle precinct. People were jumping out, calling to each other, to us.

"Tel Mason — are you there?"

I bawled an unintelligible noise.

"Are you alone?"

"No!"

Callan shouted: "I'm Tony Callan. Teutoburger is here, but he's dead. I think his wife is, too."

And then four people clattered and slithered down the steps by the light of a good torch.

"Christine Bouderon!" I called as I recognised her. "Have you come to save us?"

"I said I would. But where's my boss?"

There was so much to tell: how Flight-Lieutenant Hollis from 23E Squadron, Euroluftwaffe, reasoned in the night what was wrong with his machine and put it right within minutes. How Bouderon had realised where Teutoburger would have hidden his hostage. And confirming that Frau Louisa Teutoburger had indeed died of exposure during the night. Annette Dugard claimed the dead man's socks and the dead woman's shoes.

"What about Euroslavia?"

"Finished!" Bouderon and Dugard shouted together.

Suddenly I remembered. "But where's my wife? I'm sure she would have tried to get to Brussels Airport."

Bouderon stared. "Then we must get back at once. She could be in trouble on her own." She and I, and the man wanting a lift home, clambered into the helicopter, leaving Annette Dugard and Callan in the market square and the two bodies in the cell. Flt. Lt. Hollis increased thrust until the machine slowly rose, amid the usual shower of snow. When it cleared, I looked down on the hilltop fort and the small town clinging at its base, and I saw two figures on the steep road waving their arms at us.

"Hold it," I called. The machine slid down towards the two and I quickly recognised one of them. "It's my wife! It's Lisa! How the devil did she get here? Can you land — quickly?"

NINETEEN

THE EMERGENCY OVER, we left the helicopter by the castle and all trudged through the snow for hot meals in a smart bistro at the foot of the hill where the modern town of Montmédy clusters, while Lisa told us her story and Callan couldn't understand why she had run away from him.

And then we had to begin the remainder of our lives. Annette Dugard took a taxi to her parents' home in a guest-house a kilometer out of town on the Longuyon road. Christine Bouderon invited us to her own family home in the tiny village of Thonne-les-Près on the other side of town, but we promised to come back some other time. She said she would report the two bodies in the dungeons after we'd left.

And then Flight-Lieutenant Hollis and I, Lisa and Heinz Müller, Tony Callan and the man still hoping for a lift back to England, clambered up the snow-covered hill again and flew to Douzy where we dropped Müller amid a welter of handshakes and good wishes. Then we flew leisurely back to the Royal park in Brussels where Bridget Norris was making some soup on the camping stove. Callan chose to drive his precious car home, but Mrs Norris and Sir John Faulds hitched a lift with Lisa and me — and the man begging a lift — to 23 Squadron's base at Lintkasteel where the pilot refuelled. There was no mechanic available to check the machine, so we all took a chance and flew with him to Manston in Kent.

ON WEDNESDAY, THE SECOND of November, 2005, with a light dusting of snow across the eastern part of England and Scotland, the Prime Minister of England and Wales called an emergency meeting of his emasculated Cabinet. Most ministers were in their constituencies but almost all managed to reach the Palace of Westminster by late evening.

Prime Minister William Hague gave his Cabinet the latest information on the European situation.

"As I'm sure you all know, virtually every European Union building has been destroyed by fire. The European Parliament in Brussels, and its new building; the European Commission; the Council of Ministers; the European Investment Bank in Luxembourg destroyed by a suicide car bomb, after which the crowd set fire to the Court of Justice with the Court of Auditors badly damaged by petrol bombs; the Economic and Social Committee on fire. Only the Palace of

Europe in Strasbourg was untouched. Crowds are still surrounding the Bundesbank in Frankfurt."

He paused for effect before telling them more of what they already knew. "I very much deplore the loss of life, and I must inform you that the President of the European Union and every commissioner died in the rioting. The losses among the members of Parliament have not yet been assessed, but it is around half. As yesterday, Tuesday, was a public holiday, very few of the civil servants were on duty, and we have no reports at all of any being attacked. It seems that the targets were firstly the unelected autocrats who have ruled the Union, and secondly the elected members whom the Eurocitizens now see as impotent figureheads. I know I speak for every member of this Cabinet, of this Party and of the House of Commons when I totally deplore this killing."

He acknowledged the muted cheers and applause.

"However, we must look at the facts as they now stand. The European Union is effectively dead, and I am sure that none of us here has any regrets on that score. You already know that there has been an overwhelming loss of confidence in the euro, triggered by the Saudi Arabian withdrawal of all its available funds — and that was instigated by the Ambassador to the Sterling Zone in an attempt to weaken the Union and allow Britain, eventually, to escape from the irrevocable situation — I quote Chancellor Helmut Kohl, of course.

"I therefore propose that this Government declares its signatory of the Treaty of Rome and all subsequent treaties to be null and void.

"Tonight, there is no European Union so there is nobody with whom we can negotiate, nobody who can deny us the right to unilateral revocation of the treaties."

"Hear, hear."

"Ladies, gentlemen. There is still a long way to go before we get back to the situation that prevailed before our unfortunate entry into the Common Market, but we have, at last, begun that long road back to the future — with some considerable help from our Arab friends to whom we owe a special debt. Yesterday we had the powers of a county council and the rights of a debating society. Today we are once more the lawful government of England and Wales, and I trust Edinburgh will make the same moves to become the government of Scotland. And if either of us ever again negotiates unions, it shall be between us two, and no others."

The Cabinet room echoed to the shouts of approval.

Of course, Euroslavia's affairs would take much longer to sort out. Every one of the member states — even Luxembourg and Ireland — signed treaties annulling the entire idea of the Union and set in motion the task of refunding the national reserves held at Frankfurt.

Early in the New Year, after the crowned heads came home, there was a spate of general elections, with Christine Bouderon gaining a surprise victory in La Meuse, but everybody knew it would take several parliaments to shake off the shadow that Euroslavia had cast over a continent, threatening the Third World War within a hundred years.

SO NOW YOU KNOW

THE BOOK YOU have just read is a work of fiction, but it is based very closely on fact, and on a future projection of those facts.

Everything I claim that the European Union has done up to the date of first publication of this book, is true. Things that I claim the Union has done *after* that date one may logically expect to be possible, although they may never happen.

The Eurosicherheitsdienst, the European Security Service, is one such nightmare that should stay within the bounds of fiction. In a pure and simple form it could result from Chancellor Kohl's 1996 call for a pan-European police force. As I write there is no suggestion that a kind of Gestapo was intended, but in the absence of public accountability such a force could emerge. It happened in the 1930s.

The technology exists at the moment to have a security device which would immobilise vehicles *en masse,* and the EGNOS satellite navigation system exists.

The Franco-German Brigade has existed for years — have you heard of it? — and there are calls for an integrated European Defence Force, so the RAF could become part of the Euroluftwaffe. I am fully aware of the emotive nature of the word *Luftwaffe*, particularly among those people who remember World War Two, but it means nothing more than 'air force'.

If full European integration is achieved according to the rules at present laid down, then the head of state of the EU *must* be appointed from within the autocracy, and the President of the European Commission is the most likely choice although in 1997 a supreme President of the European Union was suggested: appointed, of course, not elected. As I write the post of President of the Commission is held by Jacques Santer, but Neil Kinnock is being tipped as his successor in 1999. Kinnock may even become the supreme President, if such a post is created, and if the single currency has heralded federation, President Kinnock could become the most important head of state in the world.

With the head of state in charge of Britain being the president of an autocracy in either form, there will be no need for monarchies. England, Scotland and Northern Ireland — and Wales? — would become separate 'provinces' within Europe, and a province cannot support its own monarchy — can you imagine the King of Normandy surviving in today's Republic of France? Can you imagine a mere province of the European Union being called the United Kingdom? Is this the true reason behind New Labour's Scottish and Welsh devolution proposals —

to split Britain ready for full integration in Europe? The British Royal Family — and the monarchies of Spain, Benelux, Denmark and Sweden — would be surplus to requirement. With no monarchy, there is no aristocracy. The House of Lords is automatically abolished: it is far too democratic for Europe.

The regions I mention are already in existence, on paper. According to the regional map, Spain has claimed Gibraltar as Region ES63, and France has claimed the Channel Islands as part of Region FR25. According to the map, what is currently Britain has claimed the Isle of Man. As Britain already administers Value Added Tax in the island, this could hold sinister bodings for all Manxmen. And women. Andorra, Liechtenstein, San Marino and Monaco are still free — but the EU map to which I referred also claims the Gallipoli Peninsula of Turkey as part of Greece. If this is a mistake rather than a subtle statement of intent, it shows either appalling proofreading or abysmal knowledge of European geography — or both.

The extracts from the Maastricht Treaty are genuine. Read the original if you possibly can — it makes terrible bedtime material.

France has caught its *départements d'outre-mer* of St Pierre et Miquelon, Guyane, and Réunion in the Euro net and Spain has brought in the Canaries, Melilla and Ceuta in north Africa, and the fortified rocks of Peñon de Alhuceimas (pop 366), Peñon la Gomera (pop 450) and Las Chaffarinas, three islets near Algeria, population 610; none of these is shown on the EU's map of the regions. As Rhodes and other of the Greek islands are geologically in Asia, this means Euroslavia has spread its tentacles into every continent except Australasia and Antarctica. God help us!

Notable non-members of the European Union: Andorra, Falkland Islands, Faroe Islands, Greenland, Iceland, Liechtenstein, Malta, Monaco, Norway, Republic of San Marino, Switzerland. The Channel Islands — Alderney, Guernsey, Jersey and Sark — and the Isle of Man, are affiliated, but are not members, and are not subject to the diktats coming from Brussels. Gibraltar has accepted some of the conditions but has stopped a long way from full membership. With one exception, none of these territories has adopted the European Union's own tax, Value Added Tax, which is the true mark of membership. The exception is the Isle of Man which had VAT imposed upon it for historical reasons.

At the time of publication, the European Commissioners — nominated by member states and appointed by the European Parliament — are:

> President: Santer, Luxembourg
> Vice-President: Brittain (UK)
> Vice-President: Marín (Spain)
> Commissioners: Bangemann (Germany)

EUROSLAVIA

Bjerregaard (Denmark) (female)
Bonino (Italy) (female)
Cresson (France) (female)
Fischler (Austria)
Flynn (Ireland)
Gradin (Sweden) (female)
Kinnock (UK)
Liikanen (Finland)
Monti (Italy)
Oreja (Spain)
Papoutsis (Greece)
Pinheiro (Portugal)
Silguy (France)
Van Den Broek (Netherlands)
Van Miert (Belgium)
Wulf-Mathies (Germany) (female)

How many names are familiar to you?

A Member of Parliament at Westminster represents his constituents and is ultimately responsible to them. A European Commissioner is required to sign an oath putting *Europe's* interests foremost, regardless of whether they conflict with those of the country which nominated him. He has no constituents to whom to be answerable.

All the main characters in this book, except Terry Mason who closely resembles me, are totally fictitious, but all the offices of state mentioned up to 1997 are real. Among the minor characters, Padré Fermín Yzurdiaga really was active in the Spanish Civil War. I therefore apologise to any holders of such office at the time of writing who may find themselves replaced by fictional characters only a few years hence. Opinions expressed by these creations of my imagination have no relevance to opinions held by the contemporary holders of office.

The history of places such as the Isle of Man, the Falklands, the Basque land of Euzkadi, Gibraltar, Andorra, Liechtenstein, Brussels, Montmédy, etc, is correct to the present, except that Father Zimmerman's Church of Sankt Maria does not exist and I have taken great liberties with the interior of Montmédy Castle.

In sounding out public opinion in Britain while writing this book, I found one person in a hundred in favour of joining the single currency. A slightly larger percentage was in favour of a *parallel* European currency, managed by economists rather than politicians. This benign euro would need a uniform interest rate and must be available across the continent of Europe, and probably beyond. The essential difference between this and the obligatory euro is that it would be run *in sympathy*

EUROSLAVIA

with national currencies, which would remain in use and be under the control of their national governments — the present member states.

This new euro would be accessible through banks for a nominal fee and would be useful for tourists and business people; some companies may choose to keep some of their currency readily available in new euros, and Luxembourg may choose to adopt this as its national currency.

But hold on! All we need to do is modify the traveller's cheque system and the credit card, perhaps merge them — and there is your new euro, without the fudged convergence criteria or loss of sovereignty!

Doesn't that prove that the euro is being created for *political* aims, rather than economic?

This is a summary of the European Union's member states:
AUSTRIA: population 8,100,000; 1 Commissioner; 21 MEPs; 12 members of Committee of the Regions.
BELGIUM: 10,000,000; 1 Com; 25 MEPs; 12 CoR.
DENMARK: 5,200,000; 1 Com; 16 MEPs; 9 CoR.
FINLAND: as Denmark.
FRANCE (with Reunion, Guyane, St Pierre & Miquelon): 60,750,000; 2 Com; 87 MEPs; 24 CoR.
GERMANY: 82,000,000; 2 Com; 99 MEPs; 24 CoR.
GREECE: 10,000,000; 1 Com; 25 MEPs; 12 CoR.
IRELAND: 3,500,000; 1 Com; 15 MEPs; 9 CoR.
ITALY: 56,300,000; 2 Com; 87 MEPs; 24 CoR.
LUXEMBOURG: 400,000; 1 Com; 6 MEPs; 6 CoR.
NETHERLANDS: 15,000,000; 1 Com; 31 MEPs; 12 CoR.
PORTUGAL (with Azores, Madeira): 10,150,000; 1 Com; 25 MEPs; 12 CoR.
SPAIN (with Canaries & North African possessions): 38,300,000; 2 Com; 64 MEPs; 21 CoR.
SWEDEN: 8,300,000; 1 Com; 22 MEPs; 12 CoR.
UNITED KINGDOM: 58,000,000; 2 Com; 87 MEPs; 24 CoR.

My apologies to Susan Nelson and David Pollard of Nelson & Pollard Publishing for borrowing the word Euroslavia from their book *The Unseen Treaty*. My thanks to the Clacton Police and Pc Derek Lee, for advice and for help with the cover, and my gratitude to the Referendum Party for much information. I'm sorry you didn't make a bigger impact, or this book may not have been necessary.

But, as things stand, Euroslavia is still out there, waiting.
Run — or fight.